SECRETS OF THE TOMBS

BOOK 3

THE SERPENT KING

Also by Helen Moss

SECRETS OF THE TOMBS
The Phoenix Code
The Dragon Path

ADVENTURE ISLAND
The Mystery of the Whistling Caves
The Mystery of the Midnight Ghost
The Mystery of the Hidden Gold
The Mystery of the Missing Masterpiece
The Mystery of the Cursed Ruby
The Mystery of the Vanishing Skeleton
The Mystery of the Dinosaur Discovery
The Mystery of the Drowning Man
The Mystery of the Smugglers' Wreck
The Mystery of the Invisible Spy
The Mystery of the King's Ransom
The Mystery of the Black Salamander
The Mystery of the Secret Room
The Mystery of the Phantom Lights

SECRETS OF THE TOMBS

BOOK 3

THE SERPENT KING

Helen Moss

Orion
Children's Books

First published in Great Britain in
2016 by Hodder and Stoughton

1 3 5 7 9 10 8 6 4 2

A CIP catalogue record for this book
is available from the British Library.

ISBN 978 1 4440 1043 5

Typeset by Input Data Services Ltd, Bridgwater, Somerset

Printed and bound in Great Britain by Clays Ltd, St Ives plc

The paper and board used in this book are from well-managed forests
and other responsible sources.

MIX
Paper from
responsible sources
FSC® C104740

Orion Children's Books
An imprint of
Hachette Children's Group
Part of Hodder and Stoughton
Carmelite House
50 Victoria Embankment
London EC4Y 0DZ

An Hachette UK Company

www.hachette.co.uk
www.hachettechildrens.co.uk

1

TOMB

RYAN FLINT HAD to hunch double to avoid hitting his head on the roof of the steep tunnel. The air was so thick with dust that it was like trying to breathe through a duvet. 'Are you sure this leads down to another tomb?' he panted. 'If we go much further we'll come out in Australia.'

Cleo was hurrying along in front of him, stumbling on the uneven steps. 'The writing on the stone tablet that Roberto Chan found clearly states that we have to *search deeper to find the tomb of the Serpent King.*' She spoke without slowing down or looking back. 'And this,' – she patted the stone walls on either side – 'is the "*deeper*" part. This steep tunnel represented the journey down to the underworld – or

Xib'alb'a, as the Maya called it. *The Place of Fear*. I can't wait. Just think! Nobody has entered this tomb since the eighth century.'

There's probably a good reason for that, Ryan thought. *The Place of Fear doesn't exactly sound very inviting*. But he couldn't turn round now even if he wanted to. Most of the team of archaeologists were up ahead – or rather, *down* ahead – but two of the workmen were right behind him, struggling with boxes of equipment. 'And anyway,' Cleo went on, 'if we kept going we wouldn't end up in Australia. The other side of the planet from Mexico is somewhere in the middle of the Indian Ocean. Of course, we'd burn to a crisp at the earth's core long before we got there . . .'

Ryan almost laughed out loud. Cleo was always so literal. He also wondered, not for the first time, how she managed to fit so many random facts into her brain. Especially when his own brain was so overheated it was practically toast. Never mind the earth's core; it was sweltering down here. 'I'm starting to feel pretty *crispy* already,' he muttered.

I suppose I should be used to it by now, he thought. For the first fifteen years of his life, the nearest Ryan had come to the tomb of an ancient ruler was watching old *Indiana Jones* movies. But since meeting Cleopatra McNeil last year, getting up close and personal with long-dead royalty had become something of a habit. There'd been Smenkhkare and Queen Nefertiti in Egypt, then the First Emperor of China. Now, if Roberto Chan – the young Mexican archaeologist in charge of the dig – was right, they were about to enter the secret tomb of King Jaguar Paw, also known as the Serpent King, or Lord of The Snake Kingdom.

'The ancient Maya built excellent ventilation shafts,' Cleo

said. 'They're all blocked with rubble now, though.'

Ryan was about to point out that knowing that the tunnel had been fitted with high quality air conditioning more than a thousand years ago wasn't helping, when Cleo slipped and sat down hard. Ryan almost fell over her and bumped his shoulder on a jutting rock. Enraged cursing wafted up from further down the tunnel as Max Henderson, the dig photographer, tried to squeeze his cameras and lighting rig round a tight turn. Roberto and his men had been excavating for months. They'd shored up the roof with wooden props and installed hand-holds and a string of spotlights, but this was the first descent for the whole team with all their kit.

At last they were on the move again. The tunnel made a final turn, levelled out and came to a low archway. Everyone crowded round waiting for Roberto's signal that they could enter. Cleo's green eyes glittered in the spotlight. *'This is it!'* she breathed. 'King Jaguar Paw's burial chamber.'

Cleo's excitement was catching. Ryan felt his heart flutter as he ducked under the archway and came out in a long, narrow room with a vaulted roof, like a small, dark chapel. They swept their torch beams across the painted walls. Shades of blue and green, rust brown and mustard yellow still glowed beneath thick veils of dust. Maya characters in enormous plumed headdresses marched with banners and staffs or sat cross-legged, holding bowls, shields and other objects Ryan could only guess at. Blocks of writing had been squeezed into every space. The Mayan symbols, or glyphs as Cleo insisted he call them, bristled with life; faces, beaks, fins, wings, tails, hands, teeth, claws – all tangled up with whorls and dots and basket-weave lines.

'This lady is presenting the crown to a new king . . .' Cleo's

3

mum, Professor Lydia McNeil, was dashing from scene to scene like a toddler in a toyshop. 'And look, here's a flap-staff dance and a blood sacrifice. This is Sky Witness. And over here, Scroll Serpent . . .'

Roberto Chan stared as if in a trance. 'These wall paintings show the entire dynasty of the Kingdom of the Snake . . .' He wheeled round in slow motion. Everyone followed his gaze. In the centre of the chamber stood an enormous sarcophagus on a stone platform, bordered by life-sized carved heads, some human, others animal; snarling monkeys, alligators, and snakes with gaping jaws dripping with fangs. A chill scurried down Ryan's spine in spite of the heat. The heads had clearly been placed here to guard the coffin and, from the look in their eyes, they were not at all impressed at being disturbed by a bunch of twenty-first century intruders. *The Place of Fear,* he thought, suddenly remembering that he really didn't like tombs very much.

Cleo had no such worries. She had grown up around archaeological digs and looked totally at home in a burial chamber. She rushed over to the sarcophagus to join her mum, who was already kneeling down to study the inscriptions that covered the sides. Cleo took a small brush from her trusty leather tool belt – or *bum bag,* as Ryan always called it, just to wind her up – and began to sweep dust from the stone surface.

Cleo could read Mayan glyphs, of course. She could also read Egyptian hieroglyphs, Chinese characters, Latin, Greek and several other languages Ryan had never even heard of. *On the other hand,* he thought, *she has the fashion sense of a beige pop sock.* In addition to the tool belt, she was sporting her usual stylish combo: zip-off hiking shorts, and a charity

4

shop t-shirt so faded that it would have taken scientific tests to guess at its original colour. The two long black plaits that hung from beneath her hard hat were lop-sided and pale grey with dust.

'The stone is cracked right through at this end!' Pete McNeil – Cleo's dad – looked up from examining the lid of the sarcophagus. Being a paleopathologist – an expert on ancient death and disease – Pete was more interested in the body *inside* than the carvings on the outside. The same was true of his research student, Alex Shawcross, who was bouncing with impatience at his side. She flashed a winning smile at Roberto Chan. 'Ooh yes, if we shimmy this piece to one side we could have a teeny-tiny peek inside, please say we can . . .'

Ryan willed Roberto to agree. It wasn't that he wanted to see the body (Ryan had had enough of mummified corpses to last a lifetime). But Cleo had told him all about the stone tablet, known as the Snake Stone, that Roberto had recently discovered. As well as telling them to *search deeper for the tomb of the Serpent King,* the Snake Stone also spoke of *secret knowledge* and the *prize that all men desire*. Surely that must mean treasure of some sort. Ryan glanced around. The wall paintings might count as secret knowledge, he supposed. But he hadn't seen much sign of treasure yet. It must all be hidden inside the coffin. He was sure it would be spectacular. Heaps of gold and silver and jade, probably . . . those seemed to be the 'prizes' that ancient royalty usually went in for . . .

Roberto's face was as smooth and brown as if carved from polished wood, and as stern as the stone heads around the sarcophagus. But at last he nodded. 'We'll try to move it just a little.' He spoke slowly, with a strong Spanish accent. 'But

5

we must be careful not to cause more damage.'

Everyone joined forces to push against the huge slab of limestone. A deep, rumbling sound echoed around the walls of the tomb as the lid began to move.

'Max!' Pete shouted to the photographer, who was lying on the ground taking photographs of the sarcophagus. 'Can we get some light up here?'

Max Henderson hauled himself up. 'I'm getting too old for this lark,' he puffed, struggling to set up the stand for a spotlight. Rivulets of sweat trickled down his pouchy face and darkened his beard. 'I can't get this confounded contraption to stay in place.' He pushed a long metal arm with a light on the end into Ryan's hand. 'Make yourself useful, lad. Hold this up. High as you can. Left a bit. Don't move! I said *don't move!*' Max shoved a second light into Ryan's other hand. 'Hold this one out to the other side . . .'

By the time Ryan looked down through the gap in the lid, he was a human lamp stand, balancing on one leg, all four limbs pointing in different directions, as if he'd been freeze-framed halfway through a star jump.

All he could see was a mass of gleaming red.

The ancient coffin was full of blood.

2

JAGUAR

BLOOD? RYAN'S HEAD swam. His thoughts raced. *That can't be possible! How can a thousand-year-old corpse be lying in a pool of fresh blood?*

He started to reach up to touch the St Christopher medal that he wore round his neck, but then he remembered he had a spotlight in each hand. Dad had given him the silver St Christopher – the patron saint of travellers – before he'd left for the last time. Not that Ryan had *known* it would be the last time, of course. It was just another work trip. Dad was always going on work trips. Only this time he didn't come back. That was six years ago . . .

'Hold that light still! Stop wobbling about!'

7

Ryan snapped back to the moment.

Pete and Alex had swooped in on the coffin of blood like vultures on a kill. Ryan knew that death was their job – but did they really have to *enjoy* it quite so much? Alex had pulled off her hard hat and was leaning so far in through the gap that her head had disappeared. When she came up for air her golden curls were tinged with scarlet. 'It's not blood,' she said, sounding rather disappointed. 'It's red powder.'

Pete McNeil nodded. 'Ground cinnabar, no doubt.'

Cleo shielded the light from her eyes and looked up at Ryan. 'Otherwise known as mercury sulphide.' But he already knew what cinnabar was. They'd come across the poisonous powder before, in a cave called The Kitchen of Eternal Life in China. 'The Maya associated the colour red with death and rebirth,' Cleo went on. 'They often used cinnabar to coat the body.'

You might have mentioned that before we opened the lid! Ryan grumbled to himself. He passed the lights back to Max, who had finally managed to get the lighting rig set up, and tried to shake some feeling back into his arms.

Roberto was busy handing out disposable gloves and paper face masks to protect against the cinnabar. The team stood around the sarcophagus looking down at the body, like surgeons about to perform an operation. *Although it's a bit late for this guy,* Ryan thought. Beneath the cinnabar, the age-browned skeleton poked out from the shreds of the animal pelts that had once wrapped it. Jade ornaments had been laid out on top of the corpse but now lay scattered among the bones – pendants, ankle cuffs, a heavy belt adorned with carved jade heads. There were vases and bowls too, and some mean-looking thin black blades.

Cleo's mum pointed at the magnificent mask of square tiles of smoky green jade that covered the face and translated the ancient glyphs that ran around the edge. *'The white soul breath of Jaguar Paw has died. Here he lies. Yuknoom Yich'aak K'ahk, Lord of the Snake Kingdom.'*

Roberto smiled for the first time. He even did a small air punch. 'Yes! I knew it! This proves it's King Jaguar Paw. Now they'll have to believe me! The Snake Stone was right. We searched deeper and we've found the tomb of the Serpent King.'

Ryan exchanged a glance with Cleo. She had told him some of the background to this dig. Many other archaeologists had doubted that the stone tablet Roberto had discovered last year was genuine. There were rumours that he had fallen for a hoax, or even worse, that he'd faked the Snake Stone himself. Most people still believed that King Jaguar Paw was the body buried in the tomb above this one, higher up inside the pyramid, which had been excavated years ago.

Ryan looked back down into the coffin. Was he imagining things or had the jade mask moved a little? Suddenly he realised why. Alex had been gently nudging the mask to one side. She blushed as she saw that Ryan had caught her out. 'Oh dear!' she said, as she gave a final little push. 'The mask seems to be slipping off!'

Ryan closed his eyes. Not fast enough. The mask fell away to reveal the skull beneath. The image was now imprinted on the backs of his eyelids. Empty eye sockets. A gaping hole for a nose. A grin full of jade fangs. Red smudges around the bony mouth. The vampire effect was the stuff of nightmares.

Pete McNeil craned over for a closer look. 'This skull is a most *peculiar* shape.'

Alex looked as if Father Christmas had just appeared down the chimney. 'Ooh, cranial deformation? How *super!*' Her old-fashioned BBC newsreader voice made *cranial deformation* sound like something she was being offered at an afternoon tea party.

'Cranial deformation?' Ryan asked Cleo. 'Is that what I think it is?'

'If you think it's changing the shape of the skull, then yes. It was a common practise in many cultures . . .'

'The Maya were rather keen on a wide, flat forehead,' Alex cut in. 'It was a sign of high status. They'd bind the child's head with wooden paddles like this.' She pressed her hands against the front and back of her head. 'Babies' skulls are surprisingly soft, you know.'

Ryan couldn't think of anything he'd ever wanted to hear about *less* than baby-squashing, but Alex was on a roll. 'It might be because they wanted to mimic the flat shape of a jaguar's face . . . The jaguar was a sacred animal, a symbol of power.'

While they were talking, Pete had been peering further under the lid. He looked up, the spotlight flashing off his round wire-framed glasses. 'Sorry to be a party-pooper, but this isn't King Jaguar Paw!'

Lydia laughed. 'Pete, stop messing about. We know it is. His name's on the mask and it's all over the sarcophagus too.'

Roberto Chan stared at him. 'What do you mean?'

Pete shrugged. 'Let's just say that if this guy was trying to look like a jaguar he made a pretty thorough job of it. He's grown two extra legs for a start.'

Roberto made an odd choking noise. With a burst of superhuman strength, he shoved the lid further back. Now they could all see the entire skeleton beneath its tattered shroud.

Ryan was no expert on anatomy, but even he could make out that there were four legs. There was also a long curved line of small bones extending from the spine. 'Is that a . . .'

'Rather splendid tail?' Pete finished the sentence for him. 'Yep!'

Roberto swallowed hard. 'So . . . they placed some jaguar bones inside the sarcophagus with the body. That's not unusual in royal Maya burials. Any part of a jaguar was a valuable object . . .'

Cleo's dad shook his head. 'These aren't extra bones. It's all one skeleton. And there's no cranial deformation either. This skull hasn't been shaped to *look like* a jaguar skull, it *is* a jaguar skull.'

3

BLOOD

YES, IT WAS obvious, Cleo thought. Now that she could see the skeleton properly it was clearly not human. She stared down at the bones with a mixture of excitement and confusion. Jaguars were of great importance to the ancient Maya, of course, but she had never read of one being given a full royal burial before. It was an extraordinary discovery. She just wished she knew what it meant.

Roberto Chan clearly felt the same way. 'I don't understand!' he cried, throwing up his hands. 'This burial makes no sense!' His dramatic gesture knocked a spotlight flying from its stand. Ryan dived to save it, but Max Henderson made a grab for it at the same time. Ryan caught the spotlight. Max caught Ryan's nose. Ryan yelped, dropped the light, and clapped his hands over his face. His white paper mask – protection against cinnabar dust – was no protection against Max's fist and was already turning bright red. *'Doze beed,'* he mumbled, gazing down at the blood splashing into his hands.

'Sorry, lad! Your face got in the way of my hand.' Max examined the light. 'I hope this bulb hasn't broken.'

'Stand back from the sarcophagus!' Roberto snapped. 'You're dripping on the artefacts.'

Ryan backed into the corner of the tomb. 'I'll just go over here and bleed to death quietly, shall I?'

Cleo couldn't help smiling. Ryan always went in for wild exaggeration. No one *died* of a nosebleed! But he was going to make it worse if he kept sniffing like that. She handed him some tissues from her tool belt. 'Sit down. Put your head back and pinch the bridge of your nose.'

Ryan groaned.

Cleo knew that you should talk to a patient to take their mind off their injury. She sat down next to him. 'Actually, blood was central to ancient Maya culture,' she said, choosing a topic that seemed relevant. 'They offered it up to the gods. Obviously, they would use a sharp blade, rather than a thump on the nose. They collected the blood by letting it soak into strips of bark paper.'

Ryan's eyes widened behind the bundle of blood-stained tissues. *Good,* Cleo thought, *he's interested.* 'The Maya saw blood sacrifice as a great honour. They believed that human blood nurtured the gods and kept the world in balance. All those long black blades in the sarcophagus aren't weapons, they're lancets specially designed for bloodletting rituals.

They're made from obsidian, a volcanic glass.'

Alex couldn't resist joining the conversation. 'It's razor sharp. You'd hardly feel it slice through your skin.' She stuck out her tongue and stabbed at it with her finger. 'This was the usual place,' she lisped.

Ryan gurgled and waved his hands about. Cleo guessed he needed another tissue and handed one over. 'The priests gathered the pieces of blood-soaked paper into special bowls,' she went on. 'They added rubber and copal resin, and burned them like incense. It produced a lovely thick smoke, perfect for seeing visions in . . .'

'On special occasions,' Alex chipped in, 'they would pull a rope of ceiba tree thorns through the tongue to produce even more blood.'

Ryan dropped the tissues. His face had turned an unusual shade of greenish-white. He mumbled something that sounded like, *'Really . . . not . . . helping . . .'* Then he was scrabbling to his feet and lurching out of the chamber.

Cleo and Alex looked at each other and shrugged.

Must be the heat down here, Cleo thought as she went back to clearing dust from the sarcophagus. It was hard work, and by midday she began to feel hungry and made the long climb back up the tunnel. She emerged through the floor of the upper tomb via a trap door, which had been hidden for over a thousand years until it had been unearthed by Roberto's excavations. She helped herself to packed lunches from a large icebox and climbed a second tunnel – shorter, but just as steep – to come out onto a wide stone platform.

Cleo stood for a moment, blinking in the dazzle of the sunny January afternoon. The platform was about two thirds of the way up the vast temple-pyramid known as

14

Structure Two, in the heart of the ruined city of Calakmul. Looking down, the wide grey stone steps that flanked the pyramid stretched away dizzyingly towards the ground far below. Looking up, the pyramid rose even higher in a second stage, with more stairs leading to the flat peak. Ryan was sitting with his back against a crumbling wall almost at the top.

The rise of each step was so high that Cleo had to push up with her hands on her knees. By the time she sank down next to Ryan on the sun-warmed stone, she was out of breath. His nose had stopped bleeding and his face had returned to its usual colour – fair with a hint of sunburn and freckles – although, now with added smudges of dried blood. 'You look as if you've been daubed with cinnabar,' she puffed.

'Cheers! It's my dead jaguar look. I'm still working on it.' Ryan had his sketchbook open on his knee but he hadn't drawn anything yet. He was tilting his head to one side and squinting through narrowed eyes.

'What are you doing?' Cleo asked, handing him a bottle of water and a taco wrapped in greaseproof paper. 'Your nose is all right now, isn't it?'

'I'm looking at the trees . . . they're just so *green*.'

Cleo wondered whether Ryan had lost more blood than she'd thought. They were looking out over a forest canopy that stretched as far as the horizon in every direction. Calakmul – the modern name for the capital city of the Snake Kingdom – was in the middle of a vast jungle on the Yucatán Peninsula of Mexico. The main structures had been cleared, but trees still grew among the ruins. The snake-like roots of strangler figs wrapped themselves around monuments and burst through walls. 'Trees usually *are* green,' she pointed out. 'It's chlorophyll, the pigment needed for photosynthesis . . .'

'It's not just *any* green,' Ryan interrupted through a mouthful of corn tortilla, fried chicken and beans. 'It's mega-green, like someone's been into Photoshop and turned the saturation up to maximum. It's a massive tree *ocean*.' He swept his arms out over the panorama. 'The tops of the other buildings are like little islands poking up through the waves. And look! There are even ghostly black pirate ships racing about.'

Cleo gave Ryan a long, hard look. He really was rambling now. 'Those "black ships" are just cloud shadows,' she explained as slowly and clearly as she could. She pointed at the sky, which was deep blue and dotted with fat little white clouds. 'The the wind is blowing the clouds past the sun . . .'

Ryan took a glug of water and almost choked with laughter. 'You don't say!' he spluttered. 'Imagination really isn't your thing, is it?'

Cleo couldn't see what imagination had to do with it. Cloud shadows weren't *imaginary*. It was basic physics. She decided to change the subject. 'The Maya kings and priests performed their ceremonies up on these high platforms on the pyramids,' she said. 'The crowds all gathered in the plaza below to watch. Important events would be marked with rituals involving bloo—'

Ryan held up his half-eaten taco and the water bottle in a cross sign. 'If you say the b-word one more time, I'll have to push you off the edge.'

'B-word?' Cleo echoed. 'Oh, do you mean *bloo*—'

Ryan clapped his hands over his ears. *'La-la-la! I'm not listening.'*

Cleo wondered when Ryan had suddenly developed this irrational fear of blood. She gazed out over the forest. The only sounds were the whistle and cackle of birdsong and a muffled word or two floating up from the handful of tourists milling about far below. Calakmul was an hour's drive along a single-track road from the nearest highway; few visitors made it this far.

Ryan broke the silence. 'Just think! King Jaguar Paw could have stood on this exact spot, looking out over this scene.'

'Actually it would have looked completely different then,' Cleo pointed out. 'The trees were all chopped down to make room for wide plazas and avenues. The pyramids were painted white and red and there were huge stone masks of *Witz* monsters down the sides, their mouths gaping open to symbolise caves on a mountainside.' Cleo's thoughts drifted back to the discovery deep inside the pyramid. 'I can hardly believe what just happened down there.'

'I know! Max thumped me right on the hooter. I'll be scarred for life.'

Cleo frowned. How could Ryan think his nosebleed was the most significant event of the day? Then she saw his mouth curl into a big grin. She wished he'd give her some sort of sign when he was joking. 'I meant the burial.'

'Ah yes, you mean the minor detail that the king appears to have turned into a whopping great jaguar. So what's *that* all about?'

'I wish I knew.' Cleo thought back over the events leading up to the jaguar discovery. Mum had known Roberto Chan since she'd met him at a conference several years ago. When he'd called and asked her to help decipher the Snake Stone she'd been happy to help. According to Roberto, he had come across the stone tablet in the storage room of a local museum where it had sat gathering dust for over fifty years. It appeared to come from Naranjo, another ancient Maya city, and was actually a fragment broken off from a larger *stela*, or stone monument. It was in the shape of a coiled snake, which was why it had come to be known as the Snake Stone.

Most of the writing on the Snake Stone recorded the battle victories of Smoking Squirrel, the great eighth-century Naranjo warlord. But one section talked of Jaguar Paw's death; *search deeper to find the tomb of the Serpent King*. Roberto was hugely excited. He'd never been convinced that the burial in the upper tomb was that of King Jaguar Paw, and this seemed to support his theory. But when he went public with his find, many people thought it was just a little too *convenient* that Roberto had happened to stumble across a stone tablet that proved him right. Mum had stood by him. She was sure that the Snake Stone was genuine. When Roberto had finally found the concealed tunnel down to the lower tomb, he had invited the McNeil team to join the dig.

It had all been going well. Until the jaguar showed up!

'The thing is,' Cleo told Ryan, 'Jaguar Paw's death was a mystery even before Roberto found the Snake Stone. This has just added to the puzzle.'

Ryan frowned. 'What's the mystery? I thought you said everyone believed he was the man buried in the upper tomb?'

'Most people did. When that tomb was discovered in the 1990s there were some grave goods in the coffin with Jaguar Paw's name on them. The date was 700AD, which seemed about right. But it just didn't look like a grand enough burial for a great king. That's what Roberto thought anyway. He published lots of articles about it.' Cleo ate the last piece of her taco and tipped out the crumbs from the greaseproof paper. 'And then there are other historians who claim that Jaguar Paw was captured in a major battle with the city of Tikal in AD 695 – which would mean he couldn't have been buried here in Calakmul at all.'

'What if he escaped and found his way home?' Ryan suggested.

'Unlikely. Calakmul and Tikal were rival states. If the King of Tikal had captured his sworn enemy he would almost certainly have sacrificed him. He probably had to play in a ritual ball game.'

'You mean football or something?' Ryan laughed. 'What's so bad about that? Unless you're a Chelsea fan, of course!'

Cleo assumed that this was a joke but as she never understood anything Ryan said about football, she didn't even try to figure it out.

'The ball game was called *pitz*.' Cleo scrunched the taco paper in her hands. 'They cut off their captives' heads and used them as the balls.'

Ryan stared at her. 'Sorry. For a moment there I thought you said *they used heads for footballs . . .*'

'That's right.' Cleo was sure Ryan had heard the first time.

Ryan nodded. 'So you're saying Jaguar Paw can't have been buried here unless he came back from the dead, reattached his head, and crawled home. It's obvious then. The man was a zombie. Either that or he had a very good stunt double!'

Cleo didn't believe in zombies and she seriously doubted that stunt doubles had been invented in the eighth century. 'The *obvious* explanation is that Jaguar Paw *wasn't* captured in that battle with Tikal. That's what most people think.'

Ryan brushed crumbs from his jeans. 'There's something

else mysterious about that burial we found today – apart from the whole jaguar skeleton thing, I mean. Didn't the Snake Stone say something about prizes and stuff that would be found in Jaguar Paw's tomb?'

'There were some words missing,' Cleo said. 'But Mum deciphered it as *there you find secret knowledge . . . the way to the prize that all men desire.*'

Ryan shrugged. 'Maybe I've been spoilt by seeing too many bling-tastic royal tombs lately, but Jaguar Paw's burial didn't seem *that* stuffed with treasure. I know there were a few jade bowls and pots, but it's not even in the same league as Nefertiti's tomb, is it? And, the First Emperor of China had a scale model of the universe made of jewels, for goodness sake!'

Cleo knew what Ryan meant. She'd expected something more spectacular too. Perhaps the *secret knowledge* would be revealed when they deciphered the writing on the sides of the sarcophagus. It would probably be a complex star chart or calendar. The Maya were highly sophisticated astronomers. 'One thing the Snake Stone *didn't* mention,' she said, watching as a grackle – a glossy black bird with yellow eyes and a long tail – landed and began pecking at the taco crumbs, 'was anything about there being an *actual* jaguar buried in the tomb!'

Ryan laughed. 'They mummified animals in ancient Egypt all the time. Cats, dogs, crocodiles. Even *birds,*' he added in a whisper, glancing at the grackle as if worried it might overhear and be upset.

'But the Egyptians didn't bury those animals inside the royal sarcophagus *with the pharaoh's name all over it,*' Cleo pointed out. 'It's as if the people who buried that jaguar actually believed it *was* King Jaguar Paw.'

'Maybe it was,' Ryan suggested. He was holding his hand out, feeding the grackle scraps from his palm. 'What if there was a spell or a curse that turned him into a jaguar *after* he was shut inside the sarcophagus? That would count as secret knowledge in my book!'

Cleo was always astonished by how willing Ryan was to believe in the paranormal. 'A spell?' she snorted. '*Magic*, you mean?'

'Why not? He could be a *were-jaguar*!' Ryan hooked his hands into claws. 'Who dares to disturb my tomb?' he boomed. 'Vengeance will be mine!' He reared back, opening his mouth to roar . . .

An explosion of growling, howling and grunting ripped through the tranquil afternoon. The grackle screeched and took off, its wings flapping against Cleo's face. Ryan spun round, eyes wide with fear. 'What . . . is . . . *that*?' he stammered.

'*Howler monkeys.*' Cleo pointed down at a spot where the treetops were swaying and bouncing. Red-brown fur flashed through the foliage. She'd heard it many times before, but Ryan and his mum had only joined the camp two days ago. This was the first time he'd heard the male howlers proclaiming their territory. And Cleo certainly wasn't going to admit that the roaring had startled her so much that for a moment – no more than a nanosecond – she'd almost *seen* the ancient were-jaguar bursting out of the pyramid to wreak revenge. 'They're one of the loudest land mammals in the world,' she said in her most matter-of-fact tone. 'The hyoid bone in the throat amplifies their call.'

She jumped up, impatient to return to the tomb. One part

of the text on Roberto's Snake Stone had proved to be true, at least; they *had* found King Jaguar Paw's burial by *searching deeper* beneath the upper tomb. If the rest of the inscription was right, there should be 'secret knowledge' and the 'prize that all men desire' waiting for them down there too.

Or, Cleo wondered, did the fact that the coffin contained a jaguar's body prove that the other archaeologists had been right all along, and that the Snake Stone was some kind of elaborate hoax. A flicker of worry caught in her throat. Sir Charles Peacocke, Mum's boss in London, had not been at all keen on her coming to Calakmul, in case the Snake Stone turned out to be a fake and she got tangled up in an embarrassing scandal. After all the problems they'd had in Egypt and China, that would be the last straw. Mum had put her reputation on the line to support Roberto.

Cleo gave herself a shake. The Snake Stone was genuine. Nothing would go wrong this time. The dig would be a great success, a major step forward in understanding the ancient Maya civilisation. They would solve the mystery of Jaguar Paw's death. *Was he the man buried in the upper tomb or had he been sacrificed in Tikal? Why had a jaguar been buried in his place in the royal tomb? What was the secret knowledge and the prize all men desire?*

Whatever the answers, Cleo was quite sure they didn't involve zombies, stunt doubles *or* were-jaguars.

4

WORLD TREE

CLEO PROPPED HER chin in her hands and frowned at the Lords of Death.

With their skeletal grins, hooked noses and smoking torches growing from their foreheads, they were a gruesome crew. The photograph was from the sarcophagus lid, one of many that Max had enlarged and printed out. They were now arranged on the table, held down at the corners with large pebbles. Cleo peered at the column of glyphs that ran down the side of the panel. All she had so far was that the axe-wielding Lord *Chac-Xib-Chac* had lured King Jaguar Paw into the Hall of Fire . . .

It was the morning after the jaguar discovery. While most

of the team had returned to the tomb, Cleo had stayed in camp with Mum to study the inscriptions from the sarcophagus, searching for clues to help solve the puzzle of the burial and uncover the secret knowledge promised by the Snake Stone. To make the most of the sunlight, they'd set up a trestle table outside the long white and silver R.V. trailer that was the McNeil family home for the duration of the dig.

The camp was in a clearing among the trees. The trailers were parked around a patch of scrubby grass, strewn with fallen leaves and seed cases. On one side a path led to a cluster of concrete block huts with roofs of dried palm fronds where most of the workmen lived while on site. On the other, was a track to the ruins of Calakmul. Although the camp was almost a mile from the central buildings, ancient half-walls and tumbledown monuments poked up through the undergrowth even here.

'*K'uhul kaanal ajaw.* Yes, yes, *Holy Lord of the Snake Kingdom,* we know that ...' Cleo talked to herself as she worked. 'But what did he *do?* Where's the verb?' Mum broke off from her own translation to help her work it out. Cleo kicked the table leg with frustration. Mum had been teaching her ancient Mayan for months now. She couldn't understand why she was finding it so much harder than all the other languages she knew.

Like Egyptian hieroglyphs, the Mayan script was a mixture of symbols that stood for whole words and others that stood for the sounds of the language – syllables in the case of Mayan. Cleo could recognise glyphs that came up regularly, such as *snake, sky, lord, jaguar, temple, blood* and *captive,* as well as numbers and the names of days and months. Beyond that, she struggled.

A cloud of yellow butterflies flitted past. *Colias eurytheme,* Cleo thought, automatically labelling them with their Latin scientific name. They landed on the branch of a dogwood tree. *Piscidia piscipula.* If only it were as easy to memorise the glyphs! They were just so complex. To make it worse, every scribe seemed to write them in his own artistic way.

Cleo tried to concentrate again, but now she wasn't even sure it was the *Hall of Fire.* Perhaps it was the *Hall of Bats.* Either way, it was all about King Jaguar Paw entering the Underworld. So far she'd found nothing useful about buried jaguars or secret knowledge. She looked up at the trailer that Ryan shared with his mum, Julie. They'd been inside all morning with the radio on full volume. She could hear every word of the Country and Western ballad over the hum of the generator that provided the camp's electricity. *Mis lágrimas fluyen como un rio,* the singer lamented. Cleo had no trouble translating from Spanish; my tears flow like a river. *Perhaps,* she thought darkly, *the poor woman's trying to read Mayan glyphs . . .*

A door slammed on another trailer. Max Henderson lumbered down the steps. 'More photographs,' he announced as he dumped papers on the table. 'These are the best I can do. That printer I've got here must be left over from the Stone Age.'

Cleo always wondered why Max had gone into a career as a dig photographer. He disliked everything about archaeology; travelling, enclosed spaces, dust, heat, foreign food . . . But Mum had worked with him for years. She said he was the best in the business, and nobody was as careful about recording every detail of information with each image. Cleo was about to point out that they didn't have printers in

25

the Stone Age when Max froze and then slowly raised the binoculars that always hung from his neck. The only thing he *did* like was birds. 'Long-billed gnatwren,' he murmured. 'On that ceiba branch . . .'

Mum turned a page of her notebook.

'Shh!' Max hissed

Cleo looked at Mum. They both raised their eyebrows, but neither dared speak. An unremarkable brown bird chirped and took flight. Max harrumphed and stomped away.

'What is this, a sponsored silence?'

Cleo swung round in her chair to see Ryan standing behind her. 'What have you been doing all morning?' she asked.

Ryan didn't answer the question, 'Ooh, I love these glyphs!' he said. 'I'm not a genius like you, so I've no idea what any of them mean, but they're so cool.' Cleo could tell he was trying to change the subject but she couldn't figure out why. Ryan pulled up a chair and pointed at one of the printouts. 'But I recognise this one. *Smug Snake Lurks under Pile of Stones.*'

Mum smiled at him. 'That's right. It's the emblem of the Snake Kingdom. It's pronounced *Kan*.'

'That explains why it's all over the place.' Ryan took out his sketchbook and turned to a page filled with beautifully-drawn glyphs. 'I copied these yesterday morning. They're from the ceiling of that little alcove in the upper tomb.'

Cleo had noticed Ryan wedged under the overhang. It was so low that he'd had to lie on his back like a mechanic under a car.

'I practically had to bend my arms into origami folds to hold the pencil.' Ryan rubbed his neck. 'Not to mention the blast of icy air coming from the wall at the back. It's given me neck ache. Yes, we artists suffer for our art!'

Cleo laughed. Ryan grumbled about the conditions on a dig almost as much as Max did. 'Icy? I thought you said it was too hot down there?'

'It was!' Ryan said. 'What is it with tombs? They can be boiling hot and chill you to the bone at the same time. It must be all the ghosts wandering around or something . . .'

Cleo rolled her eyes. Ryan was always on about ghosts and monsters and evil spirits. Before she could put him right he pointed to a glyph on the photograph she was studying. 'What does this one mean?' he asked. *'Fierce Face with Tattooed Cheek?* I've seen it a lot.'

To Cleo's relief the glyph was one that she recognised. Since Ryan had just called her a genius, she felt embarrassed to reveal how little of the script she could read. 'It's *Ix,*' she told him. 'It goes before a name to show that it's a woman. It's usually translated as *Lady.* Here it's *Lady Six Sky.*'

Mum leaned back in her chair, and fastened her hair into a bun with her pencil. 'I've deciphered most of this section from the lid,' she said. *'Jaguar Paw has descended to Xib'alb'a. But he will outwit the Lords of Death and return from the deepest waters. He will rise through the World Tree to live forever among his people.'*

'The Maya believed that the spirits of the ancestors could return to this world,' Cleo explained to Ryan. 'It was part of the ritual where they saw visions in the smoke that came from burning bloo—' She saw Ryan's face and stopped herself saying the b-word just in time. 'From burning *you-know-what.* The most important vision was a giant snake called the Vision Serpent. It opened up a portal to the Underworld so that the Ancestors could climb up through its mouth . . .'

'But it says Jaguar Paw will come back through the World Tree,' Ryan said. 'What's that?'

'The World Tree was a central feature of ancient Maya mythology,' Cleo said. 'It was believed to connect the three levels of the cosmos; the Underworld, the earth and the skies. It can appear through the portal that opens when the Vision Serpent is summoned.' She passed Ryan one of the photos. It showed the World Tree with its roots coiling among the dark waters of the Underworld, the mighty trunk sprouting up through the earth and the branches reaching into the sky, all twining scrolls and fronds, topped by a fabulous *celestial bird*.

Ryan immediately turned to a new page of his sketchbook and began to copy the intricate design.

'Ryan does have a point.' Mum frowned down at her notes. 'It *is* surprising that there's no mention of the Vision Serpent here. The next lines are puzzling too. '*To find the entrance to the Underworld, count the hidden path through the forest. Enter the mouth of the Witz monster and follow the trail of the Serpent King.*'

'The Serpent King must mean Jaguar Paw, the ruler of the Snake Kingdom,' Cleo said. 'But what does it mean by *count the hidden path*? Shouldn't that be *paths,* plural?'

'I *did* check,' Mum said, a little snappily. 'It's definitely *path.*'

Cleo wondered whether Mum had made a mistake but decided not to push it. She'd read about there being different roads to the Underworld in the *Popol Vuh,* the Maya sacred book, but there was nothing about *counting* them. She noticed that Mum had circled another glyph with red pen. 'What's that?' she asked.

'I can't quite make it out. It looks like *Wacah Chan*, which is the Mayan name for the World Tree, but it's got these extra elements here.' Mum indicated two curved bumps, one at the top left and one at the bottom left of the symbol. 'I've not seen those before . . .'

Ryan picked up the printout and squinted at it from different angles. 'Yeah, I thought so,' he said. 'Those bumps are part of the *Curly Teacup Handle* symbol. I don't know what it means but it's the same as the one over here.' He held out another page to show Cleo. 'They look like separate bumps, but they're connected. It's just that there's a chip in the stone so you can't see the middle bit.' He drew a copy of the glyph, adding in a faint line to show how the missing part fitted in. 'It's like the cup handle has broken, so that all that's left are the top and bottom bits.'

Cleo stared at the photograph. The *Curly Teacup Handle* was a silly nickname for a glyph, but Ryan was right. When you looked carefully you could see the slight change in colour where the stone had been damaged.

Mum could see it now too. 'It's the possessive pronoun!' She shook her head. 'But that's just so *weird*! It can't be.'

Ryan grinned. 'Oh no! Not the dreaded *possessive pronoun*? Quick, call the newspapers! We've got jaguars in coffins, magic trees and dead people climbing out of the mouths of snakes, and *that's* the weird part?'

But Cleo knew why Mum was so puzzled. 'The *Curly Teacup Handle* is really called the *u-glyph*. It means *his* or *her* . . .' she explained. 'So whatever word it's attached to, it means that the thing belongs to somebody. In this case, it's attached to the World Tree.' She waited for Ryan to get the point but he was still looking blank. 'How can the World Tree belong to *anyone*?' she went on. 'The World Tree is a mythical symbol. It's not a thing anyone can own . . .'

Ryan nodded slowly. 'Oh, I see. It's like saying 'his Loch Ness Monster' or 'his Father Christmas'. It doesn't make sense.'

'Actually it's *her* World Tree,' Mum said. 'This says it belonged to Lady Six Sky . . .'

'Unless it's a fluffy toy Loch Ness Monster or a plastic model of Father Christmas, of course,' Ryan went on. 'Then they could belong to someone.'

Mum laughed. 'I've never heard of a model of the World Tree. Especially not a plastic one!'

But Cleo suddenly had an idea. Ryan was right. Not about the plastic, of course. The Maya had made use of rubber and chicle, but true plastics were unknown before the twentieth century. But perhaps Lady Six Sky did own some kind of model of the World Tree. 'It could have been a beautiful artefact made of jade or obsidian or even gold,' she said. 'Don't you see? This World Tree could be the *prize that all men desire* that the Snake Stone talks about.'

Mum still looked doubtful. 'Hmm. I don't know. We didn't see any sign of it in the coffin.'

But Cleo was convinced. 'But Mum! There could be all kinds of grave goods under the rubble that we've not uncovered yet. Or maybe it's hidden somewhere else inside the burial chamber.' Her heartbeat quickened. They were no closer to solving the mystery of why a jaguar had been buried in the king's tomb. But they could be on to something even more exciting. No one had ever discovered an artefact in the form of The World Tree before. And if Smoking Squirrel, the great warlord of Naranjo, had described it as 'the prize that all men desire' on the Snake Stone, it could be something

30

really special, the Maya version of the Holy Grail . . .'

Mum nodded slowly, winding the pencil round and round in her hair. 'It *is* an intriguing idea. I need to do more work on these texts to see if there's any evidence that we're talking about an actual World Tree object here rather than the standard mythical symbol.' She shuffled her notes together. 'Let's get some lunch to keep us going.'

Cleo turned to Ryan. 'We'll help, won't we?'

Ryan looked up from shading the branches on his World Tree. 'Oh yeah, maybe . . .'

The delicious smell of fried chicken drifted from the palm-thatched kitchen gazebo where Rosita – the elderly Maya lady who was cooking for the team in camp – was preparing lunch over an open fire. As they walked over to the plastic tables set up under the spreading branches of a giant ceiba tree, Cleo wondered why Ryan was being so vague about helping this afternoon? They could be on the trail of a truly ground-breaking discovery. What else could he possibly have planned, after all? They were in the middle of the jungle, hours away from the nearest cinema or football pitch.

At the end of the meal Ryan got up quickly, 'I'm feeling a bit sick,' he said, holding his stomach. 'I think I'll go and lie down.'

Now Cleo was really baffled. He'd just wolfed down two helpings of chicken and rice.

AMBUSH

RYAN RUSHED INTO the trailer and flopped down on his bed. He didn't really feel ill. Not unless you counted the vinegary churn of dread in his stomach. But there *was* a reason he couldn't help Cleo with the sarcophagus texts this afternoon.

He was going as his mum's unofficial bodyguard to a secret meeting with a ruthless gang member.

What could possibly go wrong?

Apart from literally everything, he thought grimly.

He stared up at a fly trapped in the mosquito net.

King Jaguar Paw wasn't the only man whose fate was unknown. It was a different mystery that had persuaded Ryan's mum that they needed to come to Mexico, even though it meant Ryan missing several weeks of school; joining their friends, the McNeils at the dig in Calakmul was really only a cover story.

When Dad disappeared six years ago he'd been making a documentary film about drug smuggling gangs in South America. Mum had been trying to find him ever since. But, even though she was an investigative reporter, all her leads had led to dead ends. Then, when they were in China last year, she'd had a tip-off from a member of the Tiger's Claw gang that Dad was being held prisoner somewhere in the Yucatàn Peninsula of Mexico.

Mum had never given up hope that he would be found alive.

Ryan wasn't so sure. Or maybe it was just that he didn't dare to believe that the huge dad-shaped hole in the middle of his world could ever be filled in. He'd trained himself to stay well away from the edge of the hole in case he fell in and never climbed out; keeping busy, joking around, not letting anyone know how much it mattered. Meeting Cleo and being caught up in her world of ancient mysteries had helped more than anything. Sometimes he could almost forget the hole was even there. But it was. Always.

'Get ready!' Mum shouted from the kitchen. 'The coast's clear.'

Ryan grabbed his backpack and threw in a bottle of water. *Not that I'll care about being dehydrated when I'm getting beaten to a pulp by a gangster,* he thought. He'd be a lot safer spending the afternoon poring over ancient Mayan scripts – even if it meant listening to Cleo and her mum going on about possessive pronouns and blood rituals. But what choice did he have? If he didn't go, Mum would only go by herself. Yesterday she'd met a journalist who had tracked down a member of a notorious local gang called *Los Lobos Rojos* – The Red Wolves – who claimed to have information about Dad's whereabouts. This gang member, Miguel, was prepared to talk; at a price, of course. And only if Mum went alone.

Los Lobos Rojos specialised in drug trafficking, with a sideline in looting ancient treasures and smuggling them out of the country. They weren't the kind of people you met for a picnic tea.

Ryan had told Mum this, of course. They'd been in the trailer arguing about it all morning. He'd had to turn the radio up to full blast so that the rest of the camp didn't hear.

'What do you mean *too dangerous*?' Mum had slammed her coffee cup down so hard that the fold-out table had collapsed. 'I went undercover as a hostage on a Somali pirate ship to get a news story before you were even born! Don't you *want* to find your father?'

'Of course I do!' Ryan had yelled. Although he sometimes wondered what it would be like after so long. *What if we don't recognise each other? What if we don't get along? Worst of all, what if he's dead?* 'But at least I've got *one* parent at the moment,' he'd added, staring down at his bowl of cereal, now lying in a puddle of milk on the floor along with Mum's coffee. 'If you go and get killed I'll be an orphan.'

Mum had sighed. 'Look, I know you're worried. I'll be careful. The Red Wolves are obviously a pretty small-time operation. This Miguel guy has only asked for $300 for his information . . .'

Ryan had groaned with frustration. 'If they kidnapped Dad six years ago and have been holding him hostage ever since then they're not the local knitting club either.'

But Mum wouldn't back down. Ryan had realised there was no way of stopping her. He'd marched to the door of the trailer and reached for the handle. 'I'm coming with you!'

'No way!'

'OK, then. I'll go right outside and tell the McNeils what you're doing.'

Mum's clear blue eyes had flashed. 'Don't you dare. They'll try to stop me.'

'Exactly! So, when do we go?'

Mum had caved in at last, pouring herself another cup of coffee. 'I planned to leave right after lunch. But here's the deal. You can come. But you stay out of sight in the back of the jeep. He won't talk if I'm not alone. And I don't want you in danger . . .'

And so it had been agreed. Ryan would say he say he was feeling ill and needed to spend the afternoon lying down in his room. That also gave Mum a cover story for taking the jeep; going into town to get Ryan some medicine from the pharmacy.

He'd hated lying to Cleo but he'd gone through with it.

And now they were off.

They drove in silence along the narrow road that led towards the highway, a green tunnel with the jungle pressing in on every side. About half-way to the main junction, Mum consulted a hand-drawn map and turned off down a rutted track. It was almost an hour before they came to a fork in the road and took an even narrower track, barely wide enough for the jeep to squeeze through the dense underbrush. Mum looked around nervously as she drove. 'We're getting close. You'd better hide.'

Ryan climbed into the back of the jeep. It had been kitted out with a bench seat down each side. He stretched out on the floor down the middle, his bones rattling with every jolt. When Mum swerved to avoid a flock of wild turkeys he was bombarded by objects skidding out from under the seats – a large tool box, coils of rope, a metal jerry can of petrol, several crushed Coke cans and a pile of blankets.

At last they slowed and came to a stop.

Ryan peeped out through the back window.

The track had fizzled out in a weed-blown yard of packed red dirt. Around it, patches of jungle had been cleared to make way for small fields. Squash and tomatoes grew half-heartedly among spikey pineapple palms. Maize plants stood like tall green fountains, their pale tassels swaying in the breeze. The only sign of life was a clutch of scrawny hens scratching in the shade of a ramshackle barn.

'What do we do now?' Ryan asked, checking his phone. There was no signal, of course.

Mum raked her hands through her short blonde hair and puffed out a breath. 'We wait.'

It was hot in the jeep. They opened all the windows and listened to the rustle of maize leaves, breathing the smell of sun-baked dust mixed with scorched metal and melting rubber from a burned-out truck. The sides of the barn were open to the air and Ryan could see stacks of wooden crates inside. He shaded his eyes against the sun. At one end was a large tawny-orange object dappled with black. 'Is that . . . a *jaguar*?' he whispered, his heart jumping into his throat.

'It's a pile of jaguar pelts.' Mum shuddered in disgust. 'It looks like these Red Wolf guys go in for a bit of poaching as well.'

'They can't hunt jaguars! They're an endangered species.'
Mum gave a bitter laugh. 'You don't think they let that bother them, do you? Look at all those crates. They'll be full of drugs. Cocaine mostly. They spell misery and suffering for millions of people. But there's money in it. That's all the gangs are interested in.' Her words tailed off. A high-pitched mosquito-whine grew louder and louder until a motor scooter finally pulled into the yard, scattering the hens.

'This must be Miguel,' Mum hissed. 'Stay down.'

Ryan lay down and pressed one eye to the gap between the double back-doors. The man parked his scooter next to the barn, took a baseball cap from his pocket, pulled it on over his lank black hair and slouched into the middle of the yard, shoulders hunched like a question mark.

'Show me you have no weapon!' Mum shouted.

Miguel looked no older than a teenager. He held his arms out to the sides, skinny as old ropes and laced with inky homemade tattoos. His jeans sat so low on his hips that staying up defied gravity.

'Here goes!' Mum opened the door and got out. She stopped a few paces away from Miguel and held out her hand. She looked like a life-sized action figure. She'd dressed in combat trousers and khaki t-shirt for the mission and had pulled her bandanna up to hide her face. Miguel's eyes flicked from side to side as he dug in his jeans pocket. Ryan held his breath. Did this guy have a gun after all? But he pulled out a packet of cigarettes, tapped one out and lit it. The lighter flame illuminated an unconvincing moustache. Miguel looked, Ryan thought, like one of the boys at school who was trying to come across a lot tougher than they really were. But they could be the most dangerous; you never knew what they might do to try to prove themselves.

Mum was smiling, patting the guy on the shoulder and pulling the wad of dollars out of her shirt pocket. Ryan allowed himself to relax a notch. *We might even get out of here alive . . .* But before he could finish the thought, he heard the growl of an engine and crunch of tyres over dry leaves. A red souped-up pickup truck – all monster tyres and cow-catcher – fishtailed into the yard and screeched to a halt only centimetres away from Mum and Miguel. The doors flew open and two men jumped out.

Ryan's stomach clenched with horror. It was a set-up!

Miguel had tricked Mum into coming here so that the gang could ambush her.

EXPLOSION

THE SHORTER MAN, thickly bearded, gold chains dripping from his beefy neck, whipped a gun from his belt. But instead of pointing it at Mum, he turned it on Miguel and shouted something in Spanish. Miguel dropped to his knees, his hands on his head. The other man, whose entire head was tattooed with the face of a wolf, grabbed Mum by the shoulders.

Ryan's brain whirred in frantic overload. He had to do something. But what? There were two of them. Three if you counted Miguel. And one, at least, was wielding a sawn-off shotgun. *Don't panic,* he told himself. *Think! The only thing I've got on my side is surprise. They don't know I'm here . . .*

He scanned the back of the jeep. There had to be something he could use. *My backpack?* But it only contained water, a sketchbook, an antique archaeology trowel given to him by Cleo's grandmother, and a phone with no signal. *The rope?* He could hardly lasso the men from here. *The petrol.* He didn't have anything to light it with. *Coke cans? Blankets?* This was getting ridiculous! *The tool box?* Yes, of course, there must be something useful inside. He tugged at the black metal lid. It was jammed. He grabbed the trowel from his backpack, inserted the point into the catch and twisted it hard. The lid popped open.

Spanners, jump leads, flashlight, distress flare. Ryan was throwing them all aside – there was hardly time to set off a flare and wait for a rescue helicopter – when he noticed the safety warnings on the side of the tube. *DANGER! FLAMMABLE! EMERGENCY USE ONLY!* A diagram showed a stick-man pointing the flare at another man. They were struck through with a large red cross, the international sign for *Do Not Do This Stupid Thing. Ever!*

Except, Ryan thought, snatching the flare back as it rolled away, *in exceptional circumstances.* He knelt up and peeped out of the window. It was never going to work! The gangsters were too close to Mum. He wasn't that good a shot; he'd probably miss and hit her instead. He slumped against the door. Hopelessness was closing in fast. He looked down at the flare. Beneath the stick-men, the list of chemical ingredients blurred into a string of letters; *calciumcarbonatestrontiumnitratesulphur . . . If only Cleo were here.* She'd probably waste ages giving him a chemistry lecture, but she'd be bound to come up with a clever idea.

40

Or at least they could create a distraction between them . . .
Distraction! That's it!

Ryan looked across at the barn. The roof was made of dry palm fronds. It was stuffed full of wooden crates of cocaine. There were even some old bales of hay at one end. *Flammable,* he thought. Then he remembered the petrol can. *Especially if I help things along a bit . . .*

Without letting himself think about what would happen if this went wrong, he grabbed the jerry can, unscrewed the top, took aim and hurled it out of the window. An arc of droplets sprayed out as the can flew through the air, making a rainbow in the sunshine and painting a dark spatter trail across the dust. It landed on the barn roof, bounced once and fell to the ground. The man with the gun looked up at the noise. Wolf Head turned in confusion, loosening his grip on Mum. She kicked him and began to struggle.

Ryan uncapped the flare and pointed it towards the barn. He only had seconds before the men would be on to him. He grasped the silver tab at the end and pulled. His fingers slipped. He tried again. This time the flare fired. The inner core, packed with chemicals, rocketed out of the tube, a stream of neon orange smoke billowing out behind it, and thudded into the side of the barn, just below the point where the petrol can had landed. There was a moment of silence, like an intake of breath. Then came the explosion. Fragments of flaming palm stem, wood and sacking blasted into the air. More bangs popped like rounds of gunfire, as objects in the barn blew up in the heat.

The two men swore and ran towards the fire and began trying to pull crates from the flames.

Ryan dived into the driver's seat and turned the key. Nan had given him a voucher for an off-road driving day for his birthday last year. He tried to remember everything he'd learned ... *clutch* ... *gears* ... *brakes* ... Glancing in the rear view mirror he saw a tongue of yellow flame racing along the trail of petrol drops towards him. He'd have to remember the rest later. He slammed his foot on the accelerator. The jeep shot forward just in time to escape the fire.

Mum had seen her chance. She was already running towards the jeep. Ryan slowed just enough for her to wrench the door open and throw herself inside before he rammed his foot to the floor again. Clouds of red dust flew up as the tyres skidded over the dirt. Chickens squawked and scattered. There was another boom as Miguel's scooter caught fire and the petrol tank exploded.

'Wait!' Mum shouted, twisting to look over her shoulder. Ryan looked in the mirror. Miguel was sprinting along behind them. His baseball cap had flown off. Terror was etched all over his face. 'We can't leave him behind!' Mum yelled over the engine noise. 'They'll kill him!'

Ryan checked the mirror again. The two men were running back towards their truck. 'They're coming after us!' he shouted. 'We can't stop.'

'He's fifteen! The same age as you!'

Ryan stamped on the brake. Mum shot forward, almost hitting the windscreen. Miguel caught up and tumbled into the back of the jeep. Ryan pulled away, the back doors still flapping open, and drove as fast as he dared, bouncing over the ruts and potholes in the track. He glanced back. The red truck was not far behind. A cloud of black smoke hung in the sky like a smudge of charcoal on blue paper. *I've just sent millions of pounds worth of drugs up in flames,* he thought. *If they catch us, it's Game Over.*

At last the track joined the road that led back to Calakmul. But Ryan knew that their problems were far from over. If he led the gangsters back to camp there'd be no escape. 'We've got to lose them first,' he muttered, making a sharp left turn and speeding onwards. The red truck was still in pursuit as they joined the highway and raced on and on, overtaking lorries and buses and battered old farm trucks. Ryan saw a junction coming up, and, at the very last second, cut in between a lorry full of oranges and a horsebox. He veered onto the slip road, pulled in to a building site and hurtled to a stop behind a wall of diggers and cranes. He looked back just in time to see the red truck flying past the junction and on down the highway.

'Oh yeah!' Mum laughed. 'It'll be miles before they can get off at the next exit.' Then she frowned. 'You haven't been out joy-riding, have you? You can't have learned to drive like that from one day at the off-road centre.'

Ryan grinned. 'I got a bit of help from all those computer games you say are a waste of time . . .'

At that moment a skinny hand reached in from the back and patted him on the shoulder. He'd forgotten the young gangster was still in the jeep. 'Did Miguel give you any information?'

Mum's face suddenly contorted as if caught between many different emotions.

Ryan held his breath, afraid of what he might hear.

'He says that *Los Lobos Rojos* were given a captive by a much larger South American gang a couple of months ago. He thinks it was part of a big trade deal. It makes sense. These

Red Wolves guys don't usually kidnap people themselves.' Mum turned to Miguel. *'Eddie Flint?'* she prompted. 'You said that was the name of the prisoner?'

Miguel gave a thumbs-up and replied in a halting mixture of Spanish and English. 'Si, Eddie Flint. English man.' He held a hand above his hand. *'Muy alto.* Very tall. I see him only one time.'

'He's *alive?'* Ryan's heart flipped over. Was this really happening? He glared at Mum. 'Why didn't you tell me before?'

'I couldn't tell you when you were driving! You'd have run right off the road.'

Ryan had to admit that was true. He turned back to Miguel. 'Eddie Flint? Are you *sure?'*

'Si, alive. Yes,' Miguel said. 'For now,' he added.

'Where?'

Miguel shrugged. *'No lo se.* I don't know.'

'You *must* know!' Ryan raised his hands. For a moment he wanted to grab Miguel and shake the information out of him. This was the most important thing in the world. He couldn't just *not know!* Instead, he clutched at his own hair.

Mum took hold of his wrists. She leaned in close and spoke softly, looking straight into Ryan's eyes. 'I think Miguel is telling the truth. I've asked him over and over. The gang have a lot of small hideouts in the jungle. Dad could have been taken to any one of them. This boy is only a new recruit. He doesn't get told much.'

Ryan let his arms drop.

Mum slumped back and closed her eyes. 'But we know he's alive now! That's what matters. And we're getting close!' She opened her eyes and smiled. Then she walked round to the driver's side. 'Swap seats. We don't want you getting arrested for driving without a licence.'

When Ryan slid out of the jeep his legs gave way. Shock and adrenaline had turned them to water. But it was more than that. Every fibre of his body was struggling to take in the news that Dad was alive and not far away.

'We'll make a detour on the way back to camp to take Miguel to the bus station,' Mum said, as she started the jeep. 'He wanted to do a runner from the gang anyway. That's why he was desperate enough to talk to me for £300. After what just happened he *really* needs to get out of here.'

'I go to grandmother,' Miguel said. 'Mexico City.'

Mum gave Miguel an extra $200 and the name of a lawyer to contact if he needed help. Ryan gave him the blankets from the back of the jeep and his bottle of water. They watched the hunched figure lope across the bus station and melt into the crowd. 'I hope he makes it,' Ryan said as they headed for the snack kiosk to stock up on biscuits and Cokes for the return journey. If the Red Wolves caught up with him, Ryan was sure Miguel had about as much chance of escaping in one piece as King Jaguar Paw if he'd been captured in Tikal. Although, they might stop short of using his head as a football . . .

'He only joined the gang because his friends were signing up,' Mum sighed. 'That's what can happen if you get in with the wrong crowd and don't work hard at school.'

Ryan couldn't believe his ears. 'I've just rescued you from a gang of drug-dealers and that's your take-home message? *Do your homework!*

'I'm your mother. It's my job.' Then she grinned and pushed her bandanna up onto her head. 'But if all else fails you could have a great career as a getaway driver!'

7

COMPASS

CLEO ALSO SPENT the afternoon helping her mother, although in a slightly less explosive fashion.

She and Mum had set themselves up at the outside table again. Their mission was simple; to search the sarcophagus texts for more information about the World Tree. Cleo was convinced that Lady Six Sky's World Tree referred to a real object, a priceless treasure, *the prize that all men desire* described on Roberto's Snake Stone. Mum was not so sure.

They'd been ploughing through the photographs for what seemed like hours and Mum had just gone into the trailer to fetch some drinks when Cleo spotted a small block of writing that had been partly hidden behind one of the carved stone monkey heads. The glyphs jumped straight out at her; *Lady Six Sky's World Tree* – exactly the same as the ones they'd seen this morning.

She started trying to decipher the next few glyphs, her hand trembling with excitement as she copied them into her notebook. She found the first glyph easily. *Jewelled*. Now she had *Lady Six Sky's World Tree is a jewelled* ... Yes! This was looking promising. Cleo scowled at the next symbol. She was sure she'd never seen it before. She scanned the glyph charts with no success. She wrote the word SOMETHING into the space and moved on. Luckily the next few glyphs were familiar and required only a quick check in the dictionary. As she worked, the coil of excitement under her ribs wound tighter and tighter until, by the time Mum came back to the table, it burst out like a loaded spring. 'Look!' she cried, thrusting her notebook under Mum's nose. 'I've found something.'

Mum almost dropped the tray she was carrying. She took the notebook and began mopping up spilled lemonade with a paper napkin. But she forgot all about the mess as soon as she she read Cleo's words. *'Lady Six Sky's World tree is a jewelled SOMETHING that now lies in Jaguar Paw's final resting place in the heart of the Snake Kingdom'*.

She reached out, her fingers twitching with impatience. 'Quick! Let me see the original.'

Cleo slid the photograph across the table. Mum snatched it up and peered at it through her magnifying glass.

'If it's *jewelled*,' Cleo said, 'surely that proves it's a real object?'

'Mmm,' Mum murmured. 'Maybe ...'

'If we could just make out that next glyph it might tell us what it is.' Cleo jabbed impatiently at the mystery symbol she'd labelled as *something*. 'Do you recognise it?'

Mum shook her head. 'I've never seen it before . . .'

Cleo knew that the ancient Mayan script had only started to be decoded in the middle of the twentieth century. New ones were still being found all the time. 'Can you work out what it might mean?'

'It seems to be a combination of several glyphs. *Tree,* and *white,* and . . .' Mum flicked back and forth through the dictionary and scribbled down notes, '. . . *finding,* or *finder.* Yes, that's the closest I can get; *White Finder Tree.*' She looked up at Cleo and pulled a questioning face. '*Lady Six Sky's World Tree is a jewelled White Finder Tree?*'

Cleo was baffled too. She'd read up on Maya mythology but she'd never come across anything called a White Finder Tree.

Mum raised her lemonade glass in a toast. 'Well done! I'm starting to think you must be right. We're looking for some kind of jewelled model World Tree hidden in the jaguar tomb. That must be what it means by *now lies hidden in Jaguar Paw's final resting place in the heart of the Snake Kingdom.* This could well be what the Snake Stone meant by the *prize that all men desire.* Roberto's going to be thrilled when we tell him about this.'

Cleo did feel rather pleased with herself. She glanced across the clearing at Ryan's trailer. The blinds were pulled down at every window He'd be so annoyed he was missing the excitement. He must be having a really boring afternoon, lying in bed feeling sick. 'So why is it called the White Finder

Tree?' she wondered out loud. 'Maybe it's made of some kind of white stone like alabaster.'

Mum was already scouring through all the photographs again. 'Now we know what the White Finder Tree glyph looks like, we might find more mentions of it. A few minutes later, she stabbed a photograph with her pencil. 'Ah yes, here it is! *The directions to Xib'alb'a are written on Lady Six Sky's White Finder Tree.* How extraordinary!'

Directions? Cleo thought. That must be something to do with the *Finder* part of White Finder Tree. Perhaps there were instructions for summoning visions of the Underworld carved into the 'bark' of the model tree? Could that be the 'secret knowledge' that was described on the Snake Stone?' Suddenly she had a brainwave and jumped up from her chair. 'Bark!'

'Bark?' Mum echoed.

'The Maya used the bark of ceiba trees to make paper, didn't they? And paper is white. Maybe this White Finder Tree isn't a model, but a map . . .'

'A road map to Xib'alb'a?' Mum chewed her pencil. 'It's a good idea. But if it's made of paper, it would have rotted away long ago in the humid conditions.'

Cleo slumped back into her chair. She hadn't thought of that. It ruined everything if the White Finder Tree was a book or codex made of paper. There would be nothing left of it but shreds of decayed pulp. Any knowledge it contained – secret or otherwise – would have vanished. It would be no more useful than the soggy lump of paper napkin sitting in the pool of lemonade on the tray.

'Don't look so miserable,' Mum said. 'I don't think it's paper. It's "jewelled" remember. That sounds more like a solid object.' She brushed away a party of ants that had arrived to investigate the spilled lemonade. 'But I like your idea that it's called a *Finder* because it's used to help find the way.'

'In a vision, you mean?' Cleo asked.

'It could even be the way to a real place. It might be something to do with that odd passage I deciphered this morning about counting the hidden path through the forest.' Mum's voice sped up as she ran with the idea. 'Maybe it's a navigation instrument like a sextant, or an astrolabe. Something to help chart the positions of the stars and planets.'

Cleo instantly cheered up. Mum's idea made sense. The ancient Maya were expert astronomers. *Yes,* she thought. The White Finder Tree was almost certainly a navigation instrument, something to guide them to a place they believed to be an entrance to the Underworld. Perhaps it was a sacred cave or a sinkhole somewhere out in the jungle.

She looked over at Ryan's trailer again. Still no sign of life. She wished he'd hurry up and get better. She was sure she'd be able to figure things out more quickly if she could just talk to him. He had a knack of seeing things from a different angle. Then again, he'd probably come up with some stupid joke. He'd say that the White Finder Tree was a magic device for tracking down things that are white. *Snow, sugar, swans* . . . She could almost hear Ryan's voice; *You'd be surprised how handy it could be when you need to find some meringues in a hurry* . . .

'What are you smiling about?' Mum asked.

'Oh, nothing! I just thought of one of Ryan's jokes.'

Mum gave her an odd look. 'Don't worry. He'll be up and about again soon.'

But Cleo had stopped listening. Ryan's meringue joke had given her a brilliant idea! The White Finder Tree really *could* be for finding something white. For the Maya, each direction was associated with a specific colour; red for east, yellow for south, black for west and *white for north* . . . 'It's the *north* Finder Tree!' she blurted. 'White symbolises north. It's a compass!'

Cleo's brain fizzed with excitement. *A North Finder is the perfect description of a compass – a piece of magnetised metal that aligns itself with the earth's magnetic north pole.* But then she remembered her history. The fizzing stopped. Her lovely theory came crashing down around her. 'The Maya didn't *have* compasses in the eighth century, did they?' she sighed. 'They weren't known outside China until the tenth century at the earliest.'

But Mum was smiling. 'They *could* have found a lodestone, a naturally occurring magnet. They're produced when certain kinds of iron ore in the rock are struck by lightning.'

Cleo knew what a lodestone was, of course. She also knew that they were rare in this part of the world. Rare, *but still possible* . . .

'I can just see it.' Mum's fingers flew over the keys of her laptop as she made notes. 'A hunter or a fisherman comes across an unusual little piece of stone and notices that it always spins round to line up in a certain direction.'

Cleo took up the story. 'Maybe he gives it to a priest or a shaman, who uses it in his rituals. It's so special that he has a beautiful jewelled artefact made to house it . . .'

'In the shape of the sacred World Tree!' Mum interrupted. 'It's so precious that it's given to Lady Six Sky as a present.'

Cleo was so thrilled by the idea that the White Finder

Tree was a compass that she was going to burst if she didn't tell Ryan soon. *He's only got a stomach bug,* she thought. Julie said it was nothing serious when she went off to get him some medicine. 'He just needs to rest quietly for the afternoon,' she'd said. *But surely Ryan wouldn't mind being woken up for news of this momentousness. If the White Finder Tree is a compass, it could completely change our understanding of Maya technology. And if it leads to a real place that the Maya believed to be the entrance to Xib'alb'a, it could reveal a sacred site that has been lost for centuries! You'd have to be on your deathbed not to want to hear this! And anyway,* Cleo reasoned, *someone should go and check on him. Julie has been gone for hours.*

Minutes later, armed with a bottle of water and a banana from the fridge – just the thing for replacing fluid and potassium and other minerals lost through vomiting – Cleo hurried up the steps to Ryan's trailer. Ignoring the *Do Not Disturb* sign, she knocked on the door. There was no reply. She turned the handle, but the door was locked. Starting to worry, she walked round to the back of the trailer. She spotted a chink between the blinds at Ryan's bedroom window. She dragged over a crate, climbed up and peeped through.

The room was empty.

Cleo moved the crate along to the bathroom window and tapped on the frosted glass. There was no reply.

She jumped down from the crate to run for help. That stomach bug must have been more serious than anyone had known. It could be food poisoning. Or a tropical disease. Alex had been talking about some of the worse ones only last night; *dengue, typhoid fever, Chagas' disease, schistosomiasis . . .*

53

Ryan's been alone in the trailer for hours. He could be lying in the bathroom, unconscious, or even . . .

Cleo didn't dare finish the thought.

8

FRIENDSHIP

CLEO WAS SPRINTING across the clearing when she heard the jeep pull up. She changed course and ran to meet it. 'Ryan's not in his room,' she shouted. 'Come quick!'

Julie Flint – who, for some reason was dressed for guerrilla warfare with a bandanna tied round her head and smudges of black on her face – pulled on the handbrake. But before she could reply, Cleo glimpsed movement in the back of the jeep; movement that was coming from a large trainer-clad foot.

She yanked open the doors. Ryan was lying on his back on the bench seat with his feet propped up and a heap of ice cream and biscuit wrappers on his chest. Cleo's relief that he was alive instantly turned to fury for giving her such a fright. 'You're meant to be ill!'

Ryan made a move as if to clutch his stomach, then followed her gaze to the remains of his feast. 'Miraculous recovery?' he said weakly. 'I can explain . . .'

Cleo glared down at Ryan's upside down features.

He sat up. 'OK, no, I *can't* explain.'

'Well, I can! You didn't want to work on the Mayan glyphs with me this afternoon so you made up a stupid story about being sick to get out of it.' Cleo was starting to feel extremely annoyed with herself for over-reacting. Of course Ryan hadn't died of dengue fever! For a start, the symptoms would take much longer than that to develop.

'No, that's not true. I love Mayan glyphs. I love *you* . . . No, I don't *love you,* like hearts and flowers, *I luuuurve you,* I mean I love *working with you* on boring old history stuff. No, it's *not* boring, but it *would* be boring with anyone else . . .'

Cleo had no idea what Ryan was talking about. All she heard was *I don't love you* and *history is boring.* 'If you wanted to go into town with your mum, why didn't you just say?'

Ryan glanced over his shoulder. Julie was on her way into the trailer. 'I promised Mum I wouldn't tell anyone . . .' He fell silent as Max and Roberto walked past. 'Let's go somewhere we can talk.' He slid down from the back of the jeep and they marched in silence along a path through a stand of breadnut trees. When they came to a low mound covered in a tumble of moss-covered ruins, they climbed up and ducked through a hole in a crumbling wall. They found themselves in a small circular room, the roof of which had long since caved in. Cleo sat down, leaning against a stone platform that might once have been an altar. It was now pitted by centuries of rain and wind, and served as a sun deck for a family of small lizards.

Ryan sank down next to her. 'Why are you carrying that banana around, by the way?'

Cleo dropped the banana onto the altar. 'It's high in potassium,' she muttered. Ryan looked puzzled but she really couldn't be bothered to explain her earlier concern for his digestive system. It obviously didn't deserve it anyway.

There was a long silence. 'We were looking for my dad,' Ryan said at last.

Cleo was dumbstruck. She knew that Ryan's dad was missing. He'd told her all about it in Egypt last year. She also knew that Julie had picked up some information from one of the Tiger's Claw gangsters they'd run into in China. He'd told her that Eddie Flint might now be in Mexico. But, since arriving in Calakmul, Ryan had hardly said a word on the subject. Cleo had assumed the trail had gone cold and Julie had given up looking. 'Where?' she asked at last.

As Ryan recounted the rendezvous with Miguel, pain writhed in Cleo's chest, as bitter and barbed as a rope of thorns. Ryan was the first friend she'd ever had. She'd travelled the world with her parents all her life. She'd never been to an ordinary school. It had taken her a while to even figure out how friendship *worked*. She'd thought that she'd got the hang of it, but clearly she was mistaken. She must have done something very wrong for Ryan to have shut her out of something so important after everything they'd been through together; booby traps, labyrinths, fire-breathing dragons . . . 'I would have come with you,' she said.

'That's the whole point!' Ryan burst out. 'That's why I didn't tell you. I knew you'd want to help, but it was too dangerous . . .'

'*Dangerous?* What, because I'm a *girl?* Who pulled you out of a waterfall in China? Who saved you from a scorpion in Egypt?'

'It's not because you're a girl, you wally! And I couldn't tell you, even if I wanted to, because I promised Mum I'd keep it secret. I had to go with her. Otherwise she'd have gone charging in on her own like something out of *Rambo* . . .'

'*Rambert?*' Cleo echoed. 'The ballet company?'

'Ram*bo*. It's a film. He's like this all-action tough guy . . .' Ryan sighed. 'It doesn't matter. The point is I didn't do it for the thrills. I had no choice.'

Cleo stared down at the sunbathing lizards. 'You could have told my parents,' she said. 'They'd have stopped your mum going.'

Ryan picked a flake of mustard-coloured lichen from the stone. 'I know. The thing is,' he said eventually. 'Deep down, I didn't *want* to stop her. Just to stop her getting killed.' He reached up to his St Christopher's pendant and turned it over and over. Cleo noticed he still wore the scarab beetle amulet she'd given him in Egypt threaded on to the cord next to it, along with the lucky coins their friend Meilin had given him in China. 'If there was any chance of finding Dad,' he sighed, 'we just had to go for it . . .'

The lizards on the altar stone sensed the shadow of a hawk overhead and scurried for cover. All at once the truth engulfed Cleo like an avalanche. *Ryan is far more upset by his father's disappearance than he lets on.* He hardly ever talked about it. He was always laughing and making jokes. She had assumed he'd got used to his dad being missing and didn't think about it much any more.

She felt mean and small and guilty. A proper friend would

have known. *Of course he thinks about it! How would I feel if Dad disappeared? I wouldn't get used to it for six hundred years, let alone six.* She should have known from the psychology courses she'd studied that the jokes and the denial were just Ryan's *coping strategies.* Cleo didn't know what to say. Instead she reached out and gave Ryan's hand a squeeze. She almost pulled her hand back again. She'd forgotten that Ryan was a boy. Would he think hand-squeezing was weird or soppy?

But Ryan squeezed back. 'Miguel said the Red Wolves are holding Dad prisoner.'

Cleo stared at him in amazement. 'You mean right here in Yucatàn?'

Ryan nodded. 'He didn't know where though.' He paused, watching the lizards as they ventured back out from the cracks in the stone. 'I *want* to believe it but I'm worried that Mum's going to get her hopes up again and it'll be another false alarm . . .'

Cleo looked down at their clasped hands. From now on, she vowed to herself, she would be a better friend. 'You'll find him. But promise me you won't go on any more *Rambo raids.*' She looked up and smiled. 'Not without me, anyway!'

'It's a deal.' Ryan let go of her hand, grabbed the banana and peeled it. 'So, that was my day. What about yours? Did you manage to decipher any glyphs without my invaluable input?'

'Just a few,' Cleo laughed. 'Wait till you hear this!'

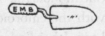

The whole team gathered under the ceiba tree for dinner that evening.

Strings of small lanterns glowed among the branches. Crickets chirped. Frogs croaked. The scent of toasting corn – a cross between popcorn and Bonfire Night – filled the warm air. Rosita was cooking tortillas over the fire, pinching off dabs of dough from a plastic tub, patting and turning them into flat discs and sliding them onto the griddle. Ryan gazed into the flames, trying to block out memories of the exploding drugs barn. Miguel's words had been replaying over and over in his head all afternoon. *Eddie Flint. Si, alive . . . Stop thinking about it,* he told himself. *You can't do anything about it now.*

Cleo sat down next to him and lounged back in her chair. She hadn't exactly dressed up for dinner, but she'd zipped the bottoms onto her hiking shorts and changed into a slightly less baggy t-shirt. 'See how Rosita has a triangle of three big hearthstones round the fire,' she said by way of greeting. 'That's an ancient Maya tradition. It reflects the creation myth in which the gods placed the three stones, representing the earth, the sky and the sea . . .'

Ryan was so relieved that things were back to normal again – or, as normal as they ever got with Cleo – that he smiled and nodded as if this riveting information about hearthstones had made his life complete. It had been torture to see the look on her face when she realised he'd lied to her about being ill. He'd felt much better once he'd told her the truth. He just wished he hadn't accidentally said *I love you.* His face burned at the memory. Luckily, Cleo didn't seem to notice. She'd now launched into a full-scale monologue on Maya culture. 'That white cotton smock with the embroidered flowers Rosita's wearing is traditional too. It's called a *huipil* . . .' She broke off, as if remembering something. Then she leaned in and treated him to a syrupy smile, the sort that news interviewers aim at people who've just been helicoptered off a sinking ship. 'How are you *feeling?*' she asked.

Ryan did a double-take. Since when did Cleo want to know about *feelings?* Was this to do with the *I love you* thing, he wondered. She'd squeezed his hand earlier too, which was surprisingly touchy-feely for Cleo. The awkward silence was broken by a cheer from the portable radio in the kitchen. Rosita's husband, Luis, the camp's handyman, was listening to a baseball game. The local team – *Pirates of Campeche* – had just scored a home run.

'Remember,' Cleo said, 'I'm here for you if you need to talk.'

Ryan shrank back in his chair. Why had Cleo suddenly started sounding like a school counsellor?

'As your *friend.*'

'Er, great. I'll bear that in mind.'

It was a relief when Rosita called that the food was ready. Ryan was first in line. Rosita smiled at him. With her twinkling eyes and glossy black hair streaked with a stripe of white, she had the look of a friendly magpie. She spooned a double helping of spicy turkey stew onto his plate, laughing and saying something in Spanish.

Cleo raised her eyebrows. 'She said it's to keep your muscles strong.'

Helping Rosita carry that enormous basket of laundry to the washing line this morning had clearly been worth it, Ryan thought. And luckily he didn't have to pretend he had a stomach upset any more!

9

MAGIC

THE CONVERSATION AROUND the table soon turned to the surprising finding in Jaguar Paw's tomb.

Pete McNeil drained his beer bottle. 'Alex and I have been examining the jaguar skeleton. He was a big old male. There are arrow scrapes on the bones from earlier hunting attempts. He'd had some lucky escapes.'

I know how he feels, Ryan thought.

'Until,' Alex said, beaming happily, 'he was whacked by something that smashed the back of his skull. A big stone, probably. *Ka-bonk! Lights out!*' She reached for a tortilla from the basket and mopped stew from her plate. 'And this is the best bit. We found a super little scrap of preserved tissue from the jaguar's intestine. There are some absolutely *gorgeous* hookworms in it!'

Ryan let the rice drop from his fork. He'd been faking his stomach problem earlier, but he was starting to feel distinctly queasy now. He remembered, too late, that he'd vowed never to eat at the same table as Alex Shawcross again, after the banquet in China, during which she'd insisted on identifying every ingredient in his bowl – including duck gizzards and tripe.

'We'll know more when we hear back from the lab in Mérida,' Pete said. 'We've sent off a sample for a full helminthological report.'

'A full *what* report?' Ryan spluttered.

'*Helminthological,*' Cleo told him. 'It's the study of parasitic worms.'

She *had* to be joking, Ryan thought. Surely that wasn't an actual *thing.* But no one else raised even half an eyebrow.

Roberto pushed his plate away, got up and paced round the table. 'That is very interesting! But it doesn't answer the question; why was a jaguar buried in a sarcophagus that was clearly intended for King Jaguar Paw? I've checked all the stonework. It doesn't look as if anyone opened it and replaced the body *after* the coffin was sealed. It would help if we had an exact date for the burial.'

Cleo's mum, Lydia, took a slice of pineapple from the fruit platter Rosita had placed in the middle of the table. 'Did you manage to get a clearer image of that section we were looking at earlier?' she asked Max. She turned to the rest of the group. 'The stone's very eroded at one end of the lid. I thought I could make out some faint numbers that might be a date.'

Max nodded. 'I've been processing the images all afternoon. They're still pretty rough but . . .'

'Let's have a look, then!' Roberto bristled with impatience. His shirt buttons – straining to close over his barrel chest – looked as if they might pop at any moment.

'Printer's playing up,' Max said. 'I told you it was rubbish.'

Roberto glared at him.

'I suppose you *could* look on the screen if you want.' Grumbling about not having a chance to finish his dinner in peace, Max fetched his laptop from his trailer and placed it in the middle of the table.

Ryan was nearest. While everyone else was still gathering round he glanced at the screen. All he could see was a photo of a smart little blue and yellow bird. 'Er, I know I'm not an expert,' he said, 'but that doesn't look like the sarcophagus.'

'Ten out of ten for observation, lad,' Max blustered. 'I've opened the wrong bloomin' folder. That's a lovely little *violaceous trogon* I spotted this morning.'

Who comes up with these bird names? Ryan wondered. *Violaceous trogon* sounded like an evil alien overlord from a Doctor Who episode . . .

'They're clever little devils. They lay their eggs inside wasp and ant nests,' Max said as he opened the correct file. The screen filled with grey stone inscribed with a series of glyphs. 'Here you go. I've zoomed right in . . .'

Lydia McNeil squinted at the screen. 'Yep, I can see it now. *Jaguar Paw departed for Xib'alb'a, 9.13.3.8.11 . . .*'

Cleo's brows furrowed for about half a second. 'That's 21st August, AD 695.'

Roberto smoothed a hand over his chin. 'That's the year

we think Jaguar Paw died. The timing's right even if it's not his skeleton.'

Ryan was still marvelling at Cleo's warp-speed mental arithmetic. 'How did you *do* that thing with the date?'

Cleo shrugged and brushed a mosquito from her arm. 'It's the Maya Long Count calendar. You just work forward from the starting date of 13.0.0.0.0. – which was 11th August, 3114 BC in our calendar – using multiples of the Maya 360-day years, or *tuns*. There are twenty *tuns* in a *katun,* four hundred in a *baktun* and so on . . .'

Ryan laughed. 'Oh well, when you put it like that, it's a piece of cake!'

'Exactly!' Cleo said. 'It's a simple numerical count . . .'

Ryan sneaked a glance at Mum. She'd been on about getting him a maths tutor for months. This was only going to encourage her. But she didn't look up from the map of the Calakmul area she'd been studying all afternoon. *Scanning for possible locations for Red Wolves hideouts.* Ryan pushed the thought away before his brain could start reliving the explosion all over again.

'Do we have any more information from the sarcophagus texts?' Roberto asked.

Cleo and her Mum exchanged excited glances. 'We've found something really interesting,' Lydia said. 'There may be a remarkable object hidden in the tomb . . .'

'It's a compass in the shape of the World Tree!' Cleo blurted. Ryan could tell she'd been bursting to spill the news since the moment they'd sat down. 'They called it the *White Finder Tree.*' She leaned across the table, her words tumbling out at a hundred miles an hour. 'Actually it was Ryan who gave me the idea, going on about a magic device for finding white meringues . . . Obviously, it wasn't *meringues*, but *white* was the symbol for *north*, so . . .'

Ryan stared at Cleo. She might be a mathematical genius, but had she totally lost her marbles? He hadn't even been there when Cleo and her mum came up with this theory, let alone spouting nonsense about meringues! But interrupting Cleo in full flow would be like trying to stop a runaway train. He let it go.

'The White Finder Tree is inscribed with directions to the mouth of Xib'alb'a,' Cleo went on, 'and it's fitted with a lodestone to help point the way . . .'

Roberto looked doubtful. 'There's no evidence the Maya used magnetic compasses.' But then he rocked his head from side to side in a *maybe* gesture. 'Although a possible lodestone device *has* been discovered at an Olmec site – and they're an *earlier* Central American civilisation than the Maya . . .'

'Goodness! It must have seemed like magic,' Alex chipped in. 'To be able to navigate in the jungle, even when they couldn't see the sun or the stars.' She raised her beer glass in Ryan's direction. 'Well done, you, for coming up with such a super brainwave!' She gave a little frown. 'Although I don't quite see where the meringues come in.'

Ryan gave up. He might as well take the credit. 'Oh, you know, just one of those lightbulb moments. So,' he added, 'this Tree was like some kind of ancient Maya satnav?'

Everyone laughed.

Everyone except Roberto. He was pacing round the table faster than ever. 'This White Finder Tree compass is obviously *"the prize all men desire"* that the Snake Stone text talks about. And you say it belonged to Lady Six Sky?' He stopped suddenly and swept a long look around the table, his face taut with emotion. 'Yes! This is the proof we needed. We know that the Snake Stone is a fragment of a monument that was put up in Naranjo to celebrate Smoking Squirrel's war victories. *Lady Six Sky was Smoking Squirrel's mother.* She was a Queen of Naranjo. That's how Smoking Squirrel knew about the White Finder Tree. It belonged to his mother.'

'Of course!' Lydia said. 'I can't believe I didn't make the link sooner.'

'But the White Finder Tree didn't just help you to find the way to Xib'alb'a,' Cleo interrupted. 'We deciphered another passage later this afternoon. It also contains instructions for special sacrifice rituals to fetch people back from the dead once you get there . . .'

Uh oh, Ryan thought, *sacrifice rituals.* Any second now Cleo and Alex would start going on about ropes of thorns again. 'Amazing,' he said, before they could even think about it. 'So it wasn't just a satnav. It had a built-in immortality app too.'

Cleo's eyes glittered the way they always did when she had a new theory. 'Exactly! Not that it was an *app*, of course. But it's all about immortality. The "prize that all men desire" isn't the White Finder Tree itself. The prize is *immortality*. The Tree contains the secret knowledge that tells you how to get it.'

'*Do* all men want to live forever?' Ryan wondered.

Max groaned and stretched. 'Not if they've got arthritis like mine, they don't. My back's playing up something rotten.'

Ryan laughed. But then he remembered the First Emperor of China. He'd been so keen to live forever that he had a whole team of experts working on producing the elixir of life. Unfortunately, their favourite ingredient was mercury, which, being highly toxic, didn't exactly have the desired effect. It seemed immortality was a prize that some people would do anything to win. And anything to keep for themselves.

Alex looked up from pouring another beer. 'Why should only *men* desire the prize? That's jolly unfair! Can't us girls live for ever too?'

'Maybe that's what Lady Six Sky thought,' Lydia said. 'The White Finder Tree was hers . . .'

Roberto finally sank down into his chair, shaking his head in wonder. '*A model World Tree, a Maya compass, directions to the Underworld* . . . This could be one of the biggest archaeological finds of the century.'

Cleo looked as if she might explode with joy.

'We haven't found it yet!' Max pointed out.

Lydia smiled. 'I'm sure it's in the jaguar tomb somewhere.'

That's when Ryan felt something furry brush against his ankle.

Cleo peered into the shadows among the feet to see what had made Ryan shoot back from the table as if he'd been electrocuted.

A pair of shiny black eyes peeped up at her from above a long tapered snout. 'It's only a tamandua,' she said.

'*Only?*' Ryan shrank behind his overturned chair. 'They have massive deadly ones round here, don't they?'

'You *can't* be afraid of anteaters!' Cleo laughed. '*Nobody's* afraid of anteaters. Well, apart from ants, of course.'

Ryan peeped over the chair. 'I thought you said *tarantula!*'

Cleo suddenly remembered her vow to be a better friend.

And friends didn't laugh at friends' phobias, however irrational and annoying they were. 'I said *tamandua*. It's a collared anteater,' she explained, in her most reassuring voice. 'It's just a baby.'

The anteater padded out from under the table on curved claws that looked several sizes too big. It had thick cream-coloured fur with a broad black band across the back. Looking up, it blinked and twitched its nose.

Ryan covered his eyes. 'It's blinding me with its cuteness rays!' He crouched down, stroked the anteater and let it nuzzle his palm. *'Eughh!'* he groaned, as a long black tongue left a trail across his hand. 'That's like superglue!'

When everyone had finished eating, they moved to sit around the fire. Cleo leaned back and gazed up through the ceiba branches. The stars were so clear here, far from the light pollution of a big city. She could make out the three bright blue stars of Orion's belt and the orangey glow of Betelgeuse.

She closed her eyes, and let the crackling of the fire lull her.

She heard a snuffling noise and sat up with a start. The baby anteater was curled up on Ryan's lap snoring softly.

'That's what you sounded like a minute ago!' Ryan teased.

'I was *not* snoring! I wasn't even asleep.' But as Cleo tuned in to the conversation she realised that maybe she *had* drifted off for a moment. 'So,' Mum was saying to Roberto, 'we can stay for another three weeks before we have to get back to London. That'll give us plenty of time to search the tomb for the White Finder Tree. That's if it's all right with you, Roberto?' she added. 'It's your dig.'

'Of course. I'd be glad of the help. The White Finder Tree could lead us to a place that the Maya believed to be the entrance to the Underworld. It might even solve the mystery of Jaguar Paw's death.'

Dad poked the fire with a stick, sending a flurry of sparks into the air. 'I suggest we keep the hunt for the White Finder Tree to ourselves for now,' he said. 'If word gets out that we're looking for some kind of ancient Maya "satnav", every crackpot and conspiracy theory nut in the world will descend on Calakmul in no time.'

Mum rolled her eyes. 'We had more than enough of that with the Benben Stone in Egypt last year. It would be even worse here since all that mumbo-jumbo about the Maya calendar prophecy . . .'

Ryan looked up from stroking the anteater. 'Oh yeah, didn't they predict that the world was going to end in 2012 or something?'

'No, they did not!' Cleo couldn't believe that Ryan had fallen for all the scare stories. 'It was just that 21st December, 2012 corresponded to the end of the thirteenth *baktun* of the Long Count calendar.'

Ryan's mum smiled. 'You'd be mobbed by journalists too. The media go mad for anything to do with Maya prophecies.'

'And then there's the treasure-hunters,' Alex added. 'If they find out that the White Finder Tree leads to the Mouth of the Underworld, *everyone's* going to be looking for it. The ancient Maya always left precious objects as offerings to the Lords of Death, along with human sacrifices. Xib'alb'a would be a gold mine for looters. Literally.'

'So, it's agreed?' Roberto fixed each of them in turn with a stern gaze. 'Not a word of the White Finder Tree to anyone outside camp.'

10

SHADOW

RYAN CRAWLED OUT from under the mosquito net and pulled on jeans and a t-shirt. He opened the door of the trailer and stood on the top step, breathing in the leafy jungle morning. Then came the tang of smoke, and onions and peppers frying over the fire. Rosita was already cooking breakfast. Even the strong coffee brewing in a pot smelled delicious, and he didn't even like coffee. Birds were shouting in the trees. It wasn't like the busy, bossy twittering of sparrows and robins back home in Manchester. Here the birds sounded surprised and excited, with fairground squeals of *wheee* and *ooooh* . . .

Suddenly the perfect morning was hijacked by thoughts

71

of Dad. *Is he out there somewhere in that vast forest? Is he listening to the same over-excited birds? Do the Red Wolves give him enough to eat?* Ryan ground the heels of his hands over his eyes. The creaking of the trailer as Mum paced around – making phone calls, sending messages, drinking endless mugs of coffee – had kept him awake half the night. The other half he'd spent worrying about all the stupid risks she might take next.

He started down the steps, tripped over a small furry object, and crash-landed on the bottom stair. A pair of bright black eyes peered down at him from above a quivering snout. 'It's you again!' Ryan couldn't help laughing. When the little anteater had waddled off into the undergrowth last night he'd assumed it had gone back to its nest or burrow, or whatever anteaters lived in. He stroked the coarse fur for a moment. Then he got up and made for the kitchen.

Rosita was sitting on a plastic chair, cracking eggs into a large bowl on her lap. '*Buenos dias!*' she greeted him in Spanish. '*Ahchab!*'

Ryan was about to reply 'Bless you!' when he realised it wasn't a sneeze. Rosita was pointing at the anteater trotting along behind him. '*Ahchab,*' she said again. 'Is the Mayan word for this animal.'

'*Ahchab,*' Ryan repeated. He'd forgotten that Mayan wasn't just the ancient language of the strange glyphs carved in the ruins. It was still spoken by millions of people in this part of the world.

Rosita shuffled to the back of the gazebo and started chopping wood for the fire. Ryan hurried to help. Rosita patted his arm as she handed him the small axe. 'This is Luis's job,' she said. 'But the *Piratas de Campeche* lost a big match

72

last night. He . . .' Rosita rested her cheek on her hands and then thumped her head, in a mime of her husband sleeping off a hangover. She explained in Mayan too. Ryan made out that *kala'an* meant *drunk* and *kaan* was *hammock*. He felt very pleased with himself. He'd now learned three words of Mayan. All he needed was the right moment to drop the phrase *there's a drunken anteater in my hammock* into casual conversation and he could pass for fluent.

When Ryan finished chopping wood and sat down for breakfast the anteater was still waiting for him.

'Maybe the mother is dead?' Rosita suggested. 'Sometimes they are hit by a car.'

Ryan picked up the little cub. 'We'll find your mum,' he promised. The anteater blinked and gazed longingly at his plate of scrambled eggs. Ryan tipped some on the floor. The long black tongue slurped up the egg in a flash.

'We're going up to the tomb straight after breakfast!'

Ryan looked up to see Cleo jogging over to join him. She pulled up a chair. 'I can't wait to start looking for the White Finder Tree and . . .' She broke off when she saw the anteater and laughed. 'Still got your little shadow?'

'Hey, that's what I'm going to call him,' Ryan said. 'Shadow! I'll join you at the tomb later,' he added. 'I'm going to search for Shadow's mum. The poor little cub's all alone.'

'Pup.' Cleo looked up from buttering her toast. 'Anteater young are called pups not cubs.'

How does she know this stuff? If it were anyone else, Ryan would suspect them of bluffing. But, knowing Cleo, she'd studied an online degree-level course in anteater biology. Shadow was climbing up his leg in search of more food. 'I know he should go back to the wild, but I'd love to keep him. He could be my little spirit animal. Like in that film, *The Golden Compass*.'

'It was a book first,' Cleo said. 'By Philip Pullman. The spirit animals were called daemons. They're based on the tradition of witch's familiars in European folklore. Many cultures have companion animals of some sort. The Aztecs called them *nahual* . . .'

Ryan braced himself for a lecture on the cultural history of animal spirits. But Cleo grabbed his arm. 'Ooh!' she cried. 'Ooh! I've just thought of something. The Maya had a similar belief. They called the animal spirit the *way*. But it wasn't so much a person's companion, as their *animal form*.'

'Fascinating,' Ryan murmured, slowly backing away from the table. 'Must go. People to see. Anteaters to find!'

Cleo pulled him back. 'Wait! Ordinary people would have a humble animal *way* like a mouse or a toad. High status people would have a more impressive *way*. This might just be the answer, don't you see?'

Well, that depends on the question, Ryan thought. *If it's 'why is a crazy girl ripping your arm off and ranting about shape-shifting?' then it might be!*

'A king would have the most important animal of all . . .' Cleo's mouth opened and closed as she tried to get all her words out at the same time. It was the expression Ryan called her Theory Face. He'd seen it many times before. 'A jaguar!' she cried. '*That's* why the jaguar is buried in Jaguar Paw's sarcophagus. They believed it really *was* Jaguar Paw, but in his *way* form.'

'You mean I was right about Jaguar Paw being a were-jaguar?'

But Cleo wasn't listening. 'I've got to tell Mum about this.' She turned on her heel and darted off across the clearing.

'Yes, Ryan, I don't know how you do it but you were right, yet again,' Ryan said, speaking Cleo's words for her. He looked down at Shadow. He wasn't listening either. He was too busy eating Cleo's leftover toast.

Ryan and Shadow roamed the vast site, from pyramids and temples right out to the fringe of scattered boulders that were slowly being reclaimed by the creeping roots and vines of the jungle.

Ryan poked a long stick into holes in the masonry and up into the overhanging branches. Shadow snuffled at every mound and burrow. Together they scrambled over fallen tree trunks and the stone *stelae* that lay like the gravestones of giants in a long abandoned churchyard, etched with traces of writing and the ghosts of figures.

Ryan knew it was probably hopeless but he couldn't give up. Maybe Shadow *was* his spirit animal. After all, a shared appreciation of scrambled eggs wasn't all they had in common. *We're both searching for a missing parent.*

They traipsed along a trail that was little more than the memory of a path, like the impression left by a rubbed out pencil line. Here and there Ryan could make out a border of chalky white stones hidden beneath the carpet of dry leaves. He'd strayed much further into the jungle than he'd intended and was about to turn back when a noise in the branches made him spin round. He heard a thwack. He saw the flash of a machete. *The Red Wolves! They've come after me!*

They want revenge for burning down their drugs barn! His heart rattled against his ribs.

'Ryan!' a friendly voice cried. *'Hola!'*

It was only Rosita! She ran a hand over the bark of a spindly tree, grey and white, and mottled like snakeskin. *'Habim.* Very good tree,' she said. 'I don't know name in English.' She looked up at the pink blossom and then knelt and hacked at the root with the machete. 'The root bark is very good painkiller.'

Ryan leaned against a tree, his legs still shaking from the scare. 'For Luis's headache?' he asked.

Rosita nodded and tipped several strips of bark into her basket. She pointed to a smooth boulder nearby. Ryan hadn't spotted it through the dense undergrowth, even though it was the size of a small car. She showed him two more, even bigger. 'These rocks make a triangle,' she said. 'Local people call them the gods' hearthstones. Inside the triangle, the best plants for medicine grow.' She winked. 'But that is my secret. Do not tell!'

Ryan held up a hand. 'Scouts' honour.'

Rosita plucked leaves from low bushes. 'This one is for skin rash. This one for infection . . .' She broke off, noticing that Shadow was sitting at Ryan's feet. 'No luck? Well, now *you* must be mother!' She tucked the machete into the woven belt she wore over her dress. 'You must show him how to find ants.'

Yeah, Ryan thought as he watched Rosita head back to camp, her flip-flops crunching on the leaves, *because ant-foraging just happens to be my best subject at school!*

But how hard could it be? The jungle was teeming with ants. He'd been covered in bites since day one. But just because he now *wanted* to find them, the place was suddenly an insect-free zone. *Never mind the gods' hearthstones,* he thought as he trailed around. *It's as if the gods' pest controllers have just turned up and fumigated the place.* He was ducking under a low branch when he spotted a blue and yellow bird flitting through the leaves. *Violaceous trogon,* Ryan thought, remembering the photo on Max's laptop. *Clever little devil,* Max had called it. *Lays its eggs in wasp and ant nests.*

Ants' nests! Ryan ran after the bird, crashing through the undergrowth. He spotted a flash of blue overhead as the trogon disappeared into the branches of a flaky-barked tree. A column of large brown ants was marching down the trunk to the forest floor.

Ryan punched the air as if he'd struck gold. He crouched down next to Shadow. 'Go on then, tuck in!'

Shadow looked up at him.

'No way!' Ryan muttered. 'Surely I haven't got to teach you *everything*?'

Shadow twitched one of his little pink ears.

Ryan knelt on all fours and stuck his tongue out, pretending to lick up the ants from among the roots. *I can't believe I'm doing this!* He couldn't help glancing around to check there were no observers lurking in the bushes. If this appeared on *YouTube* he'd have to move schools. In fact, he'd probably have to move *lives*.

At last Shadow got the idea. He thrust his nose into the ant column and gorged. Then he curled up and fell asleep. Ryan carried him back to camp, quite pleased with his first day as a mother anteater. Looking up to see Cleo running to meet him, he waved and picked up his pace.

Cleo waved back, but not in a good way. It looked more like a distress signal than a greeting. 'At last! You're back!' she shouted. 'Something terrible has happened!'

11

DISASTER

CLEO'S MORNING HAD started well.

When she'd told Mum and Roberto her theory about the jaguar being buried as the animal spirit of King Jaguar Paw they'd been so impressed that they'd talked about nothing else all the way to the pyramid.

Once inside the lower tomb the team had made good progress. There was no sign of the White Finder Tree yet, but they had been excited to find several mentions of Lady Six Sky's son, Smoking Squirrel – who was only two years old at the time of the burial – carved on a fierce stone alligator head at the end of the sarcophagus. It was yet another link with the Snake Stone Roberto had found, which had come from Smoking Squirrel's war monument. There was another name on the alligator tool; that of a boy called Radiant Turtle. Nobody knew who he was, and the stone was too damaged to read more than the name, but it was all very interesting.

Everyone had been in high spirits. Mum and Roberto swapped theories about why Lady Six Sky's White Finder Tree might have ended up in Jaguar Paw's tomb. Could Lady Six Sky and Jaguar Paw have had a secret love affair? Was Jaguar Paw Smoking Squirrel's father?

Dad and Alex were happy discussing hookworms.

Even Max was only slightly grumpy

It was only when they'd come up for a break that things had taken a disastrous turn. Mum had gone back to the trailer to check her email messages. Cleo sat on the high platform gazing out over the forest canopy. *Mega-green,* Ryan had called it. Next time they were up here she would have to point out the patches of pink dogwood and yellow mimosa blossom.

She found herself thinking about Ryan's dad. Were the Red Wolves – *Los Lobos Rojos* – really holding Eddie Flint prisoner somewhere out there among the trees? It was odd to think she could be looking at the exact spot right now. She glanced across at her own dad. He was near the tunnel entrance sorting through a tray of bone fragments, whistling *'I can't live if living is without you.'* He always picked sad tunes when things were going well. He'd caught the sun and his freckled forehead was turning red. She couldn't imagine life without him.

At that moment she heard footsteps far below and looked down to see Mum running back across the plaza. 'Disaster!' she yelled, her voice echoing from the towering stone structures all around. *'Disaster!'*

Cleo scrambled down the steep, uneven steps. Dad was right behind her. *Was it a plane crash? A bomb? Had something happened to Grandma?*

Mum slumped onto a slab of stone. Her face was granite grey beneath a sheen of sweat. 'Someone's leaked the story about the White Finder Tree!'

'What?' Cleo panted. 'How do you know?'

Mum sank her head into her hands. 'I thought it was strange when I got an email message from Suzie Beechcroft!' Cleo recognised the name of one of Mum's colleagues who worked at the British Museum. *'You've caused quite a storm with this World Tree compass. Crossing my fingers that you find it.* Suzie said she'd spotted the story on the *Classic Maya History* blog. So I went and checked.' Mum closed her eyes and swallowed. 'But it's not just on that blog. It's plastered all over the internet.'

Dad had taken his glasses off and was polishing them on his shirt hem. 'Now, don't panic. It could all be a misunderstanding . . .'

But Mum was already storming off. 'Come and see for yourself!'

Nobody spoke until they were inside the little office room at the back of the trailer. Mum threw herself down at the tiny desk, where she'd plugged her laptop into the satellite phone. There was no other internet or mobile coverage this far into the jungle. 'Oh no! It's been picked up by the BBC News now!' she wailed. 'I can't *bear* it!'

Mum could be a little over-dramatic at times, but as Cleo read the words on the screen she could see why she was taking it so badly.

ARCHAEOLOGY PROF OR TOMB RAIDER? ran

the headline above a photo of Mum that had been processed to look like a police mug-shot. *Treasure-hunter, Lydia McNeil is known to be scouring the jungles of Mexico for a mystical ancient Maya "compass" which holds the secret of eternal life* . . . the story went. *McNeil has already been linked with the disappearance of numerous priceless artefacts in highly suspicious circumstances, including the Bloodthirsty Grail in Peru and the Benben Stone in Egypt. Last year she even entered the forbidden tomb of the First Emperor of China in her hunt for treasure* . . .

'But it's all lies!' Cleo protested. 'We *know* who tried to steal the Bloodthirsty Grail and the Benben Stone. It was nothing to do with you, Mum! And you didn't go anywhere near the First Emperor's tomb. That was Ryan and me.'

Dad put his arm round her. 'I know. Don't worry. We'll get this all sorted out.'

'Don't worry?' Mum spun round and glared at him. 'There's no way I'll be able to hang on to my job after this! I had to talk Sir Charles into letting me come on this dig in the first place. He was worried about the department looking bad if the Snake Stone wasn't genuine. What's he going to say now that I've been branded as an international tomb raider?'

The computer beeped to signal that an email message had just arrived.

Mum banged her head on the desk. 'Right on cue!'

Cleo stared at the screen. The message was indeed from Mum's boss, Sir Charles Peacocke, the Minister for Museums and Culture in London. Was he emailing to give her the sack already? Cleo could hardly bear to read the words.

Dear Lidya, no doubt you have seen the stories circulating on the news wires this morning. Bad publicity of this sort reflects very poorly on the department – especially after all your previous 'incidents'. I will telephone shortly to discuss this most unfortunate situation . . .

'How many years have I worked for that man?' Mum fumed. 'And he *still* can't spell my name right. *Lidya* makes me sound like a character in a Russian novel.'

Usually Cleo was as picky about spelling as her mum, but right now, she thought, it was the least of their worries. She drifted to her room and flopped down on the bed. She tried to distract herself by studying the *Popol Vuh*, the Maya sacred book. But when she'd read the same sentence about the Amazing Twins' ball game with the Lords of Xib'alb'a six times she threw it down and ran outside to look for Ryan.

As soon as Ryan saw Cleo's expression he forgot all about his success as a mother anteater.

They headed straight for the Lizard Lounge – the name he'd given to the ruined building on the mound – where she poured out the tale of disaster. 'It's so unfair,' she concluded. 'The press are really picking on Mum. It all goes back to that time in Peru when the Bloodthirsty Grail went missing.'

Ryan nodded sympathetically. The Bloodthirsty Grail incident had taken place before he'd met Cleo, but she'd told him about it. When Lydia McNeil had been accused of stealing the grail she had lost her temper and yelled at the reporters who were hounding her. She'd also made official complaints about them. It hadn't made her very popular with the reporters. No doubt they'd been delighted to pick up another negative story about her.

'But how did the media get hold of the information in the

first place?' Cleo hugged her knees as if she were freezing, even though the sun was beating down. 'We all agreed to keep quiet about the White Finder Tree.'

Ryan stroked Shadow, who was curled up in a ball on the altar stone. 'It must be someone on the team,' he said at last. 'Nobody else knew about it.'

Cleo stared down at her walking boots.

'Let's see,' Ryan said. 'Who was there last night when you and your mum explained about the White Finder Tree?'

Cleo brightened a little. Ryan had guessed she would. She loved nothing more than a list to work through. 'Apart from us and Mum and Dad,' she said, 'there was your mum, Alex, Max and Roberto. Oh, and Rosita and Luis.'

Ryan laughed. 'Surely you don't suspect them?'

'It's important to be *systematic*,' Cleo told him. 'And a couple of the workmen came and chatted to Luis for a while. But we can probably rule them out. They don't speak English.'

'Luis was busy listening to the baseball all evening,' Ryan pointed out. 'And I can't see Rosita doing anything so sneaky.' He realised he didn't really have any evidence to back this up. Making great tortillas wasn't exactly a cast-iron defence. 'She's just too *nice*,' he added weakly.

Cleo counted off the suspects on her fingers. 'Then there's Alex . . .'

Ryan frowned. In spite of her morbid interest in death, disease and parasitic worms, Alex was one of the kindest people he'd ever met. 'Er, again, just too nice,' he mumbled.

'If Egypt and China taught us *anything*,' Cleo sighed, 'it's that *being nice* isn't a guarantee of innocence. In fact, you could say it's the opposite. Rachel Meadows was *nice*. J.J. was *nice.* Joey Zhou was *nice,* even if he was a bit cheesy. They all turned out to be criminals!'

Ryan shrugged. 'Yeah, good point. When you put it like that, maybe Rosita and Alex should go straight in at Number One on the suspect list.'

Cleo smiled. 'I don't really think either of them did it, but we'll keep them on the list as Theoretical Possibilities. What about Max?'

Ryan automatically reached up and felt his nose. It was still a little sore from Max's knuckles. Max Henderson could hardly be accused of being *nice.*

'I don't think it can have been Max,' Cleo said. 'He doesn't have a satellite phone. He borrows ours when he needs a phone or internet connection. And he didn't come round to use it last night or this morning . . .' She opened her mouth to say something else and then clamped it shut again.

'What?'

Cleo worried at her lip, catching it in the gap between her front teeth. 'Your mum has a satellite phone . . .'

Ryan stared at her. 'You think *my mum* did this?'

Cleo looked away. 'I'm just being systematic.'

'I can assure you that Mum wasn't up all night spreading gossip about the White Finder Tree.' But as he spoke, Ryan remembered Mum talking on the phone in the kitchen all night. But that was nothing to do with the White Finder Tree. 'She's got more important things to worry about,' he snapped. 'Like trying to find my dad.' As soon as the words were out, Ryan wished he could snatch them back again. 'Sorry. I know this White Finder Tree thing is important too. Your mum could lose her job . . .'

Assume the brace position, Ryan thought grimly, waiting for

85

Cleo to fly off the handle. But to his surprise her shoulders sagged. 'No, you're right. Of course Julie didn't leak the story. But I've just thought. You know who else has a satellite phone? *Roberto Chan.*'

Ryan watched as Shadow paddled his paws in his sleep, dreaming of digging up a giant ants' nest. Roberto had to be their prime suspect. Perhaps the rumours about him faking the Snake Stone were all true, and now he was up to something else. Exactly *what*, Ryan couldn't figure out. Why would Roberto want to splash the story of the White Finder Tree about when he'd seemed so keen to keep it secret? With his fierce glare and poker face he was not an easy man to read. 'I'll ask Mum to ring around her journalist friends and see if any of them can trace where the story started. Let's see if the name Roberto Chan comes up.'

'In the meantime,' Cleo said, 'we'll watch his every move.'

12

ALIEN

WHEN RYAN AND Cleo returned to camp they were greeted by shouting from Cleo's trailer.

'That's exactly why we wanted to keep the search for the White Finder Tree under wraps!' Lydia McNeil yelled. 'We knew it would create a media storm.'

They hurried over and listened outside the open window. Ryan realised Cleo's mum was on the phone to her boss, Sir Charles Peacocke. 'Of course, I want to stay in Calakmul,' she shouted. 'The White Finder Tree could be the most significant Maya discovery in decades ... Yes, I'm sure it exists! It's clearly described on the sarcophagus. There's *really* no need to send an epigrapher ...'

Ryan raised his eyebrows in Cleo's direction. 'A *pig ruffler*?'

'*Epigrapher,*' Cleo whispered. 'A specialist on writing systems.'

The phone conversation came to an end. A door slammed so hard that the whole trailer rattled. 'He's insisting on sending an *expert,*' Lydia shouted, 'to see if they agree with my interpretation of the sarcophagus texts. Does he think I'm a *total idiot* who's got it all wrong?'

'It might not hurt to have a second opinion, love,' Cleo's dad called from another room inside the trailer.

That prompted more slamming. *There aren't even that many doors in these trailers,* Ryan thought. *Lydia must be opening them and re-slamming.* 'I've already got a second opinion!' she fired back. 'Cleo agrees with me.'

'Exactly,' Cleo muttered.

'Who's he sending?' Pete McNeil asked. Ryan could hear a kettle whistling and cups clattering in the trailer kitchen.

This time it sounded like drawers being rammed shut. 'Someone I've never even heard of!' Lydia yelled. 'Sofia K. Proufork. A keen young student, apparently.'

Pete laughed. 'Well, Sir Charles has an eye for the ladies. What's the betting she's blonde and glamorous?'

Lydia finally stopped shouting and slamming. 'Like Melanie Moore, you mean?'

Ryan remembered meeting Melanie in China last year. She was Sir Charles's personal assistant and had accompanied him on his visit to Xi'an. She went in for big hair, short skirts and high heels. *Although, to be fair,* Ryan thought, *Melanie's obsession with hairdryer adaptors did give me the clue I needed to open the Dragon Path tunnel . . .*

'I'm sure Miss Proufork will be perfectly pleasant,' Pete

said. 'She might even help us find the White Finder Tree. This could turn out to be a blessing in disguise.'

Ryan was impressed. Cleo's dad was King of the Silver Lining. He could find the upside in a nuclear apocalypse.

'Blessing!' Lydia snorted. 'He could be sending Tatiana Proskouriakoff and I still wouldn't like it!'

'Who's Tatiana?' Ryan whispered. 'Does she work for Sir Charles?'

Cleo shook her head. 'She's dead now. She made some of the first breakthroughs in reading Mayan glyphs in the 1950s. She's one of Mum's heroes.'

Ryan had never met Sofia K. Proufork but he couldn't help feeling a bit sorry for her. Lydia McNeil wouldn't exactly be throwing her a welcome party.

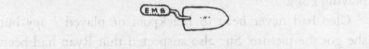

Two days later Cleo and Ryan were sitting at the table in Cleo's trailer.

Cleo was working on some new photographs from the sarcophagus. Ryan was working his way through a pack of *Pinguino* biscuits. Neither had felt like joining the excavation in the tomb. Since the story of the search for the White Finder Tree had leaked out the atmosphere in the camp had been strained. Everyone was being polite, but the knowledge that one of them had betrayed the team lurked just beneath the surface. Cleo had kept a close eye on Roberto Chan, convinced that he was the culprit. So far he'd done nothing to give himself away.

Rain drummed on the metal roof. Although it was dry season, there were occasional heavy showers. Cleo wiped steam from the window and peered out. The clearing was dark and bedraggled. *It's all my fault*, she thought. *If I hadn't persuaded Mum that the jewelled White Finder Tree was a real object, a compass to the Underworld, there would have been no story to leak out in the first place.* At least things should improve when Sofia K. Proufork arrived. Luis had taken the jeep to collect her from the airport in Mérida. When Sofia saw the sarcophagus texts she'd be bound to agree that the White Finder Tree was real; she'd soon report back to Sir Charles that Mum had been right all along.

Ryan looked up from doodling cartoons of Shadow in his sketchbook and sighed. 'This is like a wet weekend at Nan's caravan in Blackpool. If it gets any worse, we'll have to start playing *I Spy.*'

Cleo had never been to Blackpool or played *I Spy* but she got the picture. She also suspected that Ryan had been thinking about his dad. He'd been sighing and staring out of the window all morning. The trail had gone cold. The local journalist who'd put Julie in contact with Miguel had suddenly left town; no doubt because he was afraid of being found out by the Red Wolves. There were no new leads as to where the gang were holding Eddie Flint. Cleo remembered that she was trying to be a better friend and was about to say something supportive, but Ryan spoke first. 'I suppose you've seen the latest so-called news bulletin?'

Cleo nodded. The stories had continued to spread across the internet like a forest fire; and as they spread they grew wilder. Some said Mum had already found the White Finder Tree and added it to her secret store of stolen treasures. Some said that she and Roberto made the whole thing up and the

White Finder Tree was another hoax. Others were just plain weird. 'You mean the one claiming that Mum is working for aliens from the planet Alpha Centauri?' Cleo asked. 'She's here on an inter-galactic mission to retrieve items of super-advanced technology that they left behind when they last visited Earth ten thousand years ago.'

'That's the one!' Ryan laughed. 'I can just see your mum as a sort of extra-terrestrial lost property collector!' He put on a computerised voice. 'May I remind our visitors from Alpha Centauri to take all their personal belongings with them when they leave the planet . . .'

Cleo was about to list the factual errors in the story. *One, Alpha Centauri is a double star, not a planet; two, Alpha Centauri is in the same galaxy as us, so travel from there wouldn't be inter-galactic; three . . .* But she suddenly spotted something that made her forget all about alien visitations.

She stared down at the photograph in front of her. It was the section of the sarcophagus lid where they had found the burial date, 21st August, 695. Max had done more processing on the image and it was now possible to see a second date – March 21st, 697 – *and there was something else . . .* Cleo checked the glyph chart. *Yes, she was sure of it!* She slid the photograph across to Ryan. He was now half-asleep with Shadow snoozing on his chest. 'Look at this!'

'What? What am I looking at?' Ryan sat bolt upright and squinted at the page. 'A cat doing backstroke . . .'

'It's a *jaguar!*' Cleo wished Ryan would concentrate sometimes. 'It's swimming across a pool. And those glyphs underneath give its name; *Water Lily Pool Jaguar.* And the next glyph says *Way . . .*'

'*Way* as in *animal spirit?*' Ryan held up his hands to slow her down. 'I get it. You think this swimming jaguar is the *way* of King Jaguar Paw?'

'Exactly!' Cleo leaned back in her chair. 'This proves my theory. The people of Calakmul believed that the jaguar in the sarcophagus was King Jaguar Paw in his animal form as Water Lily Pool Jaguar.'

Cleo waited for Ryan to congratulate her on her brilliant research. Instead he took another biscuit. '*Water Lily Pool?* That's not a very macho name for a king's animal spirit. It sounds more like a scented candle.'

'The water lily,' Cleo pointed out as she brushed biscuit crumbs from her notes, 'was a powerful symbol in Maya mythology. Pools were seen as entrances to the Underworld. The roots of water lilies reached down into the depths.'

'Well, that solves one mystery,' Ryan said. 'We know why a jaguar is buried in the sarcophagus. Now we just have to figure out where this White Finder Tree is hidden and who the man buried in the upper tomb was and why he had grave goods with Jaguar Paw's name all over them. Oh yeah, and whether Jaguar Paw's head was used as a football in Tikal.'

Cleo smiled. 'Then our work will be done and we can pack up and go home . . .'

An odd expression flickered across Ryan's face. It made Cleo think of the cloud shadows that floated over the tree canopy. Her voice trailed off as she realised it had been caused by her careless words. *Ryan's work won't be done. He still has to find his dad. How could I have forgotten? I'm supposed to be working on being a better friend!*

'Why are you staring at me?' Ryan asked. 'Have I got chocolate all over my face?'

Cleo patted his arm. 'Don't worry. We'll find him. I'm here for you.'

Ryan gaped at her. 'OK. What have you done with Cleo? This has been going on for days now!'

Cleo had no idea what he meant. *'I'm* Cleo, of course!'

'I don't believe it. The Cleo I know doesn't do *I'm-here-for-you*. You're one of those aliens from Alpha Centuri, aren't you? You're all tentacles and slime under that disguise.'

Cleo couldn't help laughing as Ryan lunged across the table and grabbed the sides of her face, pretending to tug at her skin. 'Come on!' he cried. 'Take off the mask!'

The trailer door opened. 'Hey, kids!' Dad called. 'Luis is back with Sofia. Come and meet her! Oh, sorry if I'm er, disturbing something.' He faltered, suddenly noticing that Cleo and Ryan were locked in what was either a wrestling hold or a kiss.

Cleo jumped up. 'Ryan was just checking I wasn't an alien,' she explained. At least, she *tried* to explain, but it sounded so absurd she burst out laughing again.

They were both still laughing as they hurried outside and joined the rest of the team.

Sofia K. Proufork slammed the jeep door and strode across the clearing towards them. The rain had stopped but drops still dripped from the trees.

'There goes your dad's theory,' Ryan whispered. 'She's not exactly glamorous.'

Ryan was right. Sofia looked nothing like Melanie Moore. She wore a perfectly sensible checked shirt, jeans and trainers. Her hair was short, straight and brown. Plump cheeks and front teeth that stuck out over her bottom lip combined to give a slightly hamster-like effect.

Once the introductions were complete Sofia hoisted her enormous khaki backpack onto her shoulders. 'I'm bushed after that journey. Absolute nightmare! Where are my quarters?' She spoke with a brisk Canadian accent with a slight lisp due to the teeth.

Alex stepped forward. 'You're sharing with me. What fun! We'll be roomies.'

Sofia blanked her with a cold smile. 'I was *told* I'd have my own trailer.' She blinked behind large tortoiseshell-effect glasses, which even Cleo could tell were about thirty years out of fashion. 'I have a medical condition,' she said darkly.

Cleo glanced at Ryan and tried to keep a straight face. Sofia had definitely picked the wrong person to play that card on. Alex *adored* medical conditions.

'Super!' Alex said. 'I'll make us some hot chocolate and you can tell me all about it.'

'I can't have hot drinks.' Sofia planted her hands on her hips. 'And I'm afraid it's non-negotiable. Sir Charles gave me his personal guarantee that I'd have my own quarters.'

'I bet she was a big hit at Charm School!' Ryan whispered. 'I wonder what the K stands for. *Killjoy?*'

Alex shrugged. 'No problem. I was a girl guide. I'll pitch a tent.'

The sun was shining again when Cleo and her mum sat down with Sofia at the table outside the trailer the next morning, to go through the inscriptions on the sarcophagus. Cleo was sure that they'd soon convince Sofia that there was a compass in the shape of the World Tree buried in King Jaguar Paw's tomb. She would tell Sir Charles. Then they could get on with the search.

But it wasn't long before Cleo was having second thoughts. When she began to explain her theory about Water Lily Pond Jaguar being buried as the *way* of Jaguar Paw, Sofia brushed her away as if she were a slightly annoying mosquito. 'Yeah, yeah, all very interesting, I'm sure.' She began to riffle through the photos and sheets of notes that Mum had copied for her. 'Look, Lydia let's park the whole *jaguar-in-the-coffin* hoo-ha and cut to the chase. What's the real deal with this White Finder Tree?'

Cleo held her breath. In a moment's lull in the birdsong she could actually hear Mum grinding her teeth. Professor Lydia McNeil didn't like being told what she should or shouldn't park. But finally Mum unclenched her jaws, pushed the first photograph into the middle of the table and began to explain. 'OK. Our first clue was this line here. It talks about *Lady Six Sky's World Tree*. As you can see, there's the *u-glyph*, the possessive pronoun. That suggests it's an object that can be owned.'

'There's a chip out of the stone just here,' Cleo added. 'That's why the *Curly Teacup Handle* looks broken.'

'*Curly Teacup Handle?*' Sofia looked as if she'd just sunk her hamster teeth into a rotten apple.

Mum nodded. 'I might have missed it if Ryan hadn't spotted it.'

'And Ryan is your daughter's best friend, is he?'

Cleo squirmed. Sofia was making her feel like a six-year-old.

'He's a *family* friend. He has a very good eye for detail.' Mum said in a frosty tone. 'We believe that the White Finder

Tree belonged to Lady Six Sky of Naranjo.'

'You *believe*?' Sofia widened her eyes behind her glasses. 'So you don't actually *know*?'

'It's written on the sarcophagus,' Mum fired back. 'What do you want? A receipt from the shop where she bought it?'

Sofia held up her hands. 'No need to be tetchy. I'm just trying to get the facts straight.'

'The facts?' Mum's voice was like an elastic band stretched just short of snapping point. 'OK. How about this line? *The jewelled White Finder Tree now lies in Jaguar Paw's final resting place.* Is that fact enough for you? It was Cleo's brainwave about *white* symbolising north that led us to interpret *White Finder Tree* as a compass . . .'

Sofia shook her head. 'So you're basing your *entire* theory on a couple of teenagers' hunches. One possessive pronoun? Some fanciful notion about Maya kings wandering around with compasses centuries before they were known outside of China! This doesn't amount to a hill of beans!'

Cleo exchanged a horrified look with Mum. They were both too flabbergasted to speak.

'I don't like to undermine another scholar's work, Lydia, but you've let your imagination get the better of you. This *jewelled tree* isn't a real object. This simply refers to a vision of the World Tree conjured up during the blood-letting trance. *The path through the forest? The entrance through the mouth of the Witz monster?* It's all perfectly standard Maya mythology about the spirit's journey to the Underworld after death. Listen to yourself. A compass that points to Xib'alb'a? Next you'll be telling me that you've found the keys to Father Christmas's workshop. Or the plans to Tinkerbell's fairy dust mine!'

Mum didn't say a word. She got up and stormed into the trailer with a slam of the door.

Sofia directed a toothy smile at Cleo. 'Sorry. I can see you're kind of sold on this whole magic compass thing. I just don't want your Mom making a fool of herself over this. Her track record isn't exactly squeaky clean as it is.'

'I don't believe you can't see it!' Cleo stammered.

Sofia K. Proufork scooped up the papers. 'Hey, as a favour, I'll take all this lot and have another look through tonight.'

But next morning at breakfast Sofia hadn't changed her mind.

Perhaps the K stands for *Know-it-all,* Cleo thought bitterly.

And just when she thought things couldn't get any worse, they did.

Roberto Chan hurtled into the clearing, knocking over a plastic chair in his haste. 'The jaguar tomb has been burgled. Someone must have got in during the night. The jade mask has been stolen!'

13

ESCAPE

YOU KNOW THINGS *aren't going well,* Ryan thought, *when the highlight of the day involves parasitic worms.*

The test lab in Mérida had called Pete McNeil to say the report on the hookworms in the jaguar corpse was complete. But for some reason to do with a computer breakdown, they had sent it by fax to a hotel in Xpujil, the nearest town. When Alex said she was going to pick it up and asked whether anyone would like to go with her, Ryan was in the jeep with his seat belt fastened before she could finish the sentence. He'd stopped only to drag Cleo along with him.

He propped his feet on the dashboard and popped open a

can of Coke. *This must be how prisoners feel when they get out on day release.*

The atmosphere in camp had ratcheted up from tense to toxic. Cleo and her mum had been stomping around like thunderstorms in human form since Sofia K. Proufork had refused to believe that the White Finder Tree existed. Meanwhile, the site had been besieged by reporters and photographers and coachloads of mystical Maya fanatics who were equally convinced that the Tree *did* exist and longed to witness its magical powers. Roberto and Luis spent all their time turning them away.

And then there was the disappearance of the jade mask from the jaguar tomb last night. Roberto had immediately called the police in and everyone had been required to give a statement about where they'd been during the hours of darkness. They'd all been asleep in their trailers, of course. (As Max had grumbled; *we're in the middle of the bloomin' jungle. Where do they think we'd be? Catching a late-night opera with Prince Charles?*).

Police Chief Garcia had informed them that The Red Wolves were her prime suspects. The gang was known to have been operating in the area lately. Ryan had felt a prod of fear at the thought that members of the Red Wolves might have entered the camp. He didn't *think* that Wolf Head and the beefy guy had seen him throw the distress flare from the jeep, but he couldn't be sure. And Mum's *bandanna-over-the-face* disguise hadn't exactly been foolproof either. Her spikey blonde hair was pretty distinctive.

That wasn't the only reason Ryan hoped that the Red Wolves were not responsible for stealing the jade mask. Mum had finally tracked down an ex-gang-member who now lived in Los Angeles. He had hinted that he had information about where exactly the Red Wolves might be holding Dad prisoner, but so far he was refusing to say any more over the phone. Ryan couldn't help worrying that if the police started closing in on the Red Wolves about the jade mask, the gang might panic and move Dad to another location – or even kill him – before Mum could persuade her contact to tell her more.

The only member of the camp who *wasn't* having a bad day was Shadow. Ryan had left him on his bed sleeping off the effects of an *all-you-can-eat* larvae buffet, after digging up a termite nest behind the equipment stores.

Alex turned the key in the ignition. 'Wagons roll!'

They'd just started to pull away when they heard a shout. 'Hey! Wait up!' A short figure in checked shirt and jeans was jogging up to the jeep.

Alex braked. The door was yanked open and Sofia K. Proufork's chipmunk face peeped round it. 'Room for a little one?' she asked. 'Downloading files from my satellite phone is an absolute nightmare! I need to use the hotel WiFi in town. Sorry kids, I'll have to sit up front. I get travel-sick. It's my medical condition.'

Cleo didn't utter a word as they moved to the back but if eyebrows could kill, Sofia would be dead in her tracks.

An hour and a half later they were driving into Xpujil, rattling over speed bumps, where farmers had set up stalls to sell pineapples and fresh coconut. Alex steered the jeep through an obstacle course of juddering tankers, dusty trucks, skinny dogs and boys on over-sized yellow tricycles fitted with wide racks, on which they carried everything from crates of oranges to elderly relatives until, at last, they pulled in under a row of spindly palm trees.

Alex and Sofia headed off to find the Royal Maya hotel in search of the fax machine and WiFi. Ryan and Cleo drifted along the main street past flat-roofed block houses, painted in shades of pink, turquoise, primrose-yellow and mint-green, small cafés, and hardware stores overflowing with engine parts and wheelbarrows. The air was thick with warm tarmac, petrol fumes and overripe fruit. On every corner something was halfway through being built or knocked down. Hammering and sawing blended with the beep of traffic, crowing of cockerels and the squeals of children from a school playground. It wasn't exactly Manchester Piccadilly on a Saturday but it felt like big-city life after the jungle.

They wandered through a busy market until they came out into a courtyard overspread by an enormous tree smothered with shocking pink puffball-explosion flowers.

'*Pseudobombax ellipticum,*' Cleo muttered. 'Shaving brush tree.' She sighed, stuffed her hands in the pockets of her shorts and moved on, kicking at the fallen blossom that lay like tassels torn from carnival costumes.

She must really be feeling down, Ryan thought. Bamboozling him with scientific names was usually guaranteed to put Cleo in a good mood. He wished there was something he could do to cheer her up . . . 'Wait there,' he told her. He darted back into the market and wove his way through stalls piled high with fruit or fish or baby clothes or bike tyres or tins of cooking oil until he arrived at one with long, white cotton scarves hanging from a rail. They were just like Cleo's old favourite; the one he'd ruined in Egypt after diving into the River Nile on a rescue mission. He'd bought her a replacement, but that had ended up as a bandage when he was scorched by dragon fire in China. *Third time lucky,* he thought. He pulled several scarves from the rack. They were all embroidered with rainbow-coloured flowers at each end.

The old lady sitting on a plastic chair nearby looked up from her sewing. 'For girlfriend?' She thrust a scarf into his hands. 'I made this one. Very special. Traditional Maya style.' It had the biggest and boldest flowers of all. Cleo would hate it. *Floral* was definitely not her look. But Ryan didn't have the heart to refuse. He handed over the money, which the old lady carefully stowed in a battered tin. He was on his way back to the courtyard, wishing he could have found a plain white scarf, when he passed a butcher's stand. A short man was standing on a box hacking at a pig's head with a machete. Strings of chicken carcasses hung all around him like grisly bunting. Ryan was about to scoot quickly past when he had an idea. Glancing over his shoulder to make sure the old embroidery lady wasn't looking, he held out the scarf to the butcher . . .

Two minutes later he was back in the courtyard.

'I was beginning to think you'd got lost!' Cleo complained.

Ryan handed over the scarf, now minus its flowery ends. Cleo smiled – the first Ryan had seen all day – and wound it round her neck. She sniffed. Ryan held his breath. Had she detected essence of pig head? 'I love the smell of new cotton,' she said. 'Thank you! I've missed having a scarf.'

Result! Ryan thought. The day was starting to pick up. He reached for his St Christopher. Yes, he had a good feeling. They'd get back to camp and find that Mum had managed to get the guy from Los Angeles to talk on the phone. He'd have told her exactly where Dad was being held . . .

But as they stepped back out on to the main street, he saw

something that knocked the good feeling right back out of him.

He grabbed Cleo's arm and pulled her behind a parked truck.

14

MIND MAP

RYAN PEEPED OUT from behind the truck.

On the other side of the road a man had emerged from the double swing doors of a small bar called La Luna – the name was painted in white on the peacock-blue wall above a crescent moon – along with a burst of swirling Mexican folk music. Sporting baggy jeans and a basketball vest he slouched against the wall, smoking a cigarette, looking around as if waiting for someone. *Maybe it's not him,* Ryan told himself. But then the man turned round. Tattooed on the back of his head was the face of a wolf.

'What is it?' Cleo hissed.

'See that guy?' Ryan whispered over the wild pounding

of his heart. 'He's one of the gangsters who turned up at the meeting with Miguel.'

Ryan didn't dare leave the cover of the truck in case Wolf Head looked over and recognised him. Ten long minutes ticked by. Still Wolf Head waited. 'This is crazy!' Cleo said. 'I'll go and ask him the time or something. See what he's up to.'

Ryan grabbed her arm. 'You can't! He's dangerous.'

Cleo pulled away. 'Nothing can happen in the middle of the street. And he has no idea who I am.' Before Ryan could stop her she was crossing the road. He watched in horror. Cleo was trying to do a casual saunter but she might as well have been carrying a banner saying '*Look at Me! I'm Up To No Good!*' There was no way she'd be able to talk to Wolf Head without giving the game away; she was the worst liar he'd ever met.

At that moment, a Coca-Cola lorry rumbled past. When it had gone Wolf Head had vanished. The doors of the bar were swinging. He must have gone back inside. Cleo was still hovering in the road. *Surely she's not thinking of following him!* Ryan was taking no chances. He dashed out into the traffic, ignoring the volley of furious horn honking, and bundled her into the nearest café.

The café was no more than a few small tables under a palm-thatched porch. Ryan steered Cleo to a table as far from the road as possible, sank into a chair and sighed with relief.

Cleo seemed unruffled by her close encounter with the criminal underworld and ordered drinks and snacks in fluent Spanish.

'Maybe the police are right,' Ryan said when the café owner had placed a platter of tortilla chips, salsa and lime wedges on the table. 'If it was the Red Wolves who stole the jade mask from the tomb last night, Wolf Head could have been meeting a contact in La Luna to sell it on . . .'

'I don't believe it was them,' Cleo said. 'Why would they have just taken the mask and left all the other grave goods behind?'

Ryan bit into a freshly fried tortilla chip so delicious that he vowed never to buy them in a packet again. 'You think it was an inside job?'

'I don't know.' Cleo snapped a tortilla chip in half and then half again. 'Chief Garcia phoned this morning to say that someone had called the police station with an anonymous tip-off. This unknown informer said that Mum must have stolen the jade mask, since she has a track record of artefacts "disappearing" when she's around. Luckily Chief Garcia didn't seem to be taking it too seriously.'

The informer does have a point, Ryan thought. The McNeils were a magnet for bad luck. It wasn't just this dig. There was Rachel Meadows and her crazy Eternal Sun group stealing the Bloodthirsty Grail in Peru and the Benben Stone in Egypt, and the Tiger's Claw gang taking the Immortality Scroll in China. 'Your parents must have done something really bad in a previous life,' he said. 'Like being mean to kittens or something.'

'Bad *karma,* you mean?' Cleo started destroying another tortilla chip. 'There's no scientific evidence that doing bad deeds will bring bad things to you later, or that good deeds will produce good. And anyway, Mum and Dad have never harmed any kittens. They like animals.'

Ryan laughed. Sometimes he forgot just how literal Cleo

106

could be. 'So you're saying it's a complete coincidence that things keep going wrong?'

Cleo reached for another tortilla chip. Ryan nudged the plate out of the way before she could reduce them all to crumbs. They were too good to waste. 'No, I'm convinced there's a connection,' she said. 'In fact, I've made a mind map of all the events and all the people involved to see if we can detect a pattern.' She pulled a roll of paper from her shoulder bag and unfurled it on the table. It was covered in a spaghetti tangle of circles, arrows and lines. It was, Ryan thought, a thing of beauty. It also looked as if the world's reserves of highlighter pens had been sacrificed in its name.

'Question One,' Cleo said. 'Did the person who leaked the story about the White Finder Tree also steal the jade mask?'

Ryan thought for a moment. 'Roberto Chan is still our chief suspect for spilling the story. But why would he have stolen the mask from his own dig?'

'Good point.' Cleo added a line to the mind map. 'What about Sofia K. Proufork? She could have taken the mask. But she can't be the one who leaked the story about the White Finder Tree. That happened before she even arrived in Calakmul.' She squeezed more squiggles into the mind map. 'Question Two. If the problems that are happening here in Mexico are related to the problems on the earlier digs, who or what is the link?'

Ryan slurped orange juice through his straw, distracted for a moment by a burst of folk music somewhere along the street.

'Rachel Meadows would be the most obvious connection, of course,' Cleo went on. 'She stole the Bloodthirsty Grail and the Benben Stone. But she's locked up in prison now.'

'She could be working with an accomplice on the outside?' Ryan suggested. 'Or what about Joey Zhou?' The leader of the Tiger's Claw gang was still on the loose. It seemed he'd mysteriously vanished. 'Perhaps he's made his way to Mexico and is still in the tomb raiding business?'

'Mind if I join you?'

Sofia Proufork sat down without waiting for an answer. 'I've finished at the hotel. Alex wanted to pick up some supplies so I thought I'd come and hang out with you guys.'

Cleo snatched the mind map off the table.

But she was too slow. 'What's that you're working on?' Sofia asked.

'Oh, nothing!' Cleo said. 'It's just a list of, er, some people that we, er, know . . .'

Ryan silenced her with a kick under the table. Cleo's lies never made any sense! Who sat around making lists of people they knew? 'It's for a party,' he improvised desperately. 'When we get back to London. We're trying to decide who to invite.'

Sofia arched her eyebrows behind her chunky glasses. She must have seen some of the names on the mind map. 'You're friends with Joey Zhou?' she asked.

Ryan did his best to hide his surprise. Was Sofia about to admit to being best buddies with the leader of a Chinese criminal gang? 'Oh, do you know him too?' he asked casually.

'I met him at the Asian Archaeology conference in Hong Kong last year.'

Well, that's fair enough, Ryan thought. Joey had been posing as an archaeology student. That's how he'd tricked his way into working as a guide for the McNeil team in Xi'an. He'd been using the same identity to go to the conference.

Sofia would have no reason to suspect that Joey Zhou, the friendly young student with the leather jacket and quiffed hair, wasn't quite what he seemed.

But Cleo perked up like a terrier after a rabbit. 'Did you speak to him?'

Sofia shrugged. 'Only to say hello and good-bye. He was the translator for some of the talks I went to.'

'And you must have met Sir Charles Peacocke there too?' Cleo asked. 'He went to Hong Kong to the conference just after visiting us in China. He was with his assistant, Melanie Moore.'

Ryan cringed. Cleo's attempt to sound as if she was making friendly chit-chat was more like a police interrogation.

'Oh, er, yeah, sure. Goodness, it's hot here.' Sofia grabbed a menu and fanned her face. 'Talking of Sir Charles, I just called him from the hotel. He's really losing patience with your Mom over this White Finder Tree business. He thinks it's a wild goose chase.'

'Only because *you* told him that.' Cleo grabbed another tortilla chip and snapped it into tiny pieces.

'That's right, Cleo. I speak as I find. Do yourself and your Mom a favour and talk her into dropping this whole thing. The good news is, Sir Charles told me that if you guys can be packed up and out of Mexico within a week he's prepared to pull some strings so your Mom can join the dig at Amphipholis. They're looking for an experienced archaeologist like Lydia . . .'

'Is that the amazing tomb in Greece where Alexander the Great might be buried?' Ryan asked. 'Your Mum was talking about it the other day, saying how much she'd love to go . . .' He let his voice tail off. *Probably not helping . . .*

Cleo scowled at the crushed tortilla crumbs. 'Sir Charles thinks he can *bribe* Mum to leave?'

'It's called *incentivisation*.' Sofia gave an icy smile. 'But maybe your Mom would rather hang around here longer and then just go back to London? Sir Charles mentioned a mountain of musty old paperwork in the basement of the British Museum that needs cataloguing . . .' She stood up, flicking her hair as if she were in a hairspray advert even though it was short and so clumpy it could have been cut with a knife and fork. 'See you back at the jeep.'

As soon as Sofia had gone Cleo pulled her mind map out of her bag and began adding more lines. 'Sofia was at that Asian Archaeology conference last year!' she muttered. 'Suspicious or *what!*'

Ryan knew why Cleo was so interested. When Joey Zhou had ambushed them at the Dragon Path tunnel in China last year, he'd somehow managed to have a perfect alibi for the time of the attack. Several people – including Sir Charles Peacocke and Melanie Moore – had seen him at the conference in Hong Kong, thousands of miles away, at exactly the same time! How Joey had done it remained a mystery to this day. And now Joey had yet another witness; Sofia had seen him at the conference too. It was baffling, but Ryan couldn't see how it cast any suspicion on Sofia. 'She's interested in archaeology,' he said with a shrug. 'Why *shouldn't* she go to an archaeology conference?'

'Point one,' Cleo said, jabbing a yellow highlighter pen in the air. 'Sofia K. Proufork's name was *not* on the list of conference delegates that your mum got hold of for us when we were trying to figure out what Joey Zhou was up to. I would remember; it's not exactly a common name. So she

110

must have been there under a false name for some reason. Point two: did you notice her reaction when I asked if she'd seen Sir Charles and Melanie Moore there? She went all red and flustered.'

'Maybe it's her medical condition,' Ryan offered.

Cleo snorted impatiently. 'She couldn't change the subject fast enough. She's definitely hiding something.'

Ryan had a feeling that Cleo might be a little biased. She disliked Sofia K. Proufork so much for raining on her parade about the White Finder Tree that she'd have happily pinned the Great Fire of London and the sinking of the Titanic on her if she could. But he decided to let it go. And anyway, there was something else that was bothering him. 'Does Sofia seem sort of *familiar* to you?'

Cleo chewed the highlighter pen. 'No. How do you mean?'

'It was the way she flicked her hair. I just got this feeling I'd met her before.'

'Have you been to Saskatchewan?' Cleo now looked as if she were wearing luminous daffodil-coloured lipstick.

Ryan hadn't even heard of it.

'The University of Saskatchewan is where Sofia works in Canada. I've looked her up.'

Ryan shrugged. 'It must be my imagination. She probably just looks like someone on TV . . .'

Cleo wasn't listening. 'I got us into this. I have to get us out of it,' she said. There's only one thing for it. We'll just have to find the White Finder Tree ourselves.'

15

MOONLIGHT

AT FIRST RYAN thought Cleo was joking. But Cleo wasn't big on jokes. She was deadly serious. 'We just find the White Finder Tree ourselves?' he repeated. 'Of course! Simple! Why didn't I think of that?'

'It's not simple, but we might have a chance.'

'But Roberto and the others have been looking for days,' Ryan pointed out. 'There's no sign of it.'

'I've got a theory.'

'That's what I was worried about . . .' Cleo's theories had a habit of landing them in trouble.

'We could have been looking for the White Finder Tree in the wrong place,' Cleo explained. 'The text on the jaguar sarcophagus says the White Finder Tree *lies in Jaguar Paw's final resting place*. What if the 'final resting place' doesn't mean the jaguar tomb? Maybe it's talking about the place where King Jaguar Paw's *human* form ended up, not his *animal* spirit. That could mean the upper tomb. Everyone assumed that the man buried in there was Jaguar Paw – until Roberto found the Snake Stone. Perhaps they were right. He was buried with Jaguar Paw's plates and vases, after all. Maybe the White Finder Tree's in there too.'

Ryan watched a flock of grackles fighting over tortilla crumbs at the next table. 'Wouldn't the archaeologists have found it when they excavated that tomb back in the 1990s?'

'They didn't know what they were looking for. It may be quite small. It may be well hidden.'

Ryan knew there was no point arguing with Cleo when she'd got a theory. And anyway, it would be easy enough to help her look around the upper tomb tomorrow. *Unless,* he thought, *Mum really has managed to talk to the ex-Red Wolves guy in Los Angeles and find out where the gang's keeping Dad.* In which case he'd have far more important things to do, like . . . Ryan suddenly realised he wasn't sure *what* Mum planned to do when they finally did pin down Dad's location. Surely that would be the time to get the police involved. Although, knowing Mum, she'd be thinking of storming in on her own to rescue him. *I'll have to stop her doing anything crazy again . . .*

'So, obviously we'll have to go secretly in the middle of the night.'

'What?' Ryan realised he'd zoned out for a moment. 'Go *where* in the middle of the night?'

Cleo sighed. 'The upper tomb, of course! I just explained all this. If we're right, and Roberto is the one who leaked the

113

story about the White Finder Tree, then we have to assume we can't trust him on anything. Until we know what he's up to we have to keep all our plans to ourselves. For all we know, he could be working with the Red Wolves!'

The mention of the Red Wolves made Ryan nervous again. He leaned forward in his chair and glanced up and down the street. There was no sign of Wolf Head.'But the entrance to the tomb is locked at night,' he reminded Cleo.

'I know the combination. I've seen Roberto use it loads of times. I can't believe he picked such an obvious number.' Cleo lowered her voice to a whisper. *'Three, one, one, four.'*

'And that's obvious because . . .'

'It's the first year of the Maya Long Count calendar. It's BC 3114 in our Gregorian system . . .'

I've created a monster, Ryan thought. When he'd first met Cleo and suggested she 'borrow' the key to Smenkhkare's tomb so that they could check out her theory about the Benben Stone, she'd acted as if he'd asked her to steal the crown jewels *and* the Queen's corgis. Now she was talking about a midnight tomb raid as if it was popping to the fridge for a late night snack.

Cleo jumped to her feet. 'So, that's agreed. We start the search tonight.'

Ryan perched on a step at the base of the pyramid and waited for Cleo.

Light from a full moon filtered through the foliage, dappling the ancient ruins with splotches of ivory and silver. The spindly trunks of the trees that grew up through the stone glowed as if with their own pale light.

They'd agreed to meet at three a.m.

When they'd returned from Xpujil, Mum had not greeted him with good news. There'd been no further information from her contact in Los Angeles. Ryan was starting to think the ex-gang member had just been stringing her along. He probably didn't have any information about Dad at all. Ryan felt so deflated he'd been tempted to back out of Cleo's midnight raid. But he hadn't been able to sleep anyway. At least sneaking into the tomb was better than lying awake all night, worrying about Dad and listening to a deranged owl hooting outside his window.

He strained his ears for footsteps above the fluting and flitting sounds of the secret night-time world. Something scurried over his foot. At last he heard a crackling of dry leaves. Shreds of grainy shadow gathered together to form a figure. It was human, but its shape was strangely mutated. He wished the moonlight hadn't started him thinking about were-jaguars again. Then Cleo stepped into view. She'd crammed so much extra stuff into her bum bag that her silhouette had hips the size of small icebergs.

Within moments they were climbing the pyramid. The steep steps were doubly treacherous in the dark, their edges uneven and weathered, like lines drawn without a ruler, the stone slick with the night dew. They'd almost reached the top of the first stage when Ryan's foot slipped. He shot out a hand, felt the root of a strangler fig, grabbed it, found his footing again and was still lying on his stomach catching his breath when Cleo hissed in his ear. 'Don't move! It's a snake.'

'Yeah right!' Like he couldn't tell the difference between a root and a snake! He could feel the hard gnarly surface digging into his palm.

'Not the one you're holding. Just next to it.'

Ryan slowly lifted his head and scanned the welter of twisted roots cascading down the steps. But they weren't *all* roots. The one almost touching his right hand had stripes. It also had eyes. And they were looking straight back at him.

Ryan's insides whirled as if being sucked down a drain. 'Is it poisonous?' he asked through his teeth.

'Has it got red, yellow and black stripes?'

In the moonlight the snake's bands were black and two shades of grey, one light, one darker. They could be yellow and red. 'I think so.'

Cleo edged closer. 'Are the red bands touching the yellow?'

'Who cares?' Ryan whispered. Only Cleo could be obsessing about the precise order of the stripes at a moment like this. *If she even thinks about telling me the Latin name I'm never speaking to her again . . .*

'It's important! If the red stripes are next to the black it's a milk snake. They're harmless. If the red are next to the yellow, it's a coral snake. They're . . . not.'

Ryan strained his eyes, peering at the stripes. *Black, light grey, mid-grey, black, light grey, mid-grey.* He gulped. 'It's the bad one.'

'Keep still. It won't attack unless it feels threatened.'

Ryan heard Cleo's footsteps moving away. *What was she doing?* The snake's tongue flicked in and out. The edges of the stone steps were digging into his shins. His mind conjured up images of the emblem of the Snake Kingdom, *Smug Snake Lurks Under A Pile of Stones*. It was as if the emblem had come to life to protect the tomb of the Serpent King. Ryan felt extremely threatened.

A dark shape lunged past his eyes. He reared back in panic. There was a moment of freefall and then a painful, *thwump* as Ryan landed on his side, rolled, and came to a stop on a flat ledge. Below him, endless steps, so steep that they were almost a wall, disappeared into the dark. He twisted and looked up to see Cleo holding a long forked stick.

'I've got it pinned at the neck.' She flicked the stick and sent the snake skittering away. 'It'll be OK,' she said. 'I didn't hurt it.'

Ryan crawled up the steps and sank down next to her. 'Tell me it wasn't really that deadly.'

Cleo took a bottle of water from her tool belt and offered it to him. 'Coral snake bites contain a potent neurotoxin similar to that of the cobra.'

Ryan took a swig. 'There's an anti-venom though?'

'There is, but I doubt we'd have made it to a hospital in time.'

Ryan hoped for the sake of all the patients in the world that Cleo never became a doctor. She had the bedside manner of a serial killer. *Nope, sorry, there's no cure. Get used to it!* He hauled himself up and continued the climb, his legs still as watery as overcooked spaghetti. They came at last to the entrance to the upper tomb. The small opening in the wall that ran along one side of the flat platform had been fitted with a wooden door and secured with a padlock. *'Three, one, one, four . . .'* Cleo murmured as she turned the wheels.

Nothing happened. 'That can't be ... I *know* that was the number Roberto used.'

'He must have changed the combination after the jade mask was stolen,' Ryan said.

Cleo gave the padlock a furious rattle and slumped against the wall. 'There are ten thousand possible permutations. It'd take us hours to go through them ...'

'Maybe we can guess. You said Roberto chose something obvious before?'

Cleo nodded. 'The start of the Long Count calendar.'

'So maybe he went for the obvious again? What about 2012, the end of the ...' Ryan tried to remember what Cleo had called the time unit that had caused all the *end-of-the-world* panic.

'The thirteenth *baktun* ... surely that would be too simple?' Cleo toggled the wheels to give it a try anyway. She shoved the padlock away. 'That's not it.'

Ryan racked his brains for other significant Maya-themed four-digit numbers. There wasn't exactly a stampede. 'How about the end of the *next* thirteen baktuns?' was the best he could do.

Cleo began muttering to herself. 'That's thirteen times four hundred years. Maya years were 360 days, not 365. Add that to 2012. That comes to the year 7138.' She turned the wheels. 'Seven ... one ... three ... eight ...'

To Ryan's astonishment the padlock fell open. He held up his hand for a high five. But Cleo was already digging in her tool belt. She pulled out two head torches, passed one to Ryan, and within seconds they were making their way down the cramped entrance tunnel. The smell of the cold, ancient stone was even mustier than in daylight. They came out into the upper tomb, the beams of their torches strobing over the walls. Panels of writing and traces of sacrifice scenes slid in and out of view.

'Where do we start looking?' Ryan spoke in a whisper, as if the long-dead souls buried deep inside the pyramid might be listening in.

Cleo hurried to the empty sarcophagus and began poking about at the base with her trowel. 'Just look for any little cracks or niches where a small object could be hidden!'

Ryan hesitated.

'Don't worry,' Cleo told him. 'There isn't a body in here. It was removed to a museum years ago, along with the grave goods.'

They'd been searching in silence for several minutes when Ryan thought he heard something. He stepped back from the sarcophagus. There it was again. A soft slap. And then another and another.

Cleo looked up at Ryan, dazzling him with her head torch. 'Footsteps!' she breathed.

Possibilities – none of them good – hurtled through Ryan's mind. *The police? Roberto Chan? Newspaper reporters? The Red Wolves gang?*

One thing was certain: *someone* had followed them down the tunnel.

16

DANGER

CLEO CONSIDERED HER options.

Any moment now someone was going to step out of the entrance tunnel into the tomb. She could stand her ground and explain that she and Ryan were simply trying to help by finding the White Finder Tree. But they'd broken into a locked tomb in the middle of the night. No amount of explaining was going to make that look good. *They'll think we stole the jade mask and have come back for more.* That left Option Two. Hide! *But where?* Cleo glanced around the tomb. The beam of her head torch skated across the trap door that led down to the jaguar tomb. But the heavy slab was firmly in place. It would take too long to lift it out . . .

'Down here!' Ryan's voice was muffled. Cleo couldn't work out where it came from. But then she saw his legs sticking out from the wall. He'd crawled under the low recess where he'd spent so long copying glyphs on his first day at the tomb. 'We can't both fit in there!' she hissed. 'It's far too small.'

'I know that!' Ryan whispered from deep under the wall. 'But there's a gap at the back. I could feel the cold air coming through it when I was under here before. I don't know where it goes but if we can just squeeze through . . .' His legs began to disappear, as if being sucked into the stone. *Come on!*

Every neuron in Cleo's brain screamed that crawling through a small hole into the unknown was a *really bad idea*. But the footsteps in the tunnel were ringing louder and louder . . . She switched off her head torch, dropped to her stomach and wormed into the alcove, her nose bumping against the soles of Ryan's trainers in the dust-thick darkness. She groped for the edges of the gap in the wall at the back and began to wriggle through. Ryan's hand closed around her own and pulled. In a frenzy of writhing and scrabbling she was through.

Cleo sat huddled against the wall on the other side, as if pinned to it by the smothering blackness that engulfed her. Her heartbeat throbbed in her ears.

'We'll have to switch a torch on for a second,' Ryan whispered. 'Just to make sure we're not on the edge of a massive drop.'

Cleo shrank back in terror. She hadn't even thought of that possibility. She fumbled for her head torch and flicked it on. *Solid stone floor, walls, roof, a long raised platform . . .* With a flash of relief she realised where they were; not on the edge of an abyss but in the Tomb of the Unknown Woman and Child, a small burial chamber that had been discovered alongside the main upper tomb in 1997.

Ryan reached up and turned her head torch off for her. 'Is there a way up to the surface through that doorway on the other side?' he whispered.

'No. That tunnel was closed off years ago.' Cleo had heard the story of this chamber from Roberto. Tomb robbers had stolen the contents centuries ago. Only the mummified skeletons of an unidentified young woman and small child had remained. After the two bodies had been removed to safety, the entrance from the surface had been sealed off to prevent unwary tourists stumbling into it. 'There's no other way out,' she groaned.

A light flickered through the gap in the wall behind them. Whoever had followed them down the tunnel was now moving about in the upper tomb. 'Do you think they saw us?' Cleo whispered.

'I don't know. We should hide, just in case.'

Clinging tightly to Ryan, Cleo felt her way around the platform that had once held up the sarcophagus, and hunkered down. The stone floor had hollowed out with time and they were able to wriggle right under the platform. The chill of the stone seeped into Cleo's skin. She listened to footsteps tracking back and forth on the other side of the wall. *Who could it be?* She counted seconds but gave up at seven hundred and twenty.

'What's that weird noise?' Ryan breathed in her ear.

Cleo couldn't hear anything. Knowing Ryan, his mind was tricking him with the ghoulish moans of long-dead Maya kings. His imagination got the better of him at times. But then she heard it too. A deep rumble vibrated through the stone. 'They're lifting the slab from the trap-door,' she whispered. 'They must be going down to the jaguar tomb.'

'Come on!' Ryan was already on the move. 'Now's our chance to get out while they're down there!'

Cleo clambered to her feet and headed for the gap in the wall. But then she stopped. Was this the right way? She turned back, groping in the dark. Her knee struck the side of the platform. She swivelled round, flailing her arms, but there was nothing . . . *nothing* . . . *anywhere* . . . Panic pushed the air from her lungs, chased the blood through her veins . . .

Suddenly Ryan grasped her by the shoulders. For once Cleo didn't mind being pushed around. She didn't even object when he bundled her through the gap in the wall like a letter into a post box.

The upper tomb was as dark and empty as they'd found it. Cleo switched her torch on. The stone slab lay on the floor next to the square hole that led down to the jaguar tomb. *Maybe,* Cleo thought, *we could just have a quick look down there and see who it is . . .*

'Don't even think about it.' Ryan pulled her away. 'We're out of here!'

Cleo gave in and sprinted up the tunnel after Ryan. At the surface, they stood for a moment, catching their breath in the cool night air. Cleo began to relax. They'd made it out. And they'd have plenty of time to get back down the pyramid before their stalker emerged from the depths of the jaguar tomb.

But they'd barely started hurrying down the steps when she glanced back to see a figure standing next to the tomb entrance. She dived behind a protuberance of stone that had once been an enormous Witz monster head, dragging Ryan with her. 'There's someone up there,' she hissed.

Ryan knelt up and peeped out through the hole where the mighty jaws had once gaped open. 'I can't see anyone . . .'

Cleo looked over his shoulder. The figure had vanished. Had it been a trick of the light? In the grey pre-dawn, edges were smudged and shapes insubstantial. *After all,* she thought, *we'd have heard footsteps behind us if someone had followed us back up the tunnel.* But then there was a movement and the figure reappeared, short and stocky, silhouetted against a lighter section of stonework. 'I can't make out who it is . . .'

'Nor me.' Ryan grimaced. 'But as long as they stay there we're stuck *here*. They'll see us if we break cover.'

Cleo looked around for another way down. Below them a narrow ledge ran horizontally round the pyramid, shielded from view from above by an overhanging lip of crumbling stone that was once the base of a wall. 'If we can make our way round on that ledge we could climb down the back of the pyramid . . .'

Ryan eyed the route for a moment. Then he nodded. He slid down and helped Cleo after him. Together they inched their way along the ledge like rock climbers traversing a cliff. At last they rounded the corner. Unlike the front of the pyramid, which had been cleared of trees, the back slope still belonged to the jungle, as thickly wooded as a natural hillside.

As they scrambled down through the strangler figs and brambles, Cleo simmered with irritation. Her search for the White Finder Tree had been completely ruined. Now she wished she'd ignored Ryan and marched down into the jaguar tomb to find out who had the nerve to creep around after them in the middle of the night . . . She was so busy seething that she didn't notice where she put her feet; until one of them disappeared over the edge of a deep narrow fissure.

Cleo fell. Her arms flew up to protect her head. She clawed for a handhold. Her frantic fingers found nothing but the pebbles and lichen that skittered down after her. Screwing up her eyes, clenching her muscles, Cleo braced for the smash and crash at the bottom of the plunge, when suddenly something halted her fall with a force that jerked her upwards. Her teeth clattered. Pain shot through her body.

'Don't move!' Ryan shouted. 'Your bum bag has caught on a root.'

Cleo opened her eyes and tried to piece together what had happened. She was hanging from a tree root by the leather tool belt threaded through the double-stitched loops of her polyester cotton hiking trousers. If any one of those elements failed, she would be swallowed up by the stone.

'Reach for my hand!'

Cleo stretched but felt nothing but the cold, rough wall of the crevasse.

Slowly she looked up. Ryan was reaching down to her, his fingers splayed with effort. She heard a creak and felt a small heart-stopping drop. Something was giving way. There was another creak, another drop. She felt the skin on her wrist burn as Ryan grabbed and pulled. He dragged her upwards, her knees knocking and scraping against the stone. She managed to get an elbow over the side, heaved and kicked, until she was lying in a tangled heap. She clung on to Ryan, her head pressed into his chest, breathing in the safety of his t-shirt.

'Are you OK?' he asked.

125

Cleo sat up and brushed bits of stone from her knees. 'Just a few bruises.' She rolled her neck. 'And minor whiplash.'

Ryan grinned. 'Not to mention the world's biggest wedgie?'

Cleo hadn't heard the term *wedgie* before, but she could guess what it meant. It was not a phenomenon she wished to discuss, although there *had* been a moment as she dangled, when she'd feared her hiking trousers might need to be surgically removed. She quickly changed the subject. 'Thank you for saving me.'

'You're welcome. It's been a while since I had to pull you out of a hole. I was starting to miss it.'

'I haven't fallen down *that* many holes!' Cleo protested.

Ryan sat up and counted on his fingers. 'The deadfall in Smenkhkare's tomb? And then there was that cliff in China? And the giant's head . . .'

'That wasn't a hole it was a booby trap,' Cleo pointed out. 'And Meilin pulled me out of it, not you. Anyway, I've saved you more times than you've saved me. Remember the scorpion? And the giant salamander and the dragon fire? And don't forget the coral snake tonight.'

Ryan laughed. 'OK. Let's say we're about quits.'

Cleo felt that she was technically ahead but she decided a good friend wouldn't push the point. She took a bottle of water from her tool belt, drank, and then passed it to Ryan.

He took a swig and gazed out into the distance for a long moment. 'Wow!' he said. 'How did the light get to be so *beautiful*?'

The sky had lightened from grey to opal and pale pink. The sun, huge and red, was nudging above the horizon. The tree canopy below flamed as if on fire and the mottled stone of the pyramid glowed rose and gold. 'Light from the sun travels further to reach us at sunrise,' Cleo explained, 'so more of the shorter wavelength blue light is scattered by the molecules in the air, making it seem more red . . .' Why was Ryan giving her that look he did when he thought she'd said something funny? She'd only tried to answer his question. A twinkle of pink caught her eye. A ray of light was glinting on something among the trees. 'I wonder what that is,' she murmured.

Ryan shaded his eyes. 'It looks like a dome on top of a tower . . .'

But the light had already shifted. The building – if that's what it was – melted back into the foliage. It was time to go. Cleo was getting up when her boot scuffed against a small round object. Ryan dived and caught it before it rolled down the slope.

'What's that?' Cleo asked.

'It's an old cup of some sort.' Ryan held it out to show her. 'It was digging into my back when we were hiding under the platform so I picked it up.'

Cleo frowned in surprise. 'You took it from the tomb?'

'I didn't mean to! I forgot all about it until we were on our way out so I just shoved it in my hoodie pocket.'

Cleo took the small ceramic pot. The unusual spouted lid had broken and half of it was missing. As she turned the pot over something rattled inside. *Could it be the White Finder Tree?* Cleo held her breath. Hope flickered through her. She tipped the cup up. Several small discs clattered into her palm and hope died away. She rubbed a crust of dried dust from one of the discs with her thumb. 'It was a necklace,' she said, her voice flat with disappointment. 'Made of spiny oyster shell.'

127

'How can you tell?' Ryan asked. 'They look like fossilised crisps to me.'

'A small hole has been drilled near the edge of each piece to thread it onto a cord.' Cleo held up a shell to catch the light. 'And see how it's sort of rusty red? Spiny oyster shells were highly prized for their orangey-red colour. Actually, spiny oysters are more closely related to the scallop than the true oyster . . .'

They hurried the rest of the way back to camp in silence. As they approached the clearing Cleo could smell wood smoke and coffee. Rosita must already be up, preparing breakfast.

They tiptoed round the back of the trailers, past Alex's tent. A light shone through the canvas. *Was it Alex who followed us to into the tomb?* There was a zipping sound and the flap opened. Alex's head popped out, her golden curls tied up in bunches. 'Goodness!' she laughed, patting her hand on her heart over her red gingham pyjama jacket. 'You two frightened the life out of me. I thought I was about to be set upon by a wild beast.' She waved a sheaf of papers. 'I was reading this. It must have sent my imagination into overdrive!'

Cleo glanced at the top page. 'The helminthological report?'

'It looks as if some of the hookworms in the jaguar's intestine were of a type that infest *humans*, not jaguars! It's such a super find. I was too excited to sleep. It means the jaguar in the sarcophagus was almost certainly a *man-eater!*' Alex paused. 'What are you two doing up at this hour?'

'Oh, just a walk,' Ryan said quickly. 'Admiring the sunrise.'

'Looks like you're not the only ones.' Alex nodded towards

128

the clearing. Roberto Chan was on his way to the kitchen. He picked up a mug of coffee from Rosita and headed for his trailer.

'Don't worry, your secret's safe with me!' Alex said.

Secret? Cleo thought. *Does she know we entered the tomb?* Then she saw Alex wink at Ryan before ducking back inside the tent. Cleo blushed. 'What did she think we were . . .'

But Ryan cut her off. 'It was Roberto who followed us!' he whispered.

'I think so too,' Cleo said. Roberto was her Number One Suspect. He was short and stocky like the figure she'd seen next to the tomb entrance. And here he was, up at dawn. Then again, he could have just fancied an early cup of coffee.

'I wish we could be sure . . .'

'We can,' Ryan said. 'Did you see his trainers just now?'

'His *trainers?*'

Ryan nodded. 'They were bright red.'

17

CINNABAR

'RED?' CLEO ECHOED. 'What does the colour of Roberto's shoes have to do with anything?'

Ryan leaned against a tree trunk enjoying the moment. Cleo hated it when she wasn't the one with all the answers. 'Cinnabar dust,' he said. 'They were covered in it. He must have picked it up from the jaguar tomb.' Ryan was so relieved it hadn't been Wolf Head or Beefy Guy from the Red Wolves following them that he couldn't resist adding a joke. 'Never mind being caught red-handed! We've got him red-*footed!*'

Cleo didn't laugh. 'You're right,' she said. 'So that *proves* it. Roberto was the one who followed us into the tomb. I *knew* he was up to something. He must have faked the Snake

Stone after all. I think he was starting to worry that he might be found out, so he leaked the story about the White Finder Tree to cause a distraction.' She paused, her brows furrowed. Ryan could almost hear the cogs whirring in her brain. 'Then, in case that wasn't enough, he decided to "steal" the jade mask as well. Roberto knew about all the problems Mum's had on previous digs with artefacts going missing. He thought he could frame her for the theft of the mask. Of course!' Cleo's eyes gleamed in the gathering light as she continued to put the pieces together. 'He's the one who called Chief Garcia with the tip-off that it was Mum who stole the mask! I bet that's why he was sneaking into the tomb tonight. He wasn't following *us*. He went to steal another artefact to frame Mum for a second crime!'

Ryan was impressed. Cleo's story was a masterpiece, worthy of a twelve-part crime series on TV. But he didn't believe it. Yes, Roberto was at the tomb, but the other details just didn't add up. If Roberto Chan had forged the Snake Stone, why would he have invited Lydia and Pete McNeil to join the dig? Wouldn't that just increase the chance he'd be found out? And Lydia had been one of the few people to support Roberto's theory about Jaguar Paw being buried in the lower tomb. Why would he want to make trouble for her?

'We've got to warn Mum and Dad about this!' Cleo jutted out her chin as if daring Ryan to disagree. 'Who knows what Roberto Chan is planning to do next?'

'Hang on! Let's think this through ...' Ryan felt something nudge his foot. He looked down to see Shadow peering up at him. He'd left the anteater pup curled up on his bed. He scooped him up. It had been a long night. Ryan was exhausted and Shadow's furry warmth felt as comforting as his old teddy bear, Mr Scruffy.

Meanwhile, Cleo had gone quiet.

Please tell me I didn't just say the teddy bear thing out loud. Ryan glanced up to check Cleo's expression. But she wasn't there.

He whisked round and looked across the clearing. Cleo was marching up the steps of her trailer. It didn't look as if *thinking through* was top of her agenda.

He caught up with her as she threw open the door.

To Ryan's surprise, Cleo's parents were already up, although still in dressing gowns. In fact, the trailer was *full* of people. Max Henderson and Sofia K. Proufork were also jammed in around the little table. Even his mum was there. She'd pulled on a crumpled grey tracksuit, and her short hair – now creosote brown instead of its usual blonde – was sticking out at random angles. Ryan had bought the hair dye in Xpujil yesterday and persuaded her to use it, in case the Red Wolves showed up and recognised her. *What is this?* he wondered. *A pre-breakfast prayer meeting? A surprise pyjama party?*

'What?' Cleo spluttered. Then she pulled herself together. 'Actually, it's good that everyone's here. We can tell you all at the same time.'

Five worried faces turned to stare as if expecting a dramatic *Eastenders*-style declaration; *we're in love and we're running away together. And we're taking Shadow with us . . .*

'Roberto Chan can't be trusted,' Cleo announced. 'He's the one who told the press that we're looking for the White Finder Tree. He faked the Snake Stone. He stole the jade mask and tried to make it look like Mum did it.'

Ryan had expected Cleo's accusations to be greeted with shock. Possibly some disbelief and anger too. What he *hadn't* expected was an awkward sort of silence. Max Henderson – attired in an odd combo of old England rugby shirt over tartan pyjamas – stared down at the table like a kid caught stealing gobstoppers from the sweet shop. Cleo's dad wiped his glasses on the lapel of his dressing gown for the third time in a row.

'We can *prove* it,' Cleo said. 'He's got cinnabar on his shoes!'

Cleo's mum dropped her head into her hands. She was sporting a kaftan-style nightdress and a serious case of bed hair. 'Cleopatra, I don't know what you're talking about. We *know* Roberto Chan didn't leak the story . . .'

'Because we know who *did* do it,' Sofia interrupted. She was the only one of the adults who was fully dressed in shirt and jeans, topped with a padded body-warmer. 'It was Max!'

Ryan stared at Max. They'd crossed him off their suspect list ages ago. He wasn't even one of Cleo's *Theoretical Possibilities*.

Cleo shook her head. 'No, you *can't* have done. You didn't borrow the satellite phone that day. You couldn't get on the internet.'

'I didn't want to wake you all up so I used Roberto's phone instead.' Max spoke quietly. The effect was unsettling from a man whose voice was normally set at foghorn volume.

Cleo leaned over the table until her nose was almost touching Max's. 'But why would you do that? You're Mum's friend!'

'It wasn't *deliberate*.' Max's bulldog jowls drooped more than ever. 'I was only trying to upload some photos to a bird-watching website. *Yucatán Wings,* it's called. But I sent the wrong bloomin' files. I fired off pictures of the sarcophagus texts by mistake.'

'That's *your* story,' Sofia said sharply. 'We only have your word that it was a mistake!'

For once Lydia agreed with her. 'It does seem a little odd, Max. You're always so organised.'

Suddenly Ryan remembered something. He *knew* Max was telling the truth! *'Violaceous trogon!'*

Max looked as if he'd seen – or rather heard – a ghost. 'That's right, lad! I was trying to send pictures of the trogon. How did you know?'

'You opened a photo of it the other day when you meant to show us a picture of the sarcophagus. Blue and yellow bird? Hangs out in ant and wasp nests? Some of your files must have got muddled and saved with the wrong names.'

'Now do you believe me?' Max appealed to the group.

'And you just *happened* to include all the details of the translation of the texts and Lydia's theory about the White Finder Tree with the photos?' Sofia scoffed.

But Lydia was back on Max's side now. 'Actually, that's why he's the best photographer in the business,' she snapped at Sofia. 'Max always logs detailed notes on every image. It saves me no end of time . . .'

Ryan still didn't understand. 'But how did the story spread all over the internet?' he asked. 'Why would the people who run some random bird-watching website care about the search for the White Finder Tree? Why didn't they just delete the sarcophagus photographs and forget about them?'

It was his mum who answered. 'It wasn't the guy who runs the website. It was his wife.' Mum swirled the dregs in a large mug of coffee. 'I couldn't sleep so I did a bit of digging around last night.' Ryan had almost forgotten that he'd asked her to see whether any of her journalist friends knew where the story had come from. She must have been trying to keep busy while she was waiting to hear from the Red Wolves guy in Los Angeles. 'I got a call-back from a contact an hour ago and came straight round here to let Pete and Lydia know.' Mum gave Lydia McNeil an apologetic smile. 'Sorry for waking you up so early, by the way. My contact told me that the bird-website-guy's wife is a journalist. She saw Max's sarcophagus pictures when they came through to her husband's computer. She thought they looked interesting and showed them to a friend with an archaeology blog. The rest is history . . .'

Lydia stood up, pushed her hair off her face and smiled. 'What a relief! I feel a lot better knowing it was all a genuine mistake. Now, what were you saying about Roberto?' she asked. She looked from Cleo to Ryan. 'And where have you two been off so early? It's only just light out there.'

'Oh nowhere much,' Ryan said quickly. 'Just out looking for ants.' He held up Shadow as evidence, his fingers crossed under the thick fur. 'Dawn is the best time to find them.'

'Would you take that animal outside,' Sofia sniffed. 'It's setting my allergies off.'

Ryan backed out of the door, aiming a small kick at Cleo's shin on the way out, just in case she had any ideas about staying and trying to explain anything else.

He headed for the breakfast buffet under the gazebo and loaded his plate with tacos. Cleo was too distracted to notice what she was taking and grabbed a random assortment of fruit, boiled eggs and sugar sachets.

135

It was so early that all the other tables were empty. 'We need to revise our hypothesis,' Cleo said, drenching a slice of mango in hot chilli sauce. 'Max Henderson's mix-up with his bird photos may explain how the White Finder Tree story went public. But that's only a fraction of what's going on.' She almost choked on the mega-spicy mango. 'I'm sure Max didn't steal the jade mask,' she spluttered. 'And that wasn't Max we saw up at the tomb. It was someone shorter . . .'

Ryan agreed. Max Henderson was at least six foot tall. 'That was Roberto Chan,' he said, shovelling down the delicious pepper and chorizo stuffed tacos. 'We know from the cinnabar on his trainers. The question is *why* was he there?'

Cleo tore the corner off a sugar sachet. 'I say we take the direct approach. We confront Roberto and ask him exactly what he was doing.'

But Ryan had seen enough of Cleo's *direct approach* for one day. 'There's still a chance that Roberto didn't see that it was *us* that he followed into the tomb. If we go storming in we immediately give away the fact that it *was*.'

'You have a better idea?' Cleo took a bite of her boiled egg, realised she'd sprinkled sugar all over it, and dropped it under the table for Shadow.

'Actually, I do,' Ryan said.

Ryan's plan wasn't rocket science. It simply involved striking up a conversation with Roberto Chan and steering it towards the topic of late-night tomb visits, to see what the man had to say for himself. The first requirement of this sounding-out operation was to catch their prey alone. The chance didn't arise until after lunch, when Roberto headed off to the big metal equipment store at the edge of the camp and began sorting through shovels, sifting screens and electrical survey tools.

Ideally Ryan would have worked alone, but Cleo insisted on joining him. 'Leave the talking to me,' he whispered as they drew near.

Roberto looked over his shoulder as he heard them approach.

'Would you like a hand with that?' Ryan asked.

'Sure. I'm doing a routine check to make sure all the equipment is in order.' Roberto held up a clipboard. 'Health and Safety requirement.' He handed over a box of flashlights. 'You can test the batteries in those for me.' Then he wheeled out something that looked like a large red lawnmower and began to check the controls.

'That's ground penetrating radar,' Cleo told Ryan. 'GPR. It maps features beneath the surface. Perhaps if you are *looking for something that is difficult to find . . .*' She fixed Roberto with a narrow-eyed glare and stressed each word with all the force of a sledgehammer. It was, Ryan suspected, Cleo's version of being subtle. He threw her a look. She pretended not to notice.

Luckily Roberto didn't seem to notice either. He wasn't the easiest man to engage in light-hearted banter, but Ryan knew he had to try something before Cleo waded in again. 'Do you think that GPR could detect termite nests underground?' he asked.

Cleo rolled her eyes. 'Termites build massive mounds. You can't miss them!'

Cheers, Ryan thought. *Big help!* He soldiered on. 'I just wondered because I have to find food for Shadow. Actually, we were out before sunrise this morning looking for ant nests.' Having used this cover story once already, it didn't feel like a lie any more. 'We thought we saw someone . . .'

'Someone *CLIMBING UP THE PYRAMID TO THE TOMB . . .*' Cleo weighed in.

Ryan groaned to himself. *Why do I bother?*

Roberto made a note on his clipboard. 'I know you two entered the tomb,' he said quietly. 'I'm impressed you figured out the combination to open the lock.'

Ryan felt skewered to the spot. Roberto had seen them! Before he could make up his mind whether it would be better to deny everything or confess, Cleo took the decision out of his hands. 'We knew it was you!' she exclaimed. 'You followed us!'

Roberto wheeled the GPR back into the shed. 'Not exactly,' he said. 'I didn't follow *you.* I followed Sofia Proufork.'

18

QUESTIONS

CLEO STARED AT Roberto Chan in disbelief. 'You were following *Sofia Proufork*? But that can't be right. Sofia was with Mum and Dad in the trailer when we got back.'

Roberto pulled an old oil barrel from behind the shed and sat down heavily, resting his elbows on his knees. 'So, she must have hurried down from the pyramid and arrived back in camp before you did.'

'And *Sofia* didn't have cinnabar on her shoes.' Ryan's gaze dropped to Roberto's trainers. Traces of red still showed on the white leather.

Roberto nodded slowly. 'That's because Miss Proufork didn't go down into the jaguar tomb.'

139

There was a long silence, filled only by the hum of the electricity generator as Cleo turned these points over in her mind. She couldn't deny that they were logically possible. But she still didn't trust Roberto. 'So what was Sofia doing up there in the middle of the night?'

'That is what I wanted to know,' Roberto said. 'Which is why I followed her. I heard someone moving around the camp and went out to investigate. I thought it might be looters. The police warned me that if it was *Los Lobos Rojos* who stole the jade mask, they may well come back for more. But when we came out from the trees into the moonlight, I saw that it was Miss Proufork. She climbed the pyramid so I crept up behind her. She was about to enter the tunnel to the tomb when she spotted me.'

'What did she say?' Cleo was going to burst if she didn't find out what Sofia was up to soon.

'Sofia told me that she was following you two. She said she had spotted you climbing the pyramid and she had come to warn you that it was dangerous. At first I didn't believe her. But she showed me that the padlock had been opened.' Roberto frowned, two deep lines scoring his smooth forehead. 'Of course, I was very worried to hear this. If an accident happens on the site it is my responsibility. So I told Sofia to stay where she was and I went down the tunnel. I searched both the tombs, but I couldn't find you. I returned to the surface and was about to raise the alarm when I saw you climbing round the pyramid.' Roberto almost smiled. 'Tell me. How did get out of the tomb without me seeing you? I've been trying to figure it out.'

While Ryan explained how they'd hidden in the Tomb of the Unknown Lady and Child, Cleo's thoughts ran on ahead. Roberto's story stacked up. The short figure she'd seen standing near the tomb entrance must have been Sofia. It was her puffy body-warmer that had made her look so stocky. Cleo had wondered how their follower could've made it back up from the jaguar tomb so quickly without being heard. The answer was that there wasn't *one* follower but two. Roberto had entered the tomb. Sofia had remained on the surface of the pyramid the whole time. But there was one thing that didn't make sense. 'Why didn't Sofia just go and tell our parents instead of snooping around after us?'

'I agree. Her behaviour was a little strange.' Roberto rubbed his jaw. 'That's not the only odd thing I have noticed . . .'

'Have *you* told our parents that we broke into the tomb?' Ryan interrupted.

'Not yet,' Roberto said. 'I thought I would give it one day to see if you came to tell me what you were up to before I decided how to handle the situation.' He looked up expectantly. 'That was your cue. Are you going to tell me?'

Cleo glanced at Ryan. Ryan nodded. They might as well tell Roberto the truth, since he knew so much already, she supposed. 'We were searching for the White Finder Tree,' she said. 'Everyone's saying that Mum's either stolen it or made the whole thing up. If we don't find it soon, we'll have to go home and Mum will probably get the sack. That's if the police don't arrest her for stealing the jade mask first.'

'I'll do my best to make sure that doesn't happen. I am very proud to have Professor McNeil here on the dig. And the rest of the team, of course.'

'I don't mean to be rude,' Ryan said, 'but you don't *seem* that thrilled to have us here.'

Roberto sighed. 'I am sorry. I know I have been a bad host, but I have been under a lot of pressure.' A muscle flickered along his cheekbone. 'I was caught out by a hoax once before. Two years ago some builders brought an ancient book, a codex, of Maya prophecies, to show me. They said they had found it in the cellar of an old church. I believed it was real. I was young and enthusiastic and I didn't check carefully enough before I told the world about it. It turned out to be a clever fake.' Roberto stared down at his upturned hands, as if he should have seen the truth in the lines on his palms. 'I was a laughing stock, of course.'

'So that's why people jumped to the conclusion that the Snake Stone was a fake too?' Ryan asked. 'Because you'd been conned before.'

Roberto nodded. 'It was very difficult to get funding for this dig. It would not have been possible without Lydia's support. If it is a failure – if I do not solve the mystery of Jaguar Paw's death or discover an important artefact like the White Finder Tree – then I will never get the chance to lead another excavation. I might lose my . . .' His voice caught on a sob and trailed away.

'You might lose your job?' Cleo prompted. So that's why Roberto always seemed so tense. He was in the same boat as Mum.

'Much worse than that.' Roberto spoke so softly that Cleo had to lean in to catch his words. 'I might lose my son.'

'Your *son*?' Ryan stammered. 'How?'

'Alejandro has leukaemia.' Roberto looked up from his hands. 'He is in the hospital in Mérida. Without my job I cannot afford to pay for his medical bills.'

'How old is he?' Ryan asked.

Roberto smiled. 'He is just nine.'

'You should be with him!' Ryan shouted. He clenched his fists and raised them at his sides. For a moment Cleo thought he was going to hit Roberto.

Roberto didn't flinch. 'His mother is with him.' He got up and locked the equipment shed. 'I need to be here to make sure that the dig is a success.'

Ryan unclenched his fists. 'We'll do anything we can to help.' He turned to Cleo. 'Won't we?'

Cleo nodded. She'd just figured out why Ryan had been so upset. His dad had disappeared six years ago. Ryan had been nine years old.

The following morning Cleo woke before it was light. She had barely slept, her brain tormented by questions that buzzed like the mosquitoes circling the net above her bed. One big puzzle had been solved. They now knew who had leaked the story of the search for the White Finder Tree. It was simply Max's mistake. But other mysteries remained; ancient ones that skulked in the shadows – *Where was Lady Six Sky's White Finder Tree hidden? What was the true story of Jaguar Paw's death?* – and new ones that popped up at every turn – *Who stole the jaguar mask? Can we really trust Roberto Chan? Why did Sofia Proufork follow us in the middle of the night? What was she planning to do if Roberto hadn't intercepted her?*

Cleo couldn't shake the feeling that these questions were somehow all connected. Like mushrooms, she thought; they looked like separate organisms from above, but they all sprouted from the same *mycelium*, the vast, fungal network growing out of sight under the ground.

Suddenly she sat up. Tracking back and forth over her thoughts, something had snagged, like a ruck in a carpet. It was something to do with Sofia at the tomb. *Her behaviour was strange,* Roberto had said. *That's not the only odd thing I have noticed . . .* What did he mean? What else had Sofia done that was odd?

Cleo resolved to ask Roberto first thing in the morning. It was still dark outside but there was no chance of getting back to sleep now. She was reaching for the *Popol Vuh* when she remembered the little cup that Ryan had picked up from the Tomb of the Unknown Woman and Child. She'd stuffed it in her tool belt and forgotten all about it. She turned on her bedside lamp and examined the cup under the pool of yellow light. Through the coating of grime, she could make out a row of glyphs around the rim and another near the base. Taking a small brush she swept away centuries of dust. Then she wiped gently with a soft cloth until the entire text was visible, the red-brown ink still clear against the mottled clay.

It's probably nothing of great interest, Cleo thought, as she gathered dictionaries and notepads. But it would keep her occupied until morning. Sitting cross-legged on her bed she set to work.

The texts were in traditional 'codex vase' style, recording information such as the owner of the vessel, the date it was made and the contents it was designed to hold. Cleo found herself using Ryan's trick of giving the glyphs nicknames to help remember them. *Toothy man with quiff,* she murmured. *That's K'inich, meaning Radiant or Sun-faced. Flowered purse with fruit on top. That's Ak, meaning Turtle . . .*

144

When Cleo next looked up the sun was pouring in through the blinds.

She'd missed breakfast. But she'd deciphered enough of the text to realise that the cup was far more interesting than she'd thought. She knew what it said. Now she needed to talk to Ryan to figure out just what it *meant*.

19

TURTLE

MEANWHILE, RYAN WAS playing baseball. He'd gone out straight after breakfast to escape from the trailer. Mum was sitting at the table under a black cloud so dark that even the fresh pot of Rosita's coffee he'd fetched her couldn't lift it. The ex-Red Wolves member in Los Angeles had backed out. He was too frightened to talk. They were back to Square One.

Ryan had felt the familiar weight of disappointment settle in his bones. There'd been so many false alarms before. This time he'd allowed himself to believe they might really be getting close to finding Dad. *I should have known better,* he told himself.

He'd been on his way to find Cleo when the sound of whoops and cheers had led him to a patch of ground behind the huts, where the workmen had marked out a baseball diamond. Ryan had no idea how to play, but he'd asked if he could join in. At home playing football was one of the best ways he knew to shake off his worries; he was sure baseball would have the same effect.

The men were delighted to teach him the game, shouting their instructions in a hodgepodge of Spanish, Mayan and English. Once Ryan figured out it was basically *rounders-with-attitude*, he soon got the hang of it. He'd just scored a home run, and was high-fiving his teammates, when he spotted Cleo lurking under the trees at the edge of the diamond.

'Come and join in!' Luis called.

Cleo shook her head. Ryan suspected that she had never watched a team sport in her life, let alone *played* one. She was looking on with a sort of puzzled concentration, as if analysing an obscure ritual practised by a lost Amazonian tribe. At the end of the innings he made his excuses and retired from the game. They wandered into a glade among the trees and sat down on a huge gnarled stump. Bromeliad plants sprouted from the branches overhead, like green spiders dangling among the foliage.

Cleo opened the pocket of her bum bag, took out her new white scarf, and unbundled it to reveal the little cup that Ryan had accidentally pinched from the tomb. She must have cleaned it up a bit, as the shades of bronze and ochre were now much brighter. She pointed to the row of glyphs around the rim. 'It says that this drinking vessel belongs to Radiant Turtle . . .' She gazed intently up at him in a way that told Ryan this was Highly Significant. He had no idea why. 'Radiant Who?'

'Radiant Turtle. Don't you remember? His name is carved on the jaguar sarcophagus.' Cleo paused. 'Oh yeah, you were out searching for Shadow's mum that day ...' They both glanced across the glade at Shadow, who was balancing on a log trying to prise ants out from under the bark. 'Anyway, nobody knew who Radiant Turtle was.' Cleo jiggled the cup at Ryan. 'Until now! This says it belongs to Radiant Turtle, *the son of King Jaguar Paw*. This is really important.'

'If you say so. What's this bit say?' Ryan asked, indicating a glyph that looked like a fat fish swimming into a comb.

'It tells you what the cup was used for.' Cleo opened her notebook to show him her translation. 'It says *kakaw*. It's the word we still use: cocoa.'

Ryan took the ancient cup and peered inside. It was extraordinary to think that it had once been filled with something as familiar as drinking chocolate.

'It also gives the date of Radiant Turtle's birth,' Cleo went on. 'AD 693; and the date the cup was made, which was 695.'

'He was just two years old.' Ryan ran his fingers over the broken lid and the little spout. 'Wow! It's a prehistoric sippy cup.'

'It's not *prehistoric*,' Cleo corrected him. 'Prehistoric means from the time *before* humans recorded history in writing.'

'Yeah, yeah! I just meant that it's really old ...' Ryan's words died away. He could feel tiny dents in the spout where a toddler's teeth had chewed. Icy tingles prickled his scalp. He felt as if Radiant Turtle were actually there with them in the glade, his chubby hands clamped round the cup, his face smeared with chocolate ... Ryan tried to shake off the uncanny feeling by examining the pictures on the side of the cup. They were all battle scenes, including a warrior cutting off the heads of his enemies ... 'It's not exactly age appropriate, is it?' he said. 'What's wrong with *Winnie the Pooh* or *Thomas the Tank Engine*?'

Cleo didn't seem to have heard. 'This cup must have belonged to the Unknown Child. It must have been in the sarcophagus with him and fallen under the platform.'

'Which means he's not *unknown* any more,' Ryan pointed out. 'He's Radiant Turtle, the son of King Jaguar Paw.'

'No wonder there are no other records of Radiant Turtle anywhere,' Cleo said. 'He died as a child. Unlike Lady Six Sky's son, Smoking Squirrel, who grew up to be a ruthless warrior king. There's a famous carving of him when he was fourteen, already torturing a rival leader, Shield Jaguar of Ucanal.'

Ryan grimaced. 'Sounds like a nice guy! Perhaps good old Smoking Squirrel killed Radiant Turtle? Or Jaguar Paw? Or both of them?'

From somewhere high above came the tapping of a woodpecker at work. 'I don't know,' Cleo murmured, 'but I'm sure there's a connection. The *mycelium* just keeps on growing.'

'*Mycelium*?' Ryan asked. Was this some new Maya god he hadn't heard of?

'It's a huge underground network of fungal rhizomorphs,' Cleo explained. 'There's a mycelium of honey mushrooms in Eastern Oregon that's three and half miles across. It's the largest living thing on Earth.'

Ryan simply didn't know how to follow that piece of

information. He watched as Shadow lost his balance and fell off the log. He lay on his back happily licking ants from his fur. Ryan picked up Cleo's pen and began doodling cartoons in the margins of her notebook. He sketched a villainous squirrel in a Viking-style helmet threatening a puny jaguar with a sword. He added a speech bubble: *Now we squirrels will rule the world! Mwa ha ha!* Something was missing, he thought. The forces of good had to save the day. He added a turtle, complete with mask and fluttering cape, leaping on to the scene with the words, *Not so fast, Smoking Squirrel!*

Cleo elbowed him in the ribs. 'I'm not sure you're taking this seriously.'

'You're right,' Ryan said. 'Turtle-Man couldn't have saved the day, could he? He died as a child . . .'

But Cleo had grabbed the notebook and was staring at it as if it were a priceless manuscript. 'Wait! I think you might be on to something . . .'

'Are you feeling all right?' Ryan laughed. 'I was making it up as I went along!'

'Yes, I know *that!* But maybe Radiant Turtle *did* save King Jaguar Paw.' Cleo began leafing back through the notebook. 'Remember what the sarcophagus texts said about the instructions written on the White Finder Tree?' She read the lines that she and her mum had translated. '*Jaguar Paw has descended to Xib'alb'a. But he will outwit the Lords of Death and return from the deepest waters.* Ah yes, here it is, the next bit. *On the Tree are inscribed special sacrifice rituals that will bring King Jaguar Paw back . . .*' She looked up at Ryan, her eyes wide. 'What if the "special sacrifice rituals" meant giving Jaguar Paw's son to the Lords of Death in exchange for the king? Maybe that's what it means by *outwitting* them.'

Ryan shuddered and felt for the St Christopher pendant around his neck. He thought about his own father. Was he still out there somewhere in the forest? He thought about Roberto, so worried about his son in hospital. A lump rose in his throat as he rolled Radiant Turtle's sippy cup over in his palm. He needed to change the subject. He spotted a glyph that he recognised. 'Is that our old friend, *Fierce Face with Tattoo on Cheek*? The one that means *Lady*?'

Cleo tucked a strand of hair behind her ear. 'Yes, that's right. Actually that's another really interesting thing about this cup.'

'If it involves sacrifices, I don't want to know.'

'No, it's nothing like that,' Cleo laughed. 'Do you see that glyph just before *Lady*?'

Ryan checked the cup. '*Currant bun with wings on top*?'

'That's the one. It's pronounced *U-tziib*. It means, *this was written by . . .*'

'Like a signature?'

'Exactly. It says *this was written by Lady Mountain Star.*'

Cleo was doing that thing again where she said the words in slow motion, accompanied by her *you-know-this-is-important-right?* stare. He returned it with a blank look.

'Writing was a man's job, of course! I don't think there's ever been evidence of a *female* Mayan scribe before. It's highly unusual . . .'

Ryan took a closer look at the two glyphs that made up the signature; a bug-eyed creature with three rows of buttons on

151

its stomach, followed by a diamond and circle pattern. 'Does that bit say *Mountain Star*?'

Cleo nodded. 'Why?'

'It's just that I've seen that name somewhere before.'

MESSAGE

'YOU'VE SEEN LADY Mountain Star's name?' Cleo almost
fell off the tree stump and ended up among the leaves with
Shadow. 'Where? In the jaguar tomb?'

Ryan hadn't expected her to be quite so excited about a
name. Then again, you never knew with Cleo. 'No, it wasn't
there . . .' He closed his eyes and scrolled back through his
memories for the glyphs that matched the signature on the
cup. A stretch of crumbling stone started to come into focus.
It was low down in the undergrowth, draped with vines . . .
Suddenly it came to him. 'It was carved onto a wall,' he said,
'in a ruined building at the edge of the site. I saw it the other
day when I was out searching for Shadow's mum.'

Cleo sprang up. 'Show me!'

'What, *now*?' Baseball was hungry work and it was almost lunchtime.

But Cleo didn't look in the mood for a lunch break. 'Lady Mountain Star could be the key to finding the White Finder Tree.'

'How do you make that out?' Ryan couldn't see what decorating a child's sippy cup had to do with knowing where a magic compass had been hidden.

Cleo was already heading out of the glade. Sunlight splashed her long black hair with golden dapples, like jaguar markings in reverse. She stopped, waiting for Ryan to catch up. 'Mountain Star painted that cup for the king's son. The royal family wouldn't have given that job to just *anyone*. She must have been of high status. She might even have been a princess. It says on the cup that it was made in 695. *That's the year that Jaguar Paw died, according to the jaguar sarcophagus!* That means Mountain Star was around at the critical time. If that wall carving you saw commemorates some important event involving Mountain Star, it might well talk about Jaguar Paw as well. He was the king, after all. It could give us more information about what happened to him and where the White Finder Tree ended up . . .'

You can't argue with that, Ryan thought. Especially not when Cleo had that look in her eye. They agreed to meet in ten minutes and then he ran back to the trailer to check on Mum. She'd been so miserable earlier he half-expected to find her still slumped over the table. The empty coffee pot was still there, along with a note. *Gone into town for supplies.* Ryan cursed under his breath. He'd have gone with her. Those *supplies* were almost certainly a cover story. She'd been talking about asking around the shops and bars, trying to pick up more information about the Red Wolves. A lot of local people were bound to be involved with the gang, or at least know someone who was. *I could have helped,* he thought. *More to the point, I could have tried to keep Mum out of trouble.*

But there was nothing he could do now she'd gone. *And I did promise to help Roberto to find out what happened to King Jaguar Paw. If it means he can keep his job and pay for his son's medical bills then I'll do what I can to solve the mystery.*

As they followed the narrow path that led past the main pyramids and temples to the remoter reaches of the ruins, Ryan noticed that Cleo kept glancing over her shoulder as if worried they were being followed. 'It's only Shadow,' he told her. 'He thinks we're off on an ant safari.'

Cleo's eyes darted from side to side. 'We can't be too careful,' she muttered. 'There's something I forgot to tell you. When we were talking to Roberto yesterday he mentioned that Sofia had been behaving oddly. So I went and found him this morning while you were playing baseball and asked him what he'd meant . . .'

'Ooh, was it to do with her mystery medical condition?'

'No, it's *much* more interesting than that!' Cleo stopped and looked round again before continuing. 'Roberto thinks that Sofia K. Proufork might not be quite the expert epigrapher she makes out. The other day he asked her about an inscription on a jade ear spool and he's sure *she got it completely wrong*. Roberto isn't trained in reading glyphs himself, but he speaks modern Yucatec Mayan, and a lot of the words are still the same . . . He knows enough to spot obvious mistakes . . .'

What was the big deal? Ryan wondered. He couldn't

see why an ear spool – whatever that was – mattered so much.

'If Sofia can't read glyphs very well, how could she be so sure that Mum and I were wrong about the White Finder Tree being a real object?' Cleo asked. 'Now I think about it, she barely glanced at our notes on the sarcophagus texts before declaring they were all rubbish. *She didn't actually decipher anything herself.* She was bluffing! The woman is a *total fraud.*'

Ryan wasn't so sure. 'You said that about Roberto yesterday, remember? The *total fraud* part, not the *woman* part,' he added. 'You're starting to develop paranoid tendencies.'

Cleo marched along the path at double pace. 'Don't forget Sofia tried to follow us into the tomb. She would have done, if Roberto hadn't stopped her. What was she even doing wandering about at that time of night?'

'Perhaps she's a werewolf,' Ryan joked, hurrying to catch up. 'It *was* a full moon, remember. Of course! *That's* Sofia's medical condition.'

'For goodness' sake,' Cleo sighed. 'Sofia is *not* a werewolf!'

'It would explain why she demanded to have her own trailer.'

Cleo laughed. She even attempted a joke. 'Maybe the K stands in Sofia K. Proufork stands for *Kveldulf!*'

Ryan shrugged. 'Who?'

'He's a character from Icelandic sagas. It means *Evening Wolf*. He could transform into a wolf in battle ...' Cleo stopped so suddenly that Ryan barrelled into her. 'Oh, wait! Forget about werewolves! I've just figured out how Sofia knew we were going to the tomb. She must have overheard us at the café in Xpujil. We were planning it just after she left us. She could have just slipped round the side of the café and eavesdropped on our whole conversation.'

It's possible, Ryan thought. But he still wondered whether Cleo was being over-suspicious of Sofia, simply because she didn't like her. After all, Cleo had looked up Sofia's qualifications and they all checked out; she was from that university in Canada. And Sofia had been personally selected for this job by Sir Charles Peacocke; surely she was the real deal if the Minister for Museums and Culture himself had drafted her in as an expert?

It wasn't long before they reached the spot where Ryan remembered seeing Mountain Star's name. A maze of low stone walls, swagged with creepers and vines, was all that remained of a cluster of buildings. He entered the skeleton of a small, round structure and retraced his steps. He knelt down, brambles snatching at his jeans, and worked his way along the base of the wall, looking for the tracery of glyphs he'd spotted before. He'd been searching for something very different then, of course; an injured mother anteater. At last he found the place. 'Over here!' he called.

Cleo crouched next to him. Holding her hair back from her face, she peered down at a stone that had somehow remained free of the patchwork of yellow and green lichen and unsullied by black watermarks from dripping rain. She took her trowel from her tool belt and slashed back a clump of thorny scrub for a better view. 'These glyphs don't look like a carving on a monument,' she murmured. 'They look as if they've been scratched in a hurry . . .'

'Like graffiti?' Ryan asked.

Cleo nodded She stretched out on her side, her nose almost touching the stone. 'The writing is so low down on the wall.

157

It's almost as if it wasn't *intended* to be seen.' She sat up again. 'I can see Mountain Star's signature. You were right. It's the same as on the cup. But the rest is so faint, I can hardly make it out.'

Ryan had an idea. He took his sketchbook from his pocket, tore out a page, held it to the wall and rubbed over it with the side of a soft pencil. Ghostly lines began to emerge in the graphite grey on the paper. Cleo watched, entranced. 'I can see now.' She pointed to a row of glyphs. 'Yes, I knew it! That says *King Jaguar Paw* . . . And yes,' she breathed, 'there's a date . . . *March 23rd, 697* . . .'

'Wasn't that the mysterious second date on the lid of the jaguar sarcophagus!' Ryan burst out. Perhaps Cleo was right. Maybe these lines – as delicate as slug trails – really did hold the key to unlocking the mystery of the death of King Jaguar Paw and the fate of the White Finder Tree.

'It's not the *same* date,' Cleo corrected him. 'It's two days later. The date on the sarcophagus was 21st March. This is definitely 23rd.' She took the sheet of paper and pored over it again. 'It says something about *stones* . . . and a *road* . . . I'll need to look some of these glyphs up, but I know this one here. It's *bak*. That means *captive*. Then there's this number . . . twenty-two.' She pointed at an arrangement of four lines and two dots. 'The lines represent fives and the dots are ones.'

'So this could be something about twenty-two prisoners?' Ryan asked.

'*Prisoners!*' Cleo repeated the word under her breath. 'That could be it.' She began to stride around the 'room' inspecting the stonework and poking at the rubble. She pointed out a neat round hole in the wall. 'That was for piping in the steam.' She pulled away more undergrowth. 'There's another one here. Yes, I'm sure of it. This was a prison.'

'*Steam?*' Ryan echoed. 'Like a *sauna,* you mean?' Everything he'd heard about the ancient Maya made him highly doubtful that they'd equipped their prisons with luxury spa facilities.

Cleo made a face that told him he wasn't going to like the answer. 'The steam was to clean the captives ready for sacrifice. The gods wouldn't be pleased with impure offerings.' She looked around. 'There's probably a *cenote* around here somewhere – a big natural sinkhole in the limestone – the Maya saw them as entrances to the Underworld. They used to throw sacrifices and other offerings into the water that pooled at the bottom.'

Above the background of jungle bird song and insect drone Ryan could hear Shadow snorting as he excavated a termite mound on the other side of the wall. Had Mountain Star been held prisoner in this cell? Was *twenty-two* a tally of the days she spent on Death Row? He could almost see the thick white steam gushing in through the pipes; feel its scalding embrace, stewing him like a lobster in a pot. He tried to focus on the pencil and paper rubbing in his hands. Beneath the glyphs Mountain Star had etched a long line of little circles. Was it another tally or just a pattern? He started to count the blobs but they blurred before his eyes.

'Let's go!' Cleo called. 'I need to get back to decipher the rest of this text. It must be important if Mountain Star scratched it on the wall of her prison cell.'

Ryan didn't move.

'We're late for lunch too.'

Ryan's stomach curdled at the thought of eating.

Shadow looked up at him and grunted contentedly. Gobbets of termite larvae were smeared all over his snout. It would take more than a bit of sacrifice and steam to put an anteater off its food.

By the time they got back to camp Ryan's appetite had returned. It was past two o'clock and lunch had been cleared away, so he headed for the kitchen to see what was left. Rosita looked up from cleaning plates, called *hola!* and went back to singing along to the radio.

The sound stopped Ryan in his tracks. It was just one of those swirly Mexican folk songs, as bright and cheerful as a fairground ride. So why, he wondered, was it giving him the creeps; as if it were the scary shark music from *Jaws?* He listened carefully. He'd heard this tune before somewhere . . . *now it was coming back to him* . . . yes, it had blared out of La Luna bar in Xpujil when Wolf Head had stepped out onto the street. That had been quite a hairy moment! Pleased to have solved that puzzle, Ryan picked up a plate. Then he dropped it. The plate smashed.

That wasn't the *only* time he'd heard this tune.

Sitting in the café with Cleo, just moments before Sofia K. Proufork had appeared and asked to join them . . . he'd heard a blast of the same music from down the street.

Had Sofia just stepped out of La Luna?

Was it a coincidence that she'd been in that bar at the same time as one of the gangsters from *Los Lobos Rojos?* Or had she been meeting Wolf Head? Had she been handing over the stolen jade mask? Or telling him about other treasure that could be plundered from the site?

Maybe Cleo wasn't being over-suspicious about Sofia, after all.

I was joking about Sofia being a werewolf, Ryan thought, *but maybe I was nearer the mark than I knew. She could be a Red Wolf instead.*

21

WASP

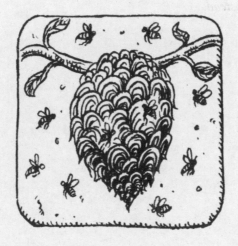

CLEO LOOKED UP from the Mayan dictionary and glanced out of the window again.

She'd been on high alert ever since Ryan had told her about Sofia K. Proufork's meeting with Wolf Head in La Luna bar. She was now convinced that Sofia was a fully paid up member of *Los Lobos Rojos*. Perhaps, Cleo thought grimly, that K stood for *Killer* . . .

The only thing that stopped Cleo marching straight over to her trailer – where her parents were having a meeting with Roberto – and announcing that Sofia was, in fact, a professional tomb robber was the memory of marching over there and falsely accusing Roberto yesterday. Just thinking about it brought on a heatwave of embarrassment. She couldn't live with the humiliation if she got it wrong again. This time she'd wait until she had rock solid proof.

Cleo and Ryan were using Ryan's trailer as their base for deciphering Mountain Star's prison message. Julie had gone into town with Alex to pick up supplies so they had the place to themselves. Ryan had posted Shadow on lookout duty, in case Sofia came snooping, although Cleo suspected he was curled on the top step snoring. He'd just got into the fridge and polished off an entire pack of bacon. There was a good reason, she thought, that anteaters hadn't been domesticated at any point in human history.

Cleo sighed as she puzzled over another glyph. There were just so many unanswered questions. *Who had stolen the jade mask and tried to frame Mum for the crime?* Sofia looked like a strong contender now, but Cleo still felt there must be a connection to the earlier thefts in Peru and Egypt and China. Sofia had not been around then. *Where was the White Finder Tree?* The sarcophagus text said it was in King Jaguar Paw's final resting place. *But where was that? The jaguar tomb? The upper tomb? A ball game in Tikal?* They would only know when they solved the mystery of how Jaguar Paw died. And then there was Ryan's dad. *Were the Red Wolves really holding Eddie Flint prisoner?* Cleo had her mind map open on the table and she drew in another line from Sofia's name. If Sofia was working with the gang, could she be connected with Ryan's father's disappearance too? The mind map was so crowded it looked like a tangled ball of wool.

Cleo turned her attention back to Mountain Star's message.

She had scratched it on the wall of her cell on 23rd March, 697, only two days after the date on the jaguar sarcophagus. Surely that wasn't a coincidence. It must hold a clue to Jaguar Paw's death. It could be a way in, a way to start unpicking the tortuous knot of questions.

An hour later, Cleo had managed to decipher the complete sequence, all bar one glyph, which was obscured by a crack in the stone.

'Go on, spit it out!' Ryan crunched on a tortilla chip from the freshly cooked batch he'd acquired from Rosita. 'I can tell you're on to something. You can hardly sit still. It's about Jaguar Paw, isn't it?'

Cleo smiled. Ryan was right. She'd found the clue they were looking for. The problem was she had no idea what it meant. *'To learn the truth about the SOMETHING of Jaguar Paw,'* she read out, *'follow the white road past the stones of creation to the wasp nest.'*

'The *something* of Jaguar Paw,' Ryan repeated. 'What's that? The *jumper* of Jaguar Paw? The *jam tart* of Jaguar Paw?'

'Why would Mountain Star waste her time writing about jam tarts?' Cleo interrupted, before Ryan could reel off any more irrelevant objects beginning with J. 'I'm sure they didn't even have jam tarts in the classic Maya period. Or jumpers, for that matter. No,' she said, lowering her voice, in case Sofia was outside with her ear to the wall. 'I'm sure the missing word must be *death*. The question is, where are we meant to find this truth? Mountain Star has obviously made these directions a bit obscure in case the guards spotted her message.'

'A bit obscure?' Ryan snorted. 'It looks like one of those

impossible riddles to me.' He sank his head on his arms. 'Typical!' he grumbled. 'I hate riddles.' Then he looked up and grinned. 'Luckily, we're brilliant at cracking them. Remember the Scorpion Papyrus in Egypt and the Immortality Scroll in China? This can't be any worse than those brain-manglers.' He tapped a pencil on Cleo's notes. 'Start at the beginning: to *learn the truth follow the white road.*' He threw back his head and burst into song.

Cleo stared in astonishment. Why on earth, she wondered, was Ryan warbling about following a *yellow* brick road? Mountain Star clearly specified that it was white.

Ryan stopped singing mid-note. 'Don't tell me you've never seen *The Wizard of Oz?* An everyday tale of a Kansas girl who gets hit on the head by a window frame in a tornado. She follows the yellow brick road to find the wizard . . .' He ground to a halt. 'It's better than it sounds, honest.'

Cleo still wasn't sure what this had to do with Mountain Star's message. 'The Maya wouldn't have used *yellow* bricks,' she pointed out. You'd need clay for that. This area is all limestone.'

Ryan laughed so loudly that Shadow woke up and scratched at the door to come in.

What's so funny about bricks? Cleo wondered. 'Actually, *sacbe* – meaning *white road* – was just the word the Maya used for all the roads and raised causeways they built through the jungle between settlements. They were surfaced with chalky limestone, so they were always white.'

'What about the next bit?' Ryan asked. '*Past the three stones of creation?*'

Cleo was pretty sure she knew what this meant. '*The three*

stones of creation was the name the Maya gave to the triangle of three bright stars in the constellation of Orion; Alnitak, Saiph and Rigel.'

Ryan banged his forehead on the table. 'I should have known that the stones weren't actually going to be *stones*. Oh no, we're on Planet Riddle now; that would be far too easy. Stones have to be bread rolls or badgers or . . .'

'They're not badgers!' Cleo wondered whether she'd ever be able to make sense of Ryan's thought processes. *Jam tarts, yellow bricks, badgers* . . . It was quite worrying at times. 'They're *stars*,' she said slowly. 'They're called *the three stones of creation* because of the Maya creation myth. At the beginning of our current world, the gods placed three sacred stones around a fire. That's why it's traditional in Maya homes to have a triangle of three hearthstones . . .'

'Hearthstones?' Ryan murmured, his face still pressed to the table. 'Maybe we're overthinking this.' He looked up, brushed tortilla crumbs from his forehead and grinned. 'And when I say *we*, I mean *you*, obviously. What if the stones of creation are just *stones*?' He took three tortilla chips from the bowl and arranged them in a triangle. 'There's this place out in the jungle with three giant boulders. Rosita told me that local people call them *the gods' hearthstones*. It's where the best herbs grow, apparently.' He clapped his hand over his mouth. 'Oops, that was meant to be classified information! Don't tell Rosita I told you.'

Cleo adjusted the tortilla chips so that the triangle was equilateral. 'What about the last bit; the wasp nest?'

Ryan shook his head. 'I know we've been through some pretty death-defying situations together but I draw the line at sticking my hand into a wasp nest! Even if the

Holy Grail *and* next week's lottery numbers are hidden in there.'

Cleo laughed. 'I'm sure Mountain Star didn't hide the truth in an *actual* wasp nest. It would be too risky. The nest could break or rot or get eaten . . .' She sighed. 'But I've no idea what else she could have meant.' She began to gather up her notes. 'Let's start by having a good look at those giant hearthstones.' It didn't seem like much to go on, but it was all they had. Maybe when they got there *something* would turn up that would lead to Morning Star's 'truth'. Cleo looked out of the window. Dusk was already gathering. 'We'll go first thing tomorrow morning.'

Ryan and Cleo set out for the gods' hearthstones straight after breakfast.

They wandered around the triangle of giant boulders looking for inspiration. A big shiny arrow with THIS WAY TO THE TRUTH carved in metre-high capital letters would have been just the thing, Ryan thought.

Cleo paced up and down reciting Morning Star's message over and over – *follow the white road past the stones of creation to the wasp nest* – as if it were a magic spell that could conjure the answer out of thin air.

Even when they found a wasp nest – a smooth grey sack hanging from a tree with lacy leaves – it didn't help. It was just a wasp nest. Vicious-looking red and black wasps swarmed busily around the opening. Even Shadow decided to leave them alone.

Cleo dropped to her knees and began rooting among the

dead leaves. Don't just stand there!' she grumbled. 'Come and help.'

'Help *what*?' Ryan asked.

'Look for the white road, of course.' Cleo pushed Shadow's snout out of her face. He thought she was foraging for ants and was joining in with gusto. 'Mountain Star says the *sacbe* goes past the stones. If we're in the right place it must be buried under all this leaf litter. Look for any sign of chalky stone . . .'

Ryan took a few steps. 'Like this, you mean?'

Cleo ran to his side, looked down and then frowned up at him. 'Why didn't you mention this before?'

'I only just remembered. I saw these bits of white stone under the leaves after I bumped into Rosita when she was collecting herbs. I was looking for ants.'

'This must be the *sacbe*!' Cleo breathed. 'We're back on track. If we follow this road past the stones it'll take us to the wasp nest . . .'

Following the white road was easier said than done. It kept disappearing under roots and vines and clumps of thick, sharp grass. Here and there, the trail broke off completely and they had to search for the next white stone. Ryan stopped and took the compass he still carried around from his old Cub Scout days from his backpack. They were in dense jungle now and only tiny shreds of blue sky were visible through the tree canopy. They were heading due east. Without the compass it would be easy to wander in circles for days. No wonder that the White Finder Tree – with its North-pointing lodestone – had been such a precious object.

He slapped a mosquito from his ear and wished he'd

thought to wear a hat. Another homed in on his neck. Or full body armour.

Cleo handed him a bottle of insect spray from her bum bag. 'This is *hopeless*,' she fumed. 'We don't even know that this is the right road. We don't know what we're looking for. We'll never find the White Finder Tree. We'll have to go back to London. And Mum will be unbearable if she's stuck at the British Museum doing paperwork. That's if she doesn't lose her job or get arrested for stealing the jade mask or both.' She kicked a fallen branch, her boot shattering the rotten wood. 'This is all my fault. I wish I'd never seen that bit about the jewelled White Finder Tree on the sarcophagus.'

Ryan was starting to agree. He'd lost track of how far they'd walked. He looked around for a sturdy tree, checked it wasn't booby-trapped with thorns, ants, wasps or other jungle hazards and climbed up to get his bearings.

He swung up onto the highest branch and looked out over the treetops bouncing in the breeze. Looking back towards Calakmul the top of the pyramid rose up like a sheared-off mountain peak. Was anyone up there now, he wondered, looking out, just as he and Cleo had done after their tomb raid? He remembered the first light flooding the sky, the sun glinting on a dome hidden in the trees. 'If we keep going east,' he called down, 'we should come to that tower we saw from the pyramid.'

Cleo didn't reply. He scrambled down and found her fighting through the trees. 'Where are you going?' he shouted.

Cleo wiped sweat from her face with her scarf. 'The tower . . .' she panted. '*Sun rise . . . wasp . . . east . . . it all fits . . .* that's where we've got to go!'

Ryan pulled her back. 'One, if you're trying to go east, that's the wrong way. That's south. Two, any chance of a clue as to you're talking about?'

'That tower we saw . . . it must have been an observatory . . .' Cleo paused to tear a sap-covered vine out of the path. '. . . where astronomers would go to study the movements of the planets.' She attacked a swathe of bushes. 'Sky watching was really important to the Maya. They used the celestial cycles to measure time and decide the dates of rituals and battles . . .'

'Am I missing something?' Ryan asked. 'What's that got to do with a wasp nest?' He leaped back. Cleo was swinging a stick like a scythe and it was getting far too close to his knees for comfort.

'One of the most important planets was Venus. It was known by many names, but one was *Xux Ek,* the Wasp Star.' Cleo kept slashing at the undergrowth as she explained. 'The Wasp Nest would be a perfect name for an observatory where they studied Venus, especially one that was located to the east. *Wasp Star* was what they called Venus when it was in its morning phase, appearing above the *eastern* horizon before dawn.'

Ryan held aside a switch of whippy brambles for her. 'Why did they call Venus the Wasp Star?' He could almost see the sci-fi film playing before his eyes; a planet inhabited by giant wasp-like aliens, planning to take over the universe with their evil insect powers . . .

Cleo ducked under his arm. 'When the Sky Watchers plotted the movements of the planet Venus from one night to the next, they thought it looked like a wasp dancing in front of her nest.'

Ryan liked his version better. But he agreed that the Wasp

170

Nest seemed as good a name as any for a tower for observing the Wasp Star. And it was the only idea they had. He checked the compass again and they pushed on in silence.

The underbrush was so dense that they didn't see the tower until they were almost on top of it.

22

SKULL

THE TOWER'S CURVED walls were smothered beneath a thick green tapestry of moss and fern and creeper. It was like an illustration from an old fairy tale. Except, Ryan thought, that *Sleeping Beauty*'s palace had only been overgrown for a hundred years. The Wasp Nest had drowsed under a sleeping spell for over a thousand.

He helped Cleo squeeze in through a gap and they clambered over mounds of rubble and chunks of stone. Ryan hardly dared to breathe in case the tower crumbled to dust. It felt as if the only thing that held it up was the living scaffolding of root and vine. The green gloom was sliced with stripes of light from high windows as tall and narrow as arrow slits.

Birds gurgled and hooted from roosts under the spiral-shaped dome. Lizards flitted across the walls. Even though he knew that the Wasp Nest was only a name, Ryan couldn't help straining his ears for angry buzzing. He'd seen pictures of supersized mutant Japanese hornets on the internet. One sting could kill you. They'd started invading other countries too. He just hoped they hadn't made it to Mexico.

Cleo grabbed a stick and started poking at the fallen stonework. 'Come on, start looking. Watch out for scorpions, though.'

'If it's not a dumb question,' Ryan asked, 'what exactly are we looking *for*?'

Cleo's expression suggested that it was, most definitely, a dumb question. 'The truth, of course.'

'What does the truth look like?'

Cleo jabbed her stick at a broken lintel. A cloud of dust swirled up and glimmered in a shaft of light. 'We'll know it when we see it. Look for a plaque or a *stela*; anything with writing on. Mountain Star's "truth" about Jaguar Paw's death must be here somewhere.'

The air hung heavy and still. Cleo darted about, rooting into crannies and crevices. Ryan drifted. He couldn't help feeling that it was hopeless; they were looking for a truth-shaped needle in a massive haystack. *The story of my life,* he thought. The search for Dad had been hopeless too. Mum had been fooling herself. It seemed obvious now that Miguel hadn't really seen Dad at all. He'd just wanted the money so that he could leave the Red Wolves. Dad must have been dead all along, probably killed the day he went missing six years ago. Ryan closed his eyes, gulped down a lungful of warm dust and forced himself to back away from the edge of the dark, gaping void inside. *Focus on something else,* he told himself. *Help Cleo find this truth she's after. Help Roberto pay for his son's treatment* . . .

Ryan opened his eyes and ran his hand over the wall. A row of raised round grapefruit-sized decorations had been carved into the stone about a metre from the ground. They weren't *exactly* round, though, he noticed, as his fingers met bumps and hollows. He looked more closely. The *grapefruits* had teeth and noses and eyes. They were human skulls.

Cleo scrambled over to see what he was looking at. 'These must be prisoners captured in battle by the armies of Calakmul,' she said. 'Their heads were chopped off and then the sculptor would have carved these portraits of their skulls as a war record.'

Ryan shuddered. *Brilliant!* he thought. *Just what I needed to take my mind off Dad being killed by his kidnappers.* The features had eroded over time, but it was still possible to see that each skull was an individual. They were all carved in profile, as if gazing at the same point in the distance. 'I thought Venus was the goddess of *love*, not mass slaughter.'

'That's in the Greek and Roman tradition. For the Maya, Venus was associated with war. Battles were timed to take place at certain points in the Wasp Star's journey across the sky.' Cleo waved her stick up at the tall windows. 'Those openings are especially aligned for observing Venus. That's why the battles were known as *Star Wars.* Although,' she added. 'Venus is a planet, of course. Technically, they should be *Planet Wars.*'

'*Planet Wars?*' Ryan repeated. 'No, that just doesn't have the same ring to it.' He began humming the theme from *Star*

174

Wars. Cleo took no notice. She had to be the only person he knew who'd never seen a *Star Wars* film. 'We seriously need to have a movie marathon sometime soon,' he said.

Cleo rolled her eyes. 'We're meant to be looking for the *truth*, remember?'

Ryan did his best. He pictured Mountain Star kneeling to scratch her secret message on the wall of her cell. *What was she trying to tell us? And why did she make it so difficult to find?* As he thought, he stared at the wall. The row of skulls blurred into circular blobs. They reminded him of something. *A row of circles . . .*

He grabbed his backpack and pulled out the rubbing from Mountain Star's cell. He studied the row of little circles beneath the glyphs. *Yes, it was as he remembered!* One of them had a tiny line above it, as if marking it out from the others. He counted the circles. There were fifty-three. Then he counted the skulls. *Eighty-six.* 'Drat!' he muttered. He'd really thought he was on to something.

Cleo looked up from investigating a shattered stone column. 'What are you doing?'

'I just had this stupid idea that each of these circles on Mountain Star's message could stand for one of the skulls.' Ryan showed her the rubbing. 'See how the thirteenth circle seems to be marked? I thought something could be hidden on the thirteenth skull. But it doesn't work. There are far more skulls than there are circles.'

Cleo ran to the start of the row of skulls and began to count. 'It doesn't matter that there are too many,' she said, breaking off as she reached ten. 'They would have added a new crop of skulls after every battle. Maybe there *were* only fifty-three in Mountain Star's time.'

'So my theory might be right!' Ryan joined the count, their voices growing louder and louder as they chanted, '. . . eleven, twelve, *thirteen* . . .' Heavy jawbone, deep eye sockets and sloping forehead; the thirteenth captive looked quite a bruiser. *How did he die?* Ryan pushed the question out of his mind. He brushed his fingers over the stone. His other hand automatically reached for his St Christopher medal. Then he touched the scarab beetle amulet and the Chinese lucky coins that hung next to it. 'Unlucky thirteen.'

'Actually, the Maya saw thirteen as lucky,' Cleo said. 'It was the number of the heavens . . .'

'It wasn't for this guy!' Ryan felt round the edge of the carving. 'I think there's a join here!'

Cleo leaned in so close that her ear brushed against his face. She wiped dust from the stone with her scarf. 'Yes, you're right. There's a hairline crack . . .'

Ryan dug in his backpack. Cleo rummaged in her tool belt. Both pulled out their trowels at the same moment. Ryan laughed. 'Snap!'

'After you!' Cleo said. 'It was your idea.'

Ryan inserted the tip of the trowel into the join, but it immediately met solid stone. It wouldn't go in more than the depth of the pinch of grime it had dislodged. Cleo inserted her trowel a little lower and jiggled it impatiently. Suddenly both trowel blades slid in. The skull stone popped out and dropped onto the ground between their feet.

Ryan punched the air.

Cleo clapped her hands. 'The truth awaits!'

Then they both whisked round in terror as the tower erupted in a pandemonium of noise and movement.

Cleo's thoughts whizzed about like atoms in a particle accelerator. *Someone's followed us! It's Sofia! She's with the Red Wolves!*

But as she glanced around, she realised that they weren't being ambushed by heavily armed gangsters. A troupe of young spider monkeys had exploded into the tower, squealing and chattering as they skittered up the walls and swung from creepers like hyperactive trapeze artists.

Ryan laughed. 'Oh no! The attack of the killer spider monkeys!'

Cleo smiled but her heart was still beating as if a hummingbird were trapped in her ribcage. 'I had a feeling someone was following us.'

Ryan looked up at the cute pink face of a small monkey hanging by its tail. 'Yep. These guys are smart. They've tracked us down!'

'*Something* must have spooked them,' Cleo pointed out. 'Or *someone!*'

Ryan shrugged. 'Probably just Shadow.'

But Cleo knew that Shadow was asleep in a pile of leaves. She ran to the entrance and looked out. There was no one there. But in jungle this dense, an entire army could be hiding two metres away and remain invisible. She returned to Ryan's side. 'Hurry up,' he grumbled. 'Or I'll find the truth without you.' Using his trowel he reached inside the gap in the stone, which had been left by the thirteenth skull.

Cleo took off her scarf and held it out to catch anything that fell.

Ryan scooped. A shower of leaves and dead ants tumbled out. Then came crumbly fragments like pale brown confetti.

Oh no, Cleo thought. *It's paper. It's rotted to pulp in the humid air.* But there was something else too. A collection of round flat objects clattered into the scarf.

Ryan picked one up and turned it over. 'It's those fossilised crisps again.'

'Pieces of spiny oyster shell,' Cleo murmured.

Ryan sat back on his heels. 'They're exactly the same as the ones we found in Radiant Turtle's sippy cup.'

Cleo looked closer. It was true. The pieces of shell had been drilled with holes to thread them on to a necklace. But there was one big difference. These shells were covered with row upon row of tiny glyphs.

Ryan counted the shells. 'Twenty two,' he said.

Cleo leaned back against the wall of skulls. 'The same number as the tally Mountain Star scratched on the wall of the prison.'

'Could be a coincidence?' Ryan flopped down next to her and took a bottle of water from his backpack.

Cleo didn't believe in coincidences. It seemed Ryan agreed with her this time. 'No,' he said, answering his own question as he passed her the water bottle. 'I think Mountain Star was wearing this necklace when she was taken prisoner.'

Cleo nodded. 'It was the only thing she had to write on.'

'She must have smuggled the shells out somehow . . .'

They sat for a long while, both contemplating the same question. *What happened on the twenty-third day?* It was Ryan who broke the silence at last. 'If these shells are from the same necklace as the ones in the cup from the tomb of the Unknown Lady and Child, does that mean . . .'

178

Cleo finished the thought for him. 'The Unknown Lady was Mountain Star! I'm sure of it. She must have been wearing what was left of the spiny oyster necklace when she was buried with Radiant Turtle. The shells probably fell off into the cup when the bodies were moved to the museum.' She ran her fingers through the discs of shell. They were rough and dull with age now, but when Mountain Star wore them they would have been polished to a rich red sheen.

'Do you think she was his mum?' Ryan asked quietly.

It made sense, Cleo thought as she drank from the bottle of water. If Mountain Star was Radiant Turtle's mother, that made her Jaguar Paw's wife. It would explain why she'd been buried in a chamber next to the king's tomb. Although, Cleo reasoned, she was probably only a minor wife, as it was not an elaborate burial. Had little Radiant Turtle been locked up in the prison with her? Why had King Jaguar Paw imprisoned his own wife and son? Had they both been sacrificed to bring Jaguar Paw back from the dead? Cleo stared down at the broken necklace. *This is what Mountain Star wanted us to find. The truth about Jaguar Paw's death is locked up in these tiny glyphs. All I have to do now is decipher them.*

Even the thought of it was exhausting.

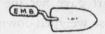

The return trek was much easier. They simply followed the trail they'd hacked and trampled on their way to the Wasp Nest. Even so, by the time they approached camp they were hot, tired and thirsty. Ryan could almost feel the cold can of Coke in his hand. It was almost lunchtime. A plateful of Rosita's chicken stew was just what he needed.

'Looks like we're just in time,' he said as they entered the clearing. Everyone was sitting around a big table under the gazebo.

Cleo raised her eyebrows. 'It's a bit early for lunch.'

'I'm not complaining!' Ryan quickened his step. Cleo could be such a stickler for routine at times!

'Something's wrong,' Cleo murmured. 'It's too quiet.'

Suddenly Ryan realised she was right. The usual lunchtime chatter and clatter was missing. There was a sort of anxious hush, like a doctor's waiting room. And why was Police Chief Garcia standing at the end of the table?

'Ah, there you are,' Pete McNeil called, turning in his chair. A shaft of sunlight shone through a gap in the palm thatch, glinting on his glasses. 'Come and sit down. Chief Garcia needs to ask us some questions . . .'

'What's going on?' Ryan looked from face to face. Lydia and Pete McNeil, Alex, Max, Roberto, Sofia, Rosita, Luis and the whole team of workmen and diggers. Mum was there too. She answered him with a shake of the head that could have meant *don't ask* or *don't worry* or both.

Chief Garcia squeezed back into her chair. Already quite short and round, the bulky bulletproof vest she wore over her short-sleeved shirt gave her the look of a navy blue armadillo. She was also weighed down by a thick black belt, which bristled with even more gadgets than Cleo's bum bag: a serious-looking gun, a radio, a big bunch of keys, handcuffs . . .

There was a sudden commotion as a small crowd of reporters who'd been hanging around ever since the White Finder Tree story leaked out, appeared as if from nowhere, and began shouting questions at the police chief. Three

180

officers jumped out from police cars parked near the jeep and shooed them away.

Chief Garcia cleared her throat. 'Another important artefact has gone missing.'

23

EAR SPOOL

ANOTHER MISSING ARTEFACT?

Guilt lurched through Ryan's body like a tremor from an earthquake.

This had to be about the sippy cup. He began to run through his defence. *I didn't mean to take it. It was just digging into my shoulder. We were going to hand it in.* But then he'd have to explain to the police that they'd been hiding in the Tomb of the Unknown Lady and Child in the middle of the night. Roberto knew already, of course. But he'd let them off with a stiff health and safety lecture, since no harm had been done. Ryan had a feeling Chief Garcia would be a lot less understanding. He was so busy figuring out how he was going to talk his way out of this one, that he almost missed Roberto Chan's words. 'A very important jade ear spool has been stolen from the safe in my trailer.'

An ear spool? Ryan was so relieved that he laughed out loud. Of course it wasn't about the cup! Nobody could know it had gone missing because nobody knew it was in the tomb in the first place.

Sofia Proufork, Chief Garcia, Lydia McNeil and Cleo all freeze-dried him with disapproving looks. Apparently there was nothing funny about ear spools. 'It's a form of body adornment,' Cleo explained under her breath. 'Worn in the ear. Often in the shape of a flower or trumpet.'

'This ear spool came from the jaguar tomb,' Roberto went on. 'It's particularly valuable, as it is very large and is inscribed with a ring of glyphs.' He scrubbed his hands over his face. His skin looked dingy now, as if he'd rubbed away the polish, and there were dark circles under his eyes. Ryan felt a spike of anger. Roberto Chan had enough on his plate, with Alejandro being in hospital. Whoever kept nicking things from this dig should go and do their looting somewhere else and give the man a break.

Roberto turned to Sofia Proufork. 'In fact, it is the ear spool that I showed you the other day.'

Sofia blinked at him through her glasses. 'Ah yes, a very fine piece.'

Ryan felt Cleo stamp on his foot under the table. He stamped back. There'd been no need for the reminder; he hadn't forgotten Cleo's conversation with Roberto yesterday. Roberto had shown Sofia some writing on an ear spool and she'd made a mistake in reading it. It had got Cleo even more convinced that Sofia was an imposter. Ryan watched Sofia's face for signs that she was a Red Wolves gang leader plotting her next move, but he just couldn't believe it. She looked the same as ever, with her podgy cheeks and big teeth, smiling to herself like a slightly smug squirrel.

'Thank you, Mr Chan.' Chief Garcia rearranged some papers on the table. 'Now, you said that the ear spool was taken yesterday afternoon?'

Roberto nodded. 'It was there when I checked at lunchtime yesterday, but it had gone when I looked in the safe first thing this morning. It couldn't have been taken during the night. I was in the trailer.'

'Me too,' Max put in. 'I share that trailer with Roberto. I'd have heard anyone break in.' He glanced around the assembled group. He was obviously still feeling a bit sensitive about the trouble he'd caused by muddling the sarcophagus photographs with the *violaceous trogon*.

'I need to know where everyone was yesterday, during the . . . er . . .' Chief Garcia reached for the word in English. Roberto said something to her in Spanish. 'Ah yes, thank you during the *critical time period*.'

Alex Shawcross raised her hand as if she was at school. 'I went into Xjupil with Julie yesterday.'

Mum confirmed with a slight roll of the eyes. 'That's right. We were there for *hours*.' She'd complained to Ryan last night that Alex had insisted on so much shopping that she had barely had a moment to herself to sound out any locals about their Red Wolves connections. Ryan had been relieved. If Mum was going to go round town asking dangerous questions he wanted to be with her.

'There's a super butcher in the market where you can buy tripe and whole pig heads,' Alex said. 'I do think offal's under-rated, don't you?'

Chief Garcia didn't look very interested in meat products. 'Miss . . . er . . . Proufork. How about you?'

Sofia sighed. 'Oh, I've been laid up with a stinker of a migraine. *Absolute nightmare!* I've been lying in the dark in my trailer for the last twenty-four hours.' She massaged her temples. As her chunky glasses flipped up to her forehead for a moment Ryan was hit by the same flicker of familiarity he'd felt in the café in Xpujil. Had he met her somewhere before? He didn't usually forget a face. 'Alex can vouch for me,' Sofia went on. 'I asked her to pick up some painkillers in town for me.'

'That's right. She did.' Alex smiled at Sofia. 'I was rather tempted to buy a pig head and bring it back for Rosita to cook up for you. Brain broth is a jolly good *pick-me-up* when you're feeling a bit peaky. But Julie wouldn't let me.'

Mum laughed. 'That pig head stank. I didn't fancy an hour's drive home with it in the jeep!'

'Anyway,' Sofia told Chief Garcia, 'anyone who's ever suffered migraines like mine would know I couldn't have left my trailer . . .'

Ryan and Cleo exchanged glances. Should they tell the police chief their suspicions about Sofia being an undercover tomb robber? Ryan shook his head. It was best to hold off for now. For a start, what evidence did they have against her? 1) She might not be as good at reading Mayan glyphs as she was hyped up to be. That wasn't a crime. 2) She *might* have met a man from The Red Wolves gang in a bar in Xpujil the other day. Then again, it was quite possible that she hadn't. Someone else could have opened the door to La Luna, letting the sound of folk music spill out into the street, just before

Sofia showed up at the cafe. *And,* Ryan thought, *it raises the awkward question of how I happened to recognise Wolf Head as a gang member.* Blowing up a barn with a distress flare was not the sort of episode you wanted to share with the police, even if the barn in question was stuffed with drugs and jaguar furs . . .

Pete McNeil wiped his glasses with a paper napkin. 'As for Lydia and me, we spent yesterday afternoon having a meeting with Roberto in our trailer, discussing plans for preserving the wall paintings in the tomb.'

The police chief pointed at Cleo and Ryan. 'What about you two?'

Cleo sat to attention. 'We were in Ryan's trailer.'

'Doing what?' Chief Garcia asked.

Ryan knew he had to jump in before Cleo launched into one of her terrible cover stories, or even worse, tried to tell the truth; *deciphering the message from the prison cell, which we discovered because of the writing on the cup that Ryan accidentally stole on our midnight tomb raid* . . . 'Oh you know,' he said casually. 'Just chilling.'

'That's right,' Cleo said, in a bright voice. 'It did go a bit *chilly* yesterday. That's why we stayed inside.'

Sofia smiled. 'You weren't in the trailer *all* afternoon. I saw you walking back from somewhere at around two. You missed lunch.'

Ryan tried to read Sofia's expression behind those clunky glasses. *Was that just an innocent comment or is she trying to land us in trouble? But if Sofia really wanted to make us look suspicious,* he figured, *she could tell everyone that she saw us enter the tomb the other night. Come to think of it, why hasn't she? Is it because she doesn't want anyone asking questions about why she was sneaking about up there too?* It was all too confusing! But this was definitely not the moment to reveal that they'd been out looking for Mountain Star's name. 'Oh yeah, I forgot, we just went for a quick walk.' Ryan's words blurted out too fast. They sounded about as convincing as *the dog ate my homework*.

It was Rosita who came to the rescue. 'I asked Ryan and Cleo to go pick some wild herbs for me.' She turned to Chief Garcia. 'I can tell you what I was doing yesterday afternoon. Cooking! And that is what I should be doing right now. Lunch is late. I have hungry people to feed.' With that she bustled off to the kitchen. Ryan sent her a silent thank you for inventing a cover story for them.

'So you don't know *anything* about the missing item?' Chief Garcia asked.

'Of course not,' Ryan and Cleo chorused. It was true. They didn't have a clue about what had happened to the ear spool. Of course, there was the issue of Radiant Turtle's sippy cup. And then there were the shells from the Wasp Nest. They hadn't declared those yet. But for now, by unspoken agreement, they decided to keep their findings to themselves. If Cleo was right and Mountain Star's shell necklace contained the truth about Jaguar Paw's death and the White Finder Tree, they couldn't risk having it taken away before they'd unlocked its secrets.

Chief Garcia delivered her parting words over her shoulder as she headed back to her car. 'I no longer think that the Red Wolves are involved in these thefts. I'm now certain that this is an inside job. We are dealing with a very clever thief here.' Her hand slid to her gun. 'But they will not get away with it for ever!'

Ryan couldn't help noticing that the police chief was looking directly at Cleo's mum as she spoke. Had she received another anonymous tip-off that Lydia McNeil had stolen the ear spool as well as the jade mask?

24

NECKLACE

CLEO UNWRAPPED THE twenty-two discs of spiny oyster shell from her scarf and arranged them on the altar stone in the Lizard Lounge. The lizards watched curiously from the edge of the stone. She was armed with dictionaries, charts, notebooks and a powerful magnifying glass, but even so, the task of deciphering the filigree of tiny glyphs that covered the shells was a daunting one. She let the magnifying glass drop. 'I don't even know where to start.'

Ryan settled against a comfortable moss-cushioned stone that he'd picked out as his own personal armchair. He took the magnifying glass and examined the nearest shell. He peered at a second and a third. 'Elementary, my dear

189

Watson! We start at the beginning,'

Elementary? That, Cleo thought, was easy for Ryan to say. He wasn't the one who had to do the deciphering! And she still hadn't admitted that she wasn't quite such a genius at ancient Mayan as he took her for. Cleo frowned at Ryan's eye, which loomed huge and blurry through the magnifying lens. 'That's precisely the problem,' she pointed out. 'The beginning could be any one of these shells.'

'Unless,' Ryan said, 'they happen to be ordered by date.'

Cleo swiped the magnifying glass and chose a shell at random. Sure enough, the first line started with *Six Muluc*, the day name and number in the *Tzolkin* calendar, followed by *Eighteen Cumku,* the month name and number in the *Haab* calendar, and the Long Count date. She examined another. That was headed with the date too. Ryan was now reclining against the cushion of moss again, sunlight dappling his face. 'How did you know?' she demanded.

Ryan slowly pushed up on his elbows. 'You keep telling me how the Maya were obsessed with time and calendars and stuff. I figured that no self-respecting scribe would write a message without putting the date on. So I had a quick look at the first line on each shell. They all have those little number bars and dots in them . . .'

Cleo was furious with herself. It was so obvious! Why hadn't she thought of looking for dates? Her cognitive functions were clearly not firing at full capacity. She wished Ryan wouldn't look quite so smug about it though. She was quite sure that gloating was not best practice for being a good friend. She scooped up all the age-crusted shells, identified the date on each one and sorted them into chronological order. At last all twenty-two were lined up along the rock.

'They start from 1st March, 697,' she told Ryan. 'Then there's one every day until 22nd March.'

Ryan puffed out a breath. 'That's one day before Mountain Star wrote the message on the wall of the cell.'

Cleo gazed down at the array. 'It's also one day *after* the date on the jaguar sarcophagus. That was March 21st.' She thought for a moment, realising the significance of the date. 'March 21st is the Spring Equinox. It's when night and day are of equal length. It would have been an auspicious day for rituals . . . Maybe that was the date that the jaguar was buried.'

'I don't think it was an auspicious day for Mountain Star.' Ryan picked up the twenty-second shell and weighed it in his palm as if it might actually be heavy with doom. 'Whatever happened, she fell silent one day later.'

Cleo thought of Mountain Star in her prison cell. Etching the tiny glyphs into the hard surface of the shell would have been hard work. What tool had she found to trace such intricate lines? The answer came to her in a flash. *It must have been a bloodletter!* A high status woman like Mountain Star – assuming she was Jaguar Paw's wife – would have owned a personalised lancet made of razor-sharp obsidian. It would probably have been one of the few possessions she was allowed to keep with her, so that she could perform her ritual offerings to the gods. Cleo looked through the magnifying glass again. The scratched symbols had been inked like a tattoo, with a coffee brown substance. Had Mountain Star managed to find some ink? Or had she stained the glyphs with her own blood?

Cleo decided not to share this thought with Ryan.

She picked up her notebook and got to work deciphering

the first shell. Meanwhile, Ryan copied out larger versions of the miniscule glyphs on the next shell so that they'd be easier for Cleo to see. 'Just call me the Human Microscope,' he laughed.

They worked in silence for several hours. At last Cleo sat up and stretched. 'Listen to what I've got so far. *I, Lady Mountain Star, eldest daughter of King Jaguar Paw, born in the year 683 . . .*'

Ryan's eyes widened. '*Daughter* of Jaguar Paw? Not wife? So she wasn't Radiant Turtle's mother, she was his big sister. And if she was born in 683 she was only fourteen when she wrote this.'

The same age as me, Cleo thought. Somehow, knowing that Mountain Star had been so young transformed her from a name into a real person. Her words spoke louder, as if the centuries between them had telescoped to days. *Stop being so sentimental*, Cleo told herself. *Just focus on the facts.* She went back to reading from her notes. '*I, Mountain, Star, Scribe and Sky Watcher of The Kingdom of the Snake . . .*'

'Wow, she was a sky watcher as well as a scribe?' Ryan interrupted. 'Wasn't that a man's job too?'

Cleo nodded. That was another thing that made Mountain Star so real. No doubt the royal family expected girls to sit around looking decorative, and then married them off to some doddery old lord from a neighbouring kingdom. But Mountain Star was determined to study instead. Perhaps that's what had landed her in prison. 'She obviously refused to conform to the limited roles open to women in a patriarchal society.'

Cleo noticed Ryan's eyebrows twitch. Perhaps he wasn't familiar with the word patriarchal. 'A society in which men hold all the power,' she explained.

Ryan grinned. 'Yeah, I guessed that. It sounds like Mountain Star was a bit of a rebel. Not to mention a brainbox. You two would have been BFFs.'

'BFF?' Cleo asked.

'*Best Friends Forever.*'

Cleo pretended to take no notice, but secretly she was pleased. Ryan thought she would make a good BFF! All her efforts to be a better friend must be working ... 'Listen to this,' she said. *'I am held prisoner at the order of Lady Six Sky. I fear I may not live to tell my story so I will write it here. The guards will not notice that one shell disappears from my necklace each day.'*

'This is amazing!' Ryan said. 'We were right about it being her necklace. So how did she smuggle them out?' He had now shuffled over to Cleo's side and was leaning in to read her translation. She batted him away with her notebook. 'I can't read with your head in the way,' she laughed. *'When my faithful servant, Seven Rabbit, visits to bring me food each day, I will give the shells to her to take away in the empty basket and hide in the Wasp Nest.'*

'Go on!' Ryan said. 'What next?'

'That's as far as I've got,' Cleo sighed. It had taken her hours to decipher just a few lines. It would take her weeks to decipher the full story. And they didn't have weeks. In fact, they barely even had days. Sir Charles had been on the phone to Mum again last night and demanded she be back in London by the end of the week. 'I think we're going to have to tell my parents what we've found,' she said. 'Mum might be able to decipher these shells in time ...'

'It'll mean owning up to sneaking into the tomb,' Ryan

said. 'I'm not too worried about *my* Mum finding out. She'd probably have done the same herself. But *your* Mum . . .'

Cleo knew what he meant. Mum was always strict about correct procedure. They had broken all the rules in the book by entering the tomb at night. They'd also removed Radiant Turtle's cup from the tomb without permission. That wasn't going to look good with the jade mask and ear spool still missing. 'Mum will hit the roof,' she said. 'But it'll be worth it if it leads us to the White Finder Tree.'

Cleo took a deep breath and pushed open the trailer door.

Mum was sitting at the desk in the small office. Dad was standing behind her. Both were peering at something on the computer screen.

Cleo cleared her throat. 'There's something I need to tell you . . .'

Dad looked round. The words withered on Cleo's tongue. He was attempting a smile but failing to pull it off. Mum slammed her hands down on the desk, scooted back and sprang up. *She's found out already! Sofia must have told her we crept into the tomb!* Cleo braced herself for the storm. But Mum torpedoed right past without even noticing she was there.

Cleo glanced at Dad and then at the computer screen. It showed an email message from Sir Charles Peacocke.

Dear Lidya, I have heard from Sofia Proufork that another important artefact has unaccountably disappeared from the Calakmul site and that the local police suspect that you are involved. This is most distressing. I must now insist that you return to London immediately before the police start to make arrests and you drag the Department of Museums and Culture into further scandal. When I return from holiday we need a serious discussion about your future career with the department . . .

'I've booked flights for Saturday,' Dad said quietly.

'*Saturday!*' Cleo echoed. 'But that's the day after tomorrow!'

'I'm going to start packing,' Mum yelled from the other end of the trailer. The bedroom door slammed. The trailer shook.

'How dare Sofia tell Sir Charles that the police suspect Mum!' Cleo fumed. 'All they had was an anonymous tip-off. There's no evidence. I wouldn't be surprised if it was Sofia who rang in the information herself.'

Dad placed a hand on Cleo's arm. 'Don't be silly, love. Chief Garcia told me the caller was a man and he was Mexican. Don't worry. Sir Charles will soon realise that Sofia just got the wrong end of the stick. Now, why don't I make us all a nice cup of tea.' But Cleo *was* worried. She knew Dad was too, despite his rallying words. The bald patch on the back of his head seemed to have grown overnight. And he was whistling *Don't Worry, Be Happy!* as he put the kettle on. That was Dad's most cheerful tune; the one he saved for the direst of situations.

Mum was about to lose her job and be arrested as a tomb robber.

This was serious; too serious for cups of tea.

There was only one way out of this; to find the White Finder Tree and prove that Mum hadn't either made it up, or stolen it herself; along with the jade mask and ear spool. It would also prove that Sofia was an imposter who couldn't read Mayan. She'd been wrong about the White Finder Tree and was probably only in Calakmul to help the Red Wolves steal artefacts from the jaguar tomb. But it all depended on deciphering Morning Star's shells. Cleo turned and flew down the trailer steps in a single leap. Ryan would know what to do.

She found him sitting on a bench next to the campfire, stirring a big pot of corn and black-eyed pea stew. Shadow was curled up at his feet. 'It's worse than we thought,' Cleo panted. 'We've only got two days. And Mum's in no state to help.'

Ryan scooted over to make space on the bench. 'OK. What's Plan B?'

'I was hoping *you'd* have one.'

Ryan nibbled a piece of corn from the wooden spoon. 'We order another Mayan epigrapher online, express delivery?'

Cleo had an urge to grab the spoon and hit him over the head with it. She fought it back, tears pricking at her eyes. *That's not what a real friend would do.*

Ryan looked down into the stew. 'I'm sorry,' he said. 'I know it's not funny.' He looked up at the sound of a trailer door opening and closing. Sofia K. Proufork was heading for the dining area under the trees. He grimaced. 'What about asking . . .'

'No way!' Cleo hissed. 'In case you've forgotten, Sofia was seen meeting with a known member of a major tomb-robbing gang. If she reads the shells and finds out where the White Finder Tree is hidden, it'll be in the hands of the Red Wolves and smuggled out of the country in no time.'

'We didn't actually *see* the meeting,' Ryan pointed out. 'I heard some music that *might* have come from a bar that Sofia *might* have been in at the same time as Wolf Head . . .'

'Keep your voice down!' Cleo whispered. Sofia had settled at a nearby table with a book. Rosita had the radio on loud enough to drown out a brass band, but it was best to be careful.

Ryan gave the stew a stir. 'So what's Plan C?'

Cleo thought for a long moment. 'We could ask Roberto Chan?'

'But he said he's not an expert on reading ancient Mayan?'

'But he might know someone who is . . .'

'Ask me what?'

Cleo's heart almost jumped out of her mouth.

Roberto Chan was standing right behind her.

25

PLAN

CLEO SWUNG ROUND to face Roberto. 'Were you listening to us?'

He held up his hands. 'I came to see how much longer this stew is going to be. *Chulibu'ul* is my favourite and I'm starving. I just heard you say my name.'

Cleo sat back down. Ryan, meanwhile, seemed to have developed a nervous tic. He was jerking his head towards Roberto and winking. Had he got smoke in his eyes, Cleo wondered.

'Oh I give up,' Ryan said. 'I was *trying* to be subtle, but I'll just spell it out. I think we should tell Roberto everything. He might be able to help.'

'Tell me what?' Roberto asked. 'Do you know something about the missing artefacts?'

Ryan's right, Cleo thought. Roberto already knew that they'd crept into the tomb at night to look for the White Finder Tree, after all. But he *didn't* know that they'd taken Radiant Turtle's cup. He wouldn't be pleased about that, but he was their only option.

'You'd better tell me the whole story over lunch,' Roberto said. He and Ryan piled their plates with stew and tacos. Cleo was far too tense to eat. As they sat down, she was relieved to see that Sofia had left. With numerous interruptions from Ryan, she explained how the signature on Radiant Turtle's cup had led them to Mountain Star's prison cell, and then to her oyster shell necklace in the Wasp Nest tower.

'The writing on the shells will tell us the "truth" about how King Jaguar Paw died,' Ryan cut in.

Cleo talked over him. 'And once we know that we can figure out where he's buried, which is the "*final resting place*" where the White Finder Tree is hidden.'

Roberto listened carefully. 'You should have told me about this sooner. But you've done some good work. I really need some positive results to come out of this dig if I'm going to keep my job. Now that the police are involved there are even more rumours going round. Apparently I haven't only faked the Snake Stone, I've also invited gangs of tomb robbers to come and help themselves.' He stabbed beans onto his fork. 'I do know someone who could help decipher the text on the shells. A professor. He's retired now. He's very old, a little . . . you know . . .' Roberto paused, searching for the right word. He tapped his temple.

'Batty?' Ryan offered. 'Off his rocker?'

'Eccentric?' Cleo cut in.

Roberto smiled. '*Eccentric*. That's it. But he is one of the most brilliant Mayan epigraphers in the world.'

'Perfect,' Cleo breathed. 'Can you call and ask if we can see him tomorrow. It's Thursday now. Dad's booked a flight home on Saturday!'

Roberto gave a rueful smile. 'I'm sorry, that's not possible. Professor Wynne lives in Chichén Itzá. It's a six-hour drive. A lot longer by bus. You'd probably have to go via Mérida.'

'Mérida?' Ryan said. 'Isn't that where your son is in hospital? I know how much you miss him. What if you drive up to see him tomorrow? We could hitch a lift with you?'

'*Please!*' Cleo begged.

Roberto took a tortilla and mopped stew from his plate. 'Well, I *was* planning to go soon anyway. It would be a nice surprise for my wife and Alejandro. If we leave early and drive back overnight we could make it back in time for you to get your plane . . .'

If she'd been the hugging type, Cleo would have hugged them both. They had Plan C at last.

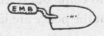

Cleo was awake before dawn for the second morning in a row. She stared up at the mosquito net. The woven mesh was like the iron grid of prison bars.

Plan C had been perfect.

Then Dad had spoiled everything by saying no.

Cleo could still hardly believe it. Dad was usually so easy-going, so ready to stand up for her when Mum was being over-protective. *What if you're delayed and don't get back in time for our flight?* he said. *Sir Charles would be furious. And the longer we stay, the greater the risk that Mum will be arrested.*

At least all was not lost. Julie had agreed that Ryan could go. They were staying on in Mexico for a few more days anyway, and she thought it was a great opportunity for Ryan to visit the world-famous Maya city of Chichén Itzá before they left. Ryan would go with Roberto and take the shells to Professor Wynne.

That almost made it worse. The pain of missing out burned deep and hot, as corrosive as sulphuric acid.

Outside the trailer the forest birds began tuning up for the dawn chorus.

This must be how Mountain Star felt, Cleo fumed. *I bet her father never let her do anything she wanted either. No doubt she had to study writing and astronomy in secret.* Cleo hated Jaguar Paw. She hated everything. She especially hated those birds. Why did they have to sound so excited just because it was another day? What was so great about flying about and eating insects anyway?

If we don't decipher those shells we may never find the White Finder Tree; Mum will always be under suspicion for its disappearance – not to mention the jade mask and ear spool. And we'll never know whether the ancient Maya had a compass that led to the mouth of the Underworld.

More birds joined in, mocking her with their squawks of joy.

Cleo made up her mind.

Mountain Star didn't give in. She stood up for herself. *And so will I . . .*

It was barely light as Ryan padded across the clearing past the silent trailers towards the jeep. He hoisted his backpack a little higher on his shoulder. The precious discs of shell were inside, carefully packed into a small biscuit tin lined with tissue paper.

Still half asleep, his heart grasshopper-jumped with fright when a door behind him opened. A patch of orange light spilled out onto the grass and a hushed voice called his name. 'Ryan! Hey, Ryan!'

Sofia K. Proufork was standing on the steps of her trailer, fully dressed in a denim shirt and brown cord trousers. Her brown hair looked even more lop-sided than usual. What did *she* want? Had she found out about the shells? Was she going to try to trick him into handing them over? 'I heard you were off on a road trip today?' she called.

'Yeah, you know, just wanted to have a look round Chichén Itzá.' Ryan gave a *no-big-deal* shrug, as if he routinely made fourteen-hour round trips to check out historical attractions.

'I don't blame you. It's an awesome sight.' Sofia fluttered her hand as if to flip her hair off her shoulders, even though it barely covered her ears. Then she beckoned to him. 'I thought you might like some provisions for the journey.'

Ryan was taken aback. Why was Sofia being nice as pie all of a sudden? 'Oh, er, thanks,' he said as he climbed the trailer steps, even though Mum had already done him a packed lunch and Rosita had loaded him up with half his bodyweight in empanadas. Alex had also given him some fossilised jaguar poo from the sarcophagus. That was for Roberto to drop off at the lab in Mérida to be tested for hookworm eggs rather than for a lunchtime snack, although you could never be sure with Alex.

'Wait there!' Sofia disappeared into the kitchen. Ryan stood in the doorway and craned his neck to see inside the trailer. He hoped to see a swag bag bulging with looted treasure, including the stolen jade mask and ear spool – or, at the very least, a copy of *Tomb-Robbing for Dummies* on the bookshelf. But there was nothing. If only he could have a nose in the other rooms. 'Can I just use the loo?' he shouted, darting inside the trailer. He locked himself in the bathroom, switched on the light and glanced around.

There were no tomb-breaking tools stuffed down the loo. No Red Wolves gangsters hiding in the shower cubicle.

Ryan peeked into the cupboard above the washbasin. If nothing else, it might hold a clue as to Sofia's mystery medical condition. But there were no oxygen tanks or exotic medicines; only aspirins, soap, toothpaste, Fixodent, cotton wool, deodorant . . . nothing to suggest a rare tropical disease or missing body part. A large flower-patterned bag hanging from a hook caught his eye. It was full of expensive-looking make-up. *Odd,* Ryan thought. *I've never seen Sofia wearing make-up.* He ran the tap for a moment then scuttled out.

Sofia was waiting outside the door, arms folded, looking like she was about to blow a gasket. 'How dare you just barge in like that!'

'Sorry,' Ryan mumbled. 'Couldn't wait.' *This woman has some serious personality issues,* he thought. *She gets up at five in the morning to make me sandwiches, but flips out when I use her bathroom! It's like Jekyll and Hyde. Perhaps the K stands for Krackpot!*

'Yeah, sure, no problem.' Sofia was suddenly doing her friendly act again. 'Here you go. Hope you like peanut butter?' She held up a foil-wrapped package. 'I'll just pop them in your backpack for you.' She patted him on the shoulder. 'I know you're in a hurry. Off you go now. Safe journey.'

'Cheers!' Ryan backed out of the door before she could change her mind and have another meltdown.

They'd been on the road for several hours when Ryan jolted awake.

'Sorry about that!' Roberto gripped the steering wheel as the jeep flew through the air and landed with a clank and a rattle. 'I didn't see those speed bumps . . .'

'Ouch! Aggh!'

The cries came from the back of the jeep. Ryan and Roberto both spun round in their seats. There was a screech of tyres as they almost veered off the road. *There's someone hiding in the back!* Ryan's thoughts scattered like startled birds. Was it Wolf Head intent on revenge? Or Chief Garcia about to arrest him for stealing Radiant Turtle's cup?

26

HELP

WHEN CLEO CRAWLED out from under the seat Ryan didn't know whether to hug her or yell at her. He settled on the yelling option. 'Are you trying to give me a heart attack? I nearly died of fright!'

Cleo sat up, rubbing her head. 'Well, I nearly died of multiple crush injuries.' She wriggled over the seat back into the front. 'Can't you slow down a bit more over those speed bumps? They're outside every village. I've been bashed to bits back there.'

'What are you *doing*?' Ryan demanded.

'Putting my seat belt on.'

'I meant what are you doing *in the jeep*?'

'That's what I want to know too,' Roberto said. 'Your father said you were not allowed to come!'

'I'm sorry but I *had* to come!' Cleo tried to wipe oil from her hands but only succeeded in spreading it over her t-shirt. 'I borrowed Luis's key – he always leaves it on a hook in Rosita's kitchen – and let myself into the jeep before it was light.' She smiled nervously at Roberto. 'I knew I had to stay hidden until we were a few hours down the road, otherwise you'd just turn round and take me back.'

'Ryan! Did you know anything about this?' Roberto demanded.

'I swear I had no idea!' Ryan stared at Cleo in disbelief. 'Your parents are going to freak out!'

Cleo chewed on her bottom lip. Her confidence seemed to be leaking away. 'We hid in the back of a pickup truck in Egypt,' she said. 'All the way to Amarna. And that worked out OK.'

'So you guys make a habit of stowing away in trucks?' Roberto asked. Ryan glanced across at him, expecting his expression to be sterner than ever. But Roberto was actually smiling. He seemed to have grown more cheerful with every mile. He was also wearing a flamingo pink shirt for the occasion. *It must be because he's on his way to see his wife and son,* Ryan supposed. 'Next you will tell me that you've smuggled that anteater in here too!' Roberto joked.

Ryan laughed. 'Rosita is looking after him for me.' He'd left Shadow curled up in a spare hammock sleeping off the effects of another fridge raid. This time he'd knocked over an open bottle of wine and snaffled down half the contents before Mum had caught him at it. Suddenly Ryan realised this was his moment! He might *never* get another chance. He could use the three words of Mayan that Rosita had taught him! '*Kala'an ahchab*,' he said. '*Kala'an ahchab kaan*.'

Roberto laughed so hard he almost ran over a lop-eared cow that had wandered into the road. '*Drunk-anteater-hammock!* Well done!'

Cleo gaped at him in astonishment. 'Since when did you speak Mayan?'

Ryan savoured the moment. 'Oh, just another of my hidden talents!'

Roberto was suddenly serious again. He handed Cleo his satellite phone. 'I'll take you to Chichén Itzá on one condition; you phone your parents and tell them you are safe.'

Cleo made the call. Ryan could hear her mum screaming at the other end. Cleo hung up. 'I'm grounded for a month after this,' she said. 'And I'm not allowed to see you any more. Ever. Not even to talk online. You're a bad influence.'

Ryan didn't know whether to laugh or protest. Cleo was the most stubborn person he'd ever met. He'd have more chance of influencing a tsunami. But Cleo looked really upset so he decided to keep this thought to himself. 'Your mum will calm down when we find the White Finder Tree for her,' he said. He pinned on his very best encouraging smile to hide his doubts; *we've got less than a day and we're not entirely certain that it even exists. So, no pressure there then . . .*

They drove on. Soon they'd left the main highway for country roads with overgrown verges carpeted with tiny yellow flowers. Now and then they trundled through small villages and towns. Ryan gazed out of the window as Yucatán life streamed by; families clearing weeds in the fields, old ladies sitting in the shade of almond trees kneading tortilla dough, boys pedalling yellow tricycles loaded with sacks of cement, old men drinking coffee in roadside taquerias . . .

The smell of frying chicken wafted in through the window. Ryan grabbed his backpack. 'Who wants something to eat? I've got empanadas from Rosita, cheese and ham rolls from mum, and some peanut butter sandwiches Sofia made me this morning.'

'*Sofia* made you sandwiches?' Cleo asked. 'I don't believe it!'

Ryan shrugged. 'She's obviously fallen for my irresistible charm.'

Cleo snorted. 'At five in the morning. You're not *that* charming!'

'Cheers!' But Cleo had a point. It did seem weird. A cold sick feeling trickled into the pit of his stomach. He remembered Sofia placing the pack of sandwiches in his backpack. Had it all been a trick? *Sofia must have reached in and stolen the shells!* Ryan could barely bring himself to look. He forced his hand inside the backpack. He felt the sandwiches wrapped in rustling foil . . . the basket of empanadas . . . the packed lunch Mum had made . . . the Ziploc bag of wormy jaguar poo . . . and then – the Hallelujah Chorus played in his head – the smooth round metal lid of the biscuit tin. He gave it a little shake to be certain. The shells were still inside!

Ryan breathed a sigh of relief. It seemed Sofia really had just been overcome with an attack of niceness. Peanut butter was his favourite too!

Roberto dropped Cleo and Ryan off at the Grand Hacienda hotel and raced away to the hospital in Mérida. Ryan had never heard of anyone *living* in a hotel before, but apparently Professor Wynne had made this his home for the last twenty years.

The *Grand Hacienda* was, indeed, grand; not in a new and shiny way, but with a faded, old-fashioned elegance, surrounded by sweeping lawns dotted with stately trees casting pools of shade. Hummingbirds flitted among flowerbeds of bright, exotic blooms. Elderly customers pottered in and out, while bellboys in white uniforms carried their matching luggage. Ryan looked down at his jeans and trainers. He felt a bit under-dressed. But he was the height of style and good taste compared to Cleo; her hiking trousers were stained with oil from hiding in the back of the jeep, and she'd ripped the sleeve of her baggy black t-shirt. Her white scarf was still dust-smeared from being used to wrap the oyster shells. He reached out and brushed a cobweb from her fringe. She looked like a TV charity appeal for teenagers living rough on the streets.

Cleo didn't care, of course.

She was already whisking through the revolving glass door and marching across the lobby. To Ryan's surprise the receptionist didn't call security, but smiled and directed them to Professor Wynne's suite.

Ryan followed Cleo along a veranda, which looked onto a central courtyard. The clink of cocktail glasses and murmur of refined conversation wafted up from beneath a canopy of scarlet bougainvillea.

Cleo knocked and they entered a room full of dark wooden furniture, the walls cluttered with bookshelves and old photographs. Professor Wynne was reclining on a velvet sofa in the bay window. He was wearing a sort of quilted maroon dressing gown, a garment that Ryan knew from old films was called a smoking jacket. He'd had no idea that they actually existed in real life.

'Come on in,' Professor Wynne said, without looking up from his book. 'Don't lurk. I can't abide lurkers.'

Ryan stared at a large grey-green lizard perched on the old man's shoulder.

Professor Wynne placed a bookmark in his book. 'This is Kylie. She's a bearded dragon.'

'Kylie?' Cleo repeated. 'As in the Australian Aboriginal Noongar language, meaning *boomerang*?'

Professor Wynne opened a plastic tub on the coffee table. His fingers hovered over it as if selecting the strawberry cream from a box of chocolates, then plucked out a live locust. 'As in the Australian popular music artist, Kylie Minogue. I'm rather a fan.' He held the locust up to Kylie. She opened her mouth and snapped it in. 'Are you familiar with her work?'

'Sure,' Ryan said. He'd seen Kylie Minogue on a couple of TV programmes. He sang a line or two of *I should be so lucky*, the only one of her hits he could remember. He could tell from Cleo's face that she'd never heard of her.

Professor Wynne smiled. 'Although Kylie herself prefers jazz-funk. Don't you?' he added, stroking the bearded dragon's head.

Cleo obviously wasn't interested in small talk, human or reptile. 'Roberto Chan said you might be able to help us. We have an epigraphic emergency.'

Professor Wynne strolled across the room. 'I met your grandmother, you know, Miss McNeil,' he said, sitting down behind a huge mahogany desk. 'Not long after the war, on the Silk Road near Kashgar. I helped her out of a spot of bother.

She'd been arrested as a spy. Remarkable woman, Eveline Bell! First-rate archaeologist too. How is she?'

'Fine,' Cleo snapped. 'We only have one day!'

Professor Wynne pushed aside a pile of papers. 'You are very like her.'

Ryan grinned. He'd met Eveline Bell in London last year. She and Cleo were indeed alike. They had the same mannerisms and the same gap between their front teeth. Both were direct, stubborn and very impatient.

The old man held out his hands. 'So, what do you have for me?'

Ryan opened his backpack and placed the biscuit tin on the desk. Professor Wynne peered inside. 'Spiny oyster,' he murmured as he extracted a disc of shell from the tissue paper with a pair of tweezers and turned it in the light. He held it up to Kylie. 'What do you think?'

Kylie blinked but kept her opinion to herself.

'They were written in prison, in 697, by Lady Mountain Star, a daughter of King Jaguar Paw of Calakmul,' Cleo explained. 'The pieces were smuggled out by her servant. We believe they explain how Jaguar Paw died and where we can find the . . .' She hesitated. 'You won't tell anyone about this until we're ready?'

Professor Wynne closed his eyes and smiled. 'This is your discovery.' He stroked Kylie. 'Our lips are sealed.'

Cleo glanced at Ryan, who shrugged and gave a thumbs-up. Professor Wynne was certainly eccentric; he had meaningful conversations with a bearded dragon for a start! But he seemed friendly enough. *Perhaps,* Ryan thought, *Kylie is his Way, his animal spirit. Who am I to judge, when mine is an anteater with a drink problem?*

211

'We're looking for something called the White Finder Tree,' Cleo said. 'We think it was a lodestone mounted in a jewelled artefact in the shape of the World Tree.'

'A compass, of sorts?' Professor Wynne asked. Kylie tilted her head as if mildly interested. Then she opened her mouth and snaffled in a stray locust leg.

'More than a compass,' Ryan said. 'It also has directions to Xib'alb'a and instructions for rituals to bring Jaguar Paw back from the underworld.'

Professor Wynne raised his bushy white eyebrows. 'Fascinating. That would indeed be a most remarkable find.' He switched on a desk lamp and hooked reading glasses over his ears. 'Well, we'd better get to work.'

An hour later Ryan was officially bored. Cleo and Professor Wynne were huddled at the desk, occasionally muttering random words and phrases. They didn't even need him to copy the glyphs out; Professor Wynne had a scanner plugged into his computer, so he could simply enlarge the images on the screen. Ryan flopped down on the sofa and hummed *I should be so lucky*. The tune had stuck in his head. It was doubly annoying, as he didn't feel *lucky* at all. In a few days he'd be heading back to Manchester with Mum. They were never going to find Dad. They were just going to have to face up to it and move on. Ryan sprang up and began picking up books from the shelves. He had to find *something* to do before those dark thoughts wrapped him in their tentacles and pulled him towards the black hole.

Cleo looked up from her notes. 'Why don't you go and look around the Chichén Itzá site? It's only a few minutes' walk from the hotel.'

Ryan shrugged. He wanted to see the famous ruins, but he

didn't fancy trailing around by himself like Larry the Loser.

Professor Wynne picked up an old-fashioned telephone. 'I'll call my granddaughter. Monique is over from France for a few weeks.'

'No need!' Ryan darted for the door. 'I'll be fine on my own.' If there was one thing worse than looking round by himself it would be babysitting some annoying little kid.

But Professor Wynne wouldn't take no for an answer. 'It's no trouble. She's only in the next-door room.'

Ryan forced a smile. 'Great.'

But when the door opened five minutes later he decided he might be a tiny bit luckier than he'd thought.

27

LOVE

MONIQUE WAS NOT a little kid. She was about the same age as Ryan, with long tanned legs and sun-streaked blonde hair. Her denim shorts, lacy white crop top and collection of silver bangles had *fashionable-without-even-trying* written all over them.

Maybe I'm not Larry the Loser, after all, Ryan thought.

They chatted about their favourite Mexican foods, ice cream flavours, and films. Unlike Cleo, Monique had actually seen *Star Wars* and *The Wizard of Oz*. She also laughed at his jokes – even the rubbish ones – and her French accent was adorable. But then she moved on to her obsession with a Korean boyband Ryan had never heard of. As they crossed the hotel garden the conversation was already flagging. By the time they reached the entrance gate to Chichén Itzá, it was fighting for its life.

Approaching the ancient city along a wide avenue of graceful trees, Ryan looked around in surprise. Unlike Calakmul, where walls, steps, ramparts, walkways and broken *stelae* all jumbled and tumbled with roots and vines in a great big untidy brawl, Chichén Itzá was orderly and well-groomed. The jungle had been pushed back and replaced with clipped lawns and smooth paths. The stonework, shorn of strangler figs, had been cleaned and patched up.

On either side of the avenue stood souvenir stalls piled high with local crafts; rainbow-painted jaguars and serpents, woven hammocks and white *huipils* with their garlands of embroidered flowers. Calendar wheels were printed on everything from tea towels to t-shirts. Ryan dawdled, automatically scanning the calendars for glyphs that he recognised.

'You're not into all that old writing, are you?' Monique sighed a sigh of epic proportions. '*Bor-ring*.'

If Cleo were here, Ryan thought, *she'd be lecturing me on the precise mathematical properties of the Maya calendar.* He was surprised to find he sort of missed it.

Monique tugged at his elbow. 'Let's look at something *normal*.' She stopped at a stall festooned with silver, jade, turquoise and coral jewellery and dangled an earring against her neck. 'What do you think?'

'Yeah, nice,' Ryan murmured vaguely.

'No, no, it's horrible.' Monique held up another. 'Is this better?'

It looked exactly the same. Ryan's gaze settled on a rack of necklaces in shades of burnt orange and tomato red. 'Ah, you like spiny oyster?' the stallholder asked. 'Good quality.'

Ryan picked up a string of red discs. The shell beads clattered softly, the surfaces polished to a soft gleam. *This must be what Mountain Star's necklace looked like.* He turned to show Cleo. Then he remembered; he was with Monique.

Monique pushed her sunglasses up onto her hair. 'I know what you're thinking!'

Ryan seriously doubted it. He was thinking of two girls. Neither of them was Monique and one of them had been dead for over a thousand years.

Monique smiled. 'You're thinking that would really suit me!' She took the necklace and held it up to her throat.

Ryan remembered something Cleo had said when they'd found the first broken shell pieces. 'It's funny because they're called spiny *oysters,*' he told Monique. 'But they're actually more closely related to scallops.'

Monique flared her nostrils in an expression he recognised from school: *Major Nerd Alert!* She tossed the necklace back onto the rack. 'Orange is so not my colour.'

'Monique!'

Ryan turned to see a group of teenagers. Monique ran to join them in a flurry of air kissing and arm-linking. 'Ryan!' Monique called. 'Come and meet my friends.'

Ryan looked up at the huge flat-topped El Castillo pyramid towering beyond the trees. He really wanted to get a closer look, and Cleo had told him not to miss the ball court or the observatory . . .

He backed away at high speed. 'I'll catch up with you later!'

Just call me Ryan 'Nerd Alert' Flint . . .

216

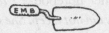

Meanwhile Cleo and Professor Wynne were hard at work.

Cleo rubbed her eyes, massaging life into her weary optic muscles. They had made good progress. She leaned back in her chair and read over the translation of the first three shells. *I have been held prisoner for many months now. I knew that Radiant Turtle and I were in danger from the moment that Lady Six Sky arrived from Naranjo, with her son. Smoking Squirrel is as cruel and ambitious as his mother. They showed up, as ill-fated as the days without names, shortly after our mother fell ill. Lady Six Sky soon cast a spell on my father, blinding his spirit. He fell in love with her.*

Professor Wynne looked up from the screen 'Time for refreshments,' he announced. 'I'll call room service. What will you have? Dry sherry? Martini cocktail?'

'Er, just a Coke, please.' Cleo turned back to Mountain Star's words. *My father could not see that Lady Six Sky was scheming with her advisors to get rid of Radiant Turtle, the true heir, so that she could install Smoking Squirrel as the new Lord of the Snake Kingdom. But then something happened that made Lady Six Sky's plan start to unravel like a torn cloak. During the star war with Tikal my father was captured and sacrificed to the gods in a ball game. I know this, because I was out of sight nearby when Lady's Six Sky's messenger brought her the news.*

Every time Cleo read over this part of the translation she was swept up on a new wave of excitement. Here it was in black and white. Jaguar Paw had been killed at Tikal. She couldn't wait to tell Roberto. They were starting to get to the truth at last!

She went back to her notebook. *I was full of grief for my father, but Lady Six Sky did not weep. She summoned her advisors. 'If word gets out that the king is dead, the people of Calakmul will call for Radiant Turtle to be crowned immediately. I need more time to remove him and set Smoking Squirrel up in his place.'*

A waiter arrived with the drinks and a huge plate of cakes. Cleo sipped the ice-cold Coke and bit into a mango tart. She couldn't help smiling; Ryan was going to be furious at missing the feast! She hoped he'd get back soon so she could tell him Mountain Star's story. He was going to love this bit; *I heard Lady Six Sky and her advisors plotting to keep my father's death a secret. They agreed to employ a man to play the part of the king until they were ready for Smoking Squirrel to be crowned.*

Professor Wynne looked up from pouring his tea into a bone china cup. 'They hired a lookalike,' he chuckled. 'Most ingenious. They even arranged for the stand-in to go off on several long royal visits to other cities, so that there was less chance that anyone in Calakmul would notice the deception.'

'But why didn't Mountain Star tell anyone what Lady Six Sky was up to?' Cleo wondered out loud.

Professor Wynne pointed to the screen where he'd started work on the sixth shell. 'It says here. She tried, but nobody believed her. Lady Six Sky made sure of that!' Cleo leaned in and read the words. *Lady Six Sky found out that I have secretly been training as a Sky Watcher and a Scribe for many years. A girl doing a man's job! She has told everyone in the palace that I am crazy, as unnatural as a monkey that wishes to lay eggs or a fish that tries to fly like a bird. My words are met with laughter . . .*

Cleo seethed with rage on Mountain Star's behalf. She got up and paced around the room, scowling at the old black and white photographs of Professor Wynne posing at various digs with other famous Mayan epigraphers. Many of them were women, Cleo noticed – Linda Schele, Merle Green Robertson, and Mum's hero, of course, Tania Proskouriakoff. Women had played a vital part in deciphering the ancient script, even if they'd not been allowed to write it in the first place. The thought reminded Cleo of a question she'd been meaning to ask. 'Professor Wynne, have you heard of Sofia K. Proufork? She's Canadian. A Mayan specialist.' *So she says,* she added silently.

The old man fed a piece of his custard tart to Kylie. 'No. But I don't keep up with all the youngsters coming through these days. I wonder what happened to the lookalike?' he said, returning to the older mystery. 'I presume that they quietly bumped him off when he was no long useful . . .'

Suddenly Cleo knew the answer. He'd played the part in death as well as life. 'I know!' she spluttered, almost choking on her Coke. Kylie eyed the display of bad manners with obvious disapproval. 'He's the man who was buried in the upper tomb at Calakmul, of course!'

Professor Wynne sipped his Earl Grey tea. 'Yes, yes, I think you could be right. That would explain why he was buried with some of Jaguar Paw's possessions, the plates and so on. It was to keep up the pretence.'

Where *had* Ryan got to, Cleo wondered. She was bursting to tell him she'd solved another part of the mystery. Even though it had been her idea that he should go off to look around Chichén Itzá, she felt a fizzle of annoyance that he'd been *quite* so keen when he'd seen Monique. Perhaps they'd stopped for ice creams. She was probably laughing at all his terrible jokes. They might even be holding hands . . .

Ryan wasn't eating ice creams or holding hands.

He was standing on the immense expanse of sun-baked grass in the ball court at the heart of Chichén Itzá. You could still see the stone hoops the players had to get the ball through, mounted high on the sloping stone walls that flanked the court. A tour guide clapped his hands to show how the stadium amplified the sound. His group all joined in, until the court rumbled as if with thunder. *It must have been like Quidditch without the broomsticks,* Ryan thought. He thought of Cleo. *I bet she hasn't even seen the Harry Potter films.* He made a mental note to add them to the movie marathon he was planning.

Drifting out of the ball court, Ryan came face to face with the skull platform. Row upon row of carved heads of captives stared out from empty eye sockets, just like those in the Wasp Nest tower. Faded crimson splashes still stained the limestone. The whole structure had once been painted blood red for added impact. Tourists crowded round to take pictures, posing with the skulls as if for a team photo. Ryan walked away. *Why were humans always so keen on killing each other?* he wondered. That's when they weren't trying to be immortal. The pharaohs in Egypt, the emperors in China, the Maya kings; they were all obsessed with power and living forever. What was it Roberto's Snake Stone had called it? *The prize that all men desire . . . And maybe all women too,* he thought, as two expensively styled ladies tottered past. Their faces were stretched and smooth, their lips plumped. *Face lifts and botox,* he thought. *People are still trying to live forever . . .*

He sank down on a bench near the foot of the mighty El Castillo pyramid. A lonely waterlogged feeling was seeping through him. He'd soon be back to maths lessons and football practise and dark January afternoons. To fend off the gloom, Ryan took his sketchbook and pencils from his backpack and began to draw El Castillo, losing himself in trying to capture the flights of ruler-straight stairs meeting at the top of the pyramid to form a square platform, the stone edges as sharp as knife blades against a perfect blue sky.

As he sketched the colossal blunt-nosed snake-heads that bordered each flight of stairs at the base of the pyramid, he half-listened to the words of an American guide nearby. 'El Castillo was a temple to the plumed serpent god, Kukulcan,' she recited in a sing-song voice. 'At the Spring and Autumn equinox, the sun shines on the edges of the stairs on the north face, at an angle that forms a "snake" of light from the top, down to the serpent head at the bottom, so it looks as if Kukulcan himself is descending the pyramid.'

Ryan glanced up. The sun wasn't in the right position today, of course. He had to imagine the sunlight zig-zagging down to the serpent head. *That's another thing all human civilisations seem keen on,* he thought. *Massive great snakes!* In Mexico it was Kukulcan, the plumed serpent. In Egypt, he and Cleo had encountered Apep, the World Encircler. In China it was dragons, but with their long serpentine bodies, they were basically snakes by another name. His chest tightened as he remembered the searing fire of the jade dragon's breath . . .

Snakes and dragons. Different names for the same beast. The thought had barely formed in Ryan's mind when another one slammed into it. It zoomed away so fast it disappeared in a blur. All Ryan caught were tiny thought-glimpses.

Sofia K. Proufork patting her hair as if it were a big movie-star arrangement rather than a badly done pudding bowl. The make-up bag in Sofia's bathroom, Sofia saying "absolute nightmare!"

'Absolute Nightmare,' he muttered under his breath. And with that he jumped up from the bench as if catapulted by an invisible ejector seat.

He had to tell Cleo before it was too late.

28

SACRIFICE

CLEO HEARD A knock. Before Professor Wynne could say 'Come in!' the door burst open and Ryan rocketed into the room. She jumped up and pulled him over to the desk. 'At last! Just wait until you hear this!'

Ryan spoke at the same time. 'She's not what you think!'

Cleo wasn't going to let Ryan get in first with an amusing incident from his afternoon with the beautiful Monique. And what could be more important than Mountain Star's message? The more she and Professor Wynne had deciphered, the more exciting the words had become. They had actually done a victory dance together – something between a highland fling and a foxtrot – around the desk at one point. 'We've found out the truth!'

'Do have a cake.' Professor Wynne offered Ryan the tray. 'There's a pineapple sponge left, and the strawberry gateau is superb.'

Ryan barely glanced at them. 'No, thank you. There's something really important . . .'

Cleo had never seen Ryan refuse a cake before. It must be serious with Monique. Perhaps he was in love. She'd read that strong attraction could cause loss of appetite. She'd keep an eye out for other symptoms; flushed skin and sweating palms. But she'd deal with that later. Her news simply couldn't wait. 'I know where the White Finder Tree is!'

That did the trick. Ryan was so surprised he sat down and took a piece of strawberry gateau. 'Wow! Where is it?'

Cleo explained how Lady Six Sky had hired a lookalike to stand in for Jaguar Paw after he'd been killed at Tikal, so that she could buy some time for her plot to line up her son Smoking Squirrel as the next king instead of Radiant Turtle.

Ryan threw out his arms, scattering a trail of strawberry glaze. 'Didn't I say that there was a stunt double right from the start?'

Cleo had to admit that Ryan was right but she didn't want to encourage him *too* much. He'd be on about his werewolf and zombie theories again soon. 'Yes, but you got it the wrong way round,' she pointed out. 'You thought Jaguar Paw sent a stunt double to Tikal to be killed . . .'

Ryan laughed. 'Details! Details!'

'It's important,' Cleo said. 'If the lookalike was buried in the upper tomb, it proves that Roberto was right. That burial was not the real Serpent King. Anyway, there's more,' she added, before Ryan could argue. '*Several months after my father's death, Lady Six Sky received a visit from her chief priest-shaman. I hid in the maid's room and listened through the curtains. The shaman had brought her a magical object of great power.*' Cleo stressed every word, looking up to make sure that she had Ryan's full attention. She did.

'*The shaman claimed that it was given to him by a travelling medicine man, who had found it in the sacred caves of the Candelaria River. Lady Six Sky exclaimed over its beauty. It was in the form of a ceiba tree with branches and leaves and thorns and roots crafted from jade, obsidian, gold and precious stones. "It is the World Tree," the shaman explained. "Inside the trunk is an enchanted serpent that always turns its head towards the white realm of the north."*'

'The *"enchanted serpent"* is the lodestone!' Ryan cried through a mouthful of gateau. 'Oh yeah! It's the White Finder Tree. We were right all along! There *was* an actual tree. And it *was* a compass!'

'It's quite remarkable!' Professor Wynne agreed. 'It's the first evidence the Maya used such advanced technology in the eighth century. Top marks for figuring that out from those sarcophagus texts!' He yawned. On his shoulder, Kylie did the same. 'All the excitement has worn me out. I need a little catnap after squinting at those infernally tiny glyphs all afternoon.' The old man shuffled over to the sofa and stretched out.

Ryan held up his hand for a high five. Cleo reached over the desk and slapped his palm. It felt a little sticky. *Sweaty palms,* she thought. *I must be right about him being in love with Monique . . .* Although maybe it was strawberry juice.

'Take *that,* Sofia K. Proufork!' Ryan laughed. 'You

don't know what you're talking about!' He glanced across at Professor Wynne, who was already snoring softly. Kylie was snoozing on his chest. 'And that's what I have to tell you ... I realised something when I was looking round Chichén Itzá ...'

Cleo could hardly believe it. This was a breakthrough moment in Maya history, and Ryan was *still* trying to tell her about his romantic afternoon with Monique. She knew she'd pledged to be a better friend, but he could be really infuriating at times.

'Hang on!' she snapped. 'We're coming to the best bit.' She handed him the pineapple cake, to stop him interrupting again, 'Right, where were we? Ah yes. Morning Star says: "*I heard the shaman tell Lady Six Sky; 'written on the bark of the White Finder Tree is secret knowledge, directions that will lead you to the mouth of Xib'alb'a and the rituals you must perform to bring a man back from the Underworld.' Lady Six Sky snatched the tree. 'Give it to me. I will use it to summon King Jaguar Paw back to this world.'*

'You must wait for the auspicious day,' the shaman told her. 'And you will need an offering, one who shares the king's blood, to trick the Lords of the Underworld into letting him go.'

"'Radiant Turtle!' Lady Six Sky replied with a smile in her voice. 'What greater honour than to take his father's place ...'"

Ryan's hands flew to his face. 'Oh no! You were right about that bit on the sarcophagus about special sacrifice rituals. Poor Radiant Turtle. He was only four years old!'

'I know,' Cleo said. 'And poor Mountain Star. She obviously loved her little brother. Listen. "*I was so afraid for my brother that I stumbled through the curtains and fell. My hiding place was discovered. Lady Six Sky ordered the guards to lock me up.*"'

Cleo paused. Late afternoon shadows were gathering in the corners of the room. Professor Wynne muttered in his sleep.

'So *that's* how Mountain Star ended up in the prison cell,' Ryan whispered.

Cleo nodded and continued to read. '"*My servant, Seven Rabbit, brought me food each day. She also brought me news. When the Spring equinox came, she told me that this was the chosen day. Lady Six Sky and her entourage were going to Xib'alb'a to retrieve my father, the king. I had no choice but to act. I pounced on my guard and cut his throat with my blood-letting lancet ...*"' Cleo glanced up at Ryan. She knew he'd hate that part. Sure enough, his face had turned mushroom-pale in the gloom. She hurried on. '"*I followed Lady Six Sky and her priests through the jungle. They were using the White Finder Tree to show them the way. After a long march we came to a cenote overlooked by a giant Witz monster carved into the mountainside. The priests lit burners of resin. Smoke rose through the branches. They chanted many spells. 'Now we pay the price that the Lords of the Underworld demand to release Jaguar Paw,' the chief shaman cried. Lady Six Sky, put on a headdress of shimmering quetzel feathers and held my brother over the water.*

I had no plan. I only knew I must stop them.

I was about to run out from cover of the trees, when there was a roar. From the mouth of the Witz monster burst a mighty jaguar."'

Ryan stared at her across the desk. 'Do you think that's the jaguar that's buried in the tomb?'

Cleo was sure of it. 'No wonder Lady Six Sky and her men believed that the jaguar was the Way of King Jaguar Paw. They were doing their best to summon him up from the Underworld and it appeared right on cue.'

'What happened next?'

'"The shaman dropped the White Finder Tree into the water,"' Cleo read. *'"Lady Six Sky dropped Radiant Turtle to the ground. Then they scattered in fright along with the priests and guards. The jaguar lunged at Radiant Turtle . . ."'*

'Oh no!' Ryan sank his forehead onto the desktop. 'We know this was a man-eating jaguar. Alex found those human hookworms in its guts. It *ate* Radiant Turtle, didn't it?'

'No, wait!' Cleo told him. 'It's not over yet. Mountain Star threw a rock at it. *"The jaguar howled, stumbled and fell like a rotten branch from a tree."'*

'Oh yeah! Go Mountain Star!' Ryan punched the air. 'She must have been a great shot. Alex said that the jaguar's skull was completely smashed. Now we know how it happened.' He took the last cake from the tray. 'So Mountain Star saved her little brother's life. It was a happy ending?'

Cleo wished she had better news. 'Yes and no.' She read out the translation of the final shell from Mountain Star's necklace. *'"I scooped Radiant Turtle up in my arms and ran blindly through the forest. But my joy was short-lived. Lady Six Sky sent her guards after me. I was soon captured and returned to my cell, this time with Radiant Turtle. We will both be killed tomorrow. I am guilty of killing the Way of my father . . ."'*

The room was now almost fully dark but for the blue glow of the computer screen on the desk. But neither Cleo nor Ryan stirred to switch on a lamp. Finally, Cleo got up and stood looking out of the French windows that gave on to a balcony. Spotlights shone on a turquoise pool. The smell of chlorine and sunscreen wafted on the breeze. Somewhere a pair of frogs struck up a duet, one croaking low, the other high. 'So now we know where the White Finder Tree ended up; at the bottom of a *cenote* in the middle of the jungle. The priest dropped it when the jaguar sprang. That's what the writing on the sarcophagus was telling us. When it said *the jewelled White Finder Tree now lies in Jaguar Paw's final resting place* it didn't mean that it was in his tomb; it meant it was deep beneath the waters of Xib'alb'a.'

Ryan padded across the room to stand behind Cleo at the window. She felt him place his hand on her arm as cautiously as if she were a wild animal that might bolt or bite. 'So, it's lost forever,' he said gently. 'Never mind. At least we tried.'

Cleo whipped round to face him. She hadn't given up yet, even if Ryan had! 'But we can still find it,' she said. 'Professor Wynne helped me to decipher one other shell which I've not told you about yet. It's a copy of the directions on the White Finder Tree. Mountain Star heard the shaman reading them out as she followed through the forest, and wrote them down. And now they're all in here.' Cleo waved her notebook at Ryan. 'They're a bit vague but I'm sure we can figure them out. We'll find the *cenote*. We'll tell Roberto about it and he'll arrange for divers to go down to look for the Tree.'

Ryan put his hands on her shoulders. 'But you fly out tomorrow night. I'll be leaving Mexico in the next day or so too. We don't have time.'

Cleo's head dropped. Ryan was right. But then she thought of something. 'But we won't *have* to leave straightaway now! We've got cast iron *proof* that the White Finder Tree exists. It's all written on the shells. Once we hand this over to Mum and she shows it to Sir Charles, he's bound to let her stay in Calakmul until we find it. And Professor Wynne can vouch that the shells are genuine. Sir Charles would listen to him. Professor Wynne is a much more distinguished epigrapher than Sofia Proufork. In fact, I don't know why Sir Charles bothered sending Sofia all the way from Canada to look at Mum's work in the first place, when there was someone like Professor Wynne so close at hand!'

Ryan snorted. 'She tricked him into it!'

'Yeah, you're probably right.'

'I *know* I'm right!'

Ryan's voice was suddenly so intense that Cleo felt a snag of fear under her ribs. 'What are you talking about?'

'It's what I've been *trying* to tell you.' Ryan's grip tightened on her shoulders. He was almost shaking her. 'It came to me when I was at El Castillo. I was thinking about snakes and dragons and how they're like the same beasts with different names. And I suddenly figured out why Sofia looked familiar.'

'So you're not in lo . . .' Cleo stopped herself saying *in love* just in time. 'Not *enlisting* Monique for any more outings?'

'*Monique?*' Ryan shook his head as if he'd forgotten her very existence. 'What's *she* got to do with anything?'

Cleo couldn't help smiling with relief. 'Nothing.'

'Sofia K. Proufork is a false identity,' Ryan said. 'She's Melanie Moore in disguise.'

PROOF

'MELANIE MOORE?' **CLEO** jolted back as if she'd been electrocuted. 'As in Sir Charles Peacocke's personal assistant?'

Ryan nodded.

'But Sofia doesn't look anything *like* Melanie. Melanie has long blonde hair.' Cleo waved her hands around her head, indicating the bouffant curls.

'So she was wearing a wig!'

Cleo's brows scrunched into a deep V. 'But Melanie's hair was real. Don't you remember in China? She was always going on about hairdryers and volumising treatments?'

Ryan could see that Cleo had a point. 'OK, so maybe Sofia's lovely brown pudding bowl style is the wig.' Now he thought about it her fringe had looked particularly wonky this morning. Perhaps she'd not had time to put it on properly.

'But it's not just the hair!' Cleo had started pacing up and down between the window and the desk. 'Melanie Moore's all high heels and tight skirts. And she definitely doesn't have hamster cheeks and big teeth.'

'It's all a disguise.' It was hard to believe, Ryan knew, but he had absolutely no doubt; glitzy, glamourous Melanie Moore had transformed herself into no-nonsense, no-frills Sofia K. Proufork. The clues had been there in Sofia's trailer this morning; he'd just not picked up on them at the time. 'There was an industrial-size bag full of make-up in her bathroom,' he said.

Cleo had reached the window again. She stopped. Ryan watched her reflection in the dark glass as she considered this information. 'But Sofia doesn't wear make-up.'

'Exactly,' Ryan said. 'And there was a tube of *Fixodent*.'

'Denture glue?'

'For sticking in those goofy false teeth,' Ryan said. 'There were foam pads for her cheeks too. No wonder she insisted on having her own trailer; she doesn't want anyone seeing her without her disguise. The only medical condition Sofia has is that she's a pathological liar!'

Cleo frowned at herself in the window. 'I agree that Sofia is a fake. I'm sure she's a thief too. But I just can't believe she's *Melanie Moore!* Melanie has worked with Sir Charles for years. I've met her loads of times.'

Behind the glass the sky was deep indigo. Fairy lights had been strung in the branches of the trees around the terrace below and twinkled through Cleo's reflection like stars, each with its own smudgy golden halo. Ryan knew he was right.

Sofia K. Proufork didn't look or sound like Melanie Moore, but her mannerisms had given her away; the way she reached up to pat her hair, followed by a fleeting look of confusion as she realised there were no big curls to puff up. And there was that phrase Sofia liked to use; *absolute nightmare*. Ryan had heard Melanie Moore say those words in just the same way in China.

'Think about it,' Ryan said. 'Working so closely with Sir Charles – the Minister for Museums and Culture – is the perfect job for a tomb robber! All these years, Melanie has had access to information on just about every major archaeological dig in the world. What better way to find out where there's treasure to be stolen? She probably has gangs of looters working for her all over the place. She's like a black widow spider –' Ryan was on a roll now. '– sitting in the middle of her web, pulling the strings . . .'

A mosquito whined and Kylie stirred in her sleep as if hearing it in a dream. Cleo was silent for a long moment and then spoke, slowly at first. 'It *would* explain why artefacts have been going missing on Mum's digs for all these years. And Melanie could easily have read all the reports that Mum sent to Sir Charles, telling him what she was looking for and what she'd found.' Cleo turned to face Ryan, her words speeding up as the theory took shape. 'Melanie could have been sending information to Rachel Meadows about our search for the Benben Stone. She could have briefed Joey Zhou about the Immortality Scroll . . .' She clutched at her hair with both hands. 'Yes! Do you remember when we were in the café, talking about the conference in Hong Kong? Sofia said that she'd seen Joey there. Then, suddenly she got all flustered and tried to change the subject.' Cleo was at full throttle now. 'I knew she was hiding *something*. Now it makes sense. Sofia *was* at that conference, but she was there with Sir Charles, *in her Melanie Moore persona*. That's why there was no Sofia K. Proufork on the list of delegates.'

Ryan grinned. 'Yeah, Melanie slipped up for a moment there. She forgot that she's being Sofia now, and that Sofia wasn't at that conference! So, you see, Melanie Moore is the connection between all the incidents . . . She's the, what's that underground fungal stuff you were talking about?'

'Mycelium?'

'That's it.' Ryan had it all worked out. 'Melanie Moore must have seen the story about the White Finder Tree that Max accidentally leaked out via the bird-watching website. No doubt she reads all the archaeology blogs to keep track of what treasures are turning up so she can decide what to go after. She must have realised how valuable the White Finder Tree would be and decided that this time she'd come to the site in person to get her hands on it, rather than working through an accomplice like Rachel Meadows or Joey Zhou. She must have quickly arranged for 'Melanie' to go on holiday or off sick for a while. Then she made up a new identity – ace epigrapher, Sofia K. Proufork – and tricked Sir Charles into sending her to Calakmul.'

'But I saw Sofia's profile on the University of Saskatchewan website . . .' Cleo pointed out.

Ryan thought for a moment. 'I'm sure it's not that hard to put up a fake web-page if you have the right connections. She must have got a forged passport as well. And then . . .' he went on, 'when she gets to Calakmul, she tells the world – including Sir Charles – that your theory about The White

Finder Tree being a real object is all baloney. Of course, that's just to put everyone off the scent so she can find it herself.' Ryan paused for breath. 'Glamorous Melanie has been running a highly organised tomb-robbing operation all along.'

Ryan sank down in a leather armchair, feeling rather pleased with himself. For once he was the one who'd figured everything out. But Cleo went back to staring out of the window. 'So that explains why Sofia followed us into the tomb in the middle of the night,' she said, talking more to herself than to Ryan. 'She thought we might lead her to the White Finder Tree. And we were right about Sofia meeting that guy from The Red Wolves in La Luna bar. He's probably working for her. I bet she instructed him to phone the police with that tip-off about Mum stealing the jade mask. It was all part of her plan to get us out of the way so that she can hunt down the White Finder Tree.' Cleo leaned her forehead on the window. 'The problem is, how are we going to get anyone to believe us? We need some sort of proo . . .' Suddenly she spun round on her heel and darted across the room.

'. . . oof,' Ryan said weakly, assuming that *proof* was the word Cleo had abandoned halfway through. Either that or she'd been overcome by an urgent desire for prunes.

Cleo flicked on the main light.

Professor Wynne sat up so fast that Kylie slid off and landed on a cushion. 'Is it breakfast time?'

Ryan blinked at Cleo. 'Can you give us some warning next time you decide to blind us.'

Cleo took no notice. 'Look!' she said, pointing at a picture on the wall. 'That's Tatiana Proskouriakoff.'

Ryan peered at the black and white photograph. A young Professor Wynne was posing in front of a ruined building. Next to him stood a slim woman with dark curly hair, a cigarette between her fingers, looking out with serious eyes.

Professor Wynne smiled. 'I worked with her in Copán. Lovely girl.'

Ryan tried to think where he'd heard the name before. Then he remembered. Cleo had said she was one her mum's great heroes. 'Ah yes, didn't Proskouriakoff make some early break-throughs in deciphering ancient Mayan glyphs?' He waited for the others to look impressed at his knowledge of the subject. They didn't.

'Tatiana *Proskouriakoff*,' Cleo repeated.

Ryan and Professor Wynne looked at each other. They both shrugged. Kylie looked up from her cushion. 'And you're telling us this because . . .'

Cleo puffed her fringe out of her eyes. 'Because it's *proof*, of course. It *proves* that Sofia is using a fake name. I can't believe I didn't spot it before. Sofia K. Proufork is an anagram of *Proskouriakoff!* She's rearranged the letters . . . the K doesn't stand for anything. It's just there to make the anagram work!'

'But why?' Ryan asked.

'Because she thinks she's clever.' Cleo began scooping the shells back into the tin. 'Using Mum's hero against her. But we're cleverer! We're on to her.'

Professor Wynne looked interested. 'We're rather partial to anagrams, aren't we, Kylie?'

But Cleo was already on her way out. 'Thank you,' she called back to Professor Wynne. 'Thank you for all your help!'

'And thank you for the cakes,' Ryan added. 'And for . . .'

Cleo ran back and pulled him out of the door.

'We *have* to warn Sir Charles about this,' she hissed as they hurried along the veranda. 'Before Sofia strikes again!'

'You mean *Melanie*,' Ryan corrected her.

Cleo waved her hand impatiently. 'Whatever she calls herself. She could have lists and lists of valuable treasures from Sir Charles's office in her possession. She probably has people working for her at digs all over the world. Who knows what she's planning to steal next.'

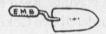

Cleo threw herself down on an elegant wicker sofa in the lobby. She was about to select Sir Charles Peacocke's number in her contacts list when Ryan pointed out that it was now the middle of the night in London. Sir Charles would be at home in bed, not in his office. Cleo had a moment of panic. Now that she knew what was going on, she couldn't bear to wait another minute before warning him about Melanie. Then she remembered; *she had his home number!* Sir Charles lived in Darlbury Hall, a mansion just outside London, and he often held official functions there. Mum had called Cleo from a dinner at Darlbury not long ago to say she would be late home, using the landline because her phone was out of charge. Cleo scrolled back through her incoming calls until she found it. 'Ha! Got you!'

Sprawling on the sofa next to her, Ryan bugged his eyes. 'You're actually going to get the Minister for Museums and Culture out of bed at two in the morning . . .'

'Of course. His trusted personal assistant is a fraud and a tomb robber. He needs to know.' Cleo listened to the ring tone and imagined it echoing round the dark corridors of Darlbury Hall. With her other ear, she was aware of the sounds of the hotel. French windows opened from the lobby to the courtyard bar. The murmur of conversation and soft rattle of ice cubes mingled with the cooing of doves and chirping of cicadas. A man in a white suit sat down at a grand piano and began to play an old-fashioned melody.

'*As Time Goes By*,' Ryan said.

Cleo raised an eyebrow, her attention still on the ring-tone.

'That's the tune he's playing.' Ryan flagged down a waiter as he glided past, and ordered two Cokes. 'We've got to make the most of this luxury lifestyle before we go back to the jungle.' He looked over at the piano. 'It's from *Casablanca*. It's a classic old film . . .'

Cleo was starting to give up hope that anyone was going to answer the phone.

'I feel like we're in a scene from *Casablanca* now,' Ryan said. 'A secret rendezvous in a hotel bar . . .'

Perhaps Sir Charles wears earplugs at night, Cleo thought.

A woman's voice crackled from the phone. '*Hello. Who is this please?*'

'I'll add it to the list for our movie marathon.'

'Shhhhh!' Cleo hissed, flapping a hand at Ryan.

'I beg your pardon!' The woman had already sounded disgruntled about being woken up. Being shushed had done nothing to improve her temper.

'I need to speak to Sir Charles. It's urgent.'

'Who is this?'

'It's Lydia McNeil.' Cleo said a silent apology to her mum for the lie, but it was a short cut to being taken seriously. '*Professor* Lydia McNeil,' she added.

238

The woman's voice softened a little. 'I see. I'm afraid he's away at the moment. I'm the housekeeper. He left for Florida yesterday. You could try calling him on his mobile. You must have the number.'

Cleo's heart sank. *Of course!* Sir Charles had said something about being on holiday in his last email to Mum. She knew she didn't have Sir Charles's mobile number. But she couldn't give up. She'd told one lie, she might as well keep going. 'The thing is I've lost my phone with all my contacts. That's why it's so urgent. We're stranded in the jungle in a storm and there's a . . .'

Ryan began doing a throat-cutting action. 'Stop!' he mouthed. 'Nice cover story! Don't ruin it.'

'Oh dear.' The housekeeper's tone was almost kindly now. 'Keep calm. I'll give you his number.'

Riding high on her success, Cleo threw in one last question. 'I don't suppose you have a number for Melanie Moore, do you?'

'I'm afraid not.' The housekeeper was sounding cagey again. 'But I do know she's away on a training course.'

Cleo thanked the housekeeper and finished the call.

'Melanie Moore on a training course!' Ryan almost choked on his Coke. 'That'd be the course on *How to Lie and Cheat Your Way to a Successful Career in Tomb Robbery.*'

Cleo stifled a laugh. She'd already dialled the mobile number and this time the answer came quickly. 'Hello. Charles Peacocke here.'

Cleo could hear voices and music in the background. Sir Charles must be in a bar or restaurant. She'd known Sir Charles since she was four years old and had only ever seen him in a bespoke suit, a handkerchief poking out of his jacket pocket, his hair groomed into a distinguished snowy wave. The image of him lounging in a beach bar in surfer shorts and flip-flops was slightly disturbing. She took a deep breath and launched into her account. 'It's about Melanie Moore . . .' she began.

Cleo had expected it would be difficult to convince Sir Charles of Melanie's double life as a tomb robber. It was, after all, a preposterous story. To her surprise he believed her almost straight away. Perhaps, she wondered, he'd already had his suspicions.

'Ah yes, Cleo, thank you for bringing this to my attention,' Sir Charles said in a grave tone. 'This is most distressing. Now, it's very important that you keep this, er, *situation*, to yourselves. No, not even your parents can know yet. This woman could be dangerous if confronted. And she'll make a run for it if she gets wind that we've rumbled her.'

'What are we supposed to do then?' Cleo asked a little crossly. 'Just let her get on with it?'

'Not at all. I'm going to deal with this myself. I'll be on the next available flight to Mexico. Then I can liaise directly with the local police. It's only a few hours from Miami. I should be there tomorrow. Sunday at the latest.'

By the time Cleo finished the call Ryan was almost sitting on her knee so that he could hear the conversation. 'Don't you think that's a bit weird?' he asked. 'Saying we can't even tell your parents about Sofia?'

'I'm sure he knows what he's doing.' Cleo wasn't sure why she was defending Sir Charles. His words had struck her as rather odd too. But he was a very important minister, not to mention Mum's boss. They couldn't just ignore his advice.

Ryan stirred his Coke with his straw. 'We're talking about a man who's failed to notice that his personal assistant is an international criminal. Maybe he's not quite as on the ball as you think?'

30

VECTOR

RYAN GAZED OUT at the night. The headlights of oncoming trucks flared past. Now and then he caught a glimpse of old men sitting in the warm glow of a roadside café, or young men gathered around a cluster of motorbikes, the glowing tips of their cigarettes bobbing in the dark.

He glanced across at Roberto to make sure that he wasn't nodding off at the wheel. It had been a long day and they'd been on the road for over four hours now. The hospital visit had been a great success. Alejandro was responding well to his treatment and they'd spent a happy afternoon playing computer games. Roberto had also been delighted to hear the story that Mountain Star's shell necklace had revealed.

The mystery of Jaguar Paw's death had been solved at last. The king's human form had been captured and sacrificed in Tikal in 695, his lookalike had been buried in the upper tomb two years later, and his *Way* or animal form – the man-eating jaguar – had been buried in the deeper tomb. For the Maya, that was the *real* tomb of the Serpent King; just as the Snake Stone had told.

Tears had welled in Roberto's eyes as he thanked Cleo and Ryan for helping prove his theory. His job and reputation would be safe and the medical bills paid. But now his eyelids were drooping. His chin was sinking onto his chest. Ryan looked at Cleo. They'd already had a near miss with a stray dog and Calakmul was still hours away. Cleo nodded and pointed ahead. 'There's a layby. You need a nap.'

Roberto was too tired to argue.

In keeping with Sir Charles's instructions, they'd avoided talking about Sofia K. Proufork and her secret identity in front of Roberto. But the moment he nodded off in the driver's seat they returned to the subject. 'I've just thought of something,' Cleo said, propping her feet up on the dashboard. 'Sofia must have faked that migraine on the afternoon the ear spool was stolen. She could easily have sneaked in and taken it from Roberto's trailer.'

Ryan slapped both palms to his forehead. 'Of course! Remember how Sofia told Chief Garcia she saw us coming back late for lunch? We were so busy trying to defend ourselves that we didn't stop to ask; *how* did she see us if she was lying down in the dark the whole time?'

'I bet she stole the jade mask too.' Cleo grabbed Ryan's elbow. 'Oh, and the spider monkeys!'

Ryan stared at her. 'She *stole* spider monkeys?'

'Not stole, *spooked*. At the Wasp Nest. I *knew* something must have disturbed that troop of monkeys. It was Sofia. She was following us. She knew we were on the trail of the White Finder Tree.'

Cleo was right, Ryan thought. It seemed that Sofia – or Melanie, to use her real name – had tracked every single step of their search for the White Finder Tree. 'We'll have to be more careful when we get back,' he said. 'If Sofia's been snooping on us she'll know all about the shells, and that we went to see Professor Wynne to decipher them. She'll be desperate to find out whether they lead to the White Finder Tree.' That reminded him. Hadn't Cleo said that she and Professor Wynne had deciphered one more shell; the one containing the directions to Xib'alb'a?

Cleo was obviously thinking the same thing. She switched on the passenger light, took out her notebook and flicked through the pages. 'Mountain Star heard the shaman reading out the directions to the Xib'alb'a cenote, and she copied them down on the shell. If we're going to find the White Finder Tree we need to figure them out, since that's where it ended up.'

Ryan pictured the shaman dropping the White Finder Tree into the *cenote* in his panic to escape from the jaguar. He could almost hear the splash as the beautiful jewelled tree hit the water and sank to the bottom of the pool. He glanced at the luminous green display on the dashboard. It was 1.30 in the morning. *We should probably wake Roberto and get going soon*. But a few more minutes wouldn't hurt. 'You said the directions were a bit vague?'

Cleo gave an apologetic smile. 'Actually *vague* is an understatement.'

244

Ryan pretended to smack his head on the dashboard. 'Oh no, don't tell me! It's a riddle isn't it?'

'No, it's some sort of schematic representation . . .'

'You mean a diagram?' Ryan rolled his eyes. Cleo never called a spade a spade if she could call it a *hand-operated-earth-removal-implement*. But he was relieved. Diagrams were much easier than riddles.

Cleo unfolded a sheet of paper and handed it to him. Professor Wynne had scanned the tiny image on the shell into the computer and enlarged it. The diagram was picked out in dark brown against a dull red background. Mountain Star had drawn a single large circle. In the middle were several glyphs, one of which he recognised as the Smug Snake emblem of Calakmul. Nine lines radiated from the centre like the spokes of a wheel, each protruding a little way beyond the edge of the circle, dividing it into unevenly sized segments. Each of the lines was labelled by a symbol made up of the little bars and dots that represented numbers.

How do we get from this to the Underworld? Ryan wondered. Maybe a riddle would have been easier after all. 'Are these numbers dates?'

Cleo shook her head. 'I don't think so. They're actually pairs of numbers. The first is a value from one to nine. The second number in each pair is much larger; in the thousands or tens of thousands.' She held out her notebook to show Ryan the copy of the diagram she'd made, with the numbers and glyphs all translated into English. 'I thought it might be some kind of star chart, since Morning Star was an astronomer. The number pairs could be co-ordinates, marking the positions of stars or planets. But I looked in some star atlases in Professor Wynne's room and those co-ordinates don't make any sense.'

Ryan suspected that Cleo was over-complicating things. 'Stars wouldn't be any use for showing you the way through the jungle,' he pointed out. 'You wouldn't be able to see them through the trees. That was why it was so important that the White Finder Tree was a compass.' He studied the diagram again. Cleo had translated the word next to the Snake Kingdom emblem in the middle of the circle. *'Blue-green,'* he read out loud. 'What does that mean?'

'The Maya associated a different colour with each direction,' Cleo explained. 'Red for east, yellow for south, and so on. Blue-green was the colour of the centre of the world.' She pointed to the left of the circle where there was a single glyph at the nine o'clock position. Below it, Cleo had written the translation: *White.* 'That means north; which you know, of course. It's how the White Finder Tree got its name.'

Ryan thought back to Mountain Star's description: *a ceiba tree with branches and leaves and thorns and roots crafted from jade, obsidian, gold and precious stones.* What if those precious stones were carefully positioned around the trunk of the tree to mark the directions, he wondered. A white jewel would mark north, a red one for east . . . and then if the branches radiating out from the tree trunk were arranged in specific ways . . . yes, it could work . . .

Ryan sat forward, his words tumbling out in excitement. 'I don't think this diagram is a copy of something that was *written on* the White Finder Tree! It's a picture of the model tree itself. Mountain Star must have had a chance to get a close look at it.' He fished in his backpack, pulled out his compass and placed it on the notebook. The needle flickered and then pointed towards the North. He rotated the notebook so the word *White* on the circle lined up with

246

it. 'Imagine this diagram is what you see if you look down on the White Finder Tree from above,' he told Cleo. 'The circle is the trunk, which is hollow . . .'

Cleo had unclipped a pen from the back of the notebook and was chewing on the end. 'A cross section, you mean?'

'Exactly. The lodestone is mounted in the middle. It always points towards the north. So you turn the tree until the north marker – a *white* jewel on the outside of the tree trunk – is lined up in the right position. And then you can use these nine lines coming out from the circle to tell you the directions you have to go in.' Ryan was sure he was on the right track. He could picture the tree, with nine straight branches made of gold or jade sticking out, corresponding to the lines on the diagram. He flopped back in his seat. 'The problem is, it only works if you know where to start from!'

But Cleo was smiling. 'That's easy!' she said. 'It tells us right here.' She pointed to the two glyphs in the middle of the circle. '*The Snake emblem. Blue-green.* For the people of the Snake Kingdom, Calakmul *was* the centre of the world. That's where you start.'

Ryan imagined Lady Six Sky and her shaman in Calakmul. The shaman held up the White Finder Tree and aligned the lodestone with the white jewel for north. Then they turned in the direction of the first branch and set off through the forest. But that immediately threw up more problems. 'Which of the nine branches do you follow first? And how do you know how far to go in each direction?'

Ryan jumped. Something had banged into the windscreen. He looked up to see soft dark wings flapping against the glass. 'A bat!' he muttered. 'I hate bats!'

'It's not a bat. It's a moth. *Ascalapha odorata*. The Black

Witch moth.' Cleo smiled at him. 'They're perfectly harmless.'

'Black Witch? That doesn't sound harmless.'

Cleo waved her hand. 'Oh yes, there's a superstition that when you see one it means someone will die. It's called the *Mariposa de la muerte* in Spanish, the butterfly of death.' Her hand flew to her mouth. 'Oh, I didn't mean . . . I wasn't thinking about your dad. Superstitions don't mean anything, of course!'

Ryan felt a shudder of dread. He quickly touched the St Christopher, the scarab beetle and the Chinese coins. Then he did it three more times. The Black Witch peeled itself off the windscreen and fluttered rather groggily away. Ryan had to stop himself thinking about what it meant. He forced a laugh. 'At least it wasn't a bat!'

But Cleo wasn't listening. 'Vectors!' she cried. She jabbed her pen up and down on the diagram. 'The lines coming out of the circle are *vectors!*'

'Right . . . yes, *vectors.*' Ryan nodded wisely. He had only the vaguest of notions as to what a vector might be. He had a feeling they might have cropped up somewhere in a maths lesson.

Luckily Cleo loved explaining mathematical concepts. 'It's basic geometry! A vector is simply a movement from one point to another. It specifies two things; direction and magnitude.'

Ryan concentrated hard, harnessing the power of geometry to block out thoughts of death.

'Morning Star has shown the *direction* as the angle of the line radiating out from the centre of the circle,' Cleo went on. 'The *magnitude,* or length, of the vector is given by the large number in the pair of numbers that labels each line.'

She looked up. 'I would have seen it much sooner, of course, but I was confused by the small number that comes first. But that's not part of the vector, it's just a numerical sequencing order ...'

'*Numerical sequencing order?*' Ryan repeated. He really was going to have to start paying attention in maths.

'Otherwise known as a list,' Cleo said with a smile. 'The numbers one to nine. They just tell you what order to follow the directions in.'

Ryan could hardly believe it was that simple! He found the line marked with a single little dot. 'So this is vector one. You follow this branch. Then you line the lodestone up with the north again and follow ...' he searched for the line marked with two dots, '... this one here, vector two.'

'And the distance is given by the second, much bigger number,' Cleo added. 'So vector one is seven thousand, three hundred and fifty.'

'Seven thousand, three hundred and fifty *what?*' Ryan asked. 'What was the ancient Maya unit of measurement?'

'I don't know. Most civilisations had units based on the human body. An arm's length, a stride ...'

A stride! Suddenly Ryan knew that was it. 'What was that inscription on the sarcophagus again? The one about the path through the forest?'

'*To find the entrance to the Underworld count the hidden paths through the forest,*' Cleo recited. 'We never did work out what it meant by *counting the paths* ...'

'But it wasn't the hidden *paths*,' Ryan cut in. 'It was *count the hidden path.* You thought it was a mistake, but your Mum was right. You have to *count the path* by counting your strides along it. That's what the big number next to each line tells you; how many steps to take in that direction.'

Cleo stared at him, her eyes wide. *'Brilliant,'* she murmured.

Ryan shrugged. 'What can I say? It's natural genius. You just have to run with it!'

Cleo wrote one to nine down the side of a new page in the notebook. Ryan read out each direction and number of steps and she filled them in. 'North, north-east, two thousand, seven hundred and fifty,' he said, reaching the final one.

Cleo gazed down at the completed list. 'We've cracked it! The *secret knowledge* of the White Finder Tree.'

Ryan grinned. 'I was right about it being like a Satnav. *Commencing in Cal-ak-mul, proceed east for seven three five zero paces,'* he recited in a computerised voice. *'You have now reached your destination. Stop here for the prize all men desire.'*

Roberto woke up with a start. 'We've reached our destination?' His hands flew to the steering wheel, as if he were still driving. 'Where are we?'

Ryan laughed. 'Don't panic. We're still in a layby in the middle of nowhere!'

Roberto sighed with relief. He stretched, started the engine and pulled back out on the road. As they drove, Cleo and Ryan explained that they had figured out the directions to Xib'alb'a. Roberto was so excited they had to shout at him to keep looking where he was going. 'Wow! Good work. Hey, there's a map of the Calakmul area in the glove compartment. You might be able to start plotting the route. We could actually find the site. That would be incredible!'

Ryan popped open the glove compartment, grabbed the map and opened it. Vast areas of green jungle were criss-crossed with a handful of narrow roads. He found Calakmul and marked it with a pencil. That was the starting point.

He checked the scale of the map; one kilometre to two centimetres.

Cleo leaned over to look. 'We'll have to convert the distances of the vectors from strides into kilometres first. But how do we know how many strides there are in a kilometre . . .'

'There are one thousand three hundred and twenty,' Ryan said.

Cleo and Roberto's mouths both fell open in matching expressions of surprise. Ryan was tempted to make out that this knowledge was evidence of the staggering mathematical powers he usually kept hidden so as not to dazzle ordinary mortals. But he couldn't see Cleo falling for it. 'OK,' he admitted. 'I know because Mum's got one of those fitness apps on her phone. It tells you how many steps you walk every day. It adds the steps up into kilometres too.' Step-counting had been Mum's favourite fad for weeks. Until she got bored of it and started doing mindfulness instead.

Cleo's pen flew over her notebook as she did the calculations. Then, starting from Calakmul, Ryan used the vectors on the diagram to plot each part of the journey on the map until he had drawn a zig-zagging nine-stage route through the jungle.' Ta da!' he said, adding a big cross at the endpoint of the final vector. 'That's it. X marks the Entrance to the Underworld!'

Cleo stared at the X in the middle of the jungle, far from any roads or other landmarks. 'X for Xib'alb'a,' she breathed. 'We've done it! We've really done it! I'm sure Mum and Dad will cancel our flights home when they see this.'

Roberto's smile was so wide that several gold fillings flashed at the back. 'As soon as we get back to camp I'll make some calls. We'll get together a search party and see if we can find that *cenote*. It's not just the White Finder Tree. We could be about to discover a highly significant ancient Maya sacred site. This is better than I could have hoped for!' He held up a hand and grinned. 'Yes, before you ask, of course you can come. Both of you!'

The sky had lightened to smokey grey. At last, they were turning off the main highway and were heading along the single-track road, through the tunnel of trees. Calakmul was less than an hour away.

Cleo was so eager to get back and share her amazing find she kept leaning forward in her seat as if she could make the jeep go faster. Ryan wished he had some exciting news to take back too. Something about Dad . . . The Black Witch moth flitted across his mind. *The butterfly of death.* He gave himself a shake. *Think positive! Maybe Mum has heard something while I've been away . . .*

'Looks like a tree has come down across the road.' Roberto was craning over the steering wheel, peering through the windscreen. He slowed the jeep to a crawl. 'I think I can just get around it.'

'Careful!' Cleo warned. 'There's a deep ditch . . .'

A movement caught Ryan's eye. A blur of red filled the windscreen. There was a squeal of tyres . . .

And then the world turned upside down.

31

GRAVITY

IT ALL HAPPENED so fast.

Cleo registered snapshot images and bursts of sound; the tree trunk in the road, the red truck coming straight at them, a shout, a thud, a squeal of tyres. Then came a tumult of motion; swerve, skid, sway, lurch, a moment of limbo and . . . everything shattered into kaleidoscope fragments as they bumped and rolled down the bank.

Then it stopped.

Cleo opened her eyes.

She was hanging at a peculiar angle, half forwards, half sideways, held up by her seat belt. The nylon webbing dug deep into her stomach.

A broad shoulder was wedged beneath her side. *Roberto!* Another body was squashing her from above. A head was jammed against her face, hair that wasn't her own draped over her eyes. *Ryan!*

Cleo tried to reach up to push the hair away. She couldn't pull her arm free.

The three of them were locked together by gravity.

The engine had stalled. It was eerily quiet, the only sounds the creak of metal as the jeep settled in the mud. Thick, dark foliage pressed up against the windscreen.

Ryan wasn't moving. *Was he* . . . Cleo fought back a dizzy rush of panic. She strained her ears to listen for breathing. But all she could hear was the frenzied thumping of her own heart. She thought of the Black Witch moth. *No, it was just an old superstition. Surely it couldn't be* . . .

'Cleo? Are you okay?'

The voice came from somewhere near her neck. A surge of joy washed over her. *Ryan's alive. Everything will be all right.*

'Cleo?' Ryan asked again, his voice shaky, his jaw jutting into her collarbone as he spoke.

Cleo ran a mental check. Ryan's forehead had slammed against her cheekbone. It was painful but probably not broken. The pressure from the seat belt was uncomfortable but not enough to have caused significant internal damage. Her right arm throbbed a little. 'I think so.'

Ryan muttered something Cleo didn't quite catch. She thought it might have been *Thank God* . . . 'What about you?' she asked.

'If you could just extract your elbow from my rib cage I'll be fine.'

Cleo tried to move her arm again. Pain shot through her

wrist. She upgraded her injury assessment to Possible Sprain. 'Sorry,' she gasped. 'I would if I could.'

'Never mind. I didn't need that rib anyway.' Ryan wriggled a little. 'Roberto!' he called out. 'Are you all right? *Roberto!*'

There was no reply.

'Oh no,' Ryan murmured. 'Is he . . . *dead*?'

Cleo closed her eyes and focussed. She could feel the rise and fall of Roberto's shoulder against her own. 'No, he's breathing. He must be unconscious.'

She felt Ryan's sign of relief against her neck. 'We need to get him out of here in case the jeep explodes.' He lifted his head. 'I think I can climb out.' He twisted his body and swung his legs up. After three attempts he managed to get a foot onto the dashboard. One more lunge and his other foot was up too. Bracing himself with his legs he reached up and grasped the sides of the open window. 'I wish . . . I'd spent more time . . . in the gym . . . doing chin ups!' he panted through clenched teeth. 'OK. Try to undo my seatbelt.'

Cleo felt behind her. Every movement sent a new bolt of pain up her arm. At last she found the buckle and pressed the catch. For a moment, she was crushed by Ryan's weight. Then with a groan of effort, he pulled himself up, until his elbow, his chest, and at last – with a kick that narrowly missed Cleo's ear – his legs, were out of the window. The jeep juddered. Ryan had the door open now and was reaching down to her. Cleo pulled away from Roberto, unfastened her own seatbelt and clambered up the seats until she was close enough for Ryan to grab her by the arms.

'Agghh!' she screamed, as his grip tightened on her wrist. But she gritted her teeth and let him haul her out. She slid down the side of the jeep and collapsed on the bank of the ditch. It was prickly, boggy and writhing with insect life, but she didn't care; it felt so good for the world to be the right way up again. She could see the muddy underside of the jeep exposed like the belly of an overturned turtle.

Ryan leaped up and hung on to one of the tyres in mid-air. 'If I can just tip the jeep back down,' he puffed, 'we can get to Roberto through the driver's side.'

The jeep rocked. Then it crashed down onto all four wheels. Mud, dust, twigs and leaves sprayed Cleo from head to toe. Ryan staggered backwards and fell onto the bank next to her. They lay still, winded and worn out, gazing up at the lattice of overhanging branches, black against the grey sky. An owl hooted in the distance. More than anything, Cleo wanted to close her eyes and sleep, but she forced herself up. They had to help Roberto.

They clambered down the bank and opened the driver's side door. The window had landed on a jagged tree stump, which had shattered the glass and gashed Roberto's temple. Blood was running down his face and neck, splotching his pink shirt with red.

Ryan pushed the seat back, pulled Roberto well away from the jeep and rolled him into the recovery position. Cleo took off her long white scarf, tore it in half and pressed it to the wound to stem the blood. Ryan found a blanket in the back of the jeep and tucked it round him. 'Wait here!' he told Cleo. 'I'll be back in a minute.'

Wait here? Cleo asked herself, as she watched Ryan slip away between the trees. *Where does he think I'd go?* She was feeling around the floor of the jeep for Roberto's satellite phone when Ryan returned. He held out his hand. 'It's *habim*,' he said.

Cleo examined the shreds of bark. '*Jamaica dogwood*?'

'Rosita told me about it. It's good for pain.' Ryan loosened the bandage and pressed strips of bark onto Roberto's temple. He added some crumpled leaves. 'I *think* these ones are antiseptic,' he said. 'Although they might be for diarrhoea.'

Roberto opened his eyes and moaned in pain. 'Diarrhoea? Am I at the doctor?'

Ryan patted his hand. 'It's OK. We'll get you to the hospital in no time.' He looked up at Cleo. 'Have you seen the satellite phone?' he whispered.

'Yes, but it's bad news.' She held up the phone. The black plastic casing had cracked right through the middle. 'It's completely dead.' She flinched at another stab of pain in her wrist.

'You've hurt your arm?'

'It's nothing,' Cleo lied. 'It just feels like a sprain.'

'Well, it *looks* like a beach ball! It's really swollen.' Ryan took the unused half of Cleo's scarf and the rest of the dogwood bark and bandaged her wrist. Cleo swallowed a lump in her throat. There was no mobile signal here and it could be hours before anyone else happened by on the remote jungle road. But she refused to cry. 'What are we going to do now?'

'I've got an idea.' Ryan ran round to the back of the jeep and came back waving a distress flare in each hand. 'I think we're officially distressed enough for these!'

Cleo felt better at once. 'Quick! Pull the tab at the bottom.'

'I *have* used one of these before,' Ryan pointed out. 'Although admittedly *not* in the approved manner.' He aimed the flare straight up and fired. The bang ricocheted around the trees. Red light tore through the grey sky, trailing a plume of strontium orange smoke and a celebratory whiff of gunpowder. Then he set off another for good measure.

All they could do was wait. Ryan retrieved his backpack and they scrambled up the bank to the roadside, where they could flag down a rescue vehicle. Cleo sat on the tree trunk that had fallen across the road. 'How did the driver of that truck not see us?' she asked. 'It would've been a head-on collision if Roberto hadn't swerved.'

'The thing is,' Ryan said as he sank down next to her. 'He *did* see us.'

Cleo frowned. 'What do you mean?'

He raked his hands through his hair and breathed out slowly. 'That's the truck Wolf Head and Beefy Guy were driving when Mum had that meeting with Miguel. It's got one of those big cow-catchers on the front. That's why they didn't care if we hit them. They knew we would just bounce off.' Ryan's usual smile had disappeared. There was real fear in his voice. 'It was the Red Wolves. They were targeting me. It was revenge for blowing up that barn full of drugs.'

'But they couldn't possibly have known that *you* were in the jeep before they tried to ram us,' Cleo pointed out.

Ryan shrugged. 'Perhaps they just recognised the jeep.' He kicked the tree trunk. 'And now Roberto's injured. This is all my fault . . .'

'No, it's not!' Cleo couldn't let Ryan take the blame. 'It's *my* fault. If I hadn't had the mad idea of going to Chichén Itzá and back in a day, this would never have happened. Wait . . .' she added, a thought suddenly striking her. 'How could the Red Wolves have *known* that we'd be driving along this road at exactly this time?'

Ryan shrugged. 'Their lucky day, I guess. Venus must be lined up with Mars or something.'

Cleo didn't believe in luck. 'No way! It's as if they were *waiting* for us to swerve round this fallen tree . . .' *In fact,* she thought, *had the tree even fallen at all?* She ran to the base of the trunk. It had been chopped cleanly through; the splinters of newly-exposed wood were still pale and raw.

Ryan joined her. 'You're right. Looks like this was all planned. You're shivering!' he added, wrapping his arm round her shoulders.

Cleo's first instinct was to pull away but the hug felt warm and safe. She leaned into it. She still couldn't stop shaking. 'Sorry, it's just a physiological shock reaction,' she said through chattering teeth.

'I know what you need!' Ryan sat down on the tree trunk again, rummaged in his backpack and pulled out a battered cardboard pack. 'A sugar fix! And I just happen to have the sweetest food item ever known to human civilisation. Behold the *Sponch!* biscuit.'

Cleo perched next to him. She selected a coconut-dusted pink and white marshmallow biscuit and was about to take a bite when she saw something that made it slip from her hand. 'What's *that*?' she breathed. 'Inside . . .'

Ryan examined his own half-eaten biscuit. 'It's jam. Strawberry, I think.'

'No, inside *there!*' Cleo snatched up the backpack and pointed to the small pocket in the shoulder strap. The Velcro fastening had come open to reveal a round black plastic device, no bigger than a pound coin, hidden within.

32

JUNGLE

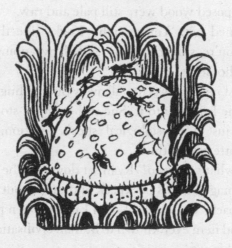

RYAN STARED DOWN at the small plastic object, 'What is it?' he asked, even though a shard of ice-cold certainty had already lodged deep in his guts.

Cleo slid the little gadget out. 'It's a listening device.'

Ryan saw himself leaving Sofia's trailer in the grainy pre-dawn light. He saw Sofia K. Proufork holding out a pack of sandwiches wrapped in foil. 'I'll just pop them in your backpack for you.' The words looped round and round in his head. Of course she hadn't made him sandwiches out of a random attack of kindness this morning. *While she was patting me on the shoulder and wishing me a safe journey, she was also busy planting a bug in the strap of my backpack.* 'But it's so *tiny*,' he mumbled, as if the size of the device made any difference. Shock had robbed him of the ability to say, or even think, anything remotely useful.

Cleo turned the bug over. 'It's got a battery, a microphone and a radio transmitter. That's all you need.' She looked up, her movements slow, as if even lifting her eyes took a huge effort. 'Sofia?' she asked.

Ryan nodded. 'She's heard everything.'

They sat in miserable silence. Ryan replayed the day's events. Every memory added to the torture. *I had the backpack with me in Professor Wynne's room. That means Sofia knows exactly what Mountain Star wrote on the oyster shells. The backpack was on the seat between us in the jeep all the way back. That means Sofia heard us figure out the directions to Xib'alb'a. We said every direction out loud. Worst of all,* Ryan realised, *she knows we're on to her. She knows that we know she's Melanie Moore in disguise.* He sank his head into his hands. 'She even knows that we phoned Sir Charles and told him.'

'Shhh!' Cleo held the bug at arm's length as it were a cockroach. 'She can still hear us!' she mouthed.

Ryan snatched the bug out of Cleo's hand and flung it as far away as he could. It flew over the jeep and landed in the jungle far beyond. He put his arm round Cleo again. Her shoulder blade felt as fragile as bird bones beneath her t-shirt. Resting his chin on Cleo's hair, he gazed down at the *Sponch!* biscuit she'd dropped. The marshmallow was now black with ants. His thoughts jumped to Shadow. Was he still dozing in the hammock or was he off on another fridge raid? *What I'd give for the simple life of an anteater right now!* 'Well that explains how the Red Wolves knew we'd be coming down

261

this road,' he said. 'We know Sofia's been working with them. She must have tipped them off.'

'You mean *Melanie*,' Cleo said. 'We've got to stop thinking of her as Sofia. There's only one reason for her to tell them to run us off the road like that; to slow us down so that she can find the Xib'alb'a *cenote* and White Finder Tree before we do. She's not going to waste any time now that we've worked out the directions for her, and she knows that Sir Charles is on his way to expose her as a fraud. We've been stuck here for hours. She's probably set off for the *cenote* already.' Cleo's voice caught on a sob. 'Melanie Moore and the White Finder Tree will both have disappeared into thin air by the time Sir Charles gets here. And who's going to believe our story then? We'll never be able to *prove* Sofia was a fake once she's gone. She'll have cleared everything out of her trailer. We don't even have the listening device!'

Ryan closed his eyes. How could he have been so stupid? He'd lobbed their prize piece of evidence into the middle of the jungle! *Melanie might even have left fingerprints on it.* 'Sorry, I didn't think ...' Something swooped past his face. It was only a bird, but Ryan felt the dark velvety wings of the Black Witch moth against his face. He couldn't hold the thought back any longer. Dad was dead. He'd probably died years ago. It couldn't be clearer. *The butterfly of death appeared to make sure I finally got the message. As soon as I get back to camp I need to have a serious talk with Mum. We have to accept it. We can't keep searching forever . . .*

Cleo seemed to read his thoughts. 'Don't give up,' she said, gently thumping his knee. 'We'll find him.'

Ryan swallowed a lump in his throat. Suddenly Cleo

jumped up. 'There's a vehicle coming!' She scrubbed tears from her eyes with her wrist bandage. 'Someone must have seen the flare.'

Ryan listened. The hum of an engine was growing louder and louder. *What if it's the Red Wolves coming back to finish off the job?* But it was too late to hide. Headlights lit up the road. The trees on either side seemed to crowd forward in a menacing pack. Cleo dashed into the road waving her arms.

The driver braked hard.

To Ryan's relief it was an ordinary grey pickup. The men crowded in the back were all sporting *Piratas de Campeche* baseball caps and were belting out rowdy songs. They weren't gangsters, but some of the diggers and workmen from the Calakmul site. When the driver climbed out, Ryan recognised Rosita's husband, Luis. He clapped Ryan on the shoulder. *'Que pasa, mi amigo?'*

Cleo began a long explanation in Spanish. Some of the men ran down the bank to the stranded jeep. 'They've been in Xpujil all night,' she told Ryan, 'celebrating after a big baseball match. They saw the distress flare and came to see what had happened. They'll turn back and take Roberto to hospital.'

As soon as the men had carried Roberto up the bank and made him comfortable in the back of the pickup, Luis started the engine. *'Vamos!'* he called, beckoning to Ryan and Cleo.

But Ryan shook his head. 'Ask him to call the breakdown service when they get to town. We'll stay here and wait with the jeep.'

Cleo looked at him as if he'd lost his mind. 'But that could be hours!'

Ryan pulled Cleo into a huddle. He'd lost all hope of finding Dad. He wasn't going to let Cleo lose the White Finder Tree as well. 'We can't let Melanie win,' he said. He took the map from his backpack and pointed to Calakmul. 'That's where she's starting from.' He traced his finger along the route he'd plotted to the X that marked the *cenote*. 'That's where she has to get to. And this,' he said, pointing to an unmarked point along the single track road, 'is where we are now.'

Cleo frowned at the map. 'So . . . Xib'alb'a is closer to us than it is to Calakmul?'

'Exactly. Xib'alb'a is north west of Calakmul. We're due north. If we start from here and head west, it's a short cut.'

'Yes, I see,' Cleo murmured. 'We'd be traversing the shorter side of a right-angled triangle . . .'

Beeeeep! The blare of the horn made them both jump. Luis slapped the truck door. *'Vamos!'*

Ryan turned back to Cleo. 'We might just beat Melanie to it.'

'But it's straight through the jungle!'

'It's not that far. I've got the compass in my backpack. We'll mark our way so we can turn back if we need to.'

Cleo's eyes were puffy and red-rimmed. One was circled by a purple bruise. But a determined glint was sparking into life. 'It's OK. You go without us!' she shouted to Luis. Then she switched to Spanish. Luis saluted his baseball cap, turned the pickup and headed back towards Xpujil.

'I said we'd stay here with the jeep until the police come,' Cleo told Ryan. 'Luis is going to phone my parents and tell them we're OK.'

Ryan watched the red taillights disappear into the trees. 'Right,' he said. 'Let's find the Underworld.'

Ryan threw all the bottles of water from the back of the jeep into his backpack along with anything he could find that might be useful; ropes, flares, and a single small machete. He found Cleo's tool belt too. She buckled it round her waist, pulled out her trowel and gave the air a couple of experimental slashes. It wasn't designed for jungle trekking, but it had a sharp edge that could cut through vines and brambles.

Dawn had crept up on them. The sky was now pale pink and the birds were all screeching and whooping along to different tunes. Ryan held the compass steady on his palm until the trembling needle pointed north. Turning their backs on the sunrise – a spiny-oyster-red blush – they headed due west.

'I've calculated how far we need to go,' Cleo said. 'It's basic geometry again. We know the distance of the longest side, or hypotenuse of the triangle from Calakmul to Xib'alb'a. We also know the distance from Calakmul to our starting point at the jeep. Using Pythagoras's theorem, the short side can be calculated as . . .'

Six and a quarter kilometres, Ryan thought. He'd already worked out the distance by the far simpler method of measuring it on the map. But he decided not to spoil Cleo's mathematical fun.

'Six point two five kilometres,' Cleo said. 'Which we'll have to measure by counting our strides. We know it's one thousand three hundred and twenty steps per kilometre . . .

That comes to eight thousand, two hundred and fifty.'

Ryan grimaced. That was a lot of steps. But he couldn't think of any other way to gauge the six and a quarter kilometres. They would have to *count a hidden path through the forest,* just as Lady Six Sky and her men had done.

'We'll have to keep a very careful count. I suggest we take turns, counting a hundred steps each.' Cleo unwound the *half-a-scarf* that bound her wrist. 'We'll use this as a *quipu.*'

'A *quipu?*' Cleo had now officially lost the plot. 'Why do we want to use a torn scarf as a giant rodent?'

'That's a *coypu!*' Cleo laughed. 'A *quipu* is an ancient Inca counting device constructed from an arrangement of strings . . .'

Ryan could only shake his head in wonder. However desperate the situation, however dire the danger, Cleo never failed to come up with a nugget of obscure information . . .

Cleo waved the frayed end of the cotton scarf under his nose. 'They recorded numbers by tying knots. I'll tie a knot for every ten strides. When we get to a hundred, I'll move on to the next thread.'

Ryan took the first step. *One*, he counted, *two, three* . . . this was going to be a long hike!

He wasn't sure which was worse, hacking through the dense underbrush or keeping track of their steps. *It's only counting,* he told himself . . . it sounded simple on paper; or even when written on an ancient jewelled tree. In practice, the terrain was so rough, the going so tough, that walking in a straight line with strides of equal length was almost impossible.

Here and there they threaded along an animal track; otherwise they slashed their way through untrodden growth.

The jungle, Ryan thought, wasn't as dramatic as it looked in the films; it was just a lot more *annoying*. It wasn't the trees that got you, but the stringy, clingy stuff in between. Everything had thorns or burrs or barbs or tiny stinging hairs. And that was just the plants. He didn't even want to think about the insect life.

'Next time I have a stupid idea . . .' he panted, 'like, *why don't we just . . . trek through miles of solid jungle . . .'* They were labouring up a slippery bank, one of a seemingly endless series of ridges and furrows. Time after time, they'd scrambled down a slope, trudged across a boggy hollow and hauled themselves up the other side, only to find another one waiting, '. . . *don't listen to me!'*

'Don't worry! *Seven thousand, five hundred and ninety-eight,'* Cleo puffed. 'I won't! Ever again! *Seven thousand, five hundred and ninety-nine.* But it can't be much farther . . . *seven thousand, six hundred . . .'* She stopped and tied a knot in her scarf, wincing as she moved her right wrist. 'We're almost at six kilometres.'

Ryan leaned against a tree and swigged from his water bottle. The scent of blossom – as sweet as rotting strawberries – saturated the humid air, clogging his nostrils. Bees thrummed somewhere above his head.

On the tree trunk, just millimetres from his shoulder, four lines had been scored into the bark. Sticky red sap oozed like blood. Ryan stared, transfixed. He'd seen that mark before! It was the 'tag' of the notorious Tiger's Claw gang. But that was thousands of miles away in China, when he and Cleo were searching for the Dragon Path. *The Chinese gangsters must have followed us to Mexico! They're working with the Red Wolves!* Reeling with confusion, Ryan wheeled round, certain he'd find himself surrounded by a murderous mob of tomb-robbing, drug-smuggling, knife-wielding hit men.

There was no one there but Cleo. 'Those look like jaguar claw marks,' she said, examining the tree trunk. 'It's how they mark their territory.'

Ryan spent a long time fiddling with the top of the water bottle to hide his relief. *You know you're not in a good place,* he thought shakily, *when an actual jaguar with razor claws and an unwelcoming attitude to visitors is the less bad option.* He glanced around. He couldn't *see* any jaguars in the murky green shade. 'Maybe it's a good omen,' he whispered, trying to rally his courage. 'According to Mountain Star, it was the jaguar that prevented Radiant Turtle from being sacrificed.'

'*According to Mountain Star,*' Cleo corrected him, 'the jaguar was going to *eat* Radiant Turtle, not protect him, if she hadn't thrown a rock at it. Let's get going. Your turn to count.' She swished her trowel at a strangler fig and took a step. 'Which is unusual,' she added over her shoulder, 'because jaguars hardly ever attack humans. They're only aggressive when they've been badly injured by hunters in the past.'

Ryan remembered the jaguar pelts he'd seen piled up in the Red Wolves' drug barn. He ran back and quickly hacked at the bark of the tree with his machete, obscuring the claw marks, to stop any passing hunters knowing that there was a jaguar in the area. Then he hurried after Cleo. *Seven thousand, nine hundred and one. Seven thousand, nine hundred and . . .*

Roo-aaaaarrrrrrrr!

Ryan froze in terror. Then he laughed out loud. 'Phew! It's a good thing I know that's only howler monkeys! I practically had a heart attack there!'

Cleo turned and looked back. When Ryan saw her face his laughter shrivelled to a whimper.

'That's *not* howler monkeys!' she said.

33

SIGN

RYAN WAS ABOUT to award Cleo a seven out of ten for her *it's-not-howler-monkeys* joke when the terrible truth hit home.

She was serious.

That roaring wasn't coming from monkey territory, high up in the branches. It was low down among the undergrowth . . . At precisely *jaguar* height.

Ryan launched himself at Cleo. Together they rolled through the brambles until they tumbled to a halt behind a heap of large boulders. He could hear Cleo's heart hammering even louder than his own. The crunch of a seedcase under his ear was like the crash of a tidal wave. Every breath was a hurricane. *Surely the jaguar can hear us.* It had stopped roaring. There was a rustling of leaves, a snapping of stems. *Is it sniffing us out? I've got Roberto's blood all down my t-shirt. Can jaguars smell a single drop from miles away? Or is that just sharks?* Nothing happened. Time passed. Ryan could bear it no longer. *Surely it's given up and gone back to its lair by now!* He untangled himself from Cleo and peeped over the stone.

At first he didn't see it. The copper and black markings melted perfectly into the dappled light. Sleek and tense, the jaguar stood contemplating the tree it had marked. It twitched its tail, lifted its head, bared its teeth and snarled. *He knows we're here,* Ryan thought. *And he's angry. We've invaded his territory. I've even hacked his warning sign from the tree.* The jaguar suddenly reared up on his back legs, gripped the tree trunk with his front paws as if in a deadly embrace, and gouged two new sets of claw marks. Then he dropped down, made a harrumphing sound like a dog settling in its basket, and loped away.

'It's gone,' Ryan whispered.

Cleo didn't reply. Ryan looked down to see that she was lying at the base of the boulder. Surely no one could be so tired they'd fall asleep in the middle of a jaguar attack? He nudged her shoulder.

Cleo looked up at him, her black eye shining purple in a shaft of sunlight. 'There's something carved into the stone down here. I think it's a glyph.'

After his close encounter with a big cat, Ryan wasn't that interested in a bit of old writing. Until, that was, he heard Cleo's next words. 'It says *Mountain Star!* She must have hidden in this very spot!'

Ryan felt as if he had fallen through a trap door into AD 697. He was crouching next to Mountain Star, peeping out over the boulder, watching Lady Six Sky march past with her guards and her shaman bearing the White Finder Tree, chanting as they counted their steps. Mountain Star's little brother was with them too. Was Radiant Turtle walking or being carried? Did he know what was in store for him? Ryan didn't have a brother of his own but his heart was turning inside out. 'Don't worry,' he murmured. 'We're coming to save you.'

'What's that?' Cleo asked.

'Nothing,' Ryan said quickly. Cleo wasn't one for spiritual time-travel moments. 'I was just making some adjustments to our course.' That part was true. If Mountain Star had hidden here, they must already have met up with the original route from Calakmul. 'We're a little further south than I thought.'

They pushed on. Two hundred steps later Cleo stopped at a flat chunk of limestone. 'There's Mountain Star's name again!' The familiar glyphs were barely visible through the brocade of yellow lichen.

Mountain Star must have been marking the route so she could find her way home, Ryan thought. A hundred steps later he pulled back a curtain of vines and found the next way-marker scratched into a craggy boulder. He was about to show Cleo when he heard a man's voice shout from among the trees.

'*Seven thou . . .*' Cleo's voice trailed off as she stopped and froze.

Ryan heard another shout and then a reply. All in Spanish. 'It must be Melanie,' he whispered. 'She's followed our directions and come looking for the *cenote*. She's brought some of her Red Wolves men with her . . .'

The voices were coming nearer. So were the thwacks and slashes of machetes. Cleo swayed. She looked as if she might throw up at any moment. 'Oh no! We've led them straight to Xib'alb'a,' she groaned though clenched teeth. 'They'll find the White Finder Tree first. And all the other sacrifice treasure in the *cenote*. They'll steal the lot.'

But Ryan had an idea. 'Not if we lead them astray. We'll take a detour, make plenty of noise and with any luck they'll follow us. Then we'll double back . . .'

Cleo looked doubtful but Ryan didn't give her time to argue. He pulled her by the hand. 'This way. And stay close!' The last thing he needed was for Cleo to get lost. She had the worst sense of direction he'd ever known.

They battled through tangled skeins of undergrowth. At last Ryan stopped. 'This should be far enough. Now to make some noise.'

Cleo pointed up at a tall tree with odd rainbow-coloured flowers. She banged on the trunk with her trowel. The tree exploded into life. The flowers were parrots! Furious at the disturbance the flock took to the air with a cacophony of squawking.

'Yep,' Ryan muttered. 'That should do it! Let's get out of here.' He consulted his compass and led the way, looping back in a wide arc to their original path. Cleo's feet dragged along the ground and she was cradling her bad wrist. 'Come on!' he urged. 'We must be nearly there!' The words were barely out of his mouth when they came out in a small glade. They stood squinting in the glare of unfiltered sunlight, free at last from the legions of trees that had imprisoned them like the bars of a cage. On the other side of the glade rose a steep slope, smothered in bright green bushes.

Cleo wiped her forehead with her scarf. 'We don't have to climb that, do we?'

Ryan opened his backpack and handed her the box containing the last two *Sponch!* biscuits. 'Eat these!' he ordered. 'You need the energy.'

Cleo took a biscuit. 'I'll be fine. I just need to sit down for a minute.'

Ryan clambered a little way up the slope to get a better view of their surroundings. To his surprise there was a wall of solid stone among the foliage. He followed the contour. It was long and rounded. He'd seen something this shape before. It was the fang of a Witz monster, just like the one on the side of the pyramid. Looking up, he could make out the darker shades of eye sockets hidden beneath the thick scrub. He pulled at a cascade of vines. Behind the fang, what had looked like the solid flank of the slope was a cave. He remembered the words written on the jaguar sarcophagus. *Enter the mouth of the Witz monster and follow the trail of the Serpent King . . .*

This was it! The mouth of the Witz monster! As Ryan scrambled back down the slope his thoughts galloped. They'd found the entrance to Xib'alb'a. All they had to do now was mark the spot on the map, then retrace their steps to the road and hitch a lift back to camp. They'd have to come straight back with Cleo's parents and the police before Melanie and the Red Wolves could help themselves to all the treasure in the *cenote*.

'We've found it! ' Ryan shouted, as he slid to the base of the slope, forgetting in his excitement that the Red Wolves might be near.

There was no reply. Cleo wasn't where he'd left her. Had she set off to explore on a *Sponch!*-fuelled sugar rush? He spun round, scanning for movement. Cleo would be lost within seconds. Panic swelled in his chest. *Or had she been snatched by the Red Wolves?*

Ryan heard a splash.

He heard a second splash, louder this time.

Ryan ran in the direction of the noise. Where was the water? *This is all my fault! I should never have made Cleo walk through the jungle. We could be arriving back at camp in Luis's truck by now . . .*

He stumbled and glanced down and suddenly he saw it. The ground beneath his feet looked like ordinary jungle floor – roots interwoven with creeping vines and suckers – but under the tangled mesh it wasn't solid earth but . . . *nothing*. Ryan found a stick and pushed it through. The stick disappeared.

Then came a small splash.

He scrabbled away handfuls of roots and leaves and peered down. Far below a glint of green water winked back at him.

He was standing above a huge underground pool.

Now Ryan knew what had happened to Cleo.

34

LOST

ONE MOMENT CLEO was looking around for somewhere to sit down, her wrist throbbing as she pulled apart the wrapper of a *Sponch!* biscuit.

The next, the ground gave way.

Thoughts of sharp, bone-breaking rocks rushed up to meet her. But when it came, it wasn't pain that struck, but cold. Cold, dark water swallowed up Cleo's legs, her arms, her chest, squeezing the air from her lungs. Cold, dark water rushed over her head. Thrashing and kicking, she struggled against the suck of the deep. Time slowed to a treacly crawl. But at last she rose and broke through the surface.

Cleo gasped for air and shook clinging strands of hair

from her eyes. She trod water, trying to make sense of her surroundings. She was in a vast underground cavern. High, high above her was a roof formed by a mat of roots and creepers. Gaps in the vegetation let in shafts of golden light, which angled down, spotlighting the water with circles of dazzling turquoise green. Clusters of enormous stalagmites towered up from the water.

It's the cenote, she thought. *The White Finder Tree is in here somewhere . . .*

Before she could take it in, Cleo was startled by a loud splash. She wheeled round. Something was swimming towards her. Silhouetted against a beam of light, all she could make out was a black shape writhing in a scatter of sparkling drops. *It's Ryan,* she thought, her heart leaping. *The idiot! He's jumped in to save me!* She paddled towards him. *But what if it's not Ryan? It could be one of the Red Wolves. Or a crocodile.*

Cleo had a strong free-style stroke, but her boots, her tool belt and her sprained wrist slowed her down. By the time she reached the side of the *cenote* she was battling for every breath. She clutched at a spur of stone and pulled herself along to a ledge that jutted out from the wall. She hauled herself up and collapsed, as limp as a stranded jellyfish. There was no sign of the other swimmer. All she could hear were drops dripping and wavelets slapping against the wall. *It must have been a crocodile,* Cleo thought, as she sat up and tipped water out of her tool belt. *It's slipped back into the depths to wait.*

Now that her eyes were used to the gloom, she saw that the limestone walls – pockmarked with crevices and holes – had been painted with hundreds of ghoulish figures. Some were skeletons. Some had flesh. Some had hook-nosed human faces or snarling monkey heads. Others wore leering white masks. They were draped in jaguar pelts and brandished burning torches, decapitated heads and fearsome axes. Slices of sunlight reflected off ripples in the water and flickered on the walls, making the figures jig about in a macabre dance. Cleo threw a stone into the water. The ripples grew and sped across the surface, sending the Lords of Death into a wild frenzy.

Clever, Cleo thought. *The more you struggle in the water, the more the figures come after you. Welcome to Xib'alb'a, the Place of Fear.*

She dragged herself to her feet and began looking for a way out. She'd just started to inch her way along the ledge when something surged out of the water, bulldozed her from behind, and knocked her off her feet.

Cleo screamed. She was pinned to the ledge by the weight of the crocodile on her back. It was trying to pull her into the water where it would roll her over and over until she drowned. Grunting in agony, she reached for her tool belt. She grasped her trowel in her left hand and stabbed up and back as hard as she could. If she could just reach its belly, the softest part . . .

'Agggghhh. That HURT!'

Cleo was cold, soaked, scared and disorientated. But she still knew one thing; that wasn't the cry of a crocodile; or any other reptile for that matter. She twisted round and found herself nose-to-nose with a furious man.

'You've stabbed my bloody leg!' The man – who had an enormous nest of straw-coloured dreadlocks and a shaggy beard – pushed away from Cleo and stared down at his thigh. An island of blood was soaking through the sodden jeans. He swore a few more times in English and then in Spanish.

278

'Sorry, I thought you were a crocodile.'

'A crocodile?' the man snorted. 'Do I *look* like a crocodile?'

'Since you attacked me from behind,' Cleo pointed out. 'I didn't have a chance to judge your appearance. Morelet's crocodiles are common in the Yucatán Peninsula. They've been known to prey on humans near water. It was a perfectly reasonable assumption.'

The man twitched an eyebrow. He shuffled round until he was sitting with his back against the wall. His clothes were tattered and his face weathered and brown. *He must be one of Melanie's henchmen from the Red Wolves,* Cleo thought. That meant he was a drug dealer or a tomb robber. Probably both. But he was obviously in pain. She unwound her scarf from her neck. It was torn in half and the frayed ends were tied into eight thousand tiny knots but it was better than nothing. 'Use this to stop the bleeding,' she said. Then she decided she ought to take no chances. 'If you're carrying a weapon,' she added, in her most authoritative voice. 'Take it out and put it on the ledge where I can see it. And don't try anything.'

The man raised a hand in surrender. 'No, no weapons.' He spoke slowly as if he'd not used English in a long time. 'You're quite a piece of work!' He took the scarf and tied it in a tourniquet above the wound. 'So, how long have *Los Lobos Rojos* been recruiting English girls?'

'*Los Lobos Rojos? The Red Wolves?*' Cleo spluttered. 'Do I *look* like a criminal?'

The man looked her up and down. This time both eyebrows twitched.

Maybe he has a point, Cleo realised. She had a black eye and a swollen wrist. Her clothes were smeared with Roberto's blood and engine oil and torn to shreds by brambles.

'So you just carry a knife for fun?' he asked.

'It's *not* a knife,' Cleo said indignantly. 'It's an archaeology trowel. It belonged to my grandmother,' she added, as if that made all the difference. 'Anyway, *you're* the one who's working for The Red Wolves!'

The man laughed. 'That's a joke!'

Cleo narrowed her eyes at him. 'You're telling me you're *not* here with Sofia Proufork – or at least, that's what she's calling herself at the moment – searching for the White Finder Tree?'

The man shook water from his dreadlocks like a large Golden Retriever. 'You've completely lost me there!' He stared out across the *cenote*. The water was calm again now and The Lords of Death had settled down to a sedate bobbing. 'Those skeleton guys are really freaking me out!' He reached up to his throat, where a coin-shaped silver pendant hung on a chain. He began to turn it over and over in his fingers.

Cleo's mouth fell open in astonishment. 'Is that a St Christopher medal?'

The man nodded. 'He's the patron saint of travellers. To be honest he's not done that great a job for me so far . . . Are you all right?'

Cleo was still staring at the St Christopher. *The twitch of the eyebrows, the laugh, the voice* . . . Cleo felt as if she'd solved Fermat's Last Theorem. The unknown variable in the equation had suddenly fallen into place. *'You're Eddie Flint!'*

The man almost fell off the ledge. 'What . . . who . . . how did you know?'

Cleo answered with a question. 'How did you get here?'

'I was hiding in the trees. I saw you trip and fall through the roots. I dived to save you. But I was too late. I lost my balance and next thing I knew I was falling in headfirst after you.'

That sounds exactly like the kind of thing Ryan would do, Cleo thought. *Charge in to help without thinking through the consequences!* 'Thank you for trying to rescue me,' she said. 'But I *meant* how did you end up here in Mexico? You've been missing for six years!'

Eddie Flint closed his eyes. His chin dropped to his chest. 'Long story.' Suddenly his head snapped up, his eyes wide open again. 'Hang on! How do you know about me?'

'Ryan told me, of course.'

'*Ryan?* Ryan's my son's name.' Eddie's weather-beaten face had turned as pale as the masks worn by the Lords of Death. He gazed down into the water as if slipping into a dream. 'He's about your age now. That's all that's kept me going; the thought of getting back to him. And his mum, of course. I don't even know if they're alive.'

Cleo dropped to her knees next to him. 'Ryan's alive. So is Julie!'

Eddie stared at her and blinked, unable to process the information.

Cleo gripped his shoulders as if she could somehow *press* the incredible truth into him. 'They're both alive. They're both fine!'

'You *know* them?'

'Yes, of course! Ryan's my . . .' Cleo searched for the right label. 'He's my *best friend*.'

Eddie fixed his eyes on hers like a hungry dog begging for scraps. They were grey flecked with amber, just like Ryan's. 'Tell me! What's he like?'

Cleo opened her mouth. Then she closed it again. How

could she describe Ryan? *He makes friends with everyone he meets. He's scared of snakes. And spiders. Oh, and bats. And don't mention blood. When he looks at things, he really sees them. He can draw anything. He makes me laugh even though I don't get most of his jokes. He thinks that life is ruled by luck and not logic. He can't resist a stray animal. He makes fun of my tool belt. He's kind and brave and makes me feel safe. He can always find his way. He hides how much he misses you.* 'He's . . . he's . . . well, he's just amazing,' she said at last.

Eddie smiled but his eyes had filled with tears. 'Where is he now?'

Cleo pointed at the roof. 'Up there.'

'Ryan's *here?*' Eddie clambered to his feet, gasping as he put weight on his wounded leg. 'Why didn't you *say?*'

'I'm saying *now.*' Cleo thought Eddie's question a little unreasonable given that she'd only met him two minutes ago, and half of that time he'd been attacking her, but she made allowances for strong emotions. She stood and looked around. They needed to find a way out of the *cenote* . . .

'*Cleo!*'

Cleo looked up at the sound of her name. Ryan's voice floated down through a gap in the ceiling of vines. 'Cleo! Where are you?'

'We're down here!' she yelled. 'You need to lower down a . . .'

Her words were drowned out by a splash as Ryan dived into the water.

'. . . a rope.' Cleo finished her sentence weakly. She turned to Eddie. 'He can also be a total idiot at times!'

35

FOUND

RYAN SWAM AS if pursued by ravenous piranhas.

He'd almost given up on finding Cleo when he'd realised that the ground was riddled with holes. And where there was a hole, it was odds on that Cleo would fall through it! He'd peered down through a gap to see, far below, a pool of dark water sun-specked with rings of green as bright as jade.

He'd yelled her name.

He'd almost cried with relief when she shouted back. But then he'd heard a man's voice down there. *She'd been captured by one of the Red Wolves.* Without another thought, he'd thrown off his backpack, wriggled through the roots and dropped into the water.

It was a lot further down than he'd expected. The water was a lot colder too.

But he was almost at the side now. He could make out Cleo sitting on a ledge. There was a man with her, a tall, thin man with mad-hermit dreadlocks and a horrible woolly beard. *He'd better not have hurt her!* Ryan wasn't sure what he was actually planning to do next. He'd just have to wing it and try to outwit Beard Face somehow. He looked up, searching for a place to climb out of the water. His heart almost stopped. Hideous figures were jumping out of the walls at him, demonic skeletons and mutant monkeys cavorting in a blood-crazed war dance. His fingers slipped from the wall. He floundered back into the water.

'Don't worry, they're only the Lords of Death,' Cleo shouted. She was hanging down from the ledge, reaching out her hand. 'They're just paintings. It's an ingenious visual illusion. The more you splash the more the light moves and the more they dance. They're designed to frighten you.'

'It's *working!*' Ryan spluttered. These guys made the skulls at the Wasp Nest tower look like a Disney cartoon. He felt a powerful grip on his arm. Beard Face was hauling him out of the water. Ryan sprawled on the stone ledge gasping for air.

Cleo knelt over him. She had a few more bruises and was shivering with cold, but otherwise looked to be in one piece. 'What did you go and jump in for?' she demanded. 'That was totally irrational. You've got the ropes from the jeep in your backpack. You could have lowered one down for us. Now we're *all* stuck down here!'

Ryan sat up and raked his hair out of his eyes. 'I thought you were being murdered by a Red Wolf! What was I supposed to do? Carry out a full risk assessment?'

Cleo glowered at Ryan and then at Beard Face. 'This is ridiculous,' she snapped. 'You *both* fell in doing your "knight in shining armour" routine. *We have to save her because she's a helpless girl...*'

'It's *not* because you're a girl!' Ryan and the man yelled in unison.

Ryan did a double take. Beard Face was suspiciously *normal* for a gangster. And how come he was speaking perfect English? *It must all be an act to catch me off my guard.* Ryan dripped to his feet and drew himself up to his full height. 'Has this guy hurt you?' he asked Cleo.

Beard Face threw back his head and roared with laughter. Had he been sampling the gang's stockpile of drugs, Ryan wondered. He seemed a bit out to lunch.

'Me hurt *her?*' Beard Face pointed at his bloodstained jeans. 'Who do you think stabbed me?'

Cleo gave a sheepish smile. 'Sorry, I thought you were a crocodile.'

And why's Cleo being all buddy-buddy with him? Ryan had heard of something called Stockholm Syndrome, where hostages make friends with their kidnappers and even end up being on their side. But Cleo had only been down here half an hour. Surely it took longer than that. 'Has he tried to brainwash you or something? And why does he keep staring at me like I've got two heads?'

Beard Face took a step nearer. Ryan backed away, unnerved by the piercing amber eyes.

'I can't believe it,' the man mumbled, his voice cracking with emotion. 'My *son!*' He smiled and shook his head. 'So tall, so grown up, so *brave* ... I've imagined this moment so many times ...'

'Your son?' Ryan echoed.

'This is your dad,' Cleo said. 'I *told* you we'd find him.'

'It can't be,' Ryan said. 'Dad's dead.'

The man patted himself on the arms and legs. 'No. A bit worse for wear, but definitely *alive*.' He was still smiling but there were tears streaming down his face.

A humming sound boomed in Ryan's ears like a swarm of underwater bees. He stared at the man. *It can't be! Dad died six years ago. I saw the Butterfly of Death.* But beneath the beard and dreadlocks, everything about that face was familiar. All at once Ryan knew it was true. He opened his mouth. *Dad?* But no sound came out. A rubbery feeling – like a badly mistimed jump on a trampoline – had taken control of his legs. They were starting to give way when he was scooped up in a giant bear hug.

The hug was the warmest thing Ryan had ever felt, in spite of the icy water that squelched from their clothes and dripped from their hair. Huge emotions wrestled in his chest. *Joy, relief, sadness for all the lost years, guilt that he'd given up hope, anger at Dad for letting it happen . . .* His throat tightened as if he were being strangled from inside. 'Dad!' he mumbled into a soggy shoulder. It felt so strange to say the word out loud. He tried it again. 'Dad!'

'I'm here,' Dad sobbed. And then, 'Your mother? Is she OK?'

Ryan wiped tears and snot from his face. 'She's fine. Well, not *fine*, like everything's hunky-dory. I mean *fine*, as in she's never given up.' He realised he was babbling. 'She's been looking for you all this time. We both have.'

'And I've been trying to get back to you . . .'

'But how did you end up down here?' Ryan asked. 'Have

the Red Wolves been holding you prisoner?'

Dad pulled back, still holding Ryan by the shoulders. 'Yes. But I managed to get away from them.'

'So Miguel was telling the truth.' Ryan grinned. 'We were so close to finding you! I even blew up one of their barns with a distress flare.'

Dad grinned and then burst into laughter. 'That was *you*? The men were all talking about it. Their boss was so angry he smashed up the whole camp!' Still laughing, he slid down the wall to sit next to Cleo who was still kneeling on the ledge smiling up at them. Ryan sat down too, and dangled his feet over the edge. Suddenly no one was laughing any more. 'So, the Red Wolves have held you captive *for six years?*' Ryan asked. It was hard not to let a hint of accusation creep into his voice. *Couldn't you have got away sooner?*

Dad shook his head. 'I've only been with *Los Lobos Rojos* for a couple of months.' He sighed. 'They're small-time. A pretty shambolic bunch really. The gang that kidnapped me in Colombia were a much more serious operation. I was making a film about drug trafficking. I was dumb enough to walk into a trap and they ambushed me.'

'So they held you to ransom?' Cleo asked.

'Yeah. It's common practise for the big drug cartels. They were demanding money from the British government for my release.'

'How come nobody knew about it?' Ryan asked. 'Mum did loads of research . . .'

'Governments keep it top secret because they never want to be seen to be "giving in" to kidnappers or terrorists,' Cleo said. 'It's happened to some of our archaeologist friends who've been working on remote digs in dangerous countries.

287

One was killed. But the others were released after a few months.'

'But *six years?*' Ryan repeated. He still couldn't take it in.

Dad smiled sadly. 'I know. The negotiations kept falling through. I was passed from one group to another, held in remote jungle camps ... Then, about six months ago a fight broke out between a couple of the bosses. It turned into a mass gun battle. In all the chaos, I saw my chance to escape ...'

Cleo handed him a bottle of water from her tool belt.

Dad gulped at the water and then passed it to Ryan. 'I stole a car and drove hell for leather. I had to stay under the radar and get as far away as possible; otherwise the Colombians would hunt me down. I knew far too much about the gang's operations by now. I was on the road for weeks. Long story short, I ended up in Mexico. I've got some old contacts here I knew would help me get back to England. I just had to find them. I was driving down a jungle road when my car broke down. I set out to walk to the nearest town but I got hopelessly lost. I ended up falling into a *cenote*.'

'You've fallen into *two cenotes?*' Ryan asked. He caught Cleo's eye and couldn't help laughing.

Dad looked puzzled. 'What's so funny?'

'It's just that falling down holes is Cleo's speciality.'

Dad smiled. 'Well, I didn't fall in this time. I jumped in after Cleo. But the first time I fell in here ...'

'You fell in *this cenote* before?' Ryan asked. Falling down the same hole twice was impressive even by Cleo's standards.

'Yeah. It's not *that* surprising! The ground is like a colander up there. I managed to get out somehow, but I was in a terrible state. I'd hit my head on the rocks. I didn't know where I was. I ended up wandering around for days. I must have collapsed and passed out, because when I woke up I was in a jungle camp. I'd been found by some guys out jaguar hunting. It turned out they were members of a local gang . . .'

'The Red Wolves?' Ryan and Cleo interrupted in unison.

'That's right. I was half-dead by then. They'd probably have just used me as jaguar bait, but it seems I was rambling on about falling into this deep cavern with weird figures painted all over the walls. They figured out that I'd stumbled onto some important Maya site.'

'You had,' Cleo said. 'The Maya believed this was the entrance to the underworld. It's of exceptional historical importance. The wall paintings are unique.'

'Yeah, well, I don't think these dudes were interested in *history*. They were just after treasure. You could practically see the dollar signs rolling in front of their eyes. It seems the Maya used to throw valuable objects into these sinkholes when they were doing sacrifice rituals.'

Cleo looked out across the water. Ryan could tell she was thinking about the White Finder Tree. From Morning Star's account it lay down at the bottom of this subterranean pool.

'We need to get back to camp,' Cleo said. 'We have to organise a team of divers . . .' Her teeth were chattering so much she could barely speak. She began getting to her feet, but sank back down.

Cleo's right, Ryan thought. *It's freezing down here.* Never mind the White Finder Tree; if they didn't get into the sun soon they'd all keel over with hypothermia. Suddenly he remembered something. 'Wait! Dad . . .' He stalled for a moment, still unused to the sound of the unfamiliar word on his lips. 'When you fell in this *cenote* before, you said you managed to get out. How?'

'There was a long tangle of tree roots hanging down, almost touching the water. I grabbed onto it and climbed up to the top.'

'Great! Let's do it!' Ryan scrambled to his feet and pulled Cleo up too. 'Show us where.'

Dad pointed to the far side of the *cenote*. 'I'm not sure that this ledge goes that far . . .'

Only one way to find out, Ryan thought. 'Can you walk on that leg?'

Eddie eased himself up and tested his weight. 'Yeah, the wound's not that deep.' He grinned at Cleo. 'You'll have to work on your crocodile-wrangling technique a bit more!'

Cleo didn't laugh.

They began to shuffle along the ledge in single file. Before long the shelf of rock became broader and flatter. 'So what happened after the Red Wolves found you in the jungle?' Cleo asked.

'They were desperate to find this place! I heard their boss talking about some rich powerful Westerner who would pay them a massive reward if I could lead them to it . . . I was their meal ticket.'

Ryan stopped and exchanged a look with Cleo. *'Melanie Moore!'* she said. 'Also known as Sofia K. Proufork!'

Dad frowned. 'I don't remember hearing those names. I got the impression it was a man. Anyway, I had to find this place again first. Every day, they'd take me out into the jungle to search; at gunpoint, of course. That's what we were doing today. I was with three of them. Then the men heard voices nearby . . .'

'That was us,' Ryan said.

'They thought we were being followed. Two of the men went off scouting around to check it out. I managed to overpower the one left behind to guard me and make a break for freedom.' Dad paused to tighten the scarf tourniquet on his leg. 'That's when I ran into you . . .'

Ryan felt a surge of pride. Not only had they found Dad. By distracting the Red Wolves men and then leading them away from the *cenote* they had actually helped him to escape. He couldn't wait to get back and tell Mum the story. Seeing her face when she realised that he'd brought Dad back with him would be almost as good as finding Dad in the first place!

To Ryan's surprise, Cleo seemed less upbeat.

She narrowed her eyes at Dad. 'So . . . when you escaped you just *happened* to be right next to the *cenote* you'd been looking for all that time? Wasn't that a bit of a coincidence?'

Dad smiled. 'Your friend doesn't miss much, does she?' Then he turned to Cleo. 'You're right. In fact I'd figured out we were almost on top of the *cenote* several weeks ago. But I wasn't going to *admit* that I'd found it! The minute the Red Wolves knew the location they'd have no use for me any more. They'd have just finished me off quietly. So I had to keep stringing them along with the search until I saw my chance to escape. Like I said, they're a pretty amateur bunch so I didn't have to wait too long.'

Dad stopped and pointed out a cluster of roots hanging down like a giant twisted rope.

Cleo sat down and began to take off her walking boots. 'We'll to have to swim from here.'

But Dad placed his hand over Cleo's on her bootlaces. 'I'm sorry,' he said gently. 'But there's no point. The water level must have dropped since I was here before.'

Ryan looked at the tangled rope. Dad was right. Even the longest roots stopped at least two metres above the water. There was no way they could reach them.

36

WILLPOWER

RYAN CROUCHED DOWN and put his arm round Cleo. She felt like a bag of frozen peas. Her skin was bluish grey apart from the black eye, which was now taking up almost half her face.

'We've *got* to find another way out of here.' Cleo said, shivering. 'Did you see a way through that cave on the slope? The jaguar sarcophagus text said *enter the mouth of the Witz monster . . .*'

'What's the jaguar sarcophagus?' Dad asked.

'Long story,' Ryan said. 'It's the reason Cleo and I are here. There was some writing on it about this ancient compass called the White Finder Tree. We think it's down there somewhere.' Ryan pointed at the water. He squeezed Cleo's shoulders more tightly. 'There's no way through the Witz monster. I was checking it out just before you decided to jump in for a swim. There was obviously a tunnel once, but there's been a huge rockfall. It's completely blocked.'

Cleo sank her forehead onto her knees. 'What are we going to do?'

Ryan didn't have an answer. How could fate be so cruel? All these years he'd been missing Dad, hiding his feelings, carefully staying away from the black hole of his absence. He'd found Dad at last. At the bottom of a black hole! It had been the happiest moment of his life. Now, just half an hour later, they were dangerously close to dying together, trapped in this stupid hole for eternity. And Cleo too. *The Black Witch moth was right after all.* He kicked his heels against the stone. The noise echoed. He glared across the water at the Lords of Death. They grinned back at him as if enjoying the joke. *At least we're handy for the Underworld,* he thought bitterly. But as Ryan watched the dancing figures, half-mesmerised by the patterns of light playing over the walls, something stirred in his memory, something he'd seen in Chichén Itzá . . . *the snake of light* . . . He jumped up, pulling Cleo with him. 'It's the next line on the sarcophagus!' he cried. '*Follow the trail of the Serpent King.* That's what we have to do!'

'But we've *already* done that part!' Cleo's voice was heavy with despair. 'The Serpent King is Jaguar Paw. We've followed the trail that his spirit took through the jungle to get to Xib'alb'a. And now we're here, stuck in the middle of it, with no way out.'

'But that's the point. We *not* in the middle of Xib'alb'a. I think this is only the outer part. Like a porch.'

Cleo looked utterly unconvinced. 'The Underworld doesn't have a *porch!*'

'OK, let's say it's like a hotel lobby then. Think about it. These ugly mugs ...' Ryan swept his arm at the Lords of Death '... are here to scare off anyone who's not allowed in ...'

'Like bouncers outside a nightclub?' Dad put in.

'Exactly,' Ryan said. At least *Dad* was on the same wavelength. 'The bit about following the trail of the Serpent King, comes *after* entering through the Witz monster. That's how we get from here into the heart of Xib'alb'a.'

Dad smoothed a hand over his beard and frowned. 'I may be missing something but we're trying to find a way out of this *cenote*. How does going further *into* it help us?'

But Cleo suddenly revived. 'No, Ryan's right. The next bit on the sarcophagus said, *Jaguar Paw will return from the deepest waters of Xib'alb'a.* We have to get to the *deepest waters* before we can get out. That must be where the trail of the Serpent King leads.' She slumped against the wall. 'But we have to find it first.'

'That's what I've been trying to tell you! It's right there!' Ryan pointed at a faint band of light that undulated round the wall of the *cenote* several metres above the surface of the water. It was the reflection of a long slice of sunlight that shone in through a crack in the limestone above the stalagmites. The movement of the water made the light waver so that the 'snake' appeared to slither along the wall. 'It's just like El Castillo in Chichén Itzá,' he said.

Dad looked blank but Cleo nodded. 'El Castillo is a pyramid,' she told him. 'The sunlight makes it look as if the snake god, Kukulcan, is crawling down the staircase from the top.' She squinted at the wall. 'I see what you mean. The reflection gives the effect of a snake. But it's so faint and blurry. Can that really be . . .' Suddenly she grabbed Ryan's arm. 'Of course! You're right! At Chichén Itzá, the pyramid is aligned so that the snake is seen at the Spring and Autumn equinox. It's the same here. Mountain Star said that Lady Six Sky came to fetch Jaguar Paw back from the Underworld on March 21st. It's the Spring Equinox. That must be when the sun is in the best position to shine in through that crack in the rock. The snake would be much brighter and clearer then.' Cleo pulled her waterproof torch from her tool belt and directed the beam along the length of the snake.

'There!' Ryan reached out and steadied her hand. At the end of the snake, lines had been carved into the wall to form the head; huge and square, with a blunt snout and gaping jaws. He scanned the snake for a clue, something that would show them how to follow the serpent trail and escape. 'There's got to be something . . .'

Cleo circled the torch beam around a dark shape between the snake's fangs. Ryan had thought it was painted onto the wall, but now he could see it was a hole in the rock. 'Are you thinking what I'm thinking?' she asked.

Ryan nodded. 'It's the entrance to a tunnel.'

'We have to climb into a snake's mouth?' Dad looked dubious. Then he shrugged. 'I guess there's a first time for everything . . .'

First time? Not for us, Ryan thought. *Cleo and I are old hands at snake tunnels!* In Egypt they'd entered through the mouth of Apep, the World Encircler, and found themselves in Queen Nerfertiti's tomb. Who knew what lay at the end of the tunnel this time? But that wasn't their first problem. The snake's mouth was on the other side of the *cenote* and several metres above the ledge.

Just getting to it would be a challenge.

Cleo had been running on adrenaline for hours. The heroic hormone had already helped her to escape from a crashed jeep, hike through the jungle, swim across an underground pool and fight off a large man/crocodile. Supplies were running dangerously low. The only fuel Cleo had left was pure willpower.

She was *not* going to give up now.

Following Ryan and Eddie, she dragged herself along the ledge around the *cenote*. In places it was so narrow they had to shuffle sideways, their backs pressed flat to the wall. But they made it, at last, to a point directly beneath the jaws of the snake of light.

'Sit down and rest for a minute,' Ryan told her. 'I'll climb up first and check it out.'

Cleo was about to protest. *Just because I'm a girl doesn't mean I can't climb* ... But her wrist was a swollen lump of pain and her legs were as heavy as sand. She flopped down onto the stone.

Eddie stooped and made a step of his hands to give Ryan a leg up. 'Ouch! Mind my hair!' he laughed as Ryan clambered up. 'I've been perfecting these dreadlocks for years!'

Eddie made another joke. Ryan laughed. They sounded so happy together; as if they were on a family outing. Cleo's head lolled. *Visit Xib'alb'a*, she thought. *A fun day out for all the family!* She closed her eyes. She was six years old, wandering the ruins of Knossos under a burning sun, lost in the Minotaur's labyrinth . . . *Cleo! Cleo!* Mum and Dad were calling her. She rounded a corner and there was Dad, his arms out. 'Dad!' she cried.

She snapped her eyes open.

It was Eddie Flint calling her name. '*Cleo!* Are you OK?'

'Fine!' Cleo snapped, furious with herself for drifting off. She might as well just wave a white flag and let hypothermia win! She scrambled to her feet. Ryan had already scaled the wall and was leaning down from the tunnel mouth. 'If Dad lifts you,' he called, 'I'll pull you up.'

Before she could argue, Eddie grabbed her by the hips and launched her upwards. As she reached for Ryan, Cleo turned and glanced down at the water. 'Wait!' she cried. 'There's something down there!'

Next thing she knew, Cleo was belly-flopping into the water. Shocked and winded by the cold, she thrashed to the surface in a froth of bubbles. 'You dropped me!' she spluttered.

'You lurched backwards,' Eddie grumbled. 'And you yelled in my ear.' He stretched out a hand to fish her out.

But Cleo had other ideas. She was in now; she was going to take a look. She was sure she'd seen something gleaming beneath the dark water. *Could it be* . . . She gulped down a long breath and dived.

There *was* something there . . . Cleo pushed deeper, reached and closed her hand around a small pale object snagged in a clump of roots; it felt soft and fleshy beneath a crinkly skin. Disappointment sucked the breath from her body. *A dead fish? A crab that had lost its shell?* Water rushed up her nose. She kicked for the surface ... *But there was something else. Those roots felt hard and smooth.* She forced herself back down, and grasped a handful. She tugged and twisted. The roots didn't budge. They were caught under a rock. Cleo tried again. Her blood roared for air ... pressure built in her lungs, her throat, her ears ... she couldn't bear it ... and then, at last something came away in her hand. Cleo burst out of the water hoisting her trophy high, like the Statue of Liberty with her flaming torch.

Eddie helped pull her out and she flopped onto the ledge.

Cleo couldn't speak. She stared at the object in her hand. It was the most beautiful thing she'd ever seen. It was about thirty centimetres high, an exquisitely carved model ceiba tree fashioned from lustrous jade; green for the spreading branches and red-brown for the roots. Blocks of glyphs had been carved into the trunk, among thousands of tiny gold thorns that pricked her fingers.

'Wow!' Eddie whistled. 'What is it?'

'White ... Finder ... Tree!' Cleo panted.

'Any chance I can get a look?' Ryan was leaning so far out of the snake's mouth he was in danger of falling headfirst. 'Or are you going to hog it for yourself?'

Cleo raised the tree above her head. 'It's got a lodestone!' she said. 'Just as we thought.' The finger of magnetic stone trembled in the centre of the hollow tree on a mounting of polished turquoise. Coloured gemstones marked points around the outside of the trunk; white pearl for north, yellow amber for south, red fire-opal for east and black obsidian for west. 'You were right about the jewels too!' Cleo counted the branches that radiated out from the top. 'Nine!' she shouted. 'Just like Mountain Star's diagram!'

Ryan cheered. 'Oh yeah! Sofia K. Proufork, eat your heart out!'

Sofia! Or rather Melanie! Cleo had almost forgotten about their duplicitous rival. Was she still searching for the *cenote*? With any luck she'd given up and gone back to camp.

'What's that in your other hand?' Eddie asked.

Cleo looked down. The soft pale object she'd found in the water was still stuck to her palm. 'It's a *Sponch!* biscuit,' she laughed. 'It must be the one I was trying to open when I fell down here.' She examined the cellophane wrapper. It was still sealed. She opened it and divided the marshmallow biscuit into three. She handed one piece to Eddie and waved another at Ryan. 'I'll bring this up to you.' Then she popped the third piece into her mouth.

She had never tasted anything so delicious.

Cleo attached the White Finder Tree to her tool belt. Powered by marshmallow, she made it into the mouth of the snake on the second attempt. Eddie hauled himself up after her.

Cleo knelt and shone her torch into the snake's mouth like a doctor examining a sore throat. The hole led to a narrow downward-sloping tunnel. Eddie insisted on going first. 'I feel as if I'm about to be eaten alive.'

'Think of the tunnel as the snake's trachea rather than its oesophagus,' Cleo told him.

Ryan laughed. 'That makes all the difference!'

Cleo didn't see what was funny. Being inhaled was obviously less unpleasant than being swallowed. Who wanted to be digested by stomach acids?

The tunnel was no more than a metre high and only wide enough for single file. Clutching the torch, Cleo felt her way along through dripping, slippery rock. At first they crouched and shuffled, but as the descent grew steeper, they gave up and slithered down on their backs. They gathered speed and were soon careening blindly down, the dark broken only by scraps of torchlight glancing off glistening black walls. At last they shot out of the chute. *Not again!* Cleo thought, as she plunged into deep icy water. Used to it now, she barely struggled, but pulled up to the surface and trod water.

'That was the water slide from hell,' Ryan gasped as he surfaced next to her. 'I'm covered in bruises . . .' He broke off suddenly. 'Get off me!' he screamed, writhing, flapping his arms, and churning the water into foam. Next to him Eddie was doing the same, swatting the air so frantically he clipped Cleo around the ear.

A swarm of soft wings brushed against Cleo's face. Small claws caught at her hair. 'It's only bats!' she shouted over the high-pitched squeaks that vibrated all around them. 'I thought you were being attacked by sharks or something!'

'Bats!' Ryan yelled. 'Not again! I had enough of these in Egypt and China. Why does the Underworld *always* have to have bats?'

'It's obvious,' Cleo told him. 'Many species of *chiroptera* colonise dark, secluded places like tombs and caves.' This really wasn't the best time to discuss bat habitats, she thought. 'Stop making a fuss. They're perfectly harmless. Well, unless they're Common Vampire bats . . .'

'Vampire bats!' Eddie and Ryan shouted as one. Their flailing grew even more frenzied.

'Don't worry! It's a myth that vampire bats suck blood.

They only make a tiny bite in the skin and lap at it.' This didn't seem to be helping. Cleo gave up. The bats were already starting to swirl back up to their roosts.

'I know I'm always saying you're rubbish at lying,' Ryan panted. 'But next time I'm being attacked by bats just *try!* Tell me they're flying hamsters or furry sparrows or something. And never, ever, say the word, *vampire* . . .'

Cleo tuned out Ryan's grumbling. She held up the torch and swept it round in a circle. Through the flittering batwings she saw that they had fallen into a second, deeper *cenote*. The walls towered as sheer and smooth as the sides of a well. Long needles of light pierced a network of tiny holes in the rock high above and slanted down to the water. They picked out a sight so breath-taking that Cleo forgot to tread water. She began to sink, and surfaced in a fit of coughing.

From the centre of the dark pool rose an enormous tree. The mighty trunk was supported by buttress roots as tall as houses and crowned with branches that spread out so far that they touched the walls. 'It's petrified,' Cleo murmured.

Ryan ducked as a straggler bat swooped past. 'Yeah, I know how it feels!'

'I don't mean *frightened,*' Cleo snapped. 'Petrified, as in *turned to stone*. Over thousands of years, the water dripping over the wood has deposited minerals that have replaced the tree's living cells. It's a giant fossil.'

As she swam towards the tree, the words from the jaguar sarcophagus played in her head. *Jaguar Paw will return from the deepest waters of Xib'alb'a. He will rise through the World Tree . . .* She clung on to a stone buttress and turned back to Ryan and Eddie. She knew what they had to do next. But she was so tired that every part of her body, from nerve endings to the marrow in her bones, sank at the thought of the energy it would need.

She was right out of adrenaline, marshmallow and willpower.

'This is the World Tree,' she said. A trembling chorus of whispers echoed round the cavernous well; *tree, tree, treeeee*. 'And we're going to have to climb it.'

37

LIFE

RYAN PADDLED TO Cleo's side.

Climb the tree. It sounded simple enough.

But this was no ordinary oak or willow. Even the lowest of the branches grew many metres above the water. The mighty trunk was deeply corrugated into ridges and runnels by the water dripping down like candle wax. *That might give some handholds.* Ryan ran his hand over the 'bark'. He snatched it back, pain darting across his palm. The stony surface was sandpaper-sharp, as if studded with broken glass. It was also covered with spikes of rock that stuck out like thorns. *Thorns*, he thought. *Perhaps it's a ceiba tree. Just like ...* He looked up and counted the branches. *Seven ... eight ... nine!*

Ryan quickly detached the White Finder Tree from Cleo's tool belt and held it up. The jade and gold and gemstones sparkled in the arrows of light from above, reflecting jewel-coloured lozenges onto the walls. He was right; the White Finder Tree was an exact replica of the fossilised World Tree. The nine branches on the model matched the shape and position of the branches on the original. 'Look!' he shouted, his voice booming around the *cenote*. 'They're the same!'

Dad swam closer. 'Yeah, I see what you mean. But I'm not sure how that helps us?'

But Ryan was one step ahead. 'The White Finder Tree is hollow. If it's an exact copy, that means the fossilised tree must be hollow too.' He turned to Cleo. 'The sarcophagus text says *he will rise through the World Tree,* doesn't it?' Cleo didn't reply but Ryan went on anyway. 'I think that means we have to climb up through the inside.' He gazed at the solid stone tree trunk. 'The question is, how do we get in?'

Dad grabbed the White Finder Tree from Ryan's hand. He turned it round and pointed at a little hole in the jade trunk low down among the roots. 'I noticed this before. I thought it must just have got chipped when it landed on the rocks, but it's been drilled.'

Ryan took the tree back. The hole was perfectly round. Next to it a glyph had been etched into the jade. He held it out to Cleo. 'Can you see what that says?'

'What?' Cleo barely looked up.

Ryan pushed the White Finder Tree under her nose. 'What does that glyph say?'

Cleo peered through half closed eyes. 'It's something like *Life.*'

305

'I knew it!' Ryan hugged her shoulders. 'It's the way out – the way back to life. There must be a matching hole in the trunk of the stone World Tree. We just have to find it and climb in and up through the middle.'

Dad was already searching for the entrance. 'Sorry,' he panted after swimming a complete circuit of the tree. 'There's nothing . . .'

'That can't be right!' Ryan examined the White Finder Tree again. The hole was right there on the jade trunk, between two twining roots. Suddenly the grim truth struck him. Most of the roots of the giant fossilised World Tree were *under* the water. 'Of course! We have to dive to find the entrance.'

'No-o-oo!' Cleo's wail of despair echoed on and on. 'I can't!'

Ryan turned to Cleo in surprise. She was barely keeping afloat. Even the parts of her that weren't bruised were blotchy and all the wrong colour. She could have passed as an extra from a zombie movie. Fear rattled around his body. He'd never known Cleo give up before. 'Yes you can!' he barked. 'You're the strongest swimmer of us all. You're like a mermaid!'

'A *mermaid*?' Cleo mumbled. 'They don't even exist!'

'All right! You're not a mermaid then!' he yelled. Cleo had to be the most infuriating person he'd met in his entire life. 'You're an Olympic champion diver! You're . . .' he racked his brain for an example. 'You're Tom Daley!' *As if,* he thought, *doing three and a half somersaults off the high board would help here* . . .

'Go without me.'

'One of us could go up to fetch help,' Dad suggested. 'And

the other wait down here with Cleo. The poor girl looks deadbeat.'

But Ryan had almost lost Cleo once before. The memory ripped through him as hot and bright as a distress flare; *Cleo being swallowed up by the giant booby trap in the First Emperor's tomb*. He'd stumbled down that mountainside thinking he'd never see her again . . . He wasn't going through that again! And there was no way he was letting Dad out of his sight either. He'd only just found him after six years. 'No!' he shouted. 'We stick together!'

Dad clapped him on the shoulder. 'OK. You're right. Let's find this entrance.'

Ryan checked the position of the hole in the trunk of the White Finder Tree. It was directly beneath the point where the highest of the nine branches sprouted. He swam until he reached the matching point on the giant fossilised tree. He pointed down. 'It should be about here.'

Dad towed Cleo to his side.

They all trod water, silently contemplating the dark surface. Ryan tried to block out thoughts of what might lurk in the fathomless depths. 'I'll dive down for a recce first,' he said, hoping he sounded braver than he felt. 'I'll come back up and let you know if we can get through.' Before either of them could argue he shoved the White Finder Tree towards Dad, sucked down a lungful of air and plunged down through the cold, dark water. Something touched his hands. He opened his eyes to see long shadowy tentacles. *A giant octopus? A nest of sea snakes?* His heart galloped out of control. *But no, the tentacles were solid stone. They were the roots of the World Tree*. He pushed on, wriggling through the roots until his outstretched fingers hit the hulking mass of the trunk. Through the gloom he could make out a blacker expanse. It was the entrance hole!

Ryan's survival instincts screamed in panic. *Don't do it! You'll get stuck! You're not a fish!* But he forced himself on and pulled himself through the gap. Terror drummed in in his ears. *What if the water is much deeper inside the trunk?* But it was too late to turn back. His body took over. His arms scooped. His legs threshed. Just when he thought his lungs would burst, the water lightened to brown and then green and gold and suddenly he was breaking the surface, gasping, choking, coughing, but *alive*. He threw back his head and let the bright, bright sunlight warm his face.

Far above, the hollow tree trunk was open to the sky.

The inside of the trunk was smothered with glyphs and scenes of grisly sacrifice rituals. Ryan tried not to look, and anyway he was far more interested in the vines that dangled down in thick straggling braids. It would be a long haul to climb to the top, but with these natural rope ladders they should be able to make it.

Ryan longed to stay and soak up the delicious sunlight. But he knew he had to go back for Cleo and Dad. The longer he left it, the weaker Cleo would be. He took a deep breath and dived back down.

'Good news!' he panted, bursting up through the water. The Underworld seemed colder and darker than ever after his brief visit to the surface. 'I found the hole. We can get through.'

Cleo clung to him, her good eye wide with terror.

Ryan held her under the elbows and spoke slowly and firmly. 'You just have to do this one thing. It's a piece of cake!' he lied. 'I'll dive with you and guide you.'

'And I'll be right behind to make sure you both get through before I follow you,' Dad said.

Ryan dragged Cleo closer to the tree. 'Take your bum bag off. It might get stuck.'

'No!' Cleo shrieked. 'I'm not dying without my tool belt.'

'Now you're just being a drama queen!' Ryan shouted. He was freezing, exhausted, fed up and furious. Cleo was making this ten times harder than it needed to be. He was starting to think that leaving her to take her chances in the Underworld might not be such a bad idea. 'Look! I'll take the bum bag,' he snapped, fumbling around Cleo's waist for the buckle. 'And you're *not* going to die, you wally! I won't let you. You're my *friend!*'

'A very substandard friend.' Cleo sobbed. 'I've been *trying* but I'm no good at it.'

'Rubbish!' Ryan strapped the tool belt across his chest. 'You're a brilliant friend. Totally weird and really, *really* annoying, but the best ever. That's why I love you.' *Oh no, I've said it again,* he thought. But there was no time to be embarrassed. He had to get Cleo out before she lost the plot even more. 'On the count of three!' he shouted. 'One, two, three . . .'

To Ryan's immense relief, Cleo didn't resist. She snatched a breath and let him drag her under the water. Dad was right behind them.

This time Ryan knew exactly where he was heading. He threaded quickly through the roots. But as he steered Cleo towards the hole in the trunk, she suddenly twisted away, her hair swirling around her head like black seaweed. Taken by surprise, water shot up Ryan's nose. He pulled her back and, in a desperate burst of panic, shoved her unceremoniously through the hole.

He felt a nudge on his shoulder. That must be Dad. He turned to give a thumbs-up.

But there was no one there.

38

INFINITY

RYAN'S THOUGHTS PULSED in time with the beat of the blood rushing in his ears. Where was Dad? And if Dad hadn't nudged him, who – or what had? He peered through the swirling water. Dark, flat-bodied *things* were circling him, cruising among the serpentine roots. *Crocodiles? Sharks? The blood-crazed, leaping Lords of Death?*

Tails buffeted his legs. Whiskers brushed his arms. The *things* were monster catfish! He glimpsed a gleam of white. One ghostly albino fish prowled among the shoal of black. Its flat face lunged at him, long barbels twitching around a wide toothless mouth. Ryan recoiled in horror as it tried to lock onto his neck. He turned and saw Dad writhing, bubbles streaming from his nose. The back of his t-shirt had caught on a root. The more he struggled the more it choked him. Hoards of smaller catfish crowded round his face, nibbling his beard. Ryan's lungs were bursting. He had to surface. But he had to free Dad. *I can't lose him. Not now!* He groped for the tool belt, ripped open the pockets, and found Cleo's trowel. With a frantic slash he chopped at the snagged material.

Suddenly released from the stranglehold, Dad shot forward, and rocketed through the hole in the tree trunk. Ryan was about to follow, when a glistening object drifted past him. *The White Finder Tree!* Dad must have dropped it. He reached down and caught it by the tip of a branch, just as the albino catfish charged from below, knocking him into a backwards roll. Disorientated and winded, Ryan spun round and round. *Where am I? Can't hold on, can't hold my breath any longer . . .*

Ryan felt something clasp his hand. *Please, not the catfish again!* But then he was looking into Cleo's eyes. She was reaching through the hole in the trunk. She pulled him through. Together they kicked for the surface.

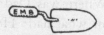

With a final heave on the rope of vines Ryan hauled himself out of Xib'alb'a. He helped Cleo up and she flopped down next to him on the jungle floor. Dad was right behind them. The climb up through the inside of the World Tree had been long and tough, but at least there had been air and sunlight; and no bats or catfish.

They crawled through a curtain of foliage and found themselves under an overhang of rock only metres away from the Witz Monster entrance. Ryan looked back at the spot from which they'd emerged. The stone twigs at the top of the fossilised tree were so well camouflaged against the undergrowth that they were almost invisible.

He sat looking around, his eyes gobbling up the blue of sky and white of cloud and green of leaves. Dad was sprawled out on a rock snoring loudly. *He's survived six years as a prisoner and escaped from the Underworld,* Ryan thought. *He deserves a snooze!* Cleo was stretched out like a starfish on a flat stone, the White Finder Tree balanced on her stomach. 'Catching some rays?' he asked.

'I'm *basking*,' Cleo corrected him. 'I'm using the warmth of the sun on the stone to increase my core body temperature. Like a lizard.'

Ryan reached out and squeezed her hand. Her skin was cold and prune-like from the water. 'You'd make a lovely reptile.'

Cleo smiled, wincing at the pain in her black eye, and squeezed back.

There weren't many girls, Ryan thought, who would consider *reptile* a compliment. Monique, for example, would not have been impressed.

'And thank you,' Cleo said, 'for not letting me give up down there. I'm sorry I was so feeble.'

'Don't mention it! I'd have been fish food if you hadn't pulled me through when that catfish attacked me.' Ryan shuddered at the memory. He had a feeling the albino catfish would be auditioning for a place in his nightmares alongside the giant salamander he'd done battle with in China. He unstrapped Cleo's tool belt and handed it over. 'I'm sorry I dropped your trowel. I know it's the special one your gran gave you. You can have mine. I'm going to give up archaeology and take up something less dangerous; like BASE jumping or shark wrestling.'

Cleo pushed up onto her elbows. 'Grandma would understand. You had to save your Dad.'

Ryan could still hardly believe it was true; Dad really was back! Every time he thought of it, he felt a new whoosh of joy. *I found Dad and I brought him back from the Underworld. Just as poor little Radiant Turtle was meant to bring his father back to life. I didn't even have to be sacrificed in the process.* And there was an added bonus! 'I guess we're immortal now,' he said. 'The jaguar sarcophagus said that if you come back from Xib'alb'a you'll live forever. We've won *the prize that all men desire.* Not that we needed any more eternal life,' he added. 'We'd already drunk the elixir of life in the Tomb of the First Emperor.'

'You don't *really* think we're immortal, do you?' Cleo asked.

Ryan was about to laugh it off when something suddenly made sense. 'How else do you explain The Butterfly of Death?'

'You mean the Black Witch moth?'

Ryan nodded. 'The Evil Black Moth of Doom came for us. We should have died. But the First Emperor's potion shielded us from its power. 'And,' he added, 'we're doubly immortal now. We'll live to infinity and beyond!'

Cleo rolled her eyes. 'There's no such thing. Infinity is . . . well, it's *infinite!*'

'You were in the tomb of the First Emperor of China?' Dad had woken up and was gaping at them in astonishment.

'Yeah. It was incredible.' Ryan couldn't help showing off

a little. 'We discovered the lost tomb of Queen Nefertiti too.'

Dad shook his head. As they dried, his beard and dreadlocks had become bushier than ever. 'We've got a *lot* of catching up to do!'

Ryan laughed and squelched to his feet. He wished they could stay sitting in the sunshine but the Red Wolves could return at any moment. And they had the long hike back to the road ahead of them.

They had just set off when Ryan remembered his backpack. He'd thrown it aside when he jumped into the *cenote* after Cleo. He had to go back for it; it contained Mountain Star's shell necklace and Cleo's notebook, not to mention the bottles of water and the machete. He picked his way carefully over the mesh of roots, until he spotted the blue nylon pack. 'The shells are safe,' he called as he headed back to Dad and Cleo. As he glanced down to check his footing he noticed a black plastic object caught in the undergrowth. He picked it up...

'Never mind the shells,' Cleo said. 'Are there any biscuits left?'

Ryan made a shock-horror face. 'You're more interested in biscuits than unique historical artefacts?'

'No. But my stomach is.' Cleo laughed. 'Must. Have. Biscuits. Now!'

Ryan took out the last packet of *Pinguinos*.

Cleo snatched them. 'What's that you've found?'

Ryan looked at the object in his hand. It was a satellite phone. Suddenly he realised he'd seen it before. 'Sofia was here,' he said. 'I mean *Melanie*.'

Cleo's mouth dropped open, showcasing the half-chewed chocolate *Pinguino*. 'How can you tell it's hers?'

'I've seen her using it. It's got an old airport security sticker on the side.'

Dad glanced over at the spot where Ryan had found the phone. The stems were flattened and snapped. 'It looks like there was a struggle. The Red Wolves must have turned on her. I know you said she's working *with* them, but they're not exactly team players.'

Ryan pressed the *ON* button, not really expecting the phone to open without a password. To his surprise the small screen lit up, revealing the most recent text message; *SEND HELP—*

Cleo peered at the screen. 'This message hasn't been sent. I think your dad's right. Sofia must have been attacked in the middle of writing it.'

Ryan scrolled up. Melanie's message was a reply to one that had arrived several hours earlier.

GET THE TREE. GET RID OF LIDYA'S KID AND THE FLINT BOY.

'Cheers!' Ryan muttered. '*Get rid of us?* What did *we* ever do?' He looked up at Cleo. 'It seems Melanie's not the Top Dog after all. She's getting her orders from this guy.' He checked the details of the message. 'That's annoying. There's no name attached to this number in the contacts list.'

'It'll have come from a stolen "burner" phone,' Dad said. 'The gangs use them all the time. They'll trash the phone after a day or two. They're almost impossible to trace. You'll probably never uncover the identity of Mr Big.'

'But I *already* know who it is.' Cleo was still staring at the message. 'There's only one person who spells my mum's name like that.'

39

BOSS

'SIR CHARLES PEACOCKE?' Ryan echoed.

Cleo could tell that he thought she was joking. She knew it sounded impossible. In fact, she felt as if the ground beneath her had turned to quicksand. She'd known Sir Charles all her life. *It can't be true.* And yet she knew beyond a glimmer of doubt that it was. The evidence was right in front of her eyes. 'Sir Charles always writes *Lidya* instead of *Lydia*, with the 'i' and the 'y' the wrong way round. It drives Mum crazy.'

Eddie Flint looked from Cleo to Ryan and back again. 'You've lost me. Who on earth is this *Sir Charles* guy?'

'Sir Charles Peacocke,' Ryan told him. 'He's the Minister for Museums and Culture. He's also Cleo's mum's boss.'

'What's he doing sending messages to tomb robbers?' Eddie asked.

'That's what I'd like to know!' Ryan frowned at Cleo. 'If you're right about this, you're saying that Sir Charles Peacocke, a government minister – a man who wears a silk handkerchief in his pocket when he's not even going to a wedding – is some kind of criminal mastermind?'

Cleo watched a large spider spinning a web between two branches. She was becoming more certain by the second. 'You said yourself that his reaction was strange when we phoned to tell him what Melanie was up to. No wonder he told us to keep quiet and that he'd sort it out in person!'

Ryan eyed the spider nervously. 'Yeah, that did seem a bit fishy. But I thought it was because Sir Charles was trying to cover up any embarrassing scandal. It wouldn't look good if it turned out that his glamorous personal assistant was a total crook. I didn't think that *he* was the one running the show!'

It was late afternoon now, and the heat was building to a thick, sweltering stew as they retraced their route to the road. Instead of steps, this time Cleo was counting the lines of evidence against Sir Charles. 'He's the *mycelium,* the connection that links all the artefacts that have gone missing on Mum's digs,' she said. 'He must have been sending orders to the tomb robbers in each country, paying them to steal the best pieces for him.'

Ryan slashed at a swathe of creepers with the machete. 'So Rachel Meadows and the other members of the Eternal Sun group were working for Sir Charles to steal the Bloodthirsty Grail in Peru and the Benben Stone in Egypt.'

'And Joey Zhou and the Tiger's Claw gang were working for him in China.' Cleo thought about how Tian Min, their original guide in Xi'an, had mysteriously disappeared. Then Joey had turned up to take his place. Sir Charles must have arranged it all. 'Joey Zhou was acting on Sir Charles's orders to steal the Immortality Scroll and to follow us into the Dragon Path tunnel on the hunt for more treasure. No wonder he was so keen to come to Xi'an and congratulate us on finding the Kitchen of Eternal Life. He was really coming to meet with Joey and see what else they could get their hands on!'

Ryan stopped, the machete still raised in mid air. 'Of course! I should have twigged. I saw Sir Charles and Joey Zhou huddled in conversation at the banquet. Then Joey disappeared, and a few hours later, the scroll did too.'

'And it explains the mystery of how Joey Zhou could have been in two places at once,' Cleo said. 'The two main witnesses who claimed they saw Joey at the conference in Hong Kong on the day that he attacked us at the Dragon Path were none other than Sir Charles Peacocke and Melanie Moore. It's obvious now; they were lying to give Joey a cover story. He wasn't there at all.'

'So Melanie has been Sir Charles's partner in crime all along.' Ryan laughed. 'It gives a whole new meaning to Personal Assistant!'

As they trudged up and down the gullies and through the jaguar glade, Cleo struggled to adjust to Sir Charles being a criminal. He'd given her a microscope for her sixth birthday. He'd arranged her a private tour of the amazing Lascaux cave paintings when she was ten. And now it was *get rid of Lidya's kid and the Flint Boy*. She wasn't sure what 'getting rid of' involved, but it sounded permanent. *The Red Wolves might just have saved our lives,* she thought. *If they hadn't turned against Melanie, she'd have been waiting for us when we emerged from the cenote. She could have picked us off with three gun shots, grabbed the White Finder Tree and been on a plane out of Mexico by breakfast . . .*

Ryan interrupted her thoughts. 'There's just no *way* anyone's going to believe this! The only evidence we have against Sir Charles is a single spelling mistake.'

But Cleo already had an idea. She grabbed the phone from Ryan's pocket, deleted *send help,* typed a new message and clicked *send.*

Ryan gaped at her. 'What have you done?'

'I've sent a reply, of course. Sir Charles will assume it's from Melanie, since it's from her phone.' Cleo showed Ryan the message.

I HAVE DEALT WITH THE KIDS AND AM NOW IN POSSESSION OF THE TREE. MEET ME AT MIDDAY TOMORROW AT LA LUNA BAR, XPUJIL; I WILL HAND IT OVER THEN.

'That's *never* going to work!' Ryan passed the phone to his dad. They both shook their heads.

'Why not?' Cleo demanded. 'Sir Charles told us he was coming to Calakmul. He'll want to meet up with Melanie.'

'He'll know this message isn't genuine,' Ryan said. 'It's way too complicated. *I am now in possession of? And* you've used a semi-colon! It's practically an essay. People don't write texts like that.'

'I do.'

'Correction,' Ryan said. '*Normal* people don't write texts like that.' He took the phone and entered another message; *ABSOLUTE NIGHTMARE HERE BUT ALL BACK UNDER CONTROL NOW. 'Now* it sounds like Sofia. Or Melanie. Or whatever her name is!'

Ryan's dad smiled. 'Don't be too disappointed if you don't hear back. It's odds on that this Peacocke guy has already dumped that phone he was using . . .'

The phone buzzed. 'Incoming message!' Cleo shouted. She swiped the phone out of Ryan's hand. There were just two letters on the screen: *OK*.

'Oh yeah!' Ryan crowed to his dad. 'Who said it wouldn't work?'

'*You* did, actually,' Cleo pointed out.

'It wouldn't have without my text as well.'

Cleo gave up. It was obviously *her* message that had done the trick. But she let it go. 'Now we just have to lie in wait outside La Luna bar at midday tomorrow and see who turns up. I'm a hundred per cent sure it will be Sir Charles Peacocke.'

Ryan grinned. 'It's genius! He's going to walk right into our trap!'

Cleo was so excited about the plan she forgot she was exhausted and pushed on at top speed. Ryan was right beside her, hacking through the brambles with superhuman energy.

'Whoah! Wait a minute, you two!'

Cleo and Ryan swung round. Eddie was standing in their trail, hands on hips.

'Sorry, Dad,' Ryan called back. 'Are we going too fast?'

'I'm talking about this plan of yours.' Eddie caught them up. 'If Peacocke really is the Head Honcho he's an extremely dangerous man. He'll be armed. He'll have bodyguards with him. I can't let you do it.'

Cleo clenched her fists. Eddie Flint had only been back a few hours and he was playing the Strict Parent card already! *Well he's not my dad*, she thought. *He can't stop me*. Then she thought of her own father. *As if Dad's going to let me hang around in a seedy bar to ensnare a master criminal either.* It was so unfair! Cleo could feel Sir Charles Peacocke slipping out of their grasp already . . .

But Eddie smiled. 'Don't look so crestfallen. I was going to say *I can't let you do it alone*. It's an excellent plan, but think about it! Peacocke's not exactly going to put his hands up and say, *I'm sorry, I've been a very naughty boy*. Look, when we get back to camp we'll all sit down together and sort it out and we'll call the police chief and do this properly . . .'

Cleo hated to admit it, but Eddie was right. They needed back-up on this one. Ryan shrugged and nodded. 'It's a deal.'

Eddie put an arm round each of their shoulders. 'Quick march then! We've got work to do!'

Mum threw open the trailer door. 'Ryan! Where on earth have you been? We heard there'd been a crash. I've been worried sick . . .' She grabbed his shoulders in something halfway between a hug and a shake.

Ryan had jumped out of the truck and sprinted to the trailer ahead of Dad. 'Guess what! We found . . .'

Mum rolled her eyes. 'The White Finder Tree?'

'Yes, but that's not what I meant. We found . . .'

Mum didn't let him finish. She began to shoo him up the steps. 'Look, I don't care if you found the Holy Grail. Honestly, love, you've got to stop these mad treasure hunts with Cleo. Why can't you stick to *normal* trouble like joy riding and graffiti? It'd be much safer . . .'

'Julie!'

Mum's words died away as she turned and saw Dad standing at the bottom of the steps.

Her eyes popped open and then narrowed as if trying to focus. Her foot missed a step. Ryan caught her by the arm. Dad had raked his hands through his beard and tied his dreadlocks back but he still looked a mess. The blood-soaked jeans didn't help.

'Is it . . . I don't . . . *Eddie?*'

Ryan gulped back tears. 'That's what I was trying to tell you. We found Dad.'

There was a long, long moment when Mum and Dad just looked at each other. At last, Dad staggered forwards and Mum sort of fell down the steps into his arms. They clung together, crying and laughing at the same time. Then they both reached out and pulled Ryan in too. He'd waited six years for this moment. He was so happy – and so squashed between his parents – that he forgot to breathe. He was in danger of being suffocated by emotion when he felt something scratching at his shins. He pulled away and looked down to see Shadow trying to clamber up his leg to join in.

Dad raised his eyebrows. 'New member of the family?'

Mum smiled through her tears. 'Let's get you two cleaned up. You both look terrible.' She peered at Ryan. 'Is that a *lovebite* on your neck?'

Ryan felt the sore patch under his jaw. 'Yeah, from a giant albino catfish.'

Mum shook her head. Then she laughed and grinned at Dad. 'Sorry, Eddie, I've done my best with him!'

Dad pulled her close. 'You've done a fine job, Julie,' he mumbled into her hair. Our son saved my life. I've never met anyone so brave.' He smiled at Ryan over Mum's head. 'He's

. . . how did your friend, Cleo, put it?' He nodded to himself. *'Just amazing!'*

Ryan glanced up at the clock on the café wall for the millionth time. Ten to twelve. Cleo was winding her plait round and round her fingers, her gaze constantly flicking across the street to the doors of La Luna. In ten minutes Sir Charles Peacocke was due to arrive at the bar to meet his accomplice Sofia K. Proufork, alias Melanie Moore.

On the building site on the corner, several workmen were busy with concrete mixers and drills. A man was washing his car outside the mini-market. Two women were buying bread from a bakery stand. It seemed like an everyday scene in Xpujil. Except they were all on high alert, surreptitiously talking into hidden walkie-talkies. Chief Garcia was co-ordinating the operation from the launderette next to the bar. Cleo and Ryan had been allowed to watch on condition they stayed out of harm's way in the café.

A lot had happened after their emotional return to camp last night.

There had been a long meeting, gathered around Rosita's campfire with the McNeils and Alex Shawcross and Max Henderson. The White Finder Tree had been passed around, gleaming green and ruby and gold in the firelight, as Cleo and Ryan told its two interwoven stories. The ancient story of how Lady Six Sky had tried to use the White Finder Tree to bring Jaguar Paw back from Xib'alb'a and how the shaman had dropped it into the *cenote* when the jaguar had pounced. And the twenty-first century story of how Melanie Moore, disguised as Sofia K. Proufork, had plotted to steal it for Sir Charles Peacocke. The fire had died down to embers and the dawn chorus was in full swing before the tales were told. *Sir Charles Peacocke?* everyone had repeated over and over. *He was behind it all? And the Benben Stone? And the Immortality Scroll?*

The flights back to London had been cancelled.

And now the trap was set. Ryan looked up at the sound of a car braking. A red and white taxi was pulling up outside La Luna.

'This is it!' Cleo murmured.

A man in a light blue linen suit, dark sunglasses and a panama hat slid out of the taxi. He paused, looking up and down the street. Then he stepped towards the saloon doors. They opened. Swirling music poured out. Suddenly there was an explosion of movement. The women buying bread charged at the man in the panama hat, waving their guns and shouting in Spanish. The car-washing guy wrestled him to the ground, one arm pinned high against his back.

Chief Garcia burst out of the laundrette, a gun in each hand. She strutted towards the man, clearly enjoying her moment.

The man looked up from the pavement. His hat had fallen off to reveal a sweep of smooth white hair.

'Sir Charles Peacocke!' Cleo breathed. 'Yes! We were right.'

As if he'd heard his name, Sir Charles looked up and across the street. He caught sight of Cleo and Ryan. A spasm of rage distorted his face. He fumbled for something in his jacket pocket. A pink silk handkerchief flew up and fluttered to the ground.

'He's got a gun!' Ryan yelled.

With a jaguar-like roar, Sir Charles fired. Chief Garcia fired at the same moment.

Ryan dived to pull Cleo to the ground.

The bullet whizzed over their heads and shattered the clock on the café wall.

Above the ringing in his ears Ryan could hear Chief Garcia shouting. 'Charles Alfred Peacocke, I arrest you on suspicion of tomb-robbing, antiquities-smuggling, money laundering and fraud.'

She hadn't even called him Sir.

40

ETERNITY

CLEO STRETCHED OUT on the sun lounger. It was three days since she'd survived the icy waters of the *cenote* and the chill still hadn't quite thawed from her bones. She gazed out over sparkling sand and turquoise sea. Beyond a row of palm trees luxury hotels sparkled white and silver against a cloudless sky.

The beach resort of Cancún was only a day's drive from Calakmul but it felt like a different world. After Sir Charles Peacocke's arrest Mum and Dad had decided they all needed a holiday, somewhere as far away from tombs and temples as possible. Cleo picked up her book. She'd swapped the *Popol Vuh* for a biography of one of her heroes:

Dorothy Hodgkin, the pioneering biochemist. She'd only read half a page when something freezing dripped on her toe. She jumped, memories of Xib'alb'a snatching her breath away . . .

'White chocolate *Magnum*,' Ryan announced, handing her the ice cream. 'You know you might need to get some therapy.'

'Therapy?' Cleo asked. 'What for?'

'This water phobia you've got.'

'It's *not* a phobia.'

'So why won't you come for a swim?' Ryan asked through a mouthful of strawberry *Cornetto*. 'The sea's really warm.'

'I'm *reading*.' Cleo wasn't going to admit that he had a point. The thought of anything cooler than a scalding hot shower gave her palpitations.

Ryan flopped down on the next sun lounger. 'Good news,' he said. 'Mum heard from Miguel today; the guy from the Red Wolves we were meeting when I blew up the drugs barn. He's made it safely to his grandmother's in Mexico City and is going back to school. We're going to send him some money.'

'I could send him some books . . .'

Cleo's words were interrupted by a buzz. Ryan pulled his phone from his shorts pocket. 'It's a message from Rosita. With a photo of Shadow.'

Ryan had wanted to take Shadow home, but had finally been persuaded that Manchester was not the ideal habitat for a young anteater. Rosita had offered to take care of him. Cleo pushed up her sunglasses to look at the screen. She wasn't wearing them so much to protect her eyes as to stop strangers asking if she'd been in a fight. The bruising round her eye was turning from purple to khaki and yellow. Combined with the bandage on her sprained wrist, it seemed no one could resist making jokes about bare-knuckle boxing.

The photo showed Shadow curled up in a hammock.

'I hope Luis hasn't been giving him beer,' Ryan said. 'It's not good for him.'

Cleo laughed. 'You sound like a strict parent.'

'Talking of parents . . .' Ryan rolled his eyes and looked along the beach to where Eddie and Julie were setting up a barbecue. They kept collapsing into each other's arms in giggles. 'Young love!' he groaned. 'They're *so* embarrassing!' Then he laughed. 'But I'm not complaining. Mum's so misty-eyed she's completely forgotten that I'm supposed to be back at school by now. We're staying here for a couple more weeks so that Dad can build up his strength.' He grinned. 'He *is* recovering from a vicious unprovoked trowel attack, after all!'

Cleo shoved him off the sun lounger. 'Unprovoked? It was self-defence. Your Dad attacked me first!'

Ryan clambered back onto the sun lounger. 'I've had a message from Roberto too.' He flicked through the pictures on his phone and showed Cleo a new one of Roberto Chan with his wife and young Alejandro. Despite the bandage round his head, Roberto's broad face was lit up by a jubilant smile. His injuries from the jeep crash hadn't turned out to be serious and Ryan's jungle leaves had stopped any infection setting in. 'They're planning a trip to Disneyland in the Spring,' Ryan added.

Roberto's money worries were over. He'd received funding from the Mexican government to study the White

Finder Tree, which was now safely stored at the Campeche Museum. He would also be in charge of a major new dig at the Xib'alb'a *cenote*, with a team of expert divers, to search for further treasures beneath the water. A television company had already asked to make a film of the project.

Cleo was handing the phone back to Ryan when another new message popped up. '*Monique?*' The last lump of ice cream fell off the stick and plopped onto the front of her swimming costume.

Ryan opened the message. 'Actually, it's from Professor Wynne. Monique's just passing it on. It's to thank us.'

'What for?'

'I sent him a thank you present from both of us. A signed photo of Kylie Minogue I found on eBay.'

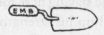

Ryan piled his plate with grilled fish and steak from the barbecue and sat down with his parents and the McNeils under a palm-thatched awning on the beach. Dad had shaved off the beard and dreadlocks, and now looked less like a Yeti. Mum had bleached the dark brown dye out of her short spikey hair and looked like her old self again. It was great to see them together; even if they did insist on staring into each other's eyes.

It wasn't long before the conversation returned to the subject of Sir Charles Peacocke. 'I've had an update from my contact back home,' Mum said. One of her reporter friends had been following the police investigation. 'They've searched his house. Darlbury Hall is a rambling old place. Apparently they've found a secret room in the basement . . .'

'Is that where he's stockpiled all the stolen swag?' Ryan asked.

Mum offered round the salad. 'Not all of it. He sold most of the artefacts on the black market. It seems he just kept certain items. Magic relics and old alchemy books and scrolls of instructions of how to make elixirs and potions . . .'

'Of course!' Ryan had suddenly figured it out. 'It was never about the money. It was about immortality! Sir Charles is just like the First Emperor of China. He wants to live forever. *The prize that all men desire,*' he added, remembering the words on the Snake Stone.

Mum nodded. 'Yeah, it certainly looks that way. They found some strange equipment in that basement too. Vats full of liquid nitrogen . . .'

'You mean for cryonic storage?' Cleo said. 'If all else failed he could freeze his body to preserve it until some future time when it can be brought back to life.'

Ryan shuddered. This was turning into something from a horror film!

'And Charles Peacocke wasn't the only one involved,' Mum went on. 'He was part of a group. Look at this! I've got a picture.' She held up her phone.

Ryan quickly closed his eyes. He didn't need to see a freezer full of the lifeless bodies of a load of Sir Charles's crackpot buddies. He heard Cleo gasp. He opened one eye to peep. But the photo wasn't of bodies in vats. It was some sort of altar painted with . . . He looked closer. *A pair of Egyptian ankh signs on a fiery sun.* The last time he'd seen that symbol it had been tattooed on Rachel Meadows's scalp. 'The Eternal Sun!' he breathed.

'Now it all makes sense,' Cleo said. 'Sir Charles was a

member of the Eternal Sun cult all along. He wanted the Benben Stone for himself so he could take part in that Return of the Phoenix ritual that was meant to grant immortality.'

'Sorry I'm late!' Alex Shawcross came hurrying across the sand. She was spending a few days in Cancún with them before going back to Campeche to study the bodies of the Unknown Woman and Child; who were, of course, no longer unknown. They had now been identified as Lady Mountain Star and Radiant Turtle, two children of King Jaguar Paw. Alex had a theory that Lady Six Sky had poisoned them both after the jaguar had disrupted her plans to bring Jaguar Paw back from Xib'alb'a. Alex loved poisons almost as much as diseases. She held up a bottle. 'Anyone like a drink? Compliments of the hotel barman. It's Mezcal, a Mexican speciality.'

'That's the stuff with the worm in the bottle?' Dad asked.

'That's right. Isn't it super?' Alex began pouring the pale gold liquid into glasses. 'Would you like to try it?' she asked Cleo and Ryan.

Ryan eyed what looked like a fat white maggot. 'No way! That's far too *helminthological for* me.'

'*Helminthology* only applies to *parasitic* worms,' Cleo pointed out. 'And, anyway, it's not actually a worm. It's the larva of the moth, *hypopta agavis*.'

Ryan laughed. 'Of course. How silly of me!'

'Have you heard the latest on the jaguar intestines?' Alex asked.

Ryan cut in with a swift change of subject. He really didn't want to discuss internal organs while eating steak. 'So was Melanie Moore an immortality nut too?'

Mum shrugged. 'Looks like she was just in it for the

money. She could sell on any artefacts that Sir Charles didn't want to keep.'

Cleo's mum agreed. 'Chief Garcia phoned me this afternoon. It seems that Melanie got away from the Red Wolves and has disappeared without a trace. She'll be travelling under a new identity, of course. Melanie Moore isn't her real name either. The police found a whole pile of forged passports in her trailer . . .'

'But they have made some progress,' Cleo's dad added, topping up his glass. 'Sofia left her laptop in the trailer. It seems that she was the technical brains of the operation. She'd hacked into databases of archaeological finds all over the world.'

'Being the assistant to the Minister for Museums and Culture must have come in very handy,' Cleo snorted. 'She had all the passwords!'

'Exactly!' Pete McNeil agreed. 'She trawled the catalogues for interesting new finds and information about the location of valuable artefacts. Then she built a 'trap door' into the software and deleted any items that she and Peacocke wanted for themselves from the database index. Basically those items 'disappeared' from the records; they wouldn't show up if anyone searched for them. Then they could arrange to steal those artefacts at their leisure – usually by sending in a local criminal gang to loot the site or break in to the museum store. Other times they'd work through an insider on the dig team . . .'

'Or Melanie made up a new identity and came to look for the treasure herself.' Lydia McNeil slammed down her glass. 'No wonder we couldn't figure out what was happening.'

Cleo dropped her knife and fork. 'That explains it!' She

turned to Ryan. 'Remember at the History of Archaeology Museum last year. I always wondered why the missing film of Lymington and Stubbs entering the dragon path tunnel didn't come up on the computer search. We thought it was just that archivist being unhelpful.'

'Anthony Chetwynd?' Ryan remembered him well. 'He *was* being unhelpful!'

'Yes, but it was more than that. Melanie must have deliberately removed that film from the computer index. No wonder the old film canister opened so easily. It struck me as odd at the time. Sir Charles must have already have watched that film and realised that the tunnel led somewhere extremely interesting. He got Melanie to "hide" the film until he could find someone to search for the tunnel in China and check out any treasure that might be down there.'

Ryan laughed. 'Then we came along and messed up his master plan by finding the film first! Wow, Sir Charles must *really* hate us! We stopped him getting his hands on the Benben Stone too. And now the White Finder Tree. No wonder he tried to shoot us the other day.'

'A toast,' Dad said, raising his glass. 'To my son Ryan. Crime-fighter and hero! And to his friend Cleo. A girl in a million.' He grinned. 'Even if she did try to hack my leg off with a trowel!'

The sun was setting, blood red in an orange sky, as Ryan and Cleo walked along the beach towards the hotel. Ryan was planning the third instalment of their movie marathon. They'd already watched *Casablanca, Star Wars* and *The*

Wizard of Oz. Tonight was zombie night. He'd picked out his top three classics. But first there was something else he needed to do. He stopped, took a tissue paper package from his pocket and handed it to Cleo. 'I brought you a present.'

'It's not a scarf, is it?'

Ryan laughed. 'No way! You can't be trusted with scarves!'

'Me?' Cleo protested. '*You* wrecked the last three.'

'It's not a scarf. Go on, open it.'

Cleo pulled apart the tissue paper and lifted out a necklace. Discs of gleaming red and orange, reflecting the colours of the sunset, hung from a delicate chain. 'Spiny oyster shell,' she breathed. 'It's beautiful. Where did you find it?'

'Chichén Itzá. I thought it looked just like the one Mountain Star wore.'

Cleo ran the smooth shells through her fingers. 'I'm sorry. I haven't got you anything.' She stared at the necklace for a moment. 'Wait. I've got an idea.' She carefully slid one of the shells from the chain. She picked up a pointed stone from the beach and etched something onto the back.

'Is it a riddle?' Ryan asked. 'Or something clever in ancient glyphs?'

Cleo gave him the shell.

'B.F.F.' Ryan read out. '*Best friends for ever!*' He swallowed a lump in his throat. He took the cord from his neck and threaded the shell onto it next to his St Christopher, the scarab beetle and the lucky coins. 'For ever,' he murmured. 'I guess we'll find out. We've drunk the elixir of life and we've escaped from the Underworld.'

Ryan helped Cleo fasten the spiny oyster necklace round her neck. The red shells glowed against the white cotton dress she'd pulled on over her swimming costume. She looked beautiful, even though half her face was green. He could think of worse people to be stuck with for eternity.

There was a long silence filled only by the lapping of the waves on the sand. Ryan wanted to say something else. He'd said it twice already but it had never come out quite the right way. *Third time lucky,* he thought. Not that Cleo believed in luck, of course. He should say it now. This was the perfect chance. Cleo and her parents would be leaving for Greece in a few days, to the dig at Amphipolis. Who knew when he'd see her again?

Cleo must have been thinking the same thing. 'You could come and join us in Amphipolis for the Easter holidays? The tombs there are amazing.'

Ryan never wanted to set foot in another tomb for the rest of his life. He took her hand. He was about to say the words when she jumped away. 'Come on! Let's swim.'

'Now?' Ryan asked. 'It's dark.'

Cleo was already running down the beach, pulling her dress over her head as she went. 'You're not afraid, are you?'

'Afraid? What of?'

'Oh, I don't know. Mutant catfish maybe? Or bats. Don't worry, I won't let them get you.'

Ryan ran after her. He'd been trying to get her to swim all afternoon. Now, just when he'd been about to have a special moment, she'd suddenly decided to hit the surf! That was so typical! 'Hang on!' he yelled.

Cleo turned. She was up to her waist in the water now. 'What?' she shouted.

'I was going to say ...' But before the next word left his mouth a rogue wave swept in and crashed over Cleo's head.

'What?' she spluttered as she surfaced.

Ryan waded into the shallows to help her up. 'Never mind,' he said. 'It'll wait.' *After all,* he thought, *we're doubly immortal. We're going to be around for a very long time.*

The Serpent King is a work of fiction. Ryan and Cleo and the other modern day characters and events are entirely the product of my imagination. But the action unfolds in real locations, and I have also woven some real characters and events from ancient Maya history into the mystery. To avoid any confusion between which parts are fact and which are fiction, I have tried to clarify in this note.

The main setting, the Maya city of Calakmul is a real place in Mexico's Yucatán peninsula. At its peak during the sixth and seventh centuries AD, Calakmul was a mighty city, the centre of the Kingdom of the Snake, one of the most powerful kingdoms of the Classic Maya period. The immense flat-topped stone pyramids, platforms, temples and giant *stelae* are surrounded by miles of dense forest, an hour's drive from the highway. Strangler figs grow up through the stone. Birds and howler monkeys call from the trees. It is the most spectacular place. I hope that one day you have chance to see it for yourself.

Chichén Itzá is also a real Maya site. You may have heard of it, because it is famous throughout the world. It is less remote than Calakmul, and is surrounded by hotels rather than jungle (several of those hotels are old and grand, like the Grand Hacienda in the story, even though the Grand Hacienda itself is fictional). The snake of light representing Kukulcan, which makes its way down the steps of the

El Castillo pyramid at the Spring and Autumn equinox is also real. People crowd there to watch this amazing sight.

Jaguar Paw (also known as Fiery Claw or Yuknoom Yich'aak K'ahk; there are several alternative names for most Maya figures) was a real Lord of Calakmul, who ruled at the end of the seventh century. An important tomb, thought to be his, was indeed discovered in the Structure II pyramid at Calakmul in the 1990s (this is the tomb I have called the 'upper tomb' in this story). The tomb of the Unknown Lady and Child is also real. Smoking Squirrel and Lady Six Sky are also real historical figures. Smoking Squirrel was a famous King of the nearby kingdom of Naranjo. He came to the throne at an early age and there are many records of his victories in battle. He certainly seems to have been a ruthless ruler. Lady Six Sky – who is thought to be his mother – was one the few women of that time for whom records exist. She seems to have been very powerful.

The idea for a mystery involving Jaguar Paw's death started to form when I read the words 'Yich'aak K'ahk's fate is uncertain.' Although archaeologists thought that the 'upper tomb' was that of Jaguar Paw (there really was a plate with his name on buried in the coffin) there was some doubt about it. Just as I explain in the story, a lintel was found at Tikal, which seemed to show that Jaguar Paw had been captured in battle in August 695 and almost certainly killed by the rival king, Jasaw Chan. How could he have been buried in Calakmul a few years later? Since that finding, historians have suggested that the man shown in the picture at Tikal may not have been Jaguar Paw himself, but one of his generals. There have also been more recent findings that suggest that Jaguar Paw was alive after AD 695 and went on a royal visit to another city.

There are many possible explanations and much is still unknown, but it started me thinking about what might have happened if Jaguar Paw had indeed been killed in Tikal. Could someone have plotted to make it look as if he were still alive? Could a 'stunt double' have made the royal visit and been buried in the upper tomb? And when I read all about the Maya belief in each person having an animal spirit or *way*, I couldn't resist bringing a jaguar into the story.

In reality there is no evidence that Lady Six Sky knew Jaguar Paw or conspired to have her son take the crown of Calakmul when Jaguar Paw died. (However, there were all sorts of alliances, rivalries, takeovers and splits between the neighbouring kingdoms, so it is the sort of thing that might have happened.) Sadly very few historical records survive from Calakmul – the inscriptions on the great stone *stelae* have been eroded by the humidity and rain. Books have rotted away or been destroyed. So we have to use our imaginations to fill in the gaps.

As with all the other modern-day characters, the young archaeologist Roberto Chan is my own invention. So is the Snake Stone, the fragment of the stela from Naranjo, that he 'discovered'. There is no real inscription about 'the prize that all men desire' and so on. Likewise, the jaguar tomb that Roberto discovers beneath the upper tomb is entirely imaginary (although much of the pyramid remains unexcavated so who knows what might be hidden within?). I based details of the tunnels, the sarcophagus, the grave goods etc. on similar burials at other Maya sites such as Palenque.

The other characters in the ancient story are my own

invention. Mountain Star, the young princess who learned to write and secretly studied astronomy, did not really exist (sadly; I wish she had!). Nor did her loyal servant, Seven Rabbit, or her poor little brother, Radiant Turtle. In reality, the Unknown Woman and Child buried in the tomb in Calakmul remain unknown.

The sacrifice rituals, the ball game, the beliefs about Xi'balb'a, the Underworld and the Lords of Death, the Vision Serpent, the World Tree, the Witz monsters and the three hearthstones are all based on features of seventh-century Maya society. The sacred book, the *Popol Vuh* that Cleo is reading throughout, is also real. It is a collection of Maya myths and stories, written down in the sixteenth century, and one of the few books to survive. There are modern translations – even a beautifully illustrated version – if you wanted to read it for yourself.

The Wasp Nest tower is my own invention, but the name, the Wasp Star for Venus, is real, as is the information about using the stars and planets to decide when to go to war (they really are known as Star Wars). The wall of carved skulls that Cleo and Ryan find in the tower is based on the real skull platform at Chichén Itzá.

I also invented the Xib'alb'a *cenote* that Ryan and Cleo find in the jungle. However, it is based firmly on the Maya belief that *cenotes* or sinkholes were entrances to the underworld, where sacrifices and offerings would be left. The steam-cleaning of captives ready for sacrifice is, rather scarily, based in reality too. You can still visit many of these amazing underground *cenotes* – you can even swim in some of them, and watch bats flying overhead. Luckily they are easier to escape from than the one in *The Serpent King*.

You may also be wondering whether the White Finder Tree, the unique artefact at the centre of the story, is a real object. Sadly it is not. I invented it for the story. However, the World Tree was a very important Maya concept, so it's plausible that an object would be made in its shape. Also, although Cleo is right when she says that compasses were not used outside of China at this time, there have been some findings of lodestone artefacts in Central America from a time of the Olmec culture – even earlier than the Maya. Some historians believe they used these to align their buildings in specific directions. It is also true that the Maya used colours (among other things) to symbolise different directions – including white for north. So, although I made the White Finder Tree up, I have tried to make it an object that fits with what we know about the Maya civilisation at that time.

The details of the Maya number system, calendar and writing system (including that all-important possessive pronoun) are all based on real research. I relied on many books and websites for this information, but any mistakes are, of course, my own. As I was reading up on all this I discovered that some scholars used nicknames to describe the complex Mayan glyphs when they were trying to decipher them, so I borrowed that detail for Ryan. (I have used the convention of *Mayan* to refer to the language, *Maya* to the people and the culture).

Other details

Tatiana Proskouriakoff really was a famous scholar who played a pioneering role in deciphering Mayan glyphs (as are the other epigraphers in the photographs in Professor Wynne's room – although not, thank goodness, Sofia K. Proufork!). Professor Wynne is a fictional character – as is his bearded dragon, Kylie – but the name comes from a real person. Serge Wynne was the winner of a drawing competition we ran in 2015. His brilliant drawing of scenes from *The Phoenix Code* won him first prize – his name for a character in *The Serpent King*.

X'pujil is a real town near to Calakmul but as far as I know there is no La Luna bar there. Mérida and Cancún are also real places. The *Piratas de Campeche* are a real baseball team.

Los Lobos Rojos or Red Wolves are entirely imaginary. Of course, there are real criminal gangs in Mexico, just as there are in many parts of the world, but I didn't base the one in the story on any specific gang.

Jaguars still live in the forests of Central America but are increasingly rare, due to hunting and loss of habitat. They are also prone to hookworms – as in the story. (Helminthology really is the study of parasitic worms, by the way.) Anteaters are more common, but sadly do sometimes get run over on the roads. Some people keep anteaters as pets and I have read that – like Shadow – they are very greedy!

Cranial deformation, shaping a child's head, really was practised by the ancient Maya. As Alex points out, it is thought that this was done to resemble the head of a jaguar.

Spiny oyster shell was highly prized by the ancient Maya and is still used for jewellery today.

I'm not sure that a real ancient Maya 'sippy cup' has ever been found. However, the object was inspired by a real drinking cup found at another Early Classic Maya site – it had a screw-top lid inscribed with the glyph for cocoa and contained actual traces of chocolate.

If you ever have the chance to go to Mexico, you will be impressed, just like Ryan, by the delicious food. All the dishes I mention are real – as are the biscuit brands!

Finally, a minor correction to a detail in Book One. It was stated that the Bloodthirsty Grail was discovered at a Maya site in Peru. In fact, it was a Moche site in Peru.

Acknowledgements

I would like to thank everyone who has helped on the long and exciting *Secrets of the Tombs* journey, especially my wonderful agent Jenny Savill, brilliant editors Amber Caraveo and Helen Thomas, and the entire team of lovely people at Orion Children's Books. I am also grateful to Leo Hartas, whose exceptional illustrations have helped to bring each book to life.

And special thanks, as always, to my husband, Mac, for his unflagging support; for being my minder, cameraman and all-round partner-in-crime.

Helen Moss, 2016